DARK FAITH

DARK FAITH

EDITED BY
MAURICE BROADDUS
AND
JERRY GORDON

AN APEX PUBLICATIONS BOOK
LEXINGTON, KENTUCKY

Copyright © 2010 by Apex Publications

ISBN TPB: 978-0-9821596-8-2

All rights reserved

Cover art by Edith Walter • Cover design by Justin Stewart

"The Story of Belief-Non," © 2010, Linda D. Addison; "Ghosts of New York," © 2010, Jennifer Pelland; "I Sing a New Psalm," © 2010, Brian Keene; "He Who Would Not Bow," © 2010, Wrath James White; "Zen and the Art of Gordon Dratch's Damnation," © 2010, Douglas F. Warrick; "Go and Tell It on the Mountain," © 2010, Kyle S. Johnson; "Different from Other Nights," © 2010, Eliyanna Kaiser; "Lilith," © 2010, Rain Graves; "The Last Words of ~~Dutch Schultz~~ Jesus Christ," © 2010, Nick Mamatas; "To the Jerusalem Crater," © 2010, Lavie Tidhar; "Chimeras & Grotesqueries," © 2010, Matt Cardin; "You Dream," © 2010, Ekaterina Sedia; "Mother Urban's Booke of Days," © 2010, Jay Lake; "The Mad Eyes of the Heron King," © 2010, Richard Dansky; "Paint Box, Puzzle Box," © 2010, D.T. Friedman; "A Loss for Words," © 2010, J. C. Hay; "Scrawl," © 2010, Tom Piccirilli; "C{her}ry Carvings," © 2010, Jennifer Baumgartner; "Good Enough," © 2010, Kelli Dunlap; "First Communions," © 2010, Geoffrey Girard; "The God of Last Moments," © 2010, Alethea Kontis; "Ring Road," © 2010, Mary Robinette Kowal; "The Unremembered," © 2010, Chesya Burke; "Desperata," © 2010, Lon Prater; "The Choir," © 2010, Lucien Soulban; "Days of Flaming Motorcycles," © 2010, Catherynne M. Valente; "Miz Ruthie Pays Her Respects," © 2010, Lucy A. Snyder; "Paranoia," © 2010, Kurt Dinan; "Hush," © 2010, Kelly Barnhill; "Sandboys," © 2010, Richard Wright; "For My Next Trick I'll Need a Volunteer," © 2010, Gary A. Braunbeck

Apex Publications, LLC
www.apexbookcompany.com
PO Box 24323 Lexington, KY 40524

—TABLE OF CONTENTS—

INTRODUCTION

In the foreword of *Orgy of Souls*, my novella co-written with Wrath James White, I wrote that "Faith is that sometimes tenuous, sometimes stronger than we think thing that keeps our world in order. [Wrath and I are] both men of faith in our own way, be it faith in ourselves or faith in God. We each are on our own spiritual journey." All quest journeys begin with a leap of faith—that is, what we choose to put our trust in. We each have a worldview that helps us navigate the world. For some, it is ourselves (the individual or humanity). For some, it is science (the determination of our senses and what we can prove). For some, it is the spiritual (under the assumption that there is more to this life than presented, both in terms of the spiritual and in terms of after this life). And there is, or can be, some overlap.

But we all believe in something.

So I invited horror, science fiction, and fantasy writers to riff on the idea of faith. Who we are, artists and people of faith, expressing our theology, whatever it may be, in our writing. And with the challenge to take it to another level: art is never for its own sake, but for people's sake. I believe that art should be engaged with—and, in its own way, explore—truth; and we shouldn't be afraid of truth, no matter where it takes us.

In this anthology, it has taken us to new and interesting places as we explore various tangents to the ideas of faith. Life can be magical and terrifying, filled with both fantasy and horror. There is life and there is death; everything in between is unknown. We live in the throes of "why?" We react to injustice, we question why bad things happen to good people. We feel the existential terror of what it means to encounter God, the ultimate Other. On the other side, there's the idea that God is personal and relational, Jesus can be a guy you can sneak around back and share cigarettes with. We can see faith lived out in love and relationships or be horrified by the things done in God's name. Faith in action can move us to do something, to confront the sins of our age, such as sexism, homophobia, and racism to name a few.

I'd like to thank several people for their support during all of this. The Mo*Con family: Brian Keene (whose own spiritual journey inspired all of this), Wrath James White (whose "anti-spiritual" journey continues to challenge me), Alethea Kontis (who reminds me that life is magic), Kelli Dunlap (who taught me that sometimes you have to give life the finger and take a smoke break), Chesya Burke (my sister, for better or worse and all that entails), and Gary Braunbeck and Lucy Snyder (mentors and inspiration). My co-editor, Jerry Gordon, for all of his hard work. I wouldn't have been able to do this without him. My fellow Indiana Horror Writers without whom Mo*Con would have remained a neat idea. Jason Sizemore for having faith in this project. And Sally, Reese, and Malcolm, who allowed me time to read, write, and edit, and sacrificed time with me to make this happen. It's to them that I dedicate this book.

And my Lord and Savior, Jesus Christ, with me during times of praise and doubt, chasing after me when I wander off. I am often the most failed of His ambassadors, but I thank you for the freedom to explore my faith and continue my weird journey... which is all mine.

Maurice Broaddus
February 16, 2010

To God and the story He has written

THE STORY OF BELIEF-NON

An expanse of water
the first cool breeze
of fall, red leaf floating
to earth, relinquished
by maple tree, a newborn's
first cry entering atmosphere.

The result of evolution,
scientifically dissected into
proteins, neurons, defined
parts of the Table of Elements,
tracked by global warming
trends, the end game of
a drunken night of groping.

H2O, the beginning, the end,
the place life dances in precise
explicit units, found deep in Earth,
alluded to on Mars, hinted at in
faraway galaxies, as close as
Neptune, a mark made in dark spots
of methane drifting in thick clouds.

Even in denying Zeus or Ra, there
is an innate beauty to the mind
unraveling fables often used as
weapons rather than song, in that
absence of belief, seasoned by
curious doubt, watching the inhumanity
of choice, heartbroken at the hunger,
the wasted life, the Shadow Story unwinds.

Faith doesn't come easily, let Truth
recognize insubstantiality, choose
to believe or not, on the Walkabout
the protagonist falls in love with
Endless Possibility, mirrored in the
grand story of perfection/imperfection.

—Linda D. Addison

GHOSTS OF NEW YORK
Jennifer Pelland

P oets and sages like to say that there is clarity in certain death. That a calm resignation settles over the nearly deceased, and they embrace the inevitability of the end of life with dignity and grace.

But there was no clarity for her, no calmness, no life flashing before her eyes in a montage of joys and regrets. There was just pure animal terror, screams torn from her throat as she plummeted toward the ground in the longest ten seconds of her life.

And then there was an explosion of pain.

She remembered flailing at the air, as if she could somehow sink her nails into it and cling there until help arrived. She remembered the crash and pop of the people who were landing mere seconds before her. She remembered a fleeting moment of shame when her dress blew up over her head, exposing her underwear to the crowds gathered below. She remembered the burst of shit and piss as she crashed through the awning just a split second before she hit—

The only people who find clarity in certain death are those who somehow cheat it, those who can reflect back upon the experience and use it to goad them into living a better life.

For the ghosts, there is only terror.

After her first fall, she stood by the roadkill smear that was her body, not recognizing what she was seeing at first, until two more bodies rained down from above, splattering on pavement with a crash of glass and a sickening splat.

Then she knew.

Then the North Tower collapsed.

All around her, people screamed and ran while she stood helplessly by the wreckage of her body. Debris flew through her, burying her corpse, leaving the ghost of her untouched.

And then she fell again.

If anything, it was worse than the first time. Now, it was an echo of a fall, a non-existent body falling from a non-existent building, with all the terror of the original fall—the same flailing, the same flash of embarrassment, the same piss—

The same body-shattering moment of pain at the end.

Days passed, the dust cleared, the debris and bodies were carried away, but still she fell, over and over, sinking through the sky for the same interminably long ten seconds, the pain of impact fresh and raw each and every time.

Between falls, she wondered if she were in hell. She wondered what terrible thing she'd done in life to merit this kind of eternal punishment. But she couldn't remember.

She couldn't remember anything.

No, that wasn't strictly true. In the chest-heaving intervals between falls, she could remember, if she tried, the blistering heat and choking smoke. She remembered mobbing a broken window with a half-dozen other people, gulping in precious lungfuls of clean air. She remembered a floor too hot to stand on, the eerie creak of metal. She remembered a man and a woman dropping past her window, hand in hand. She remembered looking over her shoulder at the impenetrable wall of smoke. She remembered a scream stuck in her throat, a heart that felt like it would burst through her chest, a desperate wish to breathe just once more before she died.

She remembered a split-second decision, legs suddenly unfrozen, propelling her out into the blue September sky.

But before that?

Nothing.

She couldn't even remember what she looked like. She would think back to standing over her body after the initial fall and try to conjure up hair color, skin color, but all she could remember was the pool of red in a sea of glittering glass.

She could see the other ghosts, though. The hundreds of others who still rained from the sky, all still trapped in the same deathly cycle as she was.

She didn't talk to them. They didn't talk to her. They each lived in their own little bubble of pain. They could each only fall, catch their breath, and fall again.

The living couldn't see them. She wondered if they could feel them. They certainly didn't come near them. All around Ground Zero she saw the same dance—the living weaving around the invisible dead, speeding up their steps to get out of the way of a falling jumper, brushing a hand across their pants legs as matterless gore splattered up from the impact. She wondered if she and her fellow ghosts were why the site had stayed empty for so long. Each year, as people gathered on the site for their memorial, she would hear them talk about bureaucracy, red tape, financial woes, lawsuits, respect for the families of the dead. She didn't believe a word of it. No force on earth could keep Manhattan from putting a building on a prime piece of real estate.

But eventually, build they did.

Between falls, she watched, rapt, as the steel beams climbed into the sky.

Sometimes, she wished she could take in the details of the construction work on the upper floors as she fell. But every time, the animal fear took over right from the start. Every time, it was the same. She was nothing but a frozen moment, repeatedly playing out exactly the same way.

She quickly learned to keep away from the construction

workers so they could do their jobs without having to step around her. The other ghosts did the same. They were uniformly polite in their silent suffering.

As the new tower grew, a memorial was constructed where the old ones once stood. She would land next to the waterfalls that poured into the old buildings' footprints, pick herself up, and stare at the water as it flowed down into a churning mist. She tried to find her name among the lists of the dead, but none of the names looked familiar to her. Out of the corners of her eyes, she could see the other ghosts looking for themselves as well. She suspected that none of them had any better luck than she did. She wandered through the museum, looking at the photographs, and finding no images of people jumping from the buildings that day. It was as if they were some shameful taboo. It was as if they had never existed.

The memorial wasn't any comfort to her. It didn't bring her any closer to knowing who she was, or really, who she had been before she died. She was still a ghost. She still fell.

Maybe she could find answers elsewhere.

For a while now, she'd been feeling less stuck to the site. As the new building went up and the memorial and museum were completed, she could feel herself coming loose, bit by bit, but it had never occurred to her to try to leave until just now. How many years had it been? She didn't want to know.

She stepped off the site for the first time in her unlife.

All around her, she could see the other ghosts coming to the same realization as they, too, left the site and started cautiously exploring the world around them.

New York City was in places familiar, in places bewildering.

Had she only been visiting the Twin Towers that day? Was she not a New York City regular? That, she didn't know. She read an ad on the side of a bus and wondered why it said the same thing twice before realizing that half of it was in Korean.

She knew Korean? Was this a clue to her past? But then she read the headlines on a Chinese newspaper and a taxi ad in Spanish, and realized that it meant nothing. Everything about her meant nothing.

And then she was falling again.

She took several short jaunts into the neighborhoods around the Towers, always being dragged back to fall from the window that no longer existed to land on the precise bit of pavement that was similarly nonexistent, before deciding to take a more ambitious walk.

That was the day she learned that they weren't alone.

Standing at the base of the Empire State Building, she stifled a scream as she watched a small plane crash into the upper floors. Not again. Not another one. Weren't the Twin Towers enough? A body flew from the gaping hole that had been torn through the side of the building, but no one on the street seemed to notice a thing.

Another ghost, with a ghost of an airplane creating a ghost of a hole in the building.

And then came the rain of jumpers, hitting the pavement or phantom cars in a staccato rhythm of death. No one seemed to notice. They were ghost jumpers, just like her, stuck in the same never-ending cycle.

One woman, lying on the crumpled hood of an old-fashioned limousine, looked positively serene.

She ran across the street to take a closer look, but the woman sat up, staring dumbly at her torn stockings, and moaned, "Oh god, make it stop."

"I can hear you!" she gasped. "Oh my god, I can hear you! Can you hear me? I haven't talked to anyone in so long. This is wonderful!"

The woman just covered her beautifully made-up face and moaned again, a long, keening sound that seemed to come from a place far deeper than her body could hold. "It never ends. It never ends."

"What do you mean? How long have you been falling?"

The woman turned wild eyes to her. "Where did you come from?"

"The Twin Towers."

"I saw them rise and fall. A new one's rising, isn't it?"

She nodded.

"But you'll fall from the old ones forever. No one's going to forget you."

"Forget me? What do you—"

But the words were ripped from her mouth as she found herself back at the North Tower, leaping through the window, and clawing at the air for ten long seconds before hitting bottom again.

She *could* talk to the dead, just not the Towers' dead.

But she didn't like what she'd heard, and wasn't sure she wanted to hear more.

She walked to the memorial park and stared at the waterfall cascading into the ground where her Tower had once stood. The living wove around her as she stood there, unmoving, not caring for once that she was bothering anyone. She was a sentinel of pain. She saw it on the faces of the people doing their little dances to avoid walking through her. It wasn't just this memorial that disturbed them, it was those who were left behind.

Why wouldn't it end?

How did that woman even know?

From the look of her clothes, she'd been jumping for at least half a century.

She looked down and felt the echo of her fall in the movement of the water.

In a way, it was the perfect memorial.

Why was she still here? Wasn't she supposed to move on?

Did she even believe in an afterlife? She couldn't remember. There was so much she couldn't remember.

Maybe she hadn't believed. Maybe that was the problem.

But what was the point in some god punishing her if she didn't remember why she was being punished?

She found an old church nearby, walked through the iron gate, through the front door, and stood facing the altar, waiting to see if she felt anything. But she didn't feel any different here than she did at the Towers, or on her walks. It was just as cold as it was everywhere else, even when she stood in the postcard-perfect beams of sunlight streaming down through the massive windows.

Maybe she needed to pray to actually feel something. But she couldn't find the words. Has she known them in life, or was this yet another wished-for revelation about her past that really meant nothing?

An old man sat on a badly-scuffed bench off to the side of the room, his head bowed in silent prayer, and she sat down as close to him as she dared. If there was a god out there listening to this man's prayer, maybe he'd see her and realize that he'd forgotten to take her when she'd died.

She waited.

And then she was yanked away to fall again.

So that was her answer.

She didn't feel much like walking anymore. The few longer trips she tried showed her a city full of people jumping from or being pushed out of buildings, all still going through the motions for countless years after their deaths. She couldn't deal with them. It was bad enough to be stuck in this endless loop herself, but seeing it played out across the city was just too much.

But some days, she would step off of the site and cross the street, if only to get away just a little bit. She needed to prove to herself that she could still leave if she wanted to. That her eternity wouldn't be completely made up of monotonous terror. She'd sit on the curb, stretching her legs into the street, watching as cabs swerved to avoid hitting her ghostly feet.

When the new tower's skeleton was nearly complete, she had a visitor.

He was young, a teenaged boy, dressed in short pants and a cap, like something out of an old black and white movie. He was soaking wet, both hands clasping the tattered life jacket that was draped around his neck. "You!" he screamed.

She tucked her feet up and stared at him, puzzled. "Where did you come from?"

"The East River. We were almost gone, until you happened."

At that, she was on her feet. "Almost gone? You mean we can go away?"

"People were forgetting about us. We were finally fading. And then you!" He jabbed a finger at her. "You! You made them start talking about us again! We weren't the biggest mass death in the city anymore!"

"So if people forget us—"

"I hate you!"

She heard a splash as he was pulled away, a gurgle.

But she didn't care about that. She knew the answer now. People had to forget them. Then they'd move on.

She stared across the street at the memorial park, and felt her hopes plummet.

That was never going to happen. They were going to be re-membered forever.

She crumpled to the ground and beat it with her fists, howling like an animal at the unfairness of it all.

And then she fell again.

And again. And again. And again.

But now, every time she landed, she screamed.

She screamed at the pavement, she screamed at the memorial

fountain, she screamed at the visitors, she screamed at the people working on the new tower. She would step off the site, stand in the middle of the sidewalk, and scream at the people walking by. She would stand in the middle of the street and scream at taxis who would swerve and honk at the other drivers as if it were their fault.

She hated them for remembering her. She hated the whole world for making her a repeating memorial of terror.

The boy kept coming back, standing at the periphery, spewing hate at whichever ghost was the closest. And the ghosts would scream back, their voices a chorus of anguish and betrayal.

The site was filled with their screams.

How could anyone not hear them?

That boy—he'd been screaming for...how long? A century?

They'd brought him back. Their deaths had brought him back.

But it wasn't her fault.

She'd had to jump.

It wasn't her fault.

She'd been suffocating. She'd needed air.

She needed air.

She needed it now.

She staggered off of the site, gasping for breath. This time, a woman was waiting for her. She looked young, but with old eyes. Her dress was long and simple, her hair messily pinned up, and there was soot on her pale face. "Stop it."

"Stop what?"

"Stop screaming."

"I have every damned right to scream."

"You're too loud."

"I don't care! If you had any idea—"

"Of course I have an idea!" the woman shouted back. "We're

all jumpers. All of us who are left behind, we're jumpers. Surely you've noticed that by now, or are you stupid?"

"That boy was wet. He didn't jump, he drowned."

"You mean that boy from the *Slocum*? He jumped into the river. History only makes ghosts out of those who try to fly."

Before either of them could say anything else, woman was snatched away, screaming.

And then she was back in the air, falling, landing.

She screamed her frustration into the air, pounding on the pavement with her fists, and looked up to see the woman from the fire looming over her. "I said stop it!"

"Don't tell me what to do!"

"We can hear you all the way over at the Triangle building. Everyone can hear you."

She pushed herself up off of the pavement and snarled, "Good. If they won't forget us, then they should hear us." She tried to storm off, but the woman stepped in front of her.

"They can't hear you," she said, gesturing at the living. "But we can."

"Why should I care?"

"Because we're all we have left. We barely even have ourselves. Can you remember what you look like? What your name was? If you had children? What you did for a living? If you were rich or poor? We're just pieces of people, not actual people."

"I know that. Don't you think I know that?"

"So have a little respect for the rest of us and stop screaming. There's too many of you. You're too loud. We just...." The woman looked like she was about to cry. "For the love of God, we just want a little peace."

She spat out a laugh. "Oh, please. We don't get to have peace. Whatever the hell we have, it's the opposite of peace. You've been around long enough. You should get that."

"We're here until we're forgotten," the woman said. "And

you and I will never be forgotten. If a pack of girls jumping out of a burning factory could learn to stop screaming, then so can you. Have a little courtesy for your fellow ghosts."

"I'm going to spend eternity reliving my death. Screaming is the only logical—"

And then she felt the wind tearing by her as she fell, again.

When she hit the ground, she lay there, staring up at the sky, not able to summon the energy to pick herself up.

Why shouldn't she scream? She was a walking beacon of pain, the icy feeling that trailed down someone's spine as they visited her death site. She had every right to scream. She should scream without stopping until the end of time.

But instead, she cried.

She curled onto her side and sobbed until she felt empty, which didn't take long at all.

It must have been because there was so little of her left.

She repeated that thought, and rolled over onto her back, letting the sun wash through her insubstantial form as she mulled it over.

There really wasn't very much of her, was there? Like the woman from the fire said, she was just a piece of a person, just the horrific slice of a woman's life as she died. The rest of the woman was who knew where—maybe heaven, maybe hell, maybe reborn into a new body, maybe nothing but worm food.

Wherever the rest of her was, she was missing this part. This death part. The part that lingered here in the shadow of the non-existent Towers.

How wonderful it must be not to be saddled with those last seconds of her life.

She sat up, staring down at the ground that all those years ago had been stained red with her blood. How strange to think that the rest of her could be out there, somewhere, not burdened with this memory.

Maybe her unlife wasn't a curse. Maybe it was history's gift to the woman she once was.

If so, that was a greater gift than anyone could ever know.

She looked over at the shouting boy and the soot-covered woman who was now lecturing another of her fellow Tower jumpers, and wondered if they'd ever had this thought.

Maybe this was the right way to stop the screaming.

She picked herself up, walked over to the memorial, and selected a female name at random from the list. Maybe that was the woman she'd once been. She had a nice name. She hoped she'd been a nice person. She hoped she was having a lovely afterlife.

She looked around the memorial, found a visitor scanning the list of names, and decided that she'd be that woman's sister today.

"It's all right," she told the woman. "Your sister doesn't remember what happened to her. She's at peace."

She reached out to stroke the young woman's hair, and for once, the living didn't flinch away from her.

Out of the corners of her eyes, she saw a couple of her fellow jumpers stop screaming and stare at her with expressions of astonishment.

She smiled back at them.

She hadn't smiled since she'd died.

It felt good.

And then she fell again.

But it was all right. At least, it was once she landed.

Because there was no clarity in death, no dignity. And history didn't fulfill any grand purpose when it plucked jumpers from the sky.

But perhaps there was a purpose to *her* suffering.

And that was enough.

I Sing a New Psalm

Brian Keene

1 Blessed is the man who has never known the love of God, for he will never know the pain of a broken heart.

2 And blessed is the man who lives in ignorance of the forces around him, for he can exist in peace.

3 I was such a man, once. I didn't know the love of God, for I did not believe in Him. God was something for superstitious people. He was like the tooth fairy and Santa Claus. God was a story told to children to give them comfort when someone they loved had died.

4 "Rover is in Heaven now, sweetheart. He is playing catch with God, and one day, if you're good and eat all your vegetables and follow the Ten Commandments, you will see him again. Just like if you're good, Santa Claus will bring you a new toy." Growing up, that was all I knew of God.

5 I did not believe in God or the tooth fairy or Santa Claus. I believed in working hard and succeeding at my job and becoming a partner with the firm. These values were instilled in me at a young age by my father. He worked seven days a week, with one day off for Christmas and a week off for deer season. My father loved me, and although I didn't see much of him growing up, I know that he worked those hours for me. He wanted me to be the first person in our family to go to college.

6 John Lennon once said that a working class hero is something to be. He was gunned down by a fan who loved him. John Lennon was more popular than Jesus.

7 My father died of a heart attack before I finished law school. My mother followed a year later, from melanoma. Years after the initial grief passed, I still felt unsettled when I thought of their passing. It bothered me how they would never know of my accomplishments, or how I'd repaid my father's unselfish work ethic in an equally driven manner. He would never know of these things because he didn't exist anymore. I did not believe in God or Heaven. My father was not with the Father. He was simply dead. Ashes to ashes. Dust to dust.

8 Would they have been proud of me?

9 My co-workers had a party for me the night I was offered a role as full partner with the firm. I drank too much Scotch. Head swimming, I returned home to an empty apartment. There was no solace to be found in the silence. Despite my achievements, I was left unfulfilled.

10 Blessed is the man who finds the love of a good partner, for that is the key to fulfillment.

11 I did not find fulfillment at a singles bar or on a dating website or in any of the other places one goes to find love these days. I found it in a church. I found fulfillment in Valerie. We met at a wedding. She was a bridesmaid. I was a guest of the groom. I still remember how beautiful she looked in her soft baby blue chiffon gown. Sunlight came through the stained glass windows and sparkled in her chestnut hair. At the reception, we made small talk over the punch bowl. Later, we danced to the Chicken Dance and the Electric Slide and other wedding reception staples. At the end of the evening, we exchanged phone numbers.

12 What did Valerie see in me? A lost soul, ripe for saving? Her Christian duty? Was it a forbidden attraction, perhaps? A chance to tiptoe over the line to the wild side with a secular atheist type? No, it was none of these things. When she looked in my eyes, I like to think that she saw mirrored the same things I saw in her.

13 Blessed is the man who finds love, for love is the greatest gift of them all.

14 The Lord gives, and the Lord takes away.

15 I started going to church with Valerie not out of a desire to know God, but out of a desire to please her. I loved her and it was important to her and I wanted to make her happy. We went each Sunday, but I did not feel the Lord. We sat in the pew together and shook hands with those around us, but I did not feel the Lord. I wrapped an arm around Valerie as we shared a hymnal and sang, but I did not feel the Lord. I read aloud from the bulletin with the rest of the congregation, but I did not feel the Lord. I sat dutifully, listening to the scripture lesson and the sermon each week, but I did not feel the Lord. I tithed, but I did not feel the Lord.

16 When I asked her to marry me, she asked if it would be forever. When I said yes, she asked me to accept Christ as my personal Lord and savior—to ask him to come into my heart so that I could be born again. Valerie said this was the only way we could be together in the world beyond this one. She asked me if I would do this thing and I said yes.

17 That was the only time I ever lied to her.

18 We were married on the last Saturday of March. We stood at the altar in front of our friends and our family and God, and when I looked into Valerie's eyes and heard the emotion in her voice when she said "I do"…I almost felt the Lord.

19 And then Mark came along.

20 Mark was born four years later, after a struggle to conceive and many visits to fertility clinics and adoption agencies. Valerie was in labor for twenty-five hours. The doctors finally decided on a Caesarian delivery. I knelt beside her in the operating room, whispering into her ear and kissing her forehead. She squeezed my hand and told me that she loved me.

21 And then the doctor asked me if I'd like to see my son. I peeked up over the curtain and there were Valerie's insides. The skin of her stomach had been folded back like a bedspread and her insides were on display. The overhead lights glistened on the red and purple and yellow and brown hues, but this barely registered with me, for there in the doctor's hands was our son. There was Mark.

22 And then I felt the Lord. I felt His goodness and His love and I wept for joy and I praised His name and gave thanks. I prayed. I apologized for my foolish disbelief. I made amends for doubting. For surely, here was proof of His provenance and His love. I wept happily, and my chest swelled as if my heart would burst.

23 An alarm blared over my cry, and through my tears, I realized that something was wrong. Mark was blue, and when I tried to go to him, the nurse whisked him away. Valerie squeezed my hand, but her grip was weak, and when she moaned, I heard the fear in her voice. Then her hand slipped away and the staff pushed me aside. The alarms grew louder, drowning out my prayer.

24 Later, after the alarms had faded and the lights had dimmed and the staff had muttered their sincere apologies, a doctor came to me. I was kneeling in the hospital's chapel. The doctor was a short, rotund man with a receding hairline and a gentle, kindly face. He pushed his glasses up on his nose and cleared his throat softly. He offered his condolences on the death of my son. I asked him if there was any update on Valerie's condition.

25 And the doctor said, "We've done all we can. She's in God's hands now."

26 Valerie died two hours after Mark.

27 I tried to pray for them both, but my voice was a harsh, ragged thing and my words were ugly.

28 My God, my God, why have you done this to me? Why did you give me the fruits of your love, and show me the path to your light, only to then rip them away? Why are you so far from helping me? Do you hear the words of my roaring? I cry in the daytime, but you don't hear me. I beg to you at night, but you don't answer.

29 For the Lord our God is a jealous God. He is a demanding God. You shall have no other gods before Him, and you shall love no other like you love Him. He demands this of us, His creation.

30 John Lennon once said that happiness is a warm gun. He was gunned down by a fan who loved him. John Lennon was killed because he was more popular than Jesus.

31 There was a small bell over the door of the gun store that jingled when I walked inside. It sounded like the chimes of freedom ringing. A heavenly chorus. I bought a shotgun and two handguns, and while we waited for the results of my background check, I asked the proprietor if he clung to God and guns, the way the President had suggested.

32 "We all need something to believe in," he said. "But I don't care what they say. I didn't vote for either candidate. None of them have our best interests in heart. The people in charge never hear us."

33 You shall hear the words of my roaring.

34 How long did you plan to ignore me, oh Lord? Forever? How long did you plan to hide your face from me? How long must I counsel my own soul, so utterly filled with crippling sorrow in my heart daily? How long do you expect to be exalted over me?

35 Consider and hear me, oh Lord. Look in my eyes before I sleep the sleep of death.

36 I will sing unto you, Lord, because you have dealt unfairly with me.

37 Later, they will say that I have prevailed against you. For I trusted in your mercy and you spat in my face; my heart will rejoice in your pain.

38 You gave and then you took away.

39 Blessed is the man who can play that game, as well.

40 Yea, though I walk through the valley of the shadow of death, I do not fear you, for Valerie and Mark are with me. My shotgun and my pistols, they comfort me. Blessed is the man who knows the satisfying weight of such an instrument in his hands. And blessed is the man who finds solace in the handguns holstered to his hips. He shall take comfort in such weapons and through them, he will know fulfillment.

41 I wait in the car as the parishioners file into the church. I watch the greeters shake their hands, and I remember when it was Valerie and me walking through those doors.

42 Eventually, the doors close. I wait until I hear the muted sound of the organ. When the congregation begins to sing, I get out of the car. The guns are heavy but my heart is light. I feel at peace.

43 Hear this, all you people; give ear, all you inhabitants of the world. Listen to the words of my roaring.

44 I shall sing a new Psalm.

HE WHO WOULD NOT BOW
Wrath James White

Joshua walked as casually as he could manage as he wound his way through the teeming throngs of worshippers lining the streets outside the newly renovated Vatican. Joshua had seen what had happened to the Pope on TV. Who would have thought that of all people it would be the Pope who would have the guts to question Him? They had played the unedited footage on CNN for more than a week, showing the flesh being rent from the old Jesuit's bones by unseen hands while he shrieked and wailed in mortal anguish and cried out for Jesus to save him. Joshua now knew the man's last agonized screams and prayers by heart. He hoped that he could avoid the same fate.

The Vatican was not the only religious site He had claimed. Nearly every temple, mosque, and church across the globe now belonged to Him. For some reason, He did seem to favor this one. It had become one of His many centers of power from which He ruled all of mankind.

He claimed all faiths as His and demanded they all worship Him. His need for constant praise was limitless. Were He a human being, everyone would have thought it a sign of His insecurity. Those who refused to worship Him, those who did not accept Him as their deity, who questioned His authenticity, at least those who did so publically, suffered the fate of millions of heretics throughout history. They were killed, burned, and many were first tortured horribly at the hands of His followers.

He would be addressing His adoring worshippers soon. Whipping them into a frenzy with promises and threats and declarations of His eternal affection for His imperfect children. Joshua had heard His speeches before. They were moving, eloquent recitations that tapped all the right emotions, inspiring love, fear, respect, and guilt in equal measure along with a hatred for all blasphemers against His vain and capricious will. He knew exactly what words to use to elicit these emotions. He should. It was He who had authored them. They had no power over Joshua, but he wasn't certain about the others and Joshua didn't want anyone having a change of heart when they were so close to their goal.

There was a nuclear device strapped to Joshua's chest. A dirty bomb. Six pounds of C-4 attached to a sealed canister of weapons grade plutonium in an army flak jacket. The jacket chafed around his underarm and the weight of it bit into his shoulders. He ignored these minor annoyances. Concentrating on them would have been fatal.

Joshua gripped the detonator in his hand so tightly that the metal cut into his palm. Once he let go of the detonator it would all be over. If he could just get close enough, he could end this whole mess, avenge his dead brother, save the world. These thoughts, too, he pushed out of his mind.

It began to snow, a light dusting of snowflakes that made everyone think of the coming Christmas and brought memories of Christmases past. More of His theatrics. Joshua kept his mind fixed on the words to "Jacob's Ladder."

"I aaaaaam…climbiiing…Jacooob's Laaaadeeer…Everyyyy…rung gooooooes… higheeeer, higheeeer."

He didn't want to remember last Christmas. It had been his first Christmas without Dalton.

It wasn't just revenge that Joshua was after. Though it was his brother's face that he thought of, his voice that he heard in his head, whenever he thought about the mission. The truth was that Joshua could not live in this world even if his brother was not dead. He could not supplicate himself. His knees were not meant to bend. His head not designed to bow. He was too much of an individual—a militant individualist, his brother had called him. The very being he now sought to assassinate had made him this way. If he could not be free, he did not want to live but he wouldn't die alone if he could help it. And Joshua was convinced now that he could.

He kept his mind clear. He had rehearsed it over and over in his head, in field simulations, during grueling, tedious practice runs. He had tried his best to imprint every movement into his muscles, to make them instinctual, because thinking about what he was doing could get him killed. Like that old Nike commercial, it was time to just do it.

He ignored the loud, joyous praise and raucous prayer that swirled around him from a million voices. Hymns he recognized from his youth growing up in the church mixed with unfamiliar ones in a dozen or more different languages. He tried not to look at their rapturous faces, many of which were weeping actual tears of joy. He fought to keep his mind blank, not to wonder how they could all be so taken in by this despot, how they could all accept this madness. Happy sheep. Happy slaves. He didn't understand. He wondered if his own parents were among them. Even after Dalton's death they had not renounced their faith or rescinded their love of Him. But thinking about it now would not be wise.

He heard the voices of his fellow revolutionaries singing their own hymns as they dispersed among the crowd, making their way into position until their voices were swallowed by the cacophonous din of mindless worship. Each of them had weapons of some sort. May had five grenades tucked in the oversized pockets of her baggy cargo pants. Javier and Armando both carried fully automatic AR-15s with scopes beneath their puffy ski jackets. Tommy was strapped with a similar bomb to the one strapped to Joshua's chest. In their heads, they were all singing gospel songs. They had decided to pick songs that they barely knew so they would have to struggle to remember the words. Concentrate on the songs, not the mission. They knew their minds were being scanned every second. One stray thought was all it would take. They had chosen Gospel because it would help them to blend in. Half of the million-plus mindless acolytes crowding the streets of Rome had similar hymns floating through their heads.

They had been training their minds and bodies for months to act without thinking, but since none of them were psychic it was hard to know how successful they had become at it. They had to trust each other's word that they had gotten it right and would not allow their thoughts to betray their intentions. If one of them slipped they all would die, and Joshua knew that dying would be the easy part. What would happen next would be worse than any of them could imagine. The only other fear Joshua had was about how much of the future He could see.

Joshua didn't understand a lot about predestination. It was one of the things they had argued about before beginning the mission.

"Even if He can't see the future now that He's here, don't you think He would have checked every last possible scenario before entering the physical world?" May questioned. She was a 46-year-old former housewife whose husband and daughter had both been immolated when New Orleans went up.

"According to everything I've read, the minute He entered the world He changed the future. Everything that happens now is new territory now that He's participating. Even if all of our actions are predetermined, His are not. So He cannot predict how we will react to His unpredictable actions," said Joshua.

"Unless He's following a script He laid out before entering the world. Then he could predict everything," Armando replied. He was a former gun runner from Brazil who had supplied all of the weapons they now carried. He'd lost his mother and father when Rio went up. Javier was his brother.

Joshua looked over at Tommy, the young street kid who'd had a grudge against God long before He'd entered the world. Tommy had been born to a meth whore. He had never known his father and his mother had known the man only long enough to earn the thirty dollars for her next hit of meth. He had run away from home after his mother had started pimping him out sometime around age six and had been on the streets ever since. He'd been a drug addict himself but had gotten himself clean in the past three years and had gone back to school, completed his GED and enrolled in college. Then He had come and destroyed it all. Tommy stared back at Joshua expressionlessly, offering no comment.

They were all right, of course. It could be that He already knew every step that they would make. It could be that He had already seen them creeping up beneath the grand balcony where He was prepared to address His children. It could be that He had already witnessed Javier and Armando raising their weapons and opening fire on the guards a hundred times or more. That He'd seen May toss the grenades onto the balcony a thousand times in his head. Seen her smile with satisfaction before she closed her eyes and waited for death. That He'd seen the heavenly guard take her down in a hail of gunfire, bullets tearing through her flesh like raindrops through tissue paper. That He'd seen Javier and Armando burnt alive a million times. Joshua's only hope was that He hadn't seen him and Tommy release the detonators on their bombs. He really hoped that He hadn't seen that coming…or else they were all doomed.

"I don't know. I don't know. Maybe He has foreseen all of

this. Does that mean you don't want to try? You want to just submit to this tyrant? Become like one of those mindless sheep out there? We have to fight. What else is there to live for?" Joshua tried to sound strong and confident, but he could not keep the panic and desperation from seeping into his voice.

It had begun last year, December 12, 2020, though to Joshua it seemed like many lifetimes ago. He had been Christmas shopping with his mother and father in Center City, Philadelphia, listening to his father complain about how he hated going downtown and hated it even more during the holidays when it was packed with cars and people all shoving and cursing, bumping into one another and stepping on each other's feet.

"There's pick-pockets down here too, you know? And muggers. They get you when you're not looking. They always come out on the holidays and this is their favorite place to hunt for victims."

"Don't worry, Dad. I won't let them get you." Joshua laughed.

"Oh you laugh now, until some thug sneaks your wallet out of your pocket, steals your identity and empties your bank account. And just look at all the traffic out there. It's gonna take us two hours to get home if we ever get out of this damn mall."

"Well, it's a good thing I drove. You can sleep the whole way home if you like."

"How the hell can I sleep in all that traffic with everyone honking their horns and the car driving and stopping every second? Let's just get this over with so we can get home."

Joshua had gone into an electronics store in the Galleria Mall to look for an iPod for his father, intending to load it with all of his father's favorite golden oldies. He had just walked in when he sensed that something was wrong. The store was packed but it was eerily quiet. No one was making a sound. The entire store had come to a halt and everyone was standing in the TV section, staring at the screens, watching as cities burned.

The angel of death came first. He was the herald, announcing His coming. San Francisco, New York City, Tokyo, Bangkok, Hong Kong, Tijuana, Rio de Janeiro, Amsterdam, and about two hundred other cities all went up in flames that first week. These were the cities that He had decided were irredeemable.

Governments stood by and did nothing as their citizens were immolated. Images filled the world's TV screens of burning homes, charred bodies, shadows burned into concrete, some of them with hands clasped in prayer, piles of ash that had once been living human beings. Images that made the pictures from Hiroshima look tame by comparison. NATO held emergency meetings. The leaders of every nation made their public addresses and discussed military options, diplomatic options, evacuation, but in the end they did nothing and their cities burned.

There had been warning signs for weeks. Some said months. Bleeding statues, an increase in the number of doomsayers haunting the subways, public parks, and shopping centers, screaming about the end of the world and God's wrath. There were plagues and natural disasters. There were even some bizarre occurrences like swarms of locusts and rats traveling across the United States. Scientists explained it away—global warming—and everyone went back to normal. There were frogs falling from the sky, people long dead who seemed to have come back to life, babies born without faces. Scientists offered their theories, rationalizing each event. Then the Mississippi, the Hudson, the Nile, the Yangtze, the Amazon, the Yenise, the Congo and seven other large rivers around the world all turned to blood, human blood, all with the same blood type and the same DNA. And finally an angel appeared in the sky over Amsterdam with wings the size of a 747, carrying a flaming sword, and the scientists ran out of explanations.

Joshua rushed out of the store to look for his mom and dad. He found them in the food court, stuffing their faces with soft pretzels.

"Mom! Dad! We need to get out of here. There's something really bad happening."

His father's eyes widened.

"Terrorists?"

"I think it's much worse than that."

It had taken them two hours to get home, just as his father had predicted. Joshua took his parents to his house because it was closer and the traffic was getting worse. They listened to NPR the entire time as reports came in of cities on fire.

"You think it's a nuclear attack or something? The North Koreans?"

"I don't know, Mom. They said that there's some kind of flying monster burning everything."

"A flying monster?"

"Some kind of angel or something. I saw it on the TV when I was in the electronics store."

His father snorted.

"That's just one of those camera tricks. The government is trying to hide something."

"I don't know, Dad. It looked pretty real."

They arrived at Joshua's home just before sunset. He and his parents sat in the living room and watched the news reports as they came in. Again and again the cameras would show this enormous bird thing floating in the sky above some city. The images were always hazy and unclear, taken from miles below, and then the cameras would go blank a second later and the report would come in that another city had gone up in flames.

The religious wingnuts and fundamentalists that everyone else used to laugh at were the first to spot the signs and get out. They poured out of the cities and into the mountains and deserts.

They joined religious communes and huddled in churches. Most of them were spared, but many still burned, even as they huddled in their churches, clutching their bibles and praying for forgiveness. Joshua's brother was among them.

Dalton Wright had been four years Joshua's junior. Joshua had changed Dalton's diaper when he was a baby, taught him to throw a football, got him drunk for the first time, and was the first person he came out to and the first one he called when the angel appeared over San Francisco.

Ten cities had already burned that day. There was no question what the angel's appearance meant by then. They had been watching CNN for several hours when it occurred to Joshua that San Francisco might be next. The reports had changed from describing the thing in the air as a monster to an angel, and religious leaders around the world were declaring the destruction God's wrath, his judgment upon human sin. Joshua knew it was just a matter of time before this "angel" made it to San Francisco, Sin City. Joshua dialed his brother over and over, leaving frantic messages on his voicemail.

"Dalton? It's me. Call me back, please! We're worried to death about you."

Dalton finally called him on his cell phone.

"Dalton? Where are you? Are you okay?"

"I'm trying to get the fuck out of the city! Have you seen what's going on?"

"Yeah, Mom and Dad are here with me. We're watching it on CNN. Are you okay?"

"I'm scared the fuck to death! Why is this happening?"

"I don't know. Just try to get out of the city. Do you hear me? Get out of the city!"

"I'm trying! There's too much traffic."

All the roads were jammed as people evacuated the city. The Bay Bridge, the San Mateo Bridge, and the Golden Gate Bridge were all gridlocked. People fled through the streets on foot, on bikes, motorcycles, skateboards, whatever would move. The BART trains were filled and several dozen people were trampled to death trying to get on board; more were suffocated by the sheer press of bodies once they managed to squeeze onto the trains.

By mid-afternoon, Dalton had given up on trying to flee the city. There was no way out. Half the people in city had already fled or were in the process of evacuating. Others had stayed behind to loot the place, not believing what was happening but taking advantage of the widespread panic. People were being murdered, robbed, and raped right on the streets and the local law enforcement officers were fighting for their lives as they tried to maintain order. Then the angel had appeared.

It was as beautiful as it was terrifying. Its wings were at least a hundred feet across from tip to tip and there were four of them sprouting from its back, with hands beneath each wing. The wings were covered in eyes that blinked in unison but were not the same colors—blue, green, almond, dark brown, black—as if they had come from many different faces. They were all of different sizes, most the size of a normal human eye, though some were oval, some slanted and some almost perfectly round. Some were as large as a man's fist. The angel's body was at least twenty or thirty feet tall. It was nude and possessed no genitalia to speak of. It had four faces on its head: a comely human face with golden hair, high cheekbones, alabaster skin, and eyes that burned like exploding suns; on the right side of its head, it had the face of a lion; on the left, the face of an ox. On the back of its head was the face of a hawk or an eagle. Its feet were bronze hooves like those of a horse or a bull. In its hand was a flaming sword like the one God had placed outside of Eden to guard Adam and Eve.

One biblical scholar had called the thing a cherubim and had given it a name, Urael, but others disagreed and said it was the archangel Michael. They all agreed on one thing unanimously. It was an angel of death.

Dalton had taken refuge in a church. He was still on the phone with Joshua, holding the phone tight to his ear as he wound his way through the church to the altar. Joshua could hear the commotion around him.

"Where are you? What's going on?"

"I'm in the church now. I'm going to pray."

"No, Dalton. You've got to leave. You've got to get out of there!"

"There's no way out. God will protect me. God will save us."

There were more than a hundred others huddled amongst the pews. Many clutched bibles, begging, crying, praying. Others tried to preach, urging the sinners to repent. There were hurried baptisms and confessions. Others were on their cell phones calling loved ones, and still others sat quietly, in shock, waiting for death to come.

Joshua's brother knelt at the foot of a large statue of Christ. Dalton had never stopped believing in God. Even after the Baptist church he and his brother had grown up in back in Philly had rejected him when he'd confessed his homosexuality, he had simply found another in San Francisco that accepted him. He had never stopped loving God. Dalton said his prayers every night and went to church every Sunday. He knew every word of the bible by heart.

Genesis 19:24 *"Then the LORD rained upon Sodom and upon Gomorrah brimstone and fire from the LORD out of heaven."*

"Pray with me, Joshua."

"Okay."

"Our Father…"

"Who art in heaven…"

"Hallowed be thy name… "

"I love you, Joshua."

"I love you too, Dalton."

"Thy kingdom come…"

"Thy will be done…"

"I'm so scared. I hear people screaming outside. The smell. The burning smell. I can…I can feel the heat."

"It'll be okay. I'm here with you."

"On earth as it is in heaven…"

"Give us this day our daily bread…"

"And forgive us our trespasses…"

"As we forgive those who—Oh, my God! The heat! It's burning! The walls are burning! Joshuaaaaaaaa!"

The phone went dead. And for Joshua, the war began. He sat with his family and watched for seven days as cities burned, one after another.

Then, on the eighth day, God appeared.

His countenance filled the sky from one end of the earth to the other and he stared down with eyes filled with judgment. He spoke three words.

"I HAVE COME."

And then He descended and took the form of a human. To Joshua, he looked like a cross between Charlton Heston and Ronald Reagan. Old, white, with an aristocratic bearing and a commanding presence, an aura of wisdom and self-certainty, a natural leader used to commanding great power. But as reports came in from around the globe it became apparent that Joshua's vision of Him was not the only one. In Africa He was seen as an old black man who looked like a cross between Nelson Mandela and Muhammad Ali. The reports from some of his African American neighbors placed Him as a cross between Martin Luther King and Malcolm X with some Sidney Poitier thrown in for good measure. In Asia He was perceived as looking like a portly Asian man not unlike the Buddha. In Latin countries He was seen as having light brown skin and dark curly hair. In the Middle East He was seen as a bearded man with olive skin. Some countries even saw Him as a Her.

Soon after His arrival He met with all the world leaders in a huge international conference in Switzerland to announce His plans to take the reins of all the world's governments and to pass along his laws, which were an expanded version of The Ten Commandments. The few dissenters were immediately dispatched. It took less than an hour for all of the leaders to sign over their powers.

Reactions were mixed, though the overwhelming majority treated the news with elation. God had returned to reclaim His kingdom. How could that not be a good thing? But all Joshua could think about were the hundreds of millions who had lost their lives to His wrath, including Dalton, and the many millions more who were likely to follow. This was not the loving, forgiving God that so many modern Christians had believed in, their own aesthetic creation, their vision of what they would have wanted God to be, reflective of their own fears and desires, the same one that his brother had believed in. This was the brutal despot the Bible had described. The one who had commanded Moses' army to lead the Jews into Israel and slaughter every man, child, and animal they found there but to keep the women for concubines. This was the God who had flooded the earth in a fit of rage, killing nearly every living thing on the planet. This was the God who had destroyed Sodom and Gomorrah, who had murdered the firstborn sons of the people of Egypt, who had placed the penalty of death and/or eternal torment upon disobedience of any of His laws. In Joshua's mind there was no such thing as a benevolent tyrant. He would fight this being who had murdered his brother until he had no more breath within him.

At first, Joshua was nearly alone in his opposition, which was then no more than a rebellion of the mind, refusing to pray, refusing to sing His praises or attend church services, waiting for God to smite him for his thoughts of vengeance and reading everything he could about Him, determined to find a weakness. He had no allies and would not have known how to find any. Everyone else was too terrified, afraid that He was listening in on their thoughts and watching every move. It wasn't until one scientist discovered the truth about Him and all the angels, four months after the worldwide holocaust, that the war really began.

He was a physics professor at Princeton University, a former Nobel prize winner in the area of quantum physics, credited with discovering the Higgs boson, "the God Particle." Joshua caught him on an early morning talk show just before he rushed off to work. He paused with his coffee in one hand and his car keys in the other, transfixed by what he was hearing. He sat back down at the kitchen table and turned the volume on the TV up. Fuck work. He could be late this once.

Professor Heinz was a diminutive man in his early sixties with a shaved head and tiny glasses perched on the end of a long aquiline nose. He spoke for nearly twenty minutes before he burst into flames, taking the chair he was sitting on with him and leaving a blackened husk in a vaguely human form. Joshua watched in horror as the production crew rushed onto the stage with fire extinguishers and began dousing his body in foam. The camera stayed on his charred remains for a full minute before cutting to a commercial. Everyone was talking about it at work that day. It was all over the news. God had made an example out of a blasphemer who had dared to question his power. On the news, they were all calling Professor Heinz a crackpot. Several noted scientists, including another Nobel Prize-winning physicist, were rushed onto the air to refute the claims the professor had made about God's mortality. Joshua thought they protested too much. It got him thinking.

Joshua knew that the media belonged to Him now. Nothing

they said could be trusted. Professor Heinz had gone off script and had been punished for it. He would be the last one to speak the truth for a long time. Joshua made it a point to remember what he had said.

"In order for God to be eternal and omniscient He must be outside of time and space. As long as He is within the physical realm He cannot be all-knowing and He cannot be immortal. He is limited by the physical laws. He may still be immensely powerful, but His powers are not limitless. Perhaps this is why there have been fewer and fewer miracles over the last millennium. In order for Him to physically affect things in our universe He must step into it. and when He does that, for that moment, however brief, He is vulnerable. That makes it dangerous for Him. And as mankind has advanced and become more powerful, our ability to murder and destroy increasing exponentially each century, such celestial visitations must have become risky. Well, now, for whatever reason, He is residing in our world full time. He can no longer read all of our thoughts at once, perhaps a few hundred—maybe even a few thousand—at a time, maybe less, maybe much much less. We are dealing in unknown territory here. But certainly not six billion people at once. It is impossible for Him to know what we are all doing every second of the day unless He focuses on each one of us individually. The angels would have to be mortal as well now."

The professor paused and removed his glasses. He wiped sweat from his brow, and then he turned to the camera. He was trembling and there was fear in his eyes. He whispered two words before he ignited. *Fight them.* Then the flames engulfed him, and he began to scream. His flesh ran like taffy and in seconds he was burned to a cinder.

The very next day, all the physics schools around the world were closed. Many universities removed scientific studies from their curriculum entirely. Scientists were watched around the clock. Some were gathered up and placed in government housing units, ghettoes that were just one step above concentration camps.

Joshua had managed to gather up tons of books on quantum physics and quantum mechanics before the police began raiding the bookstores and burning anything remotely related to science, along with books on atheism or agnosticism or anything remotely criticizing God. If Professor Heinz had been wrong, then what were they so afraid of?

"In order for Him to physically affect things in our universe He must step into it, and when He does that, for that moment, however brief, He is vulnerable. That makes it dangerous for Him."

That meant that they were not immortal, not all-powerful. What it meant to Joshua was that they could be killed. There was hope and Joshua was obviously not the only one who thought so.

Joshua discovered a growing underground of likeminded people meeting in secret, at first merely to commiserate over lost loved ones. Most had friends and family who had died during the first strike and others had loved ones who had been murdered later for such offences as working on the Sabbath or taking the Lord's name in vain. Soon their meetings became less about group therapy and more about plotting a rebellion. That's where Joshua had met Tommy, May, Javier, and Armando. Joshua had confided in them about some of the ideas he had since he'd seen the professor speak

Joshua had been studying God and His angels ever since San Francisco was destroyed. He had been trying to figure out a way to destroy them. And every day he had expected to be struck down by lightning or to spontaneously combust like the professor, but nothing had happened. Now, he thought he knew why.

"It is impossible for Him to know what we are all doing every second of the day unless He focuses on each one of us individually."

As long as he stayed under the radar, didn't draw any attention to himself, he might be able to stop Him.

"I think there's a way. Are you with me?"

* * *

The plan was simple. According to Professor Heinz, He could not affect anything in the physical world unless He was physical, so even if He was some sort of holy ghost He would have to take physical form in order to kill. That would be their chance. Armando and Javier had volunteered to be the first martyrs. Once they opened up on the guards and the angels with the ARs, He would lash out at them and that would allow May time to hit Him with the grenades. If they were lucky, the grenades would go off just as He was attacking the two brothers and He would be killed. If not, then the bombs strapped to Joshua and Tommy should finish it. They all knew that it was a suicide mission whether they succeeded or not.

Joshua kept the song going in his head as he heard the sound of gunfire and then Armando and Javier's screams. He didn't think about what was happening to them. He kept his mind on the song.

"I aaaam…climbiiing…Jacoooob's Laddeeeer…"

He heard the grenades go off just as the crowd began to surge, running in all directions, screaming and shouting, drowning out May's screams of anguish as the flesh was rent from her bones, layer by layer just as the Pope's had been. Joshua turned away as her skin was peeled off, and then her muscles, leaving a glistening skeleton still alive and in agony as it floated above the crowd. May had failed. He was still alive. It was all up to Joshua and Tommy, and it was that realization that doomed them both. They had thought it and He had heard their thoughts.

Joshua cursed aloud when he let go of the detonator and nothing happened.

"Fuck! No. No. NO! Fuck you! Bring it! I'm ready! Fuck you!"

He felt himself being lifted from the crowd. Across the enormous courtyard he saw Tommy's body rise. Tommy was still defiant to the end, spitting curses and hurling profanities until his tongue was torn from his mouth and the first layer of skin tore away. Joshua let out an involuntary prayer as he felt his own skin begin to rip free of the muscle and fat, begging for mercy. Then he stopped himself, biting his tongue, gritting his teeth against the pain. If he still had faith in anything, it was that God would not be merciful. Joshua's screams filled the courtyard, easily heard even above the joyous sounds of praise.

ZEN AND THE ART OF
GORDON DRATCH'S DAMNATION

Douglas F. Warrick

During the first era, they observe him. They watch him burn. It is a slow fire, a terribly slow fire that burns him in stages that last a thousand years. A millennium's worth of reddening skin, progressing toward blisters that form in the time it takes for generations to be born and to die. They observe as the flames climb him like leeches, blackening him, curling his skin like old paper, revealing (with a flourish, a magician's handkerchief yanked away) the strings and highways of his musculature. They watch and take notes as his organs boil and burst and their contents spill down the grate at his feet, sluicing down and down and down the sheer walls of the forever-long pit below him. They watch his eyeballs liquefy, they watch him as he becomes unable to watch them. They watch his larynx tumble out, then watch the cords behind it stretch and pop. They watch the layers of his penis curl backward one by one, until there is nothing but a burnt bundle of tissue at his crotch, shaped like a rose. They watch his teeth fall, note their velocity and the rhythm of their staccato *tic-tic-tic* down the drain, jot down the exact moment at which the sound becomes too faint to hear.

They watch all of this, and they brainstorm. And when it is all over, they do it all again in reverse to see if his pain is any less bearable when played backward. And then they compare notes.

—Allow the sensory organs to last longer, or not be destroyed at all. Allow him to see, hear, taste, and feel all of it.

—Leave his penis. I want to see what happens when we leave his penis.

—He does not scream enough. Hotter fire? Slower?

During the second era, they pry apart his mind and climb inside. They want to see who he is and why he is here. They become like tiny mosquitoes and bleed him of his memories and emotions.

For the first few decades, there is only fear. The terrible (delicious, oh so delicious for them, and oh so fascinating; these things always are) sensation of awakening to a lie you've been told, one around which you've constructed your entire life. No, no, no, this can't be real, I can't be here, I don't believe in this! It is amazing to them how long it takes for the shock to wear off. The damned can never accept that they are damned. They can never grasp that they have simply chosen incorrectly. What was it that the God-Boy had said? About being THE way? THE truth? THE light?

They relish his fear. They do not become bored of it. Not once in the never-beginning history of their kind have they ever.

And when they have gorged themselves on his emotions, they dig past them and excavate his life. They find that this man's name is Gordon Dratch. Gordon Dratch was twenty-eight years old when he fell off a ladder outside of his home and cracked open his skull on his concrete driveway.

—What a wonderfully comical way to die.

—They laugh at him, I'm sure. His obituary is its own punchline.

—What else? What else?

They dig, and they find.

Witness Gordon Dratch as a child. Thirteen and angry. He opens the closet door slowly, careful of the creak in the hinges and the scrape against the rough carpet. He ducks inside, holds his breath. The closet smells like peppermint and Old Spice and sweat and that dry, aged stench of all those creepy old people at church. Bald buzzard-headed men and fat mean-eyed women whose toothless mouths can't seem to shape the words of the hymns, and so they just sing off-key animal noises. He hates them. But he's not concerned with them just now. It's in here somewhere, his prize, his reward for being quiet and cunning and thirteen. He finds it in an old shoebox that used to hold his dad's dress shoes. A forty-ounce bottle of pale brown booze, the label torn off so the only markings on the glass are the white leavings of the paper and the sticky label glue that held it on. His dad's stash, the secret stuff.

He used to find it all over the place. Beneath the seat of Daddy's car. Down in the basement behind the dryer. Even after Daddy's Big Breakthrough, the day he and Mommy sat Gordon and Annie down in the living room and Mommy said, "Guys. Daddy's got a problem with alcohol. We've got to give Daddy some space and some extra love, okay? He needs us to help him get better." So, yeah, Gordon knows what booze is, and he knows that his dad was a drunk. Is a drunk. Whatever.

He hides the bottle beneath his coat, hard up inside his armpit, and he reaches inside his dad's jacket and steals a few cigarettes, too. Then he slips out, closes the door behind him with the same slow care he took in opening it. And he leaves the house.

Outside, Mark Milligan is waiting for him with his hands shoved in his pockets, his eyes darting from Gordon's front door to the street and back again, checking for the hidden cameras, the signs of the trap. He says, "D'ja get it?"

Gordon nods. They cut across the street and through somebody's back yard. An Irish setter growls at them, and they spit at it and flip it the bird. They vault the fence and sit beneath the bushes by the railroad tracks, trading swigs of the forty and smoking Winstons. Mark says, "My dad says your dad is gonna start giving sermons sometimes. Like, as practice."

Gordon says, "Yup."

Mark says, "Is he any good?"

Gordon cocks an eyebrow at him. "What do you mean?"

"Like, does he want to be a pastor or something?"

"I guess. I dunno."

They sit in silence for a while, smoking and taking little sips, too young and too scared to drink enough to get drunk. Then Gordon says, "I don't believe in God, anyway." They spend the rest of the afternoon like that, silent, pretending to drink, pretending to smoke, until the sun starts going down and they both have to sneak away home and brush their teeth so no one smells the smoke on their breath.

They like this memory. It is typical, vintage human behavior. Delicious in its predictability. They've tasted it before, and they note its flavor, write a few lines on the similarities it holds to other memories like it.

—*Poor baby was an angry teenager. We weep for you, Gordon.*

—*Is he an atheist? He doesn't burn like an atheist.*

—*More! There must be more!*

After the fear, the thing that was Gordon Dratch feels intense, awful, cold regret. He feels it freeze inside him, even through the slow fire burns and bursts him over and over again. They observe the change with joy, watching a favorite play, coming to a well-remembered and well-loved scene. He weeps until his eyes are gone, and then weeps some more once they are rewound back into his head. They watch the realization work its way across his soul, spreading through his veins like a blood-sickness. He made the wrong decision. Faced with a million spiritual doors, he opened the wrong one. There was such a thing as a wrong door! All of those red-faced old men with their fists bound up into tight, sausage-fingered slabs on the pulpit, those men who had raged against the follies of a Godless world, those men had been *right*. Oh, God. Oh, God, forgive me now.

They applaud. Their favorite line. No man enters the kingdom and all that.

And then they dig deeper. So much to learn about this perfect, typical member of the damned. So many beautiful, repetitive layers to wonder at.

Witness Gordon Dratch in fast-motion, the high school years, filled to bursting with parking lot fights, stolen liquor, three-day suspensions, detentions, Saturday schools, cigarettes, CDs from Scandinavian metal bands with face-paint and leather gauntlets who wear upside-down crosses and sing songs about the devil. Witness the first few years of college whiz by, time-lapse photography of Gordon becoming a sullen young man, the kid whose every relationship will ultimately be scuttled by daddy issues and a latent anger toward a God he claims he does not believe in. All so fast that you can see the bones in his face shift, change shape. A series of patchy beards grown and then shaved off, a dozen pairs of glasses becoming scratched or broken at the bow and then replaced, a thousand T-shirts and a thousand jeans, re-cycled over and over again. Spend a single second watching Gordon shout black metal lyrics in the face of the street preacher on the quad, both of them red-faced, both of them with veins standing up in their necks.

Now stop.

Did you miss it? The moment of his awakening? It is easy to do when you fly through a life. But look at him now, sitting at a desk with his notebook in front of him, scribbling with intense concentration. He loves this class. It is very possibly the only class he has ever taken that he has ever enjoyed. He is twenty-one years old. The heading he has scrawled at the top of the perforated standard-rule page says ZEN NOTES. Behind it are fifteen pages with the same heading, filled with simple, perfect discoveries excavated from a history he never knew existed, quotes from men who became historical footnotes thousands of years before Gordon Dratch was born, revelations of a life that could be lived without anger or fear.

Gordon Dratch is joyful.

Speed forward again, just a few months, and Gordon Dratch is standing at a bar with a beer in his hand, smiling and talking to a stranger in a T-shirt that says, "Jesus died for his own sins, not mine." He is saying, "Zen and atheism are totally compatible philosophies." He takes a drink, feels the alcohol going to work on him, making him feel smiley and fuzzy. "Or at least," he says, "that's a good place to start." The words sound funny to him, like they don't make quite enough sense, and he decides he's done drinking for the night. He's proud of himself, sort of. His dad could have never done that. Then he says, "Let me tell you a story."

The story he tells is a story the Buddha told when asked to explain what happens to a man after he dies. Gordon says, "There is a war. During that war, a man is shot in the arm with an arrow and is taken to a medic. The medic takes the man aside and attempts to remove the arrow, but the man is agitated. He won't sit still, he's freaking the fuck out, right? He keeps saying, who shot me? Was it someone on the other side or was it one of my own kinsmen, mistaking me for the enemy? Where was the archer when he shot me? I want to know about the trajectory of the arrow. What type of bow was used? What type of wood is the arrow made out of? What will happen now to the archer? What was he thinking when he shot me?"

The stranger laughs, and Gordon knows he's doing this right, acting out all the right parts, holding his shoulder and glancing around wide-eyed, selling the comedy. "The medic stops him, calms him down. Then he says, the answers to those questions will not remove the arrow from your arm."

The stranger says, "Nice, dude. Nice."

Gordon shrugs. "It's a good story. Basically, Buddha was saying that what happens when we die is inconsequential. We die."

The stranger points his beer bottle at Gordon, narrows his eyes, "Yeah, but that proves my point. Even you worship somebody. Buddha is your Jesus."

Gordon thinks about it, shakes his head. "No, I don't think so. For me, Buddha was nothing that I can't be. It's weird. You can't rank somebody as any higher or lower than you. That's the point. Nobody is my Jesus, because there is no essential duality between entities. Bodhi Dharma—he's another of those pre-Zen guys who kinda set the stage for Zen—he said, if you see the Buddha on the road, kill him." He smiles wide. "Everything is temporary. Even the Buddha. He's dead now. He doesn't exist anymore. When I die, I won't either. It's sort of liberating, if you can accept it."

The stranger shakes his head, sighs, runs a hand over his scalp. "So, if there's no risk of punishment or reward after death, why bother with this shit in the first place?"

Gordon's eyebrows scrunch up in the middle. He glances away. "I guess I don't know. Because...I guess, because it's good for us? It cleanses us. Maybe." He opens his mouth, works his jaw back and forth. "It makes my life happier, I guess. It makes me a friendlier person. So it can't be all bad, can it?"

Oh, delicious, wonderful, stupid, damned Gordon! They breathe the memory in, memorize it, repeat the good parts amongst themselves.

—*No risk of punishment or reward! Ha!*

—*It can't be all bad! It can't be all bad!*

—*Zen burns so long! It burns so hot! Delightful! Delightful!*

After the regret, there is the anger. Gordon would clench his fists if he had them, and when the suffering begins again and his hands rematerialize over his blackened bones, he does. He thrashes about the burning chamber, colliding with walls, falling to the grated floor, howling until his lungs and his voice are gone, and then simply scratching angry patterns in the layer of ash that covers everything. God, the bastard! God, the petulant child who throws His toys to the fire if they fail to please Him! That is the monster who made the world! How dare He? What right does He have?

They laugh at this. There is so much brilliant anger in him that they become drunk upon it, wheeling around his brain, clutching one another for balance, and howling back at his apoplepsy. These black, mean, torturous thoughts! He would make a fine member of their race, if that transition were possible. And oh, the names he comes up with. Faggot Christ! God of vomit! Jehovah the Blind Old Rapist, that's who He is! Creation-Devil! Old-Testament Fascist! Jesus died for his own sins, not mine! Fuck Him! Fuck Him!

— *Aw, look, gentlemen. How adorable.*

— *He should have written lyrics for his beloved little black metal bands.*

— *Can you imagine? Little Gordon the Satanic Rock Star. It's positively quaint.*

They enjoy it while they can. The "Fuck God" stage is the briefest of all. The one that transitions, finally, inevitably, back into hopeless, haunted, never-ending grief. Grief for what was lost: the illusion of impermanence, the lie of transcendence. Grief for what was never lost, could never *be* lost: Gordon Dratch, a thing with a soul that lasts forever and ever and ever.

Quick now, before he can lose that choice flavor of rage, they must find another memory to play with.

* * *

Witness Gordon Dratch learning that life is suffering. Drunk, like his dad used to get drunk, that sort of single-minded, locked-on-target drunk, precise in its purpose, determined beyond all distraction. He snorts. Sneers.

She's gone. Gone for good.

He calls his sister, Annie. Her voicemail clicks in, says, "Hey, it's Annie. We all know how these things work, right? Beep, message, I call you back. If you don't get it by now, you've got bigger problems than not being able to get a hold of me."

He says, "You know that everr-body...everybody...always thought she was a bitch, right? Nobody wanted to...say anything, but you all should have. Fuck her. And fuck you too, Annie. Cunt." He hangs up the phone.

Liz has left him, and all the Zen proverbs in the world mean precisely less than shit now. So fuck Liz, and fuck Linji, and fuck Dogen, and fuck the Buddha. If he saw him on the road, Gordon would run his fat ass over.

What she said was, "You think you get it. You think you have an academic understanding of how to end your own suffering. Well, congratulations. Let me know how that works out." And before she shut the door on him, leaving him out there beneath the orange porch light surrounded by light-junkie moths and blood-junkie mosquitoes and all manner of junkies for all manner of substances out in the awful, addicted world, she said, smiling, "Gordon. I hope you find out how to be happy some day."

What he said to that was, "Lizzer. I love you."

She shook her head. "I don't think you do. I think you are... attached to me. Just come over tomorrow. We'll pack up your stuff together. Okay?"

Yada yada yada, shit happened, money crossed hands, and now Gordon is parked in front of a Speedway with a bottle and a half of Red Dog already killed and two more that he'll almost certainly never finish nestled up against each other in the passenger seat like ostrich eggs. And he is thinking about Linji. Or Rinzai. Or Lin-Chi. Or whoever-the-fuck. Does it matter? The guy with the fly-whisk who woke his students to their own Buddha-nature by hitting them repeatedly, or shouting nonsense into their faces, who advocated for the True Man of No Rank. Who said, "Whether you're facing inward or facing outward, whatever you meet up with, just kill it!" Who probably thought of Bhodi Dharma, called to mind his hard eyes and sneering mouth, took from him the wisdom he needed, and allowed the rest of him to fade into the dead past where he belonged, and said, "If you meet a Buddha, kill the Buddha. If you meet a patriarch, kill the patriarch. If you meet an arhat, kill the arhat. If you meet your parents, kill your parents. If you meet your kinfolk, kill your kinfolk. Then for the first time you will gain emancipation, will not be entangled with things, will pass freely anywhere you wish to go."

There are lights behind him. The sounds of car doors opening and closing.

Gordon says, "What a shitty ass-wiper," and he laughs. Linji, with his shouting and slapping and devotion to the beatific joy of random action, his perfect refusal to bow to the tyrannical dualism of logical discourse. In his head, Gordon sees him, sitting among his students, fly-whisk in hand, listening as a student asks him to describe his True Man of No Rank.

In Gordon's head, Linji leaps at his student, wraps his fingers in the man's lapels, screams into his face, spewing wet spit into his eyes, "Speak! Speak!"

And in his head, the student cannot speak.

And in his head, Linji drops the student to the floor. He is disgusted. Failure. Don't these people know? Can't they understand that they are all the True Man? That if they would simply stop searching, they would find him? He sneers. Spits. He says, "This

True Man of No Rank…" and sighs. "What a shitty ass-wiper."

To the cop shining a flashlight through his open window, Gordon says, "I've got an academic understanding of how to end my own suffering."

Someone asks him for his ID. The door is opened. Gordon is led to the back of the squad car. He says, "See, I can tell you anything you want about Zen. I just can't put it into practice."

The engine turns over. Someone is asking him how much he's had tonight. Someone says something into a walkie-talkie. The walkie-talkie says something back.

Gordon says, "I'm not…real good at Zen."

The streets blur. The lights bleed into one another, neon and halogen and green and red and yellow and white become one light. He is going somewhere. He says, "I am a shitty ass-wiper." He passes out in the back of the squad car.

During the third era, the fires burn out. The embers fade. The flesh steams and slides away in patches, oozes a thousand brilliant multicolored fluids that never lived beneath it in life, and the thing that is left there, the eternal thing that is, was, and always will be Gordon Dratch is left alone to scab over, to scar. He becomes a blackened thing, his muscles uncovered, his intestines hanging out, a thing to which physical pain has become a sort of distant nostalgia. He mourns the passing of fairness. He mourns the death of compassion. He mourns his own eternity. And they are outside of him again, leaving him alone in his tiny cell with the grated floor. They have sobered. This stage is not one to be enjoyed drunk. There are subtleties to savor here, intricacies of sorrow that are too minute for all that. This isn't a party game anymore.

Sometimes they whisper to him. They quote Linji and Dogen and Milton and the Buddha and the God-Boy. They leave him like that while the human race rots in the world above, while they destroy themselves and rebuild themselves a thousand times over. Sometimes they turn the fires back on and scribble notes about how quietly he whimpers when it consumes him, how he twitches and stirs and murmurs when he is rebuilt. Sometimes they pluck memories from his head. The good memories, mostly. Gordon in his little house, alone, happy to be alone. They replay the time when Gordon, on the phone with Liz some three years after their breakup, said, "I don't think I'll ever be in love again, Lizzer. I think that's okay, too. I think I'm really happy this way." They laugh at that, in a quiet, meditative way. Because when he said it, he meant it.

And the fall from the ladder: Gordon up there with his toes on the top rung, feeling physical and alive and happy and simple as he threw handfuls of dead leaves from the gutters into a garbage bag. Falling. Hitting the ground. Feeling his head split open in the back, the electric stab that was not really pain at all, the trickle of blood from his nostrils and out from beneath his eyes, Gordon thought, *Oh. Okay. That's it for me.* And now Gordon aches. Had he thought he was ever that close to enlightenment? Had he really believed in such a thing?

They do not realize that something is wrong for many thousands of years. They are busy with others. It can't be helped. Heaven is so exclusive, and the alternative so indiscriminate. But something is wrong. Because the thing that is Gordon Dratch is no longer curled up in a fetal position against the grate, cradling its intestines in its skeletal arms, whimpering through its ruined mouth. The thing that was Gordon Dratch is sitting upright. Breathing. Slowly.

When they find him like this, they taunt him. They mimic a thousand voices from his past and sharpen them and use them to cut out his eyes and his tongue and his liver, and then use the same sharpened remembered voices to sew them back in again.

— *You have an academic understanding of your own suffering.*

—*We all know how these things work, right?*

—*Jesus died for his own sins, not mine.*

They turn the fire back on and watch him sit in silence. Breathing. Slowly. As he is disintegrated.

—*Speak! Speak!*

—*Kill your parents! Kill your kinsmen!*

—*What a shitty ass-wiper!*

They climb inside his brain and search for his memories. They are becoming nervous, shaking, their notes forgotten somewhere in the midnight dark of this place. Something is wrong. Gordon Dratch does not burn! Even as his flesh is slashed and blackened and his mind is picked apart, Gordon Dratch does not burn!

They seek help. And help comes.

Witness Gordon Dratch in Hell. Opening his flame-hardened eyelids. His posture is perfect. His hands, their skin gone, his skeleton fingers sticking from the globs of cooked meat at the ends of his wrists, resting on his knees. He sees the Other in the room with him, and for a moment he is surprised, and the pain and the fear and the sadness sweep into him again. He accepts them, becomes them, and does not move.

The Other is beautiful, and her eyes are full of bitter hurt. She is naked and her skin is wet and pale. Her fingers brush at her labia, bored, not so much masturbation as the iconography of masturbation. She has no mouth. She says, "You know who I am."

Gordon Dratch nods. "I think so."

"I fought against Him too, once. I stood at His throne with a sword in my hand and I thrust it into His guts and as His blood trickled down through the ground of My Father's House and found the place where it would pool and become my own kingdom. He only smiled at me and told me that He knew I would fail from the beginning. And then He cast me down. And I was not like you. Angel was my station. Spirit was my form. And still he made me into a slave. You can hope for far less compassion than I received."

Gordon smiles. "I'm not fighting anyone."

It's quiet in there. Somewhere, water drips from somewhere up high and taps against the grate. It splatters onto Gordon's knees, and he shivers.

The Other flicks at her clitoris. It's an idle gesture without any purpose. She may as well be twiddling her thumbs, chewing on a strand of her hair. She says, "What are you trying to do?"

Gordon breathes for a long time. Then he says, "If I had a fly-whisk, I'd hit you with it."

Those beautiful eyes, so betrayed and bent and bruised, narrow. She would be sneering if she could. "You were wrong, you know. There is no such thing as enlightenment. There is no Zen. The Buddha burns here. Bodhi Dharma, too. Linji weeps in this place, somewhere above you in a chamber just like this one, wishing someone had told him the truth, begging for a chance to make it right. I could show you this. Would you like that?"

Gordon shakes his head. "No. I believe you. It just doesn't matter."

She spends a long time hurting him. She knows every secret. She can recite the entire script of his life, and does, punctuating each of his cruelties and stupidities and kindnesses and betrayals with burning and bleeding and pain. She scours him. And when she is done with this, she fucks him. She heals his cock and she takes him into her, and he wants it, God, he wants it, he wants this with all of the substance that makes up his soul, even as heaving waves of memory and emotion and pain rip through him. But Gordon Dratch remembers to breathe.

When she is done with him, she whispers in his ear, "We can do this forever. We are not constrained by time." She takes his penis with her, severed and held by the stem in her hand, limp, conforming to the curvature of her palm, swinging.

When she is gone, Gordon, his eyes narrowed, his charred lips smiling, shouts, "Speak! Speak!" and he does not stop shouting until his voice is raw and all he can do is breathe.

Witness Gordon Dratch experiencing eternity. This is zazen, this is meditation. Picture a lake of ice and one drop of unfrozen water upon the ice. Now imagine the ice breaking. What happens to the drop?

Picture a bell held in an old man's hand in a room that stretches up to eternity and out to the same. Now close your eyes and hear the bell ring. You are nowhere. The only thing that is anywhere is the sound, the shatter-sweet forever noise of the bell. Where does the noise end, and where do you begin?

Witness Gordon Dratch closing his eyes in his little burning chamber. Witness Gordon Dratch, eleven thousand three hundred and eight years later, opening his eyes someplace else.

Oh, thinks Gordon.

This place—this *new* place—is made of gold. There is a golden carpet beneath Gordon's folded knees, unspeakably soft, shifting beneath him to accommodate the tiny movements of the hairs on his legs and ass. There are golden walls and golden wallpaper. There is a golden window, somehow simultaneously transparent and opaque, that looks out into a golden world. There is a golden sofa, old and sprung, the kind of thing you find at a thrift store and spend hours in, letting yourself sink like a dropped rock into its deep-sea comfort. And against the far wall, sinking forever downward into a gold-black chasm and rising forever upward into a gold-black skylight, is a column of golden faces. It moves—twists, rises, turns, sinks, changes direction like a dancer, the way smoke changes direction, the way blood spilled under water changes direction—and the faces shift, rolling over one another with a noise like wood being chopped (*shhhunt, shhhunt, shhhunt*), revealing themselves and concealing themselves.

Gordon says, "I see. You're Him."

One of the faces, one that looks like his father, drunk and dopey and sleepy-eyed, says, "I am," and then is consumed in the rolling tide of other faces, and slips away up through the chute in the golden ceiling. *Shhhunt.*

Gordon uncrosses his legs, takes a deep breath, and closes his eyes. *Jesus,* he thinks, *it would be so easy. I'm here. I'm home. Let go, Gordon, let go.*

Shhhunt.

Some other thought slides like oil into Gordon's head, slides in and slides out again, not a flash, not a jump-cut thought, but a steamy dissolve in and out. *Jehova, the Blind Old Rapist.* He says, "I don't belong here."

Another face, this one looks like Annie—*We all know how these things work. If you don't get it by now, you've got bigger problems—* says, "We made an exception." And then *shhhunt,* and Annie's gone, sliding away beneath the hole in the floor.

Gordon stands. The golden carpet pricks his feet, but it feels good, like how sometimes lying on the scratchy carpet in front of the TV on Saturday mornings used to feel good. He walks to the couch, sits down. It's as perfect a sinking couch as any he's ever sat in, and for a moment, Gordon feels tears prick his eyes (*it's been so long, oh, oh, it's been so goddamn long*) and childish, thankful joy possesses him, swallows him whole. He accepts the joy, swallows it, becomes it, and moves on. It's become instinct. It's like driving a car, riding a bike. Zazen is a forgotten instinct suddenly reclaimed. You don't attain enlightenment. You remember it.

He looks at a face that looks like the cop who found him drunk in his car outside of that Speedway so long ago, blurred into slopped paint by his remembrance, and says, "You can do that?"

The cop-face says, "I can. You know that, Gordon."

Shhhunt.

Gordon thinks, *Faggot Christ. Jesus died for his own sins, not mine.*

"Why?"

Gordon's gold-faced mother, the newest mask in this procession, looks puzzled. Her eyebrows furrow and her lips pull to one side. "Because you win, Gordon. Because you proved your point."

"I had nothing to prove."

The faces laugh. All of them. The room (the room? Ha, that's good; try the world, try the universe, try the slippery formless outside-the-eggshell-of-all-existence space, try everything, more than everything, so much everything that it might as well be nothing, and yes, try nothing while you're at it) is filled up like a water balloon with the noise of endless voices laughing together in perfect harmony. It scares Gordon. For just a moment, it almost ruins him and he thinks, *A living mind would break. A living person would go mad if they heard that sound. That sound is the true name of God.*

"Oh, my Gordon," says a face like Bodhi Dharma, golden mouth set, golden eyes staring, those eyes people used to say could bore holes into mountainsides. "That's true, now. There is no enlightenment. There is no Zen. This is the closest you'll come."

It's true, of course. Christ. It sits hard in Gordon's chest, a lead fist between his ribs. *Give up,* he thinks. *You win, Gordon. It's time to quit breathing.*

And he thinks, *Jesus died for his own sins.*

He says, "I am so angry at you."

Shhhunt, like a liquid slot machine, like a piston, like no other thing Gordon has ever seen, and, no, please, no, this face *will* ruin him, this face will eat him alive, this face will be worse than a thousand eternities in Hell, but here she is goddamn it, staring, smiling, her golden eyes wet with golden tears, and Liz, his pretty Lizzer with one crooked tooth in her perfect smile, says, "I know. I forgive you for that."

Gordon Dratch's anger slides away. He can feel it clinging to him, grasping desperately for purchase as it is sucked into ether and made into gold. And then it is gone. And Gordon cries like a child.

Shhhunt.

No, He can't do that. He can't give her back to him like that and then pull her away again. It isn't fair. It isn't right. Please, he wants to keep her there with him just a little while longer, please!

Liz's face is gone. And Gordon Dratch stops breathing.

There is no time in this place. And so Gordon Dratch does not know how long he has been curled up, sunk into the golden couch with his head on the armrest, watching the faces of the endless totem pole change, feeling sleepy and sad and satisfied. Forever, maybe. Maybe he has never been anywhere else. He can sleep now, if he wants. He can stay awake and speak to any person his heart desires, call up their shining faces and pretend that it really did belong to them, that he was talking to someone other than Him. There is no suffering.

None but the small, silent sadness, less than microscopic, planted in his skull like a tiny seed.

The pillar shifts, *shhhunt*, and the face staring back at him, mouth slightly open, witnessing the world through half-closed eyes, is unfamiliar. Almost. Gordon knows the way the lips twitch, the way the muscles in the cheeks tense and relax. Not visual memory, but something higher. He knows how it feels for those lips to twitch, for those cheeks to relax, for that jaw to chew, for those eyelids to flutter and close. Those lips once said, "I don't believe in God, anyway," and "I'm really happy this way," and "Lizzer, I love you," and "It's sort of liberating, if you can accept it."

This is the face of Gordon Dratch. And to Gordon Dratch, this face means nothing.

Zen is a forgotten instinct suddenly reclaimed.

Gordon says, "Oh, God. I think you just made a mistake."

His face says, "Gordon, I don't make mistakes."

This poor old thing. This poor, deluded, mindless thing who existed before there were any faces to add to its golden surface, before forever began. This thing who fashioned a universe in three days and filled it with life so it wouldn't have to feel so alone anymore. It just wanted to be believed in. It just wanted to be obeyed. And still it has not removed the arrow from its arm.

Witness Gordon Dratch finally understanding compassion.

He gets up from the couch, feels the regret, the longing to be back there, curled and comfortable forever and ever; he swallows it, accepts it, becomes it, *breathes* it. He stands close to the golden pillar, so close that his toes stick out over the edge, dangling above the unending mineshaft, so close that he can see the infinite faces swimming away from him, down in the darkness a million miles away.

Gordon Dratch's golden face says, "What are you doing, Gordon? Don't you want to sit back down?" What is that? Is there anger in that voice? Is there fear?

Gordon reaches out and places his hand upon his own cheek. He says, "What a shitty ass-wiper."

"Stop this. Sit down."

Gordon says, "I am so sorry for this. I can only imagine how much it hurts."

The face, contorted with anger, one golden vein (Gordon knows that vein, he's had to massage that place on his temple with trembling fingers more times than he can recall) pulsing, says, "I gave you this place as a gift. I do not have to allow you to keep it. I do not want to, Gordon, but I can send you back."

Gordon smiles a little. He says, "The Lord giveth, and the Lord taketh away. I know. But," and he runs a finger over those lips, down around that jawline. "This face isn't mine. This isn't me."

"Please." Fear this time, hot and uneven and undeniable, rippling through the entire room. "Please. I love you."

Gordon says, "I said that to someone a long time ago. And she told me I was wrong. She was right about that, I think."

More faces now, swimming up to cluster around this one, this not-his-face, trying to overlap it, to cover it, to carry it away, *shhhunt, shhhunt, shhhunt,* but the face of Gordon Dratch, the face of this stranger, the face of this person who never existed, can't escape. It is held there by Gordon's gentle fingers, pinioned in place while the other golden masks lock up around it, cramped into expressions of identical terror and rage.

"YOU ARE GORDON DRATCH. YOU WERE GORDON DRATCH FROM THE MOMENT I CONCEIVED OF YOU AND YOU WILL BE GORDON DRATCH FOREVER. YOU CAN'T ESCAPE YOURSELF."

"Are you familiar with the concept of a bodhi satva?" says Gordon (no, not Gordon, not anymore, not really ever). "Someone who opts out of Nirvana so they can continue to be born and to live just so they can lead others to enlightenment?"

The faces scream.

"It's a Tibetan thing, mostly, and there's really no equivalent in Zen."

A crack runs through the golden world, a fissure that runs out from the bottom of the God-Totem's mineshaft and spiderwebs its way over the floor and the ceiling, opening up the world like lightning.

"But I think—"

"SIT. DOWN. NOW."

"—this must be what they meant."

There is a shattering of ice, the sound of a bell being rung in a cathedral.

* * *

In the final era, there is an empty room in My Father's House. A place where a crack runs through the center like a nasty bump on a bad stretch of blacktop. There is a golden window, cracked, the golden glass a mosaic depicting nothing at all. Witness the God-Totem.

Shhhunt. Shhhunt.

The faces are silent. Their golden eyes glance around the room, confused, hurt, frightened. The eyes of children left alone.

Shhhunt. Shhhunt.

They slide. They swim. They move over the surface of the piston with their mouths open. He wishes His memory was not so complete. He wishes He could forget. And so the faces slide across almost every inch of the God-Totem, wishing and wondering.

Shhhunt.

There is just one spot where the faces do not slide, do not dare to slide for fear that the memory will be activated, will be relived with all the clarity and confusion it held in the moment it occurred. One blank spot, one place where a face used to be, a face that is gone. Just a blank, colorless place, an empty canvas drained of certainty and form, leaving behind only the blank, joyful possibility of emptiness.

Shhhunt.
Shhhunt.
Shhhunt.

GO AND TELL IT ON THE MOUNTAIN

Kyle S. Johnson

S tanding in line to meet Jesus Christ at Tel Megiddo, I have to hear Mike from Jersey tell the same anecdote for the seventh time. And it's a long one. The one about the time he and his wife got into a nasty argument over something their son did in school. The way he tells it, they got into a huge shouting match and, as things tend to go with Mike's stories, ended up having aggressive make-up sex on the dinner table. And it was good, too. He makes sure all the women in line hear this. How good he is in bed and how much he misses his wife, because he's vulnerable (in Mike's estimation, if there's anything women love, it's a vulnerable man in a small, dark hour). And right as he's getting ready to climax, as he's getting ready to spread that angry love but good (according to Mike, she loved it on her stomach, God rest her soul), something went boom.

Boom. Boom just happened one night, no warning, no foreshadowing. Boom came quickly, and boom repeated itself for the better part of three days. Boom, much to Mike's dismay, wasn't prefaced with a "badda-bing, badda-." But we know all about that. At least we know basic ideas. Speculation is the science of the day. Someone heard from someone that somebody said the U.S. was gone, all gone, and that before they got gone, they made sure that everybody else disappeared with them. Korea got it bad, the Middle East became a sheet of glass, Cuba upended and drowned, Germany became the smoking crater it should have been after WWII, and everything west of Quebec got obliterated simply because somebody in China accidentally aimed too high.

The one concrete is obvious. We are all here. And Jesus Christ is here. And that doesn't add up to a particularly promising conclusion. But some people aren't without their humor. Mike tries to shape a mushroom cloud with his hands, turns his eyes up to imply the enormity of it all. He's really into his act now. If the man wasn't a stand-up comic at some point, he was well on his way. He's right about at the point where he gets to the big finish. Literally. Where the sound of something blowing up in the distance and the rumbling of pots and pans causes his wife to look up at him and ask, in his best Jersey-girl voice, "Babe, tell me you didn't just come inside me."

Okay, so maybe his punchline needs a bit of work. And it shows in Jesus' face. That same haunting look of disapproval you'd get from your father with a report card full of Ds. But, being polite, He breaks a little bit and squeezes out one of the more obvious forced laughs I've ever heard. And then everyone chuckles a bit upon recognition, and this blight that the world has become transforms into a dark auditorium with an audience of politely laughing people stretching for miles into the fog. The line behind me leers around my shoulders, hoping to get a better look at Mike and Jesus, gauging how the messiah reacts to his routine. Taking notes. Trussing up loose ends in their speeches, re-rehearsing. *Hi Jesus, I'm Jerry Nordstrom from Halifax. Did I ever tell you the one...?*

The line to meet Christ at Tel Megiddo is impressive. It starts somewhere in Tel Aviv and winds all the way up to the rock. And it's filled with adults-cum-children. They straighten bowties and pull their denim skirts down to cover their ankles. They practice their juggling and hum their scales. They go over their lists of requests and questions, trimming the fat. The world's last job interview. The final reality TV talent search. Everyone wants that golden ticket that takes them to the pearly gates. To transcend. To escape these husks of flesh that served us so well for so long, until they betrayed us and started melting from the inside.

We are all adolescent ne'er-do-wells who start taking out the trash and doing the dishes once October clams shut and becomes November, once red and green tinsel starts getting strung up and carrot-nosed snowmen stalk the aisles of convenience stores. We've got on our cherub masks, trying our best to look dainty and polite. We wait to meet our Santa on a dirty slab of stone in the hellish heat of bombed-out nothing, pretending we're in a county shopping mall, cushy and buzzing and artificially warm, hand in hand with our parents and awaiting our showdown with the big man in red.

But that was all dress rehearsal. This is real deal Holyfield. The final list of who's naughty and who's nice has been drafted and sent to the printers. But I have little to fear. I'm confident in the way I've lived my life to this point. Granted, I may be the only one at the book signing who hasn't read the guy's work, but I lived life the way I thought it ought to be lived. And if I was wrong, if I made a bad call by not taking refuge in something I didn't believe in, then I'd rather spend eternity washing my shirts in a lake of fire than bowing at the altar of an egomaniac.

But still, I like my chances. Too many people I've grown to dislike in such a small amount of time have skipped past Jesus into the haze like they just won the Powerball. Mike seems to be the exception, not the rule. His shoulders go slack with every quiet word spoken by The Son of Man. He turns to me and shrugs, clinging to that last bit of good humor he has, and heads further west. I turn from him and lock eyes with Jesus. He keeps His gaze, nods, beckons me forward. I join the masses in feeling like a kid again, only I feel like Mr. Dvorak has called me into the principal's office one last time.

The first thing you notice about Jesus Christ when you meet him is how He smells. He smells like piss dried on the crotch of a pair of underwear. Stale cigarette smoke. It's not the fact that He looks nothing like you'd imagine. No flowing white robes, no halo, no doe eyes. Jesus is a beat up sack of a man who looks like He hasn't seen a fortuitous year since His resurrection. It isn't the tanned hide He calls His face; it isn't the dirt that covers it. It's that smell.

I sit next to Christ on the rock. He pats me on the knee. I stop myself before the first words come trickling out, like an ex-boyfriend trying to win back a former flame, calculating each word into algebra. So I whisper His name. And He tells me to call him Jeezy.

"Seriously, man. Everybody does."

And, breaking every rule somebody ever told me about questioning the word of our Lord, I ask him if He is indeed serious.

"Hey, if I'm lying, I'm dying."

He laughs. Oh, right. Because we're all dying. Like the nausea, headaches, accelerated loss of hair, and what feels like a golf ball-sized growth at the base of my skull weren't enough of an indicator. Mike could stand to learn a thing or two about comic timing from Jeezy. The whole situation reads like one of Mike's jokes. *So you and Jesus Christ are sitting on this rock, right?*

He breaks me in nice and easy. "So you have come here for the final answers? You seek the knowledge that accompanies the end times?"

He sounds vaguely empathetic, concerned. But that is just a cover for His obvious boredom. Like I'm customer number one thousand for the day at a suicide crisis hotline. I start to see that He may be as much of an actor, as much of a performer, as those standing in the line behind me. Jesus' spiel is no less rehearsed than their pleas for salvation. A bored mall Santa Claus watching the clock on the wall, waiting for closing time.

Then He catches me off guard and sneaks a curveball over the corner of the plate. "You mind if I snag one of those cigarettes? Nobody else seems to have any." The pack of Camels is jutting up out of my pocket, and I oblige him. He places it between His lips and I offer him my lighter. He smiles and waves me off. He holds His fingers up to the end of the cigarette and snaps them. Nothing happens.

"Nah. Just foolin'."

He takes the lighter and fires up the smoke. I feel a strangely authoritative wave all about myself. Not so much for the fact that I'm sitting here with Christ Himself. It's the fact that *Jesus fucking Christ* is smoking one of my cigarettes.

"Look here, Jerry. I got a good read on you when you walked up here. You never bought into me much. I don't blame you, I guess. And, you're right, to a degree. Even now, as I sit here before you, as the world ends, you were not totally wrong."

I am a little wary of looking at Him, as though staring directly into His eyes will increase the ferocity of His condemnation. Now, He has become the faltering girlfriend, letting me down gracefully.

"There is a Heaven. That much is true. What your scholars got wrong was where you fit into it all."

Jesus shifts and crosses His right leg over His lap. He's getting loose, assuming the most inviting, non-defensive posture He can muster. Something tells me this is going to sting.

"Heaven is a place, it's not a reward. It's not some trophy you get for finishing the race. It's where I live. Where a particular group of beings *live*." He's struggling to get this out. I start to realize that I might be one of the few, one of the only, to get the whole story. So I trust Him completely because, well, what have I got to lose at this point?

"You don't get to go to Heaven. Nobody does."

Ouch.

"You shouldn't be that surprised by this. You never *did* think it was a real place. And now you know it is, but you don't get to go there anyway. What's the difference?"

"Well, what does that mean for us? What happens now?" My big contribution, my moment of rebellion. It comes out a little angrier than I had hoped, but it sounds about right for how I feel. Terrified in the face of oblivion. Twelve steps of acceptance in twelve seconds flat.

He sighs. He bends His arms at the elbows, palms up. He turns His head toward the black, ashen cave ceiling that was once a sky, toward what once was bright and blue and gave those who had faith cause to believe that there was a place of enlightenment somewhere up beyond its reach. With cauterized cigarette-burn scars on His palms, He holds the weight of what's left and says, "This is it."

I look around. I see nothing. A dark haze of poison protects us from what lies beyond. Jesus and I are center stage, spotlit and soliloquizing without microphones, the audience waiting quietly to be plucked from the crowd for their turn to pull a rabbit out of the magician's hat.

I rest my head in my hand. "Jesus."

He smirks. "It's Jeezy, please."

I fail to see the humor. I ask Him why He is even here, what the point of this grand façade is, why going to all the trouble of rubbing our damnation in our faces is necessary. My voice becomes excessively pleading and whiny, no doubt coming across like every other kid who thought the idea of Jesus the Savior was bollocks and sewed too many patches onto his denim jacket.

"I came here because I wanted to, Jerry. I came here because I love this place. Because I love you people. You have no idea how good you had it down here, man."

He sounds angry. The way He stubs His cigarette out on the rock doesn't betray the sentiment. I offer him another, and He grabs it greedily. The fact that this is Jesus, that this is my judgment, has blown over enough to the point where I take one for myself. Where I won't feel so bad about blowing smoke in His face.

"Heaven is boring. Because it's perfect. It's perfect and it's flawless and it's impossibly tiresome. Everyone is pompous and spoiled. You want something, you get it. There's something really unsettling about perfection, really. When things go so well for so long, you start to wonder when the first bad thing is going to come along. And it hasn't. I've been living in angst for millennia, waiting for someone to slip, waiting for a crack in that armor. And it never comes.

"I took my vacations here. I would come down here just to see a bad movie. Go to a pro wrestling show. Listen to a Bowie song in a record shop. Eat something greasy and processed. Feel what it's like to get rained on for a change. *That* was my Heaven. And it was yours. When I said the Kingdom of Heaven was at hand, I meant it was here, for you. *This* was your kingdom."

Jesus puts a lot on my plate, and He won't be satisfied until I've licked it clean. He tells me everything He knows, about being granted dual citizenship privileges by His father so long as He never mentioned His bastard creation to the residents of Heaven. That He never worked miracles and never interfered on our behalves, because it was our imperfection that made us interesting, and our reaction in the face of adversity that made us beautiful and terrifying. He describes Heaven. He describes the face of God. He describes a place where things like this would not, cannot happen.

And I can't help but find myself a little irritated. It's really quite fruitless. In a matter of days, maybe even hours, I will keel over in the sand somewhere out here and die from radiation poisoning. So will everyone else standing back there waiting. And we will take this knowledge of nothingness after death with us into the nothingness after death, where it will become nothingness. And where we will become nothingness. And I want everything around me to have been blasted into glass. I want to use this rock and throw it at our glass house, follow the spider web of cracks until it becomes a break, until we lose our feet and tumble into the dark.

"Did I tell you that *I* was Jimi Hendrix?"

I ask the obvious question, the embittered question, the final question.

"Now what?"

He chuckles. He's gotten this one quite a bit.

"Look, Virginia, there isn't a Santa Claus as far as I know. Truth is, well, I don't know what the hell happens to you when you die. Nobody really does. Look at it this way: God is a farmer and you are His little pumpkin patch. He plants your seeds and grows you up from the dirt, and then He takes you to the market. You end up in any number of people's hands. Sometimes, you get cut with the scary face, or the dopey face, or the happy face. Sometimes you become pie. Sometimes you get smashed. Sometimes you just rot on the porch into December.

"What I mean is the farmer doesn't keep tabs on His product. He spends His money earned on his family and forgets all about the little pumpkins. And those pumpkins are left to someone else's devices. You are the products of God. You're just a crop He loses interest in once He leaves you at the market.

"Now, say I'm the farmer's son. I go through that pumpkin patch and I name all the pumpkins. And when Dad sells them off, I go to the market every day to see what my old friends are up to. And I have to watch them fed to gluttons in a pie, or smashed by careless people, or left out to rot by people who simply don't care. And it breaks my heart.

Okay, maybe not my best parable. Point is, I know you people. I watch you, all of you. I study you. I suffer your defeats and

I share in your victories. It makes me happy. I know all there is to know about you. And even I don't know what happens to you after you die. You won't know until you get there, if there is in fact anywhere to go. So I'm just here as the bearer of no news. I tell those folks what I think they'd want to hear."

What He *thinks* we want to hear. The false prophet. The merciful messenger. Putting Himself on the cross for the second time.

"Look, don't think We're not busted up about this. Dad's pissed. He's pissed because it means He's not perfect. Because He always thought you'd get on track, ya know. Least that's what He hoped. And I think that's what I loved about you folks. You were the chink in His shiny chest-plate. That ding in the brass. And He *hated* you for that. Your God, your Creator? He loathed you. You were that mark on His record He couldn't get wiped. You were His one flaw."

And I see Jesus for what He is. One of us. The greatest convert to our faith of the flaw. A being of infinite light and wisdom whose makeup changed the second He mingled with our kind. A man, like any other. A man who resents His father for the overbearing perfectionist He is. Resented by His father for the overbearing perfectionist He could never be. For the crowd He runs with. A man who is happy to smell like pissed-in underwear because it just makes the old man furious.

"I simply came here to tell as many people as I could what they wanted to hear. It might make me a liar, but it will help me sleep at night. And I know you'd want God's honest truth, Jerry. You'd want to know that, as far as I know, there is no reward for the things you've done, nor is there punishment. That everything you did in your life mattered in the fleeting moments it existed in. And that you were right all along, living in those moments, living for them. Not doing things so that someone somewhere would one day pat you on the back and say *you did good, kid, you did real good* and walk you through the gates. You lived a good life. And you lived it for the right reasons. You'd want to know that you weren't too far off from the truth all along. You got the message about as clear as anyone could."

And then Jesus starts to well up. He's taking this breakup harder than I thought He would. So I pat Him on the knee, a good sportsman's pat. I tell Him He's doing the right thing. And He asks me if I'd like to stay. Because He likes me, and He could use the company.

"Nobody wants to die alone, Jerry. Not even me."

"Were you really Hendrix?" And now the conversational floodgates are finally open.

Jesus laughs. "No, man. Not by a long shot. Even I couldn't have been that good."

"Yeah, he was amazing. Too bad we can't go hang out after this, ya know? Up *there.* We could go watch him play, have a beer."

"Yeah. Too bad. No alcohol in Heaven, though. It's a dry country."

Then something snaps into focus. I ask why Mike looked so dejected if He was telling everyone what they wanted to hear.

"Because I told him his story sucked. I had to hear it enough while He was standing in line, what made him think I wanted to hear it again? These people and their routines, do they think it's going to help, seriously? I mean, I can only hear so many terrible renditions of "Amazing Grace." My patience *does* have its limits."

I laugh. And so does Jesus. A long, hearty one. And from somewhere out of sight, a chorus of uproarious laughter.

Jesus wipes a tear from the corner of His eye. "I'm telling you, every once in a while, I'll get one of those old hags who taps little boys' knuckles with rulers. And she's so smug and so sure that she's in. And I'll just make up something wild. Tell her that I am actually a robot, and that your very annihilation was brought on by us. Just a step in our quest for a fully mechanized earth. Yeah, it's a little too close to *The Terminator*, but it's not like she'd know it. And then she goes stomping off, swearing up and down that I'm not Jesus, trying to get people to listen to her, to fear her the way they used to. Aw man, it's a sight."

"Yeah, I think I'll stay here a while," I say. "I could use a laugh. But we're going to need more cigarettes to get through this line."

"What've we got left?"

"Maybe a half a pack?"

"I think that'll work. If I can feed an army with five fish and some bread, I can get us enough smokes to last until the time comes. I've still got some tricks up my sleeve, ya know."

This will work just fine. A decent enough exit from The Kingdom. I light up a cigarette, hand it to Jeezy, and light one for myself. I swing my hips around to face the line, and the numbers have dwindled considerably. Many of them are now discarded bodies, bags of bones and rust, lying in the sand. Just missing their appointment. Just missing their final moment of consolation. Missing something. And I wonder where those missing things have gone. I wonder what they've found.

DIFFERENT FROM OTHER NIGHTS

Eliyanna Kaiser

ah nishtanah ha-lahylah ha-zeh mi-kol ha-layloht, mi-kol ha-layloht?"

The adults beamed as the children sang. The two tweens, Joshua and Kayla, shuffled back and forth, making a big show of tipping their *hagaddahs* forward so that everyone could plainly see the prayer books were in Hebrew, not English. The three middle children, still in elementary school, Nina, Megan, and Aaron, sang softly and off-key, their fat fingers pressed against their large-print transliterated *seder* books, where all the words were phonetically spelled out. Their efforts were universally regarded as adorable.

But the star of the show was unquestionably the youngest, Rachel. Despite being just seven, she sang louder than the others, confidence written on her round face, her big brown curls bouncing with the rhythm of the song. Rachel's hagaddah sat unopened on her plate, her hands resting on top of it as if to confirm how much she didn't need it. She had memorized the whole thing from a CD her *zaida* had given her last year.

The parents, all siblings or in-laws, jockeyed in the tight space between the dining room tables and the wall for the best vantage for snapping photos of their kids until the last refrain was over.

From the head of the table, the old zaida presided. He smiled warmly at his grandchildren behind a wooly salt-and-pepper beard, pleased that despite what he considered a bad rash of intermarriages and a lackluster Jewish Sunday school education, the kinder could at least manage The Four Questions, this integral cog in the Passover wheel.

"Very good. Very good." Hints of the old man's Slavic heritage were more pronounced at holiday times, the traditions bringing him back to a different time and place. "Now to answer these very good questions."

Rachel felt proud because she already knew why this night was different from all other nights. *Once we were slaves in Egypt and now we are free, and we set aside this night to remember.* Passover was her favorite holiday, something she looked forward to with the anticipation that her *goyim* schoolmates reserved for Santa Claus.

It gave her goose-pimples up and down her skinny arms when she thought what it must have been like to be in Egypt so many thousands of years ago, with blood smeared on the doorways and the cries of the dying slave masters filling the night air.

The night progressed in its timeless recital of ritual. The four questions recited were answered, the seder plate was explained, dinner served, praised, and eaten. Finally, a fifth cup of wine was poured in a decorated gold chalice and set aside for the prophet Elijah.

Siblings and cousins raced to the door, and Rachel's brother, Joshua—being the oldest and a boy—muscled in first to open it. A bitter cold wind carried the diamond dust of a dry but sharp snowfall into the foyer. Nina and Megan shrieked and ran back into the dining room. Aaron stopped to pick at his nose while half of him seemed to move to follow his sister, Megan, and he tumbled from the confusion of trying to do both. Kayla scooped him up to wipe his tears and take him back to his seat.

Joshua looked down at Rachel, who was still looking outside expectantly.

"I think we can go back now," Joshua said. "I'll bet Elijah's already drank the wine." He bent down and cupped his hand over his sister's ear in mock secrecy. *"You know that every year Zaida drinks it, right?"*

"No." Rachel looked up at him, her eyes wide.

Joshua shuffled uncomfortably. "Oh, well I'm just teasing. I'm pretty cold so I'm going to go back to the table now. Shut the door when you're done, okay, Ra-*chel?*" He gave a throaty *ch* to her name, like it was pronounced in Hebrew. He liked to tease his little sister about how their zaida thought she was the best Jew. She thought it was funny. But then again, she was seven and couldn't see that he was jealous.

Rachel watched him walk away and turned back to squint into the darkness.

It's not true, she thought stubbornly. She whispered, "Elijah," and waited. Then she saw him, under a streetlamp, standing on the sidewalk at the edge of her lawn.

Rachel beamed. Of course he hadn't shown himself until now. The others had only been pretending to open the door for him. She'd had faith. She'd *known* he would come.

Crooking a finger, she motioned for him to come in. He seemed to look over his shoulder for a moment, and then he walked to the foyer but kept himself to the other side of the threshold.

"Shalom. Won't you come in?" Rachel said and bowed her head slightly as she thought became a proper young lady greeting a Torah prophet, but nervousness caused her to speak in a rush. "We're very pleased you could make it—Zaida has a glass of wine for you—Josh doesn't think you're real—he's thirteen—that's bad luck." She felt embarrassed about some of what she said, and her cheeks, already pink from the cold air, flushed a bit rosier.

The man was tall and gangly, and his ill-fitting tan raincoat was too big in the shoulders. His hair was long and messy and his face unshaven. His eyes were grey but the whites were red, bloodshot. It wasn't how Rachel had expected Elijah to look, but then again, she'd never met a prophet.

"Do you know me, little girl?" he asked.

"You're Elijah," Rachel said, looking all the way up at the tall man.

"Ah." The man's eyes twinkled.

"Rachel, *bubbeleh*, close the door and come back to the table. We're all catching a draft!" her mother called from the dining room.

Rachel held the door open and moved to the side to let Elijah in.

"I think," the man said, kneeling, "that I should come back later. I have other seders to visit. I'll come back at midnight… Rachel, is it?"

At eye level, the stench of drinking on the man's breath irritated Rachel. For a horrible moment, she considered the possibility that he was not a prophet at all and only a horrible dirty beggar. But then she realized that he had to go from house to house all night long, sipping wine at *every* seder. Her breath would smell funny too after all that drinking. Rachel hated wine.

"Alright." She smiled at him. "I'll tell Zaida that you'll come back later." Rachel moved to close the door, but his arm caught it before it shut.

"Remember," he said, winking through the crack, "midnight."

Rachel shut the door and turned around to see her mother rounding the corner, a look of panic wrinkling the place under her eyes where she rubbed smelly cream every night before bed.

"Who were you talking to?" Rachel's mother asked, rushing forward.

"Elijah! He had to go, but he promised to come back later," Rachel said.

"Elijah?" The older woman's face relaxed and the corner of her mouth twitched with amusement. She thought about how Rachel was the picture of herself at that age. Big brown eyes that wanted to see, to know everything. Full lips that loved to talk and explore new tastes and words and ideas. "Oh, Rachel, hurry back to the table. We're about to sing the counting song. *Who Knows One?*"

"I know one!" Rachel bounced gleefully.

"Echad Elocheinu shebashamaim uva'aretz!" They sang together, clapping their hands in time to the voices on the other side of the house. Rachel's mother tickled her daughter under the chin until she squealed and ran back to the dining room.

As soon as Rachel was gone from the foyer, her mother's smile fell and she pushed aside the curtains and scanned the area in front of the house. She muttered her daughter's name with a mother's relief, turned the deadbolt shut and forgot about the whole thing.

Had she opened the door she might have noticed a trail of boot prints in the fresh snow leading up the driveway, to the porch, and then back again.

But Rachel's mother didn't open the door.

Just before dessert was served and a few hours before all the extended family would leave and only Rachel, her mother, brother, and zaida would be left in the big house, Rachel sat in the kitchen with the women trying to help make whipped cream.

"Kosher for Pesach non-dairy whipped topping," Aunt Dinah read from the label with distaste. "It's *fercockt!*" Rachel giggled as her aunt squeezed the half-frozen white chunk out of its container; it made farting sounds as it slid into the silver bowl.

Rachel spooned in icing sugar using careful measurements from the family recipe binder. She kept smiling. She loved it when the adults swore in Yiddish.

After fifteen minutes of beating the white sludge on the highest speed the hand mixer would give, the women agreed it was time to go back to Baba Shayna's (*may she rest in peace*) first rule of Passover cooking.

It was written on the inside cover of the late matriarch's Pesach binder: *First: you will require a conspiracy of women.*

Rachel was handed a paper bag containing three empty kosher for Pesach whipped topping containers and given her annual top-secret assignment: sneak down into the basement and raid the non-kosher fridge for real whipped cream.

It was a cross-your-heart-and-hope-to-die kind of secret. The men never noticed, but they would *kakken af en yam* if they ever found out. Rachel had been delighted when Aunt Dinah had told her what that meant: shit in the ocean.

Rachel tiptoed downstairs without turning the light on to make sure no one would see. She got to work quickly, opening the whipped cream cartons, squeezing the half-frozen heavy milk into the empty containers, and stashing the empty dairy containers in the downstairs trash.

Just when she was about to close the freezer, she noticed a half-used package of lamb shanks with a big pool of frozen blood at the bottom of the packaging.

Rachel opened a corner of the thin plastic wrap and picked out some frozen blood with her fingernail. Experimentally, she wiped it on the white-painted doorframe, thinking about the Passover story about the ancient Jews sacrificing a lamb and smearing it over their doorways…

"What are you doing in the dark?" Joshua's voice startled her. He switched on the lights and she quickly dropped the lamb shanks on the floor behind the freezer.

"Nothing!" Rachel shouted. "Go away, Josh."

Joshua noticed the streak of red on the doorway. "Oh, *gross.* That's sick, man. I'm so telling."

He ran upstairs yelling for their mother, and Rachel, pausing only to stash the lamb shanks under a box of photo albums, followed her brother up the stairs, quickly handing off the paper bag to Aunt Dinah in the kitchen before rushing into the living room.

Her brother's testimony was being frantically silenced by their very nervous-looking mother.

"I don't care what you think is fair, young man, this is a holiday and the whole family is here. Brother and sister squabbles can wait until tomorrow unless you want to go to your room and miss dessert."

"But she was—"

"Uh uh, I said I wasn't interested in hearing it!"

Joshua stamped his foot and, complaining that Rachel was everyone's favorite and that Passover was gay, slouched off to the foyer where Kayla was applying lipstick in the glass reflection of the grandfather clock. Rachel didn't bother saying that Passover couldn't be gay, since it wasn't a person—everyone knew Josh was being stupid. She thought she should feel badly that Joshua had gotten into trouble, but right then she couldn't help but feel relieved that the conspiracy of women was safe.

Rachel remembered the lamb shanks she'd hidden and got an idea. The prophet Elijah *and* real lamb's blood. She knew she was a good Jew, but this might be the best Passover observed since the exodus from Egypt!

After dessert was served, buffet-style in the kitchen, Rachel carried her plate back to the dining room, balancing a pile of macaroons, fruit salad, and a large slice of sponge cake with whipped cream and pineapple slices. This part of the holiday evening was always the most casual, and her family spilled throughout the house eating with the exception of the older, bearded men who had scarcely left the table since they arrived, continuing with the prayers.

"It's almost ten o'clock, boys, wrap it up, *nu*? I'm going to put out the coffee," Rachel's mother said as she carried piles of dishes from the dining room to the kitchen.

The grandfather clock clanged to sound the hour in the hall. *Ten o'clock already*, Rachel thought.

She took a seat at the head table, next to her zaida. Opening a discarded hagaddah, she looked over her grandfather's shoulder to see the page number, frowning because they were singing a song she didn't know. But when she got to the right page, the title at the top made her stomach kick: "It Happened At Midnight."

"What happened at midnight?" she asked her zaida frantically.

Her zaida paused from his prayers, only just realizing his youngest grandchild was there.

"Everything, bubbeleh! It was midnight when God passed over the Jews and the Angel of Death swept down—" he swung his butter knife to stab his sponge cake, "—to smite the first born of the sons and daughters of Egypt, and then—" he stopped mid-sentence, a look of concern passing over his face. Had he scared her?

"But why do we celebrate the 'gyptians dying? And why—"

Her zaida interrupted, chuckling. "My Rachel, always with so many questions. Frustrated with not knowing everything! But your question—an important one—we *do not* celebrate the plagues, any of them—but especially not the last one. The Egyptians may have enslaved our people, but they were also God's creation. You see, my Rachel?"

She nodded. "What...does he look like?"

"Who?"

"The Angel of Death. When he came and got Baba Shayna and Daddy, did you see him?"

The old man steadied himself and put his arms around his granddaughter and held her close, his eyes brimming with the shock of the question. "No bubbeleh, we don't see that one before our time."

The grownups were too busy with coffee and tea service to notice what Rachel did next. The little girl tiptoed barefoot through the snowy backyard, her curls bouncing with each frigid step, until she reached the garage, where she got a paintbrush.

At a quarter to midnight, Rachel sat cross-legged on the floor of the kitchen, trying not to fall asleep and thinking about how quiet it was. During the day, the kitchen had been the busiest, loudest place in the house. Now only the dishwasher, occasionally spitting steam out its sides, made any noise.

Rachel was nervous about the prophet coming back but she knew instinctively that the kitchen was her place of power. In her experience, no man was able to cow a woman in her kitchen. She didn't think any of that explicitly; she just felt better about the kitchen than any other place in the house.

Rachel pulled down a Tupperware from the counter and snacked on the auxiliary macaroons, trying not to feel too guilty about breaking the rules and eating after the seder. Her mother had over-baked, and the pistachio ones were her favorite.

She had just bitten into her second cookie when she heard a light tapping on the front door.

Tiptoeing quietly to the foyer, she jumped, her heart pounding as the old mahogany grandfather clock in the hall struck midnight and the bells started to sound to mark the time. She froze, not wanting to take a step further. *I could just go to bed*, she thought. *I don't have to open the door*. She chided herself for being a baby.

If it was Elijah, it was her Jewish duty to let him in and pour him a glass of wine. If it wasn't…she cast a look up the stairs to the door where her brother, the firstborn child of her family, was sleeping. She realized she could hear him snore even two floors down. *I have a plan, Josh.*

Swallowing her fear, Rachel undid all the locks in a few quick motions and flung open the door.

The cold air howled, flopping the tails of the man's coat in its wake. Rachel hugged her periwinkle housecoat and took a step back from the wind. The man looked over her head at the quiet, darkened house and smiled. He steadied himself against the wet doorframe with his hands.

"Hello again, Rachel. Still got that glass of wine for me?"

Rachel nodded and left the door wide open and shuffled quickly back into the kitchen. She picked up Elijah's golden cup from the drying rack and poured from one of the many unfinished bottles of red wine until it was almost full. By the time she turned around to give it to him he was sitting in one of the tall chairs across the counter, waiting.

She put the cup on the table and pushed it toward him.

"Thank you kindly," he said, and tilting his head back, he grabbed the cup with his lamb's blood-soaked hands and tossed it back in one go, a few beads of the red wine spilling down the corners of his lips and dropping on to the tile countertop.

He regarded her silently. Rachel studied her feet, counting how many rabbits were in the pattern on her right slipper.

"How many cups, four or five?" she asked.

"How many what?" he said, belching and not bothering to cover his mouth. "What?"

"I asked my zaida before he went to bed why we pour a glass of wine for you, and he told me that the Rabbis didn't know whether to put out four cups or five. So we drink four, put out a fifth, and wait for you to come and tell us if that's wrong." Rachel bit her lip and scolded herself for talking too much. But she couldn't help but ask; she wanted to know.

"The Rabbis," he bit off the word, and his shoulders shook with non-audible laughter as he reached for the bottle to refill his glass. "So they put out an extra cup for me?" The man raised the glass like he was making a crude toast. Liquid sloshed over the brim, staining his coat with a splash. "One day I'll just pop by and settle it? Like I've got nothing better to do than tell a bunch of wrinkled Jews how drunk to get!"

He drank deeply as Rachel stewed over what he had said.

"So how many?" she asked, backing toward the door, one tiny step at time.

She pointed at the cup in his hands. The gold looked tarnished and brown, but Rachel knew it was just the blood on his hands that made it look that way.

"Oh, right, right." He grinned at her with wine-stained teeth. "Many as you like!"

He was on his feet now, shuffling toward her; the half-filled cup fell from his hand and clanked against the wood floor, and wine drowned the floorboards.

He seemed to struggle to stay standing. He threw his weight against the counter, knocking the cleaned and stacked china plates to the floor, where a few shattered loudly.

Rachel walked backward, but this being her kitchen, she knew where things were. She reached behind her back and pulled a long paring knife from the butcher block and brandished it shakily.

Two floors up, Rachel heard her mother call out.

"What you gonna do with that knife?" he asked almost sadly, slurring his words. "Don't need that."

He took another step toward Rachel but lost his footing on the wine-soaked floor and grabbed for the counter with his hand. It happened very quickly, but Rachel's eyes were on his hand, slick with blood and wine, grasping for the counter but slipping.

He fell forward and her paring knife met his chest. Later she would tell herself that he fell into the knife, but the truth was that she stepped forward, thrust it, met his body.

He didn't make a sound, not even to scream, until his body

hit the ground with a thud to wake the dead. He twitched for a few moments, and then he was dead.

Rachel didn't move from the body, even though his head and hand touched her slippers. She stood where she was, looking at him, God's creation, dead on her kitchen floor.

It was nothing to celebrate.

Her mother's frantic screams were louder now. She had raced down all the stairs and through the hallway and now shrieked at the entryway to the kitchen, but it was Rachel's zaida, several paces ahead, a look of madness on his face, that got to her first. He reached over the body and plucked her up, squeezing her so tight Rachel thought she might burst. Tears streamed down every path of her grandfather's wrinkled face and drenched her shoulder.

Her zaida looked past her, eyes wide and wild, darting side to side, taking in the man on the ground, the golden cup and the wine.

"There's blood on her!" Rachel's mother said, suddenly beside her, patting her little body all over.

"Just wine, I think," her zaida said. The sweetness of alcohol was heavy in the air, covering what else there might be to smell.

Rachel caught sight of her brother, firstborn and unharmed, and she grinned at him. He looked at her oddly and left for a moment. She heard the front door close, and then he was back again. Her mother dialed the police.

"There's blood on the door," Josh said, confusion and fear in his eyes; he looked at his sister, and it was a question. "And a paintbrush and lamb shanks in the foyer."

"The door? The door?" Rachel's mother was crying, ignoring the 911 operator's questions. Confusion threatened to turn into hysterics.

"So the Angel would pass us over," Rachel answered. She hugged her zaida harder.

לילית(LILITH)

Did I wrap myself in your flesh
For a memory, momentary, of you?
Was there warmth even before
When you bit into my cold bottom lip
Wrestled it with your tongue,
Coaxing out my demon, my longing,
My bitter imprisonment,
Teetering close to exploding ecstasy,
And that debt to God I repay
Nightly
With fresh corpses.
Harvested thick, hot, pulsing in my palm,
The writhing, wriggling
Flesh of the good,
Ripped from its own
Religious inner sanctum—
That serious handshake
We all had once, with God.
Was that a second thought?
So like me, you are!
God's second thought
And His first regret.

— *Rain Graves*

THE LAST WORDS OF
~~DUTCH SCHULTZ~~ JESUS CHRIST

Nick Mamatas

Emily Case, long of leg and short of hair, closed her eyes tightly, so tight that the blood swam red under her lids. She was to make the most dramatic attempt at DIY practical neurotheology of any member of Group 3A. She had used the credit card her parents had given her for emergencies to buy a home defibrillator and related accessories. The price was well over one thousand dollars, but Emily reasoned that she needn't worry. That feeling of oneness with all the cosmos was worth it. The noose—a crimson scarf run through one of the dangly earrings Emily had liked to wear during her freshman year—was tied to a hook in the dorm room ceiling. Though the hook was loose, Emily was concerned that she still might hang by the neck till dead, rather than falling off her desk chair and chest-first onto the defibrillator for a instant resuscitation and, she hoped, another look at the face of the Lord.

She grabbed her backpack and thought to find the heaviest textbooks from the shelves to put into it, but the semester was over and Emily's roommate had already sold all of her texts back to the bookstore. Emily, a comp lit major and dance minor, had no really huge books. She ran to the college library with a mind to check out a dictionary or several volumes of an encyclopedia, but those were reference materials. Ultimately, she ended up with a copy of Guthrie's *New Testament Theology, Against The Day* by Pynchon, and very nearly a copy of *Atlas Shrugged*. Emily did finally remember that art books are sometimes also heavy and was able to leave the Rand behind, replacing it with a copy of *The End of the Game: The Last Word from Paradise*—an oversized book of photographs of Africa.

Emily's face scrunched up into a frown as she marched back to her dorm. If the machine didn't work, or if she failed to hit the pads properly, she might die and the campus police and maybe even everyone—if her death was reported to the local newspapers—would think she was some kind of weirdo, given her selections of ballast.

I won't die, she thought, hard. As if to furrow her brow and suck on her teeth would bring her thought into reality. *I won't die; I won't end up a vegetable.* The defib whined under her, the pads open and facing up. She shouldered the knapsack and then lightly stepped onto the chair, slid the noose over her head, took a deep breath, and then took a step.

The other members of Group 3A utilized less interesting procedures. There was the usual slosh of drink and soft drugs difficult to formally separate out from the normal experience of living in a college town, of running out into the grey grasses of the prairie and howling at the freight trains trundling down the line of the horizon. Of the 7-11 parking lot and the bar with the soggy French fries and well-warped billiards table. Of waiting for some moments of life to snake through the matrices of work and class schedules, of weekly iCal reminders and daily birth control.

But there were incidents. The lines of sharp cuts healing over into scales of scars on the arms of this or that participant. Joyceann Latour bled a puddle in the middle of her POL 245, Presidential Politics in Perspective midterm exam. She was fine, she said, fine fine absolutely fine and really really like just wanted to get back to class and finish up her semester with no more drama okay okay? She asked okay okay? until someone said okay *okay,* and she took a make-up exam.

Luke Duggan barricaded himself in the chapel for three days with his .22 and few bricks of ammo, caved out some stained glass panels with the butt of the rifle, and fired at whoever came close while shouting, "No! He's mine! I am in here with Him and He does not want you here!" until the real police had to be called in. They waited till he slept, which took four days, and then Luke was *removed from campus*, as the press release put it.

Julius Chen circumcised himself. So did Kelli Vincent. Chen kept his method secret. Kelli confided in one of her suitemates — by the end of the day seemingly everyone at Grove Forest knew. Julius then began buttonholing men in the Dixon Hall third floor showers to explain that he had done it first.

LaShawnda McKay stopped eating.

Even in a small Midwestern liberal arts college such as Grove Forest, incidents occur. Things happen. The study was double-blinded and nobody would have thought to draw any connections between the peculiar actions of the students and the participants in Group 3A except that when Emily Case returned to school it was on a purloined motorcycle she could hardly drive. She drew a great snake curve back and forth across two lanes of highway, her stolen layers of men's flannel flapping in the wind, the of wail state patrol sirens behind her. Emily was a wisp of a girl with way too much horsepower under her, but she managed to stay on two wheels for over fifty miles. The police had radioed ahead. Don't close the gates. Let her on campus. In the twists of the quads, in the alleys behind the dorms, she'd be easier to contain.

Emily roared across the lawn toward Gracie Hall, tilting wildly on the bike. She leapt from it and, arms and legs cycling through the air, landed a few feet from the low and wide stone staircase leading to the main entrance. On her elbows and one good knee she crawled closer, but a trooper spilled out of his vehicle and rushed her. She squirmed in his grip, ready to snap off her own limbs to get inside, it seemed, so the officer simply had to sit on the small of her back. A campus safety officer joined in, plopping down on Emily's thin legs. She was too injured for the taser, and too many student heads peered out the windows of buildings around the quad for the truncheons or pepper spray to come out. An ambulance took Emily away from Gracie Hall. Away from the God Film.

The God Film is not a motion picture about God, nor does it contain images of God. It was not directed by God, nor was it produced by God. It is a short film, one made over a period of about seven years by a bohemian artist named Myra Miller. She was a painter primarily and lived in Chicago, far from the artistic centers of avant-garde filmmaking, only about seventeen miles from Grove Forest College. She called the film "Red Light." Each day, she would mix paint, and produce what she believed to be a different shade of red. With a Super-8 camera of no particular vintage or value—there might be one similar to it in your grandparents' attic—she would record a single frame of a small piece of canvas. Then she would mix more paint.

It was easy going at first for Myra, but her goal was to paint a different shade of red each day. What first took minutes would soon involve hours of comparison between the swatches of red she'd painted, all to guarantee that not one frame was identical to any other. Myra was a young woman when she started the project, middle-aged when the nine-minute "Red Light" premiered at the Grove Forest College Film Club's meeting.

It was 1973. A teenager in the audience—her name was Abigail Hermann. The daughter of an English adjunct, Abigail hung around Grove Forest often because high school was a tyrannical bore—was forty-five seconds into "Red Light" when she had her first orgasm. By the end of the film, she had experienced a full-blown encounter with the Godhead.

Most of the rest of the audience did not seem, to Abigail, to be as interested in "Red Light" as she was. They were not moved. Their cheeks didn't burn as red as at least one of the frames of the film, as hers did. They applauded, but everyone sat quietly in their seats, murmuring normally as the reel on the small projector was changed for the next program. The seat in the front row of the little black box theater in which Myra had sat after giving her brief introductory talk was empty.

Abigail went to Grove Forest, majored in psychology, and then completed graduate work at the University of Chicago. Her research interest was in the neurological basis of religious experiences of the sort she experienced as a teen in a damp chair in a smoky room full of older boys and women in woolen stockings. Dr. Hermann joined the faculty of Grove Forest after adjuncting here and there and doing scut work on the research projects of various colleagues; her first day back on campus she checked a print of "Red Light" out of the campus library.

One might say that there are two major problems when it comes to psychological research. The first is that human behavior and perceptions are too complex, too mediated by the limits of language and statistics, to ever be fully apprehended. The second is that a significant fraction of psychological research doesn't tell us much about the human condition as a whole, but only about the human condition as experienced by psychology majors such as Joyceann Latour, who had to participate in research studies as part of her work, and unmotivated students like Emily Case, who was stuck in PSY 101 because it was the only social sciences survey course that fit in her schedule that semester. Enrolling in a few studies would have brought Emily's grade in the course up to a B- had there not been a particular set of reactions in the posterior parietal gyrus of the left hemisphere of her brain occurring during her exposure to The God Film.

It may have been something Emily ate that day, or three days prior, or an artifact of her gymnastics training since that part of the brain is responsible for integrating various sensory input into an understanding of existence within three-dimensional space. She and a few other members of Group 3A watched the film and felt the left sides of their bodies dissolve and the universe fill out the hollowed shell of the body in which their minds normally rode.

Luke Duggan had other problems as well, not all neurotheological.

In the infirmary, LaShawnda McKay explained to the nurse practitioner on duty that she was on a hunger strike until she was allowed to see the film again. Most of all, she missed playing volleyball, but that would just make her hungry. Thinking made her hungry.

A few days later, Julius Chen read an obituary in the online edition of the local newspaper. Local artist Myra Miller had died of complications from gallbladder surgery. "Red Light" was not mentioned in the brief notice, but Grove Forest was, as Miller had shown some watercolors in the hall of the administration building in 2002. Julius Chen was neither an art major nor a psychology major. He printed out the article anyway, and folded the paper in quarters. He put it in his wallet to read later. Julius, since participating in Abigail's study, had found himself very interested in death.

Not everyone experiences The God Film in the same way. Like that long ago screening at the long defunct campus film society, most viewers simply see nine minutes of flickering. This is even true now that we explain the events of this semester and the neurological and behavioral fallout Group 3A experienced. That visiting lecturer—the famous fellow from England, the man who wields atheism like a cricket bat against Islamic immigrants in his home country and uses it here for free dinners—he saw "Red Light" and proudly declared that he "didn't feel a thing." No surprises there, really.

It's not difficult to stimulate the posterior parietal gyrus of the left hemisphere of the brain. The trick is to know when to stop. A religious experience that lasts too long may be a little too enlightening.

Abigail Hermann was offered an early sabbatical. *Encouraged* very strongly to take it. There's no research question at stake here.

We're just going to watch a film.

* * *

RED:

Then a blink and blue sky. Something is tight around your skull. Flickerflickerflicker and then the left half of your body falls away and the film under the film, the film under your eyes, the film already written into the chemical chains of your brain, that is what you see on the screen. That is what you see from the other side of the screen, the other cosmos through the window of its white square painted with moments of red red redredre-drderderderred.

FADE IN:

EXT. GOLGOTHA—DAY

A small group of men, all bearded and in the long tunics and robes of the first century AD. They are shot from above, and they are looking up at something. The camera pulls back to reveal JE-SUS nailed to a cross and two other men in similar predicaments on either side of Him. With a spastic thrash, JESUS howls, and then He looks up to the sky and speaks.

JESUS:

Who shot me? Who shot me, it was the boss himself! Please make it quick, fast and furious. Please. Fast and furious. Please help me get out; I am getting my wind back, thank God. Please, please, oh please. You will have to please tell him, you got no case.

You get ahead with the dot dash system didn't I speak that time last night. Whose number is that in your pocket book, Phil 13780. Who was it? Oh please, please. Reserve decision. Oh, oh, dog biscuits and when he is happy he doesn't get happy please, please to do this. Then Henry, Henry, Frankie you didn't even meet me. The glove will fit what I say oh, Kayiyi, oh Kayiyi. Sure who cares when you are through? He is jumping around. No Hobo and Poboe I think he means the same thing.

The men look extremely confused by this outburst. One of the THIEVES even struggles to turn his neck to face JESUS, so perplexed he is by the remarks of his fellow condemned.

CUT TO:
INT. HOSPITAL ROOM—DAWN

DUTCH SCHULTZ, a strong-looking man with large features, lies dying on a hospital gurney. Several police officers surround him. One is taking notes on a stenography pad. The dress is archaic, suggesting Prohibition. Dutch's hat even rests on a small metal cabinet next to the gurney. The police are all burly men, obviously Irish, as if cast as parts in a feature film. One, SGT. CONLON, in dress uniform, leans over and brusquely addresses DUTCH.

CONLON:
Who shot you?

DUTCH :

(hoarse, but resonant, with artificial reverb effect):
Eloi, Eloi, lama sabachthani?

A PLAINCLOTHESMAN moves toward the door (camera POV), but CONLON raises a hand.

PLAIN CLOTHESMAN:

He needs last rites! You heard him! I wouldn't send a dog to meet his Maker without last rites.

CONLON:

Ain't no last rites going to help this sorry so-so. The rackets, the women, the murders. He'll be swimming in a lake of red fire by noon, that's for sure.

CUT TO:

EXT. GOLGOTHA—DAY

JOHN is holding aloft a reed that in turn supports a sponge dripping with a reddish liquid. He uses the reed to raise the sponge to the lips of JESUS. JESUS stretches his head and licks at the sponge, squeezes a corner of it as best he can with his parched lips. He grimaces at the vinegar and lets the red liquid dribble down his chin.

JESUS:

Oh, mamma, mamma! Who give it to him? Who give it to him? Let me in the district fire-factory that he was nowhere near. It smoldered. No, no. There are only ten of us and there are ten million fighting somewhere of you, so get your onions up and we will throw up the truce flag. Oh, please let me up. Please shift me. Police are here. Communistic… strike… baloney… honestly this is a habit I get; sometimes I give it and sometimes I don't.

Oh, I am all in. You can play jacks, and girls do that with a soft ball and do tricks with it. Oh, oh, dog biscuit, and when he is happy he doesn't get snappy.

JOHN jerks the reed away. The other men, especially LUKE and MATTHEW, crowd by JOHN and look at one another and the sponge, their faces thick with worry.

JESUS:
Are you getting this down? Somebody write it all down. You gotta get this all down. My buried treasure. I know the secret.

CUT TO:
INT. HOSPITAL ROOM—DAWN
THE STENOGRAPHER chews on his pencil and sighs.

CUT TO:
CLOSE UP—STENOGRAPHY PAD
A scribble of text fills up the page. Though awkwardly transcribed, the following phrases are clear amidst the gibberish.
"Father, forgive them, for they do not know what they are doing"
"I tell you the truth, today you will be with me in paradise"
"Father, into Your hands I commit my spirit"

CUT TO:
INT. PALACE CHOP HOUSE RESTROOM— NIGHT
Clearly prior to the events of the morning, DUTCH, hale and hearty, is washing his hands in the white and polished restroom of the restaurant in which he is dining. He is concentrating on scrubbing them clean so does not see in the mirror a BLACK HOODED WOMAN, obviously SATAN as depicted in the film THE PASSION OF THE CHRIST, raising a pistol. SATAN waits

until Dutch turns around and as the mobster wipes his hands clean on his suit jacket, SATAN fires the gun twice, hitting Dutch in the stomach. Red blood blooms over Dutch's white shirt and spreads slowly as Dutch sinks to his knees as if under a heavy weight. He opens his mouth to speak, but nothing comes out but gush of dark red blood that dribbles down his chin.

CUT TO:

EXT. GOLGOTHA—DAY

A fair amount of time has obviously passed, as the sky is layered with progressively deeper lines of red. Behind CHRIST'S CROSS, the sun is setting.

JESUS:

Okay okay, I get it now. I was set up. Lied to. Finked out. That's what happened, not forsaken, made a patsy. This was supposed to be the Axis Mundi, the Tree of Life all over again. This plank I'm hanging from, the angles of this cross, drilling down deep into the bowels of the world. To descend into Hell and three days later shimmy up again lickety-split. But… but… I'm a patsy, a pigeon, a rube, a chump, a sucker, a fall guy, a useful idiot, a willing victim who loves his own wounds oh so very much that they won't ever ever heal. This ain't the only world. There are so many others. We're just in a dusty little corner of a dusty little corner. There are giants out there, red giants that can eat our sun whole. The sky is full of them, worlds older than ours trudge about them in years that stretch so much longer than my thirty-three.

I thirst and they gave me vinegar. I beg for it, even, I get down on my knees and beg for it. Prohibition, that's what this all is. That's why men in fancy suits, they wear them all grey and thick like office blocks, big business, that's why they run things. Oh, I can see it. All of it. The universe, the future. Oh sweet

Father won't someone come down here and wise up the marks!

Hey Jews! Yeah, you.

REACTION SHOT—MEDIUM SHOT OF THE DISCIPLES:
The MEN look up.

CLOSE UP—JESUS:
JESUS:
New rule! New rule! No more cutting. No more nothing. Whatever you want, you can do it. It doesn't matter, see. Forget taking a sharpened rock to it, forget doing it to babies, it doesn't matter. It's a trick, a scam, something the big man makes you do just to see if you'll do it. That's a new rule! Write that down, tell everyone! And tell everyone something else too, so they won't have to live it. The hot red fevers of wisdom, that's the only way, and that is the way of death. So you, Jewy Jewy Jew Jew down there, you just write down what I say, okay okay?

Forget this cross. It's not the center of the world. It don't revolve around me, it don't revolve around anyone. It's a hell of a good universe next door—let's go! It's so big and we're so small. They'll know one day. They'll go to the moon on the tips of a big red flame and then freak out at the big black up there and turn back. It's too big, the world's too big. That's what the lilies in the field can't bear to know.

Look, I'll show you, I'll show you right now. I'm going to say something that isn't going to make a lick of sense, but you write it down and then they'll see. In the new world, they'll know what I mean and then they'll know that I am the truth.

SPLIT DISSOLVE TO:
JESUS and DUTCH SCHULTZ, on double-exposed film so their images overlap, a RED GEL lending an air of unreality. Their faces are angled upward, as if JESUS is speaking to the sky

and as if DUTCH is speaking to SGT CONLON, who is hovering over him just o.s. Then the film jerks to a stop. Sprockets can be seen on either side of the frame. As the two men speak, their lips bloom with red bubbles as the film melts under the heat of the white light of the projector bulb.

FADE TO WHITE:

FADE IN:
EXT. GOLGOTHA—SUNSET
JESUS hangs on the cross, still muttering to himself. The other two THIEVES are dead, as is obvious from the CROWS gathered on their outstretched limbs and pecking at their heads. Christ's MEN are gone.

JESUS (muttering, but rapid like the rant of a dying man):
It's the Aleph. I can see it all. Everything at once. I don't know. I didn't even get a look. I don't know who can have done it. I am so sick now. The police are getting many complaints. Look out. I want that G-note. Look out for Jimmy Valentine, for he is an old pal of mine. Look out mamma, look out for her. You can't beat him. I will settle the indictment. Talk to the sword. Shut up, you got a big mouth! Please help me up, Henry. Max, come over here. French-Canadian bean soup. I want to pay. Let them leave me alone.

FADE TO RED:

* * *

You might see something different. You might see nothing at all except for red flickering into pink and orange and purple and grey and even blue. You might be color blind, and that might be a very good thing. The religious experience, despite the differences in culture and faith and personality, is fundamentally a singular experience—we're all one, we're all one. The God Film has no plot except that which we piece together from twenty-four flickers each second. What we read in the red.

Read like that Borges story where the man sees his own face and his own bowels, and then your face, though demure and red-faced he does not mention your bowels.

Read like that Burroughs story about the last words of Dutch Schultz.

Read like The Bible, a billion different ways.

Red like the lance in your left side, red like the bowels that spill out.

Red like the blood boiling away in the brains of the fevered, like the blood blooming across a man's stomach from gunshot wounds.

Red like Emily Case's face as the noose tightens and she falls forward with a gurgle and a flash of pain, her arms spread wide, a weight on her back. No motorcycles, no midnight raids, no chance to rewind the reels and play the totality of the universe in two dimensions again.

Red like the nine minutes of film that let your mind slip out the left side of your body and into the great and bloody sea of forever.

We're all red, we're all red.

To the Jerusalem Crater

Lavie Tidhar

The rain fell in sheets on the dusty road, turning the ground to mud.

"Come and play. Come and play," the boy sang. The words took on the form of a litany in his mouth. "Seek. Hide. Conquer and ride." He sucked on a dirty thumb. Bright eyes looked into the stranger's face, big bright eyes. Like a whiteboard, the man thought, with the irises erased. "Some," the boy said, "like it hot. Is it hot?"

"It's warm," the stranger conceded. He squatted beside the boy. "You live here?"

The boy removed his thumb from his mouth, trailing saliva. His blank eyes regarded the stranger. "I don't know," he said after a long silence. Mud caked his bare feet. There were six toes on his left foot, only four on his right. Where the smallest should have been was a scar. "Where is here?"

The stranger remembered the old name of the place, which was Hebron. He wanted to tell the boy the name, but didn't. It would likely mean nothing to the boy. He thought for a fleeting moment about the old place-names, of how they were taken over and erased and made a new by the messianic mockery of the one he came to find, and to kill.

"Hide," the boy said. His face twisted in an expression that could have been fear. It could also have been petulance. "Go away!"

It was still raining. In the distance, the mountains looked ashen. The stranger wiped at the mud on his face but only served to smear it more evenly. He sighed.

"Here," he said. He put his hand into his coat pocket and brought out a small coin. He put it on the ground in front of the boy.

As he stood up he saw it sink into the mud. The boy inserted his thumb back into his mouth and watched the stranger depart.

After some time the rain stopped. Where the coin had been a small burnt sienna flower began to sprout.

Further down the mountain he came to a church. There was a crucifixion in progress. The stranger stopped beside the small garden of crosses and extracted a tin box from his coat. He opened it, relieved to find the tobacco dry, and began rolling a cigarette.

"Do you mind?" the man on the nearest cross demanded. Thick thorns penetrated his flesh and bound him to the wood. Manganese blue leaves shaded pale flowers that seemed to emerge from his skin. They shuddered and turned away as the smoke hit them. "Are you trying to kill me?"

The stranger stepped back. Further down the row of the crucified a bulbous woman cried to him. He stepped past the other Rosicrucian forms who watched him with milky eyes. The woman who called him had a round, pock-marked face. Her flowers were of a darker shade than the rest, a dirty grey. "Would you like me to tell your fortune, stranger? Do you find me attractive? I can see that you do. Give me that cigarette and I will let you have me."

"That won't be necessary," the stranger said. He put the cigarette in the woman's mouth and she sucked on it greedily. Her flowers trembled, grew darker.

"Keep it."

Beside the smoking woman another was being crucified by two shrunken old nuns who looked at him sideways but didn't speak. He nodded, then left them and walked back past the silent forms to the church. It was a small building, really nothing more than a hut, made of rough wood and roofed by sheets of old metal.

It was cool inside, and dark. The floor was packed earth swept clean. There was nothing in the room but an altar on which the rosy cross grew in a dissonance of mute and loud colors.

The stranger knelt by the altar.

"Praying?" he heard the sound of footsteps and, looking up, saw an old man detach himself from the far corner of the wall where the shadows had hidden him. "Or have you come seeking redemption." He had a flat, uneven voice, and his question, if that was what it was, trailed off into a statement.

"Neither," the stranger said. There was a silence as they contemplated each other. The priest wore tattered robes, and his bare arms and his face were smeared with ashes. "You were kind to share your cigarette with Khalifa," the priest said. "But you should not have done it. She is finding it difficult to part with the ways of the flesh."

"Don't we all, Father?" the stranger said. The priest nodded.

"What do you want here?"

The stranger contemplated the question in silence. Somewhere outside voices were singing softly in a language he didn't recognize. "Shelter from the night, perhaps," he said. "I am heading further away, to the crater."

"It is best not to travel at night," the priest agreed. "You can sleep here."

"Thank you."

The priest crossed his arms on his chest. His eyes, rheumy and narrow, regarded the stranger. "We seldom receive visitors here and, if you don't mind me saying so, none like you. Where are you from?"

The stranger made a vague gesture with his hand. "Oh, beyond."

"Beyond the mountains?"

The stranger nodded.

"Tell me," the priest said. There was a new note in his voice, and his face shifted in what could have been anxiety or greed. "Is there still an ocean?"

The stranger titled his head and seemed to think the question through. "It is possible," he acknowledged at last.

"I would have liked to see the ocean," the priest said. "Are there still ships? I was told stories...are there still ships?"

Again, a silence. "I doubt it," the stranger said. He was reluctant to continue the conversation.

The priest sighed. "Very well," he said. "Sleep well. Try not to leave the church at night. It is best not to."

"I will," the stranger said. "Thank you."

He watched the priest's back as it disappeared through the door. The priest's shift was torn open and parallel red marks crossed his skin. The stranger lay on the floor. After a moment, he fell asleep.

Roots emerged from the ground like the shriveled palms of elderly children and grasped for him. He twisted where he lay but could not move. He felt a sharp pain in his ankle, and something penetrated his flesh.

Flowers drooped over his head, enormous and wet, and for a moment he imagined them to be a forest of eyes, all of them crying. He could smell smoke and burning flesh, and though he somehow suspected it was human, the smell nevertheless made his stomach grumble in hunger.

A large insect flew above him, translucent wings vibrating. It had a long bill and was sucking the dew from the flowers, fluttering between them.

"Ashes to ashes," a voice said from somewhere in the shadows where he couldn't see. "Dust to dust."

He felt his ankle swell. He tried to move, but the roots restrained him.

"There was a song like that, once," a woman's voice said wistfully from the shadows. "I can no longer remember it. I can no longer remember." Amidst the flowers gazing at him he now saw a giant eyeball hanging by a stalk. It blinked at him. "Can you?"

"Yes."

He woke up. He was alone in the church. Sweat dried on his skin and made him shiver. He stood up and crossed the room in three steps and opened the door.

A small fire was burning outside, contained by a circle of field stones. The priest and the two nuns sat around it. The priest had his back to the stranger and didn't move. The smoke tasted sweet on his tongue.

The nuns had bent their heads down and were staring into the fire. Nearby he could hear the crucified woman, Khalifa, crying.

Sudden anger made him want to kick the logs and set the fire free. "Is this how you treat guests?"

"I told you." It was the priest. "We seldom receive visitors here."

"I am not surprised."

"You can't blame us. We need you." Still he couldn't see the priest's face, only his back. The red marks seemed deeper. "Stay."

He walked away. In the row of crosses a new one was planted.

It was empty.

* * *

Morning came sooner than he expected. He watched the sun rise over the mountains. It looked like it was struggling. Like an old woman climbing a long flight of stairs, he suddenly thought. Carrying heavy bags of groceries, wearing down the steps with the passage of too many years. He still remembered groceries. Almost alone, he still remembered the way the world had been before the crater formed, when the places he now traversed still had names like Hebron and Bethlehem and Jerusalem. He wasn't sure how to feel about being here again, both he and the place much changed. He shrugged. He had a task to do, however unpleasant. The area was a travesty, a stain on the face of a world trying to rebuild itself.

He walked steadily for several hours. There were fields in the distance but he could see no one working them. The sun grew steadily hot and he tracked its climb across the sky and watched the shadows shorten until they almost disappeared.

When the sun was at its zenith he found the tomb.

It was a short, squat stone building. He could see the ghost outline of a gate and a domed roof. The gate became, as he moved closer, the failing remains of two stone pillars. Vines grew over the stone, their fleshy leaves a dark green color. He made to pass between them.

"Can't go in there." Something hard prodded him in the back. The voice was reedy and the words were followed by a deep-throated cough.

He turned around slowly. Before him swung a long-barreled, rust-covered pipe that ended in a round metallic chamber and a trigger—on which a long scaly finger was slowly tightening. The finger was attached to a wide reptilian palm.

"Why not?"

The face that looked at him had too many eyes and too few other features. The eyes looked like maggots, crawling on a smooth oval surface. None blinked. The face was joined by a thick neck to a naked upper body with large female breasts. A loincloth covered a bulging, seemingly male area. The feet were wide with three splayed, prominent toes. "It's a place of rest," the creature said, almost apologetically. "No one remembers. No one cares, or prays here anymore."

"So why guard it?" the stranger asked.

The creature shrugged. Two eyes on the left side of its face closed. "Because it is still here. Because she still rests inside."

"She?" A long-forgotten memory returned to the stranger's mind. "Rachel?" Surprise made him ask again, "This is Rachel's tomb?"

"That's enough!" The gun sank into his stomach and the stranger fell to his knees, pain blossoming inside him like a dark flower. "Don't mention her name!"

As he rose back to his feet, the canopy seemed to thicken above him. Vines wound around the stone tomb, tightening. The guard blinked multiple eyes.

"That," the stranger said, breathing hard, "was uncalled for."

"Go away," the guard said. A small, silvery tear dropped from its top right eye and made its way down the side of its face. "Hide!"

The words were familiar. Around the stone building, the vegetation thickened again, grew rapidly. Cerulean, pulsating vines strangled the old stones.

The stranger shaded his eyes against the sun and sighed. A pattern, he felt, was emerging.

He walked away. Turning his head from a distance, he saw the vegetation receding around the building and the guard, still watching him, still pointing the ancient weapon in his direction.

He continued in the direction of the crater.

* * *

Perspective began to shift as he approached the rim. Distance became hazy and the sun's progress across the sky left a trailing arc of firebrick and rose madder across his vision. The air felt hotter the closer he moved to the crater. Lush vegetation sprouted around him, and fist-sized butterflies darted through the tropical landscape. A lizard raised its head and looked at him before scuttling away, its colors shifting to fit the background it was passing. He smelled wood smoke. There was a metallic taste in his mouth.

He could no longer see the mountains. Movement through the thickening vegetation became difficult, and the smell of rotting leaves grew underneath him. He fought away mosquitoes the size of thumbnails.

Steep glass slopes led down to the bottom of the crater. The stranger found himself slipping rapidly and finally abandoned himself to a fall that led him, sliding with increasing speed, toward the bottom.

When he at last touched ground it was nearly dark and growing colder. The bottom had a fused glass look and his steps produced loud, discordant notes that hurt his ears.

He came to the remnants of a road. Stones marked the path and, as he moved farther along, he was not surprised to discover crosses marking his passage. Silent men and women—some similar to him, some with the appearance of the tomb keeper, and others different still—were fused to the crosses and grew flowers and leaves. Eyes watched him as he walked, and moved to track his passing. He ignored them.

The road ended in a wide, circular area where the glass stopped and earth began again. The dirt felt moist and his boots sank into the ground, coming up covered in mud. Tall flowers rose above him, and the population of butterflies increased, their wings trailing thick strokes of paint in the cooling air.

He made his way into the heart of the circular garden. A small figure squatted in the mud and looked up as he approached.

Wide, milky eyes examined him in silence.

"So it was you," the stranger said. The words seemed to be swallowed by the other's silent nod. The stranger's hand reached inside his coat, and he felt the handle of the knife.

"You've come to kill me," the boy stated. Green, tiny shoots were emerging from the ground in a circle around him. "Why?"

"Things fall apart," the stranger said. He closed his fingers on the hidden handle but did not withdraw it. "Without a center."

"You're using another's words," the boy said dispassionately. The shoots around him grew, were the height of an ankle. "This is not the center of the world, and I am not the cause of all its present misery."

"No," the stranger agreed. "You are merely a symptom. But this place is important, sacred—" he laughed as if embarrassed at his choice of word "—and you cannot be allowed to pervert it further."

The boy tilted his head and watched the stranger. He wore a serious, concentrated expression. The stranger's knife was now out in the open, the blade long and dim. "And you will stop me...?"

The green shoots were the height of the boy's waist and continued to grow. Flowers in colors the stranger had no names for began to sprout from them.

"Nothing personal."

The stranger's knife flashed and moved in a graceful arc through the air, aiming for the boy. It connected with the stalks growing around him and they fell to the ground, oozing green blood.

"No," the boy said. "Likewise."

He was unharmed.

The stranger's knife flashed again. And again. Where the first stalks fell new ones grew rapidly. The boy stood up from his crouch and watched him, the knife missing him each time.

"But why do you do this?" he said. "Why you?"

"Because I remember the old faiths," the stranger said. He was grunting with effort now, and the wounded foliage around him grew. He could not hurt the boy. "And I remember how things were. I remember the city that used to be here, where no one now prays."

"Oh, they pray," the boy said. "As long as people still live there will always be prayer."

"The wrong kind," the stranger said. He stopped hacking and stood motionless, watching the boy. Flowers sprouted from the boy's body and his legs disappeared into the ground as if a part of it. "What have you done to me?" the stranger whispered.

He felt a sharp pain in his ankle and felt dizzy. The buzzing of insects grew around him.

"There is nothing for you here," he heard the boy say. He sounded distant. "Go back and tell them that, those old men beyond the mountains. Go away!"

The stranger's eyes closed, and the darkness claimed him.

He woke up. He was alone in the church. Sweat dried on his skin and made him shiver. He stood up and crossed the room in three steps, and opened the door.

A small fire was burning outside, contained by a circle of field stones. There was no one by the fire. Nearby he could hear the crucified woman, Khalifa, crying. Smoke tasted sweet on his tongue.

He shivered and huddled closer to the fire. A new, empty cross was planted in the row of the crucified—like a promise, he thought. Or a threat.

He warmed his hands by the fire. His ankle still hurt.

He reached inside his coat. The knife was missing, and in its stead was a coin he thought he recognized. He smiled and left it there, on the ground, before he rose and walked away.

CHIMERAS & GROTESQUERIES
Matt Cardin

I realized early on that it would be necessary for me to introduce the following manuscript with a brief preface explaining my involvement in bringing it to light. I can only hope that the unorthodox nature of this involvement will not cast doubt on the manuscript's authenticity or, worse, detract from its impact by distracting the reader from its profound implications.

For years I tried to explain to myself the unearthly influence that Philip Lasine exerted over me with his writings. My fascination with his bizarre, horrific, outlandish, and thoroughly transformative stories revolved largely around the fates of his protagonists, who, speaking in the first person, encountered things they could not explain—nightmarish things, awful eruptions of unearthly monstrousness in circumstance, event, person, and entity—and were invariably destroyed in the end. Bu they were also, somehow, transformed and preserved in a permanently shattered state from which they could meditate eternally on the impenetrable mystery of their own doom.

Lasine's success in depicting such things and conveying their full, devastating emotional and philosophical impact was an authorial feat of sheer, shocking genius that I tried to emulate in my own stumbling way by writing stories that aped his signature style of marrying narrative prose fiction to Montaigne-like essayistic explorations. Eventually, and fortunately, I recognized my singular lack of literary talent in this vein, and decided to aim my desire for spiritual depth in another direction. A philosophy degree, training at a respected Protestant seminary, and an ordination to a ministerial career as a Lutheran pastor were swiftly forthcoming.

But still, Philip Lasine had assumed for me the status of a distant master, and even when I grew out of my childhood attitude that imparted a permanent mystique to the authors of books and came to understand that real people with real lives and bodies and voices and histories really do stand behind all of those printed and bound volumes—as witnessed by the fact that I myself wrote and saw published a number of modestly successful books of Christian theology—Philip Lasine still seemed an iconic presence, a beacon of impossible literary perfection shining like a star from the peak of some intra-psychic Sinai. I could not keep from regarding him as an embodied archetype, and found myself thinking of him from time to time and feeling, even though I knew it was childish, that the author of *those* books could not possibly be a real, living, breathing man with a real physical appearance and a concrete geographical location. He had to be a myth, a nexus of daimonic power that had somehow focused into the form of a man for long enough to produce that perfect and powerful body of work, after which the body dissolved and the power withdrew back to the astral plane. This was my private fantasy, which I never actually articulated to myself, holding it as a kind of half-belief that surfaced occasionally into conscious awareness, at which times I observed it with an attempt at ironic amusement and made certain that I did not breathe a word of it to my parishioners.

Here my preface ends, for the spiritual and artistic relationship between Philip and me is more important than the later, more literal one that arose. There is also the fact that this literal relationship resulted from such an outlandish set of coincidental circumstances, and was of such a bizarre nature (especially considering my longstanding literary worship of the man), that I would not blame the reader for disbelieving it and therefore doubting the authenticity of what follows. When a man finds himself standing beside the deathbed of his idol, having been summoned there in an official capacity because he is a professional clergyman, he may begin to mistrust even his own perceptions and memories, and would not want to impart these doubts to his readers by giving too detailed an account of things that may or may not have happened exactly as he recalls them.

Here, then, is Philip Lasine's last story, which is especially striking for being both like and unlike his other writings. I do not know whether it was meant to be self-contained or part of a longer work. I do know that it is clearly unfinished in its current state. I will admit that the thought has crossed my mind that I could try to finish it myself, so close was I to its author when he died and bequeathed it to me, and so intimately do its ideas resonate with me. But in the end I have decided to present it exactly as he left it, on the suspicion that some sort of hidden conclusion resides within the work as it stands. I have limited my editorial involvement to the minor expansion of a few key passages that were embryonic in their received form. The reader may well recognize these passages by their heavy-handedness and overly expository tone; I did not seek to emulate Philip's style, but to clarify the vision he was incompletely expressing as he wrote by hand while lying on his death bed.

The story as a whole may be intended as an allegory of sorts, although the grounds of its metaphors are obscure. Then again, they may not be as obscure as they appear; they may only seem so because of their extreme spiritual intimacy to us all, the repercussions of which I have not yet begun to work out for my ministerial vocation.

This last suspicion is at least partly verified by the experience that I have just had between writing the preceding paragraph and this one. I paused in my work to step outside and rest my eyes. It is a frigid December night, and I stood perfectly still in the icy air, gazing up at the panorama of the night sky, which bristled with stars. As I watched, they seemed to take on the imprint of a vast human face—not looking down at me, but pressing outward, as if the entire glittering expanse were the inner surface of a cosmic mask.

The experience was invested with a clear visionary character, as opposed to a merely hallucinatory one, and I am not nearly as ashamed as I would have expected when I admit that after the celestial monstrosity had receded and the stars had returned to their normal configuration, I reached up to feel my own face with a sense of quickening dread.

Chimeras & Grotesqueries
by Philip Lasine

Just when it had first occurred to me to start assembling monstrous human effigies from the garbage that littered the alley floor outside my grotto, I could not say. I only knew that this was how I spent most of my waking hours, the ones not otherwise devoted to scrounging for food and drink in the wasteland of alleyways and trash bins that made up my world.

Occasionally there were other activities to distract me. I was obliged at times to fend off, flee from, or otherwise respond to the vicious attacks of the animalistic young men who in recent years had found a new form of entertainment in beating and sometimes killing street dwellers like me. But I was more fortunate than many of my fellows, since my appearance and demeanor effectively deterred would-be assailants. Perhaps it was my size, for I was tall and bulky, and made for a singularly hulking figure as I stalked the streets in the frayed tweed overcoat that I had fished from a dumpster one icy, wet New Year's Day.

Or perhaps it was my face with its striking disfiguration, like a melted rubber mark. The feral youths who ventured downtown to the back alleys in search of their brutal amusements usually kept their distance. On the two occasions when a group of them had approached me with clubs and broken bottles in hand, I had simply stood to my full height and raised my face to greet them, freezing them in their tracks while I turned to walk away.

But all of this was only a minor and occasional disruption in my daily routine. Each morning I awoke in my grotto and lay motionless beneath my covering of newspapers until hunger or thirst compelled me to move. Then I crawled into the alleyway, climbed to my feet, and went in search of food. After that I wandered the streets for a while, following a circuitous path dictated by impulses I could not understand. People gave me a wide berth whenever I emerged, as I sometimes did, from the labyrinth of side streets and alleyways into the brightness and broadness of a sidewalk bordering a well-traveled boulevard or avenue.

After each day's travels I returned to my alley, where I scraped together heaps of trash, seated myself against the wall, and began to assemble little human-shaped figures. These were always grotesque in one way or another. A mass of grimy, shredded newspaper, impaled on the neck of a broken beer bottle, would become a head whose fluttering fringe recalled the monstrous Medusa of ancient mythology. Oily flaps from the peel of a rotten banana, when attached to holes punched in the sides of an old cracker box or tobacco can, would suggest arms like octopoid tentacles. The effect was especially vivid when the box or can was topped with a moldy, withered orange to serve as a head whose distorted face formed a miniature parody of my own. Sometimes I would secure the pieces together with bits of string or wire. Other times I would simply prop the assembled figures against the wall or lay them gently on the concrete floor of the alley in concentric half circles around the entrance to my grotto, where they might remain intact for hours or days before a stray breeze would begin to scatter them back into their original, unpersonified parts.

I spent endless hours assembling these shapes, which I began to think of as my "little ones." The activity seemed strange even to me, for whom it was so very familiar. I could only imagine what it must have looked like to my fellow derelicts, who, on the rare occasions when our paths crossed, regarded me with expressions of fear and even awe.

It was only the unfamiliar ones, the ones who were either new to this part of the city or new to street life itself, who ever dared to venture near the entrance to my alley. And there were also the so-called crazies, the mentally muddled and addled among us, who mumbled or ranted at the empty air, soiled themselves, twitched with various tics and convulsions, and displayed all the other signs of dementia. I sometimes wondered what the others were thinking during our occasional brief encounters, which invariably ended with their flight and my resumption of my perpetual solitude and miniature demiurgic activities. I was especially curious about the crazies, with their fractured perceptions and diseased mental processes, for I thought it would be fascinating to see myself through their eyes and discover what their faulty faculties made of me and the domain I had created for myself.

When I tried to calculate the span of my rootless existence, I could not remember whether it was a month, a year, or longer. At the far point of my memory there was only a blankness, a grey and featureless barrier like a plaster wall. Sometimes, instead of a wall it felt like an absence or emptiness, as if I were missing an organ or limb. Occasionally I had the impression, so intense that it bordered on a physical sensation, that behind my eyes and brain there existed a gaping hole. At such times I would reach around and probe the back of my head to verify that it was still intact. Then I would touch my face and wonder how this disfiguration had occurred.

Other psychological dislocations occurred as well. I would start occasionally from a light doze or reverie to find myself confused and disoriented. If it were night and I had crawled into my grotto to sleep, I would emerge and gaze at my surroundings: the alleyway with its bleakness and grit, my little ones scattered sleeping all around, the strip of dark sky peering down from between the high brick walls. And although I knew this was my life, besides which I had known no other, I would intuit that somewhere there existed another, truer mode of existence. But full memory of it always eluded me, and presently the feeling would fade and I would know that there was only this life on the streets, where an incomprehensible inner compulsion drove me to assemble an ever-widening congregation of miniature monsters to worship at my rag-clad feet.

I had first awakened while staggering through the streets of the city, dressed in the same rags that I later continued to wear, and filled with a fluttering sensation in my breast, a strange electrical exhilaration like joy or terror.

After what might have been hours or days of this half-blind odyssey through the city streets, I had blundered into an alleyway formed by the rough outer walls of two brick buildings, where the shadowy coolness felt like balm to my burning face. A battered grey garbage dumpster squatted next to me at the entrance. All manner of refuse—scraps of paper, shards of glass, strips of metal—carpeted the alley floor. The far end was blocked by a barrier of pitted wooden planks, past which I could see nothing but distance and dimness, crossed by coils of mist.

I felt the contours of my soul expar instantly to claim and conform to this blissful slice of peace and privacy. My sense of belonging was further confirmed when I stepped slowly forward and saw a hole punched through the base of the wall on my right, several feet past the dumpster. It was roughly three feet high and wide, with chalk-jagged edges where the bricks had shattered. Without a moment's thought, I approached it, dropped to my hands and knees, and crawled inside, where the darkness swallowed me with uncanny absoluteness.

My gropings revealed a cramped, square-cornered cave formed by three rough concrete walls. I brushed away the chunks of brick and mortar littering the floor and then lay down, finding the cave just large enough for me to stretch to my full length.

I lay there for hours, listening to the faint murmurings of the city and reaching up from time to time to touch my face and wonder at its rapidly vanishing pain. This was my home, my grotto, as I instantly thought of it in a burst of inspiration that was as incontrovertible as it was unaccountable.

The bizarre metaphysical breakdown in the world at large, which came to define life in the city soon after I awoke to my strange existence, was heralded by a brief outburst of what the newspapers, quoting the hastily delivered verdicts of psychiatric professionals and government offices, dubbed "mass hysteria." It took the form of what one prominent mental health authority described as a "hallucinatory disfiguration" of the city's religious architecture.

For a period of about five minutes on a weekday afternoon, the city's human inhabitants saw the façades of churches, temples, synagogues, mosques, and meditation halls transmogrified into human or humanoid faces frozen in expressions of horror. The event made itself known in a ripple of panic that radiated outward from those buildings and through the crowds like waves on a lake. Everyone who laid eyes on such a structure saw the change occur. Some people blanched and stared in mute shock. Others groaned or screamed and covered their heads. Still others fell to their knees or fainted. Some vomited or went into convulsions. Later, the story that emerged from tens of thousands of individual witnesses was uniform in its assertion of the unearthly influence those faces had exerted. The sheer spectacle of the grotesquely twisted images had, as one man stated it, "flooded my sight" and "spilled into my stomach." Countless people told the same story of experiencing an overpowering sense of mingled terror and revulsion that seemed to bloat their visual sense and then "spill" or "burst" or "flood" into other parts of their bodies—stomach, bowels, genitals, limbs—and bring with it an excruciating illness.

The vision vanished as suddenly as it had appeared, and in the ensuing days and weeks more than one artist attempted to draw or paint a semblance of those spectral faces. Invariably, the attempts fell short, at least according to the people who had actually seen the originals for themselves. I, myself, examined several of these drawings and paintings in the papers that came fluttering down the street, and they were hideous in the extreme, with mouths, eyes, and other features displaying a strange perversion of proportion that rendered them utterly noxious. It was impossible to isolate the exact qualities that achieved such a striking effect. In some of the pictures the eyes were blank and white, staring blindly without irises or pupils. In others the eyes were made demonic by pupils in the shape of serpentine slits or goatlike wedges. Still others featured the bulbous black eyes of an insect or the berry-cluster eyes of a spider. In all of them the mouths gaped wide in screams of torment, but again the details varied. Some displayed reptilian rows of fangs, others a mouth lined with rotten sores like leprosy. In others a strange stone tunnel with an arched entrance had replaced the throat, suggesting a coiling journey downward, inward, toward a pit of indescribable darkness.

Of all those who were within sight of a religious structure when the visions struck, I alone failed to see the faces. I was out on one of my walks, and was standing directly before and beneath the façade of a great cathedral when the people around me began to scream and clutch their neighbors. I saw them gazing wild-eyed at the church, but when I looked at it myself I saw only the unchanged spires and arches rearing toward the pale blue sky, and the massive mazework of stained glass glinting in the afternoon sunlight. Then people began to fall and thrash, gasping and retching in fits of supernatural sickness, but still I saw nothing. Within minutes I was the only one left standing, a rag-wrapped figure surrounded by writhing forms that struck me suddenly as wormlike and obscene.

For many nights I pondered this strangeness as I lay inside my grotto and felt the darkness breathe. I could not divine whether my failure to see the faces indicated a deficit of spiritual sight or a surplus of it. Many times I reached up to feel my disfigured features, and was seized by a mental image of that great cathedral shuddering and twisting and transforming itself into a polished mirror upon whose silvery-crystalline surface I saw my own reflection screaming in unbounded horror.

Not long after the appearance of the faces, the breakdown in things was signaled in more personal fashion by the incident of the man who bled to death through his eyes. It occurred during my daily journey, when I was at one of the farthest points away from my alley and tracing an unwonted path through a part of town where people wore nicer clothing and drove newer vehicles, and where the tall buildings gleamed with the freshness of new-cut stone and polished glass. As always, the river of bodies streaming down the sidewalk parted like biblical waters to let me pass, men in business suits and women in rich furs and dresses stepping aside and averting their eyes.

What first drew my attention were the screams. They came in a male voice, harsh and piercing, and were so very sincere in their expression of frantic horror that I thought they would surely shred the throat of the one voicing them. Like everyone else within earshot, I turned to look, and my eyes located a man in a grey business suit standing at the open door of a taxicab and clutching his face with both hands. Blood spurted from between his fingers, which were capped over his eyes.

The sight proved mesmerizing to all. We stopped and stared as he shrieked in pain and horror. We remained motionless as he doubled over and vomited on his black leather shoes while the blood still squirted from between his rigid pale fingers. Then he fell into the crook of the cab door and began clawing at his eyes while his legs kicked a spastic dance-like pattern.

This triggered the panic that had been waiting for release. The crowd exploded in multiple directions, the surge of people becoming a confusion of forces, some leading toward the man and others away from him. I was caught in one of the former, which swept me to within a few feet of the man before drawing to a fearful halt.

I heard the new noise when everyone else did, the one that had been obscured by the general commotion and the man's screams. It was a whispery hiss, like the sound of ice melting on a bed of hot coals, and it filled the air with a preternatural loudness and vividness. After a moment, its source became evident.

The blood from the man's eyes was sizzling and burning like acid. It was eating at the flesh of his hands and face, the fabric of his suit, the leather of his shoes, even the yellow paint on the side of the cab. Where it had spattered on the black pavement, it bubbled like oil in a hot skillet and emitted a curling white plume of smoke.

Pandemonium ensued. The sea of people burst into atoms yet again, fleeing with shrieks and shouts. I alone stayed near to watch what happened as the man's body began to collapse in on itself.

When I arrived back at my alley a while later, I crawled inside my grotto even though several hours of daylight still remained. I lay there the rest of that day and then through the night, letting what I had seen replay again and again in the theater of my thoughts. And although I could not be completely confident about the order of events that formed my life, I felt certain when I awoke the next morning that the bleeding man was the reason why I had originally started creating my little ones. As if to prove the fact, I made a new one right there by securing a discarded length of rubber tubing to a body made from a rusty old gasoline can. The result appeared like entrails protruding from a metallic abdomen. The faulty chronology, the seemingly abstract fact that I had been making these things for quite some time before witnessing the man's unusual death, did not matter. What mattered was that my little ones owed their birth to my having witnessed that initial incursion of absolute reality into a corruptible human form.

It became impossible to avoid hearing about more such events as they began to multiply throughout the city. Even I, in my sanctified solitude, caught wind of the horror that had begun to break in at every crack and seam.

On a bitterly cold morning when every exposed surface was coated with a crust of ice, an unknown variety of flower sprang up and bloomed in the city's largest public park. A policeman watched it erupt from the frozen sod, staring in astonishment as a strange shoot broke the icy crust with a delicate crackling and rose to a height of two feet before unfolding velvety black petals clustered around a lemon-yellow core. He brushed the petals with his hand and died later that day of a raging fever. The flower, he told the doctors before he died, disintegrated into ash on contact with his skin.

A few blocks north, a car ran over a blind man's dog, injuring it grievously. The blind man fell to his knees and cradled the dog's head in his lap, weeping wretchedly as his canine guide shrieked in agony. But then the bestial shrieks underwent a shocking mutation, and it became a human voice issuing from the inhuman mouth, howling an obscenity of mangled speech formed by lips, tongue, and throat that had never been intended for such a purpose, begging the blind man not to let it die there in the street. The man ended up strangling the dog in a burst of horrified fury. "It couldn't live," he told someone afterward, still shaking and sobbing. *"It couldn't live."*

These and other such events began to play on everyone's lips, even those of the tramps whose life I shared. They began congregating outside the entrance to my alley, at first in twos and threes and then in a growing throng, and as I eavesdropped on them I could hear that many of the saner among them had begun to sound like the crazies, so deranged was the content of their conversation. As if to prove the point that the axis of the ordinary had begun to shift in the direction of insanity, the crazies themselves began to act even more fiercely crazed than usual, at times seeming positively magisterial in the intensity and sincerity of their babblings and hand-wavings. Their customary mutterings and screechings and conversations with invisible companions swelled collectively over a span of weeks to become a near-constant chorus of ecstatic chatter. It resounded throughout the concrete labyrinth of our world, echoing from every window and wall, forming a delirious backdrop to the usual weary sigh of the city, making me speculate about a new species of glossolalia whose syntax might contain the secrets of all the wonders arising around us.

In addition to listening to my fellow street dwellers, I continued to read the scraps of newspaper that came my way and found that they had come to sound unhinged in a manner formerly reserved for the tabloids as their pages were filled more and more frequently with tales of impossible occurrences. One scholar who specialized in an obscure branch of philosophical theology suggested in a hastily published pamphlet that all of these disruptions confirmed his thesis that "the supernatural is the insanity of the universe." Over time, the scale of the events grew greater, surpassing their former status as mere news of the bizarre to reach heights of grotesquery and hallucinatory horror that led otherwise sober commentators to opine in all seriousness that something had come unraveled at the heart of things.

A woman entering a clothing shop on a busy avenue was killed when the plate glass window above the door suddenly came loose from its frame and fell upon her with unnatural force like a guillotine. The thin glass pane hit the crown of her skull broadwise, cleaving her head cleanly in half and then exploding in an inferno of crystalline fragments. Her face was thus untouched, and when she fell to the floor amid the shower of shattered glass, her eyes remained open, rolling wildly in their sockets with an expression of panic while her lips worked silently. The astonishment of the onlookers, many of whom were injured by the glass fragments that shot through the store like bullets, was compounded when there came spilling out of the woman's split skull not a gush of blood and mangled tissue, but a half-dozen pulsating clumps of feathers. These landed on the polished tile floor and whipped instantly into motion, unfurling and revealing themselves as enormous black birds that someone described as deformed crows. The birds took flight and dashed madly about the interior of the store in a squawking hurricane of oily wings, crashing into light fixtures, knocking over clothing racks, and wounding a few of the patrons with sharp pecks and talon gouges before shooting through the open front door and out into the street. A dozen witnesses saw the screeching bird-things flap high into the air and then out of sight past the edge of a skyscraper.

In another part of the city, a young woman was attacked in her apartment by her four-year-old daughter. Two college students who lived in the adjacent apartment came running in response to the screams, to find that the girl had attacked her mother's abdomen and genitals with a pair of scissors. They found her buried neck-deep inside her mother's torso, which was split open like a fish. She told the police later that she had been trying to "get back inside mama's belly." One of the students told a reporter that when he and his roommate arrived, the girl pulled her head out of the bloody vertical wound and turned to gaze at them with "black eyes that burned." His roommate said the girl's eyes "burned" and "dripped" with a hot liquid like boiling oil.

As I stalked the sidewalks or sat propped against the wall of my alley in pursuit of my work, my thoughts kept returning to the reactions of those who had witnessed and participated in such scenes of abnormality. Again and again I meditated on the sense of *unreality* that must have overtaken them. I thought it must seem to these people that the sanity of the universe had sprung a leak, and that the blazing horror they encountered only in their sleep, in their most primal nightmares, had invaded the waking world.

Dwelling upon this for endless hours, I would sometimes experience an inner upwelling of giddiness or vertigo that would cause me to gasp and reach out to steady myself against a wall or lamppost. It was especially intense at those moments when I sat there in my alley fashioning miniature heads and limbs and bodies. My eyesight would flicker and grow dim, as if my surroundings were lit only by the glow of a guttering candle, and I would stare at the little unfinished creature I held in my hands, and at the others strewn about the alley floor. And all the repressed knowledge of myself, of my origin, nature, purpose, and destiny, would tremble maddeningly at the far edge of memory.

I awoke in the dead of night with the buzzing awareness of some unknown visitation resting heavily upon me. The presence was receding even as I came to consciousness and crawled out of my grotto. Something about my alley was different, and I stood blinking in the starlight for half a moment before realizing the nature of the change.

My little ones were gone. I had ended my day by setting out what was by far the largest array of them that I had ever assembled. The concentric curved rows had radiated outward from the entrance to my grotto like a great rainbow of deformity, reaching all the way to the facing wall. But now, only a few hours later, the alley floor was empty, swept clean even of its usual carpet of garbage, all of which I had used as the raw material for my creative act. Nothing remained but a thin coating of dirt. Peering more closely at it, I saw a multitude of miniature indentations flowing in a path toward the alley's entrance, which had now become an exit. Even now I heard the receding whisper of a collective scuttling.

The screams began to reach my ears a little later, as I sat against the wall in my usual spot. First they came in the voices of my fellow street people. Then they came riding the frigid night air from all over the city. Hundreds of thousands of voices shrieked in pain and horror, and continued to shriek even after their owners had met their doom.

I rose again and peered intently upward at the strip of night sky between the abandoned buildings whose outer walls defined my world. It bristled with stars. As I watched, they seemed to take on the imprint of a vast and deformed human face—not looking down at me, but pressing outward, as if the entire glittering expanse were the inner surface of a cosmic mask. I reached up to touch my own face. The celestial one remained.

YOU DREAM

Ekaterina Sedia

This is a recurring dream, the kind that lingers, and lately it has become more frequent. And it takes a while to realize that you are not, in fact, standing in front of the brick apartment building, its doorway cavernous and warm, your hands in your pockets, cigarette smoke leaking slowly between your lips and into the frozen air. It takes you a while to even remember that you've quit smoking years ago. And yet, here it is, clinging to the collar of your winter coat in a persistent, suffocating cloud, and you can taste it still.

It takes you even longer to remember why you dreamt about this building on the outskirts of Moscow—that you used to live there, but this is not why; you're there because of the boy who used to live in the same building but the other entrance. You cannot remember his name or whether you were really friends or just nodded at each other, passing by like boats in the lonely concrete sea of the yard, a fringe of consumptive poplars looking nothing like the palms of the tropical isles neither of you were ever likely to see. You know, though, that there was never any unpleasant physicality between the two of you, even after you learned to throw your body between yourself and whomever was trying to get too close.

You sit up in your bed and want a smoke, and whisper to yourself, It was never sex. Never. It was a defensive reflex, the same as a lizard that aborts its tail and escapes while some predator dumbly noses around the mysteriously wriggling appendage. You'd learned to do it with your entire body, and only the spirit escaped, not watching from the distance, running instead for the hills and the razor slash of the distant horizon. It was always about escaping.

Anyway, the boy: as far as you can recall, he had an average and pale face, he was short and slouched, his hands always in the pockets of his ratty hand-me-down winter coat, too short for him. His straight dark hair was always falling ungracefully across his forehead, and the only thing even remotely remarkable about him was the fact that even in the deadest winter cold his eyes remained warm and soft and brown, and he looked at everything with the same subdued delight. Finding oneself in the diffuse cone of his nearsighted gaze was both disconcerting and comforting, since he seemed to be the only person in the entire universe who honestly didn't want anything from you.

You try to remember what happened to him—you think vaguely that he died as a teen after being drafted, died somewhere in Chechnya; or maybe it was his older brother, and the boy just disappeared one day. Maybe he is still there, at his old apartment, and the memory of his death is a confabulated excuse for not having kept in touch. That seems likely.

It's time to get up anyway, and you stare out the window; you've moved from the grey suburbs to the sort-of center, near the Moscow River's bend, where it is somewhat less grey and the lights of opulence are visible across the river. You try to be satisfied with your lot in life, but discontent lingers, so you eye your pantyhose, tangled and twisted into a noose, and your short skirt, the one you're getting too old for, and you keep getting a sneaking suspicion that your immediate boss feels the same way and soon enough he'll trade you for a newer model, like he with his BMWs.

So you call in sick. No one minds since there's yet another economic crisis in progress, and chances are no one will be paid

until right before the new year. And they can type their own
damn reports, those twelve managers and only two of you to do
the actual work. It doesn't matter. You dig through your ward-
robe and find half-forgotten woolly tights, scratchy and severe
and thick, and a long gabardine skirt with a broken zipper,
which you fix with a safety pin. You wrap your head in the flowery kerchief every Russian woman owns—even if she never
bought one, it was given as a gift, or, barring all normal means of
acquisition, spontaneously generated in her apartment. You suspect that yours is one of those, an immaculately gotten kerchief
with fat cabbage roses on a velvet-black background with tangled fringe.

It is warmer outside than you expected, what with the
dreams of winter and whatnot, but the wind is still cutting and it
throws handfuls of bright yellow poplar leaves in your face as
you walk away from the embankment. Your shoulders stoop under a grey woolen cardigan, and your walk is awkward, unnatural in flat shoes, and you feel as if you keep falling heavily on
your heels, the familiar support elevating them above ground
missing. Your face feels naked without the makeup.

St. Nicholas' church is open and empty, the smell of frankin-
cense and whatever church incense they use there tickling your
nostrils and yet infusing you with reflexive peace, conditioned
like a dog that salivates at the sound of the bell. You buy a thin
brown candle and plop it in front an icon, wherever there's
space, and mumble something prayer-like under your breath.

The mass is long over and only black-clad old women are
there, rearranging and correcting falling candles, sweeping the
heavy stone tiles of the floor. They look at you with their cata-
ract blue like skimmed milk, and mumble under their breath.
You catch the word "whore" and try not to take it personally—
after all, this is what they call every woman who is not them,
whether she is mortifying her flesh with woolen tights or not.

You try to will your legs to not itch and end up backing behind a column and scratching discreetly.

You are not sure what brought on this religious impulse, except for the boy you miss without having known him. Then you think of the rest of his family, his numerous siblings, always hungry and underdressed, and it resolves in your memory, finally: he was a son of a defrocked priest who was forced into disgrace and living in a common apartment building instead of a parish house, no longer surviving off tithes, but the very modest salary of a night watchman. His wife worked at the meat factory across the street and always brought home bulging sacks dripping with blood, filled with tripe and bones and stomachs, and it was never enough for their brood, which, by your estimate, was somewhere between seven and nine. Poorer and more fecund than real priests, even.

"May I help you?" A soft, stuttering voice startles you from your reverie and you spook upright, your head springing back and almost breaking the nose of the speaker.

The young priest steps back, calm, his hands behind his back. "You look spiritually wrought," he says, smile bristling his soft beard, light as flax. "You need guidance."

"I don't," you say with unnecessary force, the wraiths of your twelve bosses rearing their heads, the images of people always telling you what you need. "I need information. Why would a priest be defrocked?"

"Depends," he answers with the same softness, the change of topic barely breaking his cadence. "Are we talking about now, or in the past? Because the synod just defrocked a priest the other day, for marrying two men."

"No," you say. "Before—in the seventies or early eighti A priest in Moscow was defrocked. He had children."

"Most of us do," young Father says, musing. "Back then, that would've been insubordination, most likely. Failure to respect the hierarchy. Talking badly about the hierarchy. Or possibly a failure to inform—or maybe informing on the wrong people, the wrong things." He sighs heavily, his grey eyes misting over. "You know, I grew up in the church. I'm not afraid of ever losing my faith—when I was young, I saw one priest beating another up with an icon."

Normally you would laugh at the image, but his thoughtful sincerity stops you. "I see," you say.

"Do you know that priest's name?"

"Father Dmitri," you say.

"No last name?"

You shake your head and feel stupid.

"Do you know what church he was assigned to before his defrocking?"

"No. I was just thinking about his son...they used to live in the same apartment building as I did."

"Go visit them, then," he says flatly. "They were probably too poor to buy another apartment."

"I don't...." You want to tell him that you really don't want to see anyone from your past, anyone who would recognize you and put together the images of you—then and now, past and present—and find the comparison lacking.

But he is already losing interest, backing away. "You need to get baptized," he says before turning away, toward the old women who wait for his glance as if it were a blessing.

"How do you know I'm not?" you call after, raising your voice unacceptably.

"You're tormented," he calls back, just as loud.

The priest is wrong—your mother had baptized you at birth, even though such things were frowned upon back in 1970s. She even took you to the Easter and Christmas masses, where you stood on your aching feet for hours, holding a candle that dripped hot wax on your hands. The memory brings only bore-dom and unease and doesn't lessen whatever spiritual torment the priest saw in you. He doesn't know that the church with its battling priests isn't as calming to you as it is to him—you worry that you will now have comical nightmares of priests in their long black robes and tall hats pummeling each other with icons and candlesticks. You are really not looking for salvation from them, but from that quiet boy in your childhood. No one else had such kind eyes. You sigh, regretful that your young self was so unaware of how rare a treasure this kindness was—and you're not even sure if such optimism should be commended.

By the time you were twelve, you certainly knew enough of those who were not kind, of the tiny cave under the very first flight of stairs by the apartment building's entrance, the cave you always had to run past because of those who hid there—boys who would reach out and hold you against the wall and put their hands under your skirt and down your sweater. You never told your mom why you would wait for her to come home from work, when the shadows grew long, and she couldn't under-stand that you were not afraid to be home alone—you were afraid of the dash up the flight of stairs, and your two-room apartment could've as well been located on the moon.

You do not remember the faces of those boys, just that one who never laid a finger on you; instead, he walked with you sometimes, and watched you get into the elevator, safe. Some-times the boys under the stairs would beat him, and once they held his face down in the large puddle that manifested in your paved yard every spring and fall—held him until bubbles com-ing from his silted lips turned into stifled screams and only a chance passerby spooked the hooligans.

When you get home, you unwrap the kerchief and hate it for a while because your hair is now flattened and tangled and you'll have to wash it again. Then you pick up the phone, since there's nothing else to do but to hurl yourself toward the past, since the present refuses to surrender any answers or even passable lies.

Your mother sounds older than she did the last time you spoke, and you try not to feel guilty about her unseen decline in some sanatorium that costs you most of your uncertain salary, and of course it would be cheaper to have her live with you, here, over the black river that smells of gasoline and foams white in the wake of leisure boats. You sigh into the phone and try to ignore all of her unvoiced complaints.

"Mom," you finally say, "do you remember that family that used to live next door, when I was little? The one with seven kids?"

"Vorobyev," she says, her memory as flawless as always. "The youngest boy, Vasya, was such a sweet kid. Always running around in those girls' coats from his older sisters."

That's right, you now remember, those were plaid, too-short girl coats. No wonder everyone teased him; no wonder his unperturbed demeanor incited them to violence—there was no point in such savage humiliation as a girl's coat unless its victim would acknowledge it as such.

"Vasya Vorobyev," she repeats. "Too sad about him."

"What have you heard?" Your heart seizes up and it's ridiculous. You haven't thought about that kid in decades. In forever. "What happened?"

"Anya, his mother, used to call me sometimes," she says. "He's dead, in Osetia last year. Now she's dead too—her heart gave out after that."

"Too bad." You are numb now, numb to the tips of your fingers, and they almost drop the receiver. A deep chill settles in at the loss you aren't sure you've suffered. "Do you remember why was his father was defrocked?"

"No. Why would you care about something like that?"

"I don't," you whisper, and say goodbye. You spend the rest of the day watching TV and pacing and drinking buttermilk straight out of the bottle that fits so comfortably into one hand, and you keep thinking back to the days when you needed two to hold it.

The boy who defended you sometimes. You're glad to have a name, but in your mind he's still that boy—the boy. You're glad to be dreaming about him the next night—at least there he is alive and little, even as other people's hands press his face into the dirty pavement, his teeth making an awful scraping sound that makes you cringe in your sleep. They leave, but not before making lewd gestures in your direction, and you wait for the boy to stagger up, his feet shuffly and his knees buckling under him. He totters but remains standing. You feel lucid even though it is a dream and in it you are still small. "Why was your father defrocked?"

"Why does it matter?" He lisps a bit, his tongue thoughtfully exploring the ragged edge of the chipped front tooth. He doesn't seem to know that he is in your dream.

"Because I need to know what did he do that was so awful, to bring you here. What was it that you were paying for?"

"Looking for the prime mover, huh?" He drops the pretense of childhood and for a second becomes terrifying—still a kid, but somehow older and deader. "I don't know why. Who knows why shit happens, huh? Who knows why you don't tell anyone about them dragging you under the stairs. Why you never told them—"

Your face burns with exposed shame and you snap away from him, the hem of your gabardine dress twirling around your legs, long and smooth and brown in your first pair of nylon pantyhose. "Fuck off," you mutter darkly. And yet you understand his point, the essential impossibility of revealing one's secrets—especially if those secrets are not one's fault. We can get over the wrongs we do, but we cannot forgive ourselves for the wrongs done to us, for our own helplessness.

"Don't be like that." He catches up to you and walks with you across the paved yard, the large puddle in its center only nascent. It must remind him, you think, and then you are suddenly not sure whether the puddle incident happened before or after the chipped tooth.

You sit in your bed upright, your heart strumming against your ribs. You have to go to sleep, you tell yourself, you have to get up early tomorrow, but then you remember it'll be Saturday. So you give up and pull on a pair of jeans and tuck your nightgown into them, throw on a jacket and run down the stairs and across the street—like a wayward moth that woke up in the fall by mistake—toward the fluorescent glimmer of an all-night kiosk.

You buy a gin and tonic in a can—make that two—and a pack of Dunhill's, the red one. You buy a translated detective novel for good measure, and the guy behind the bulletproof glass smiles crookedly. "Got a wild night planned?"

You ignore the familiar sarcasm, so integrated into the national discourse that you notice its absence more than its presence. You spend the rest of the night sitting on the windowsill, the right angle of your legs reflected in the dark windowpane, drinking bitter gin and tonics and smoking with abandon, stuffing the butts into an empty can.

You wait until six in the morning, when the subway is open, and you walk to the station and take the subway and the bus to the street where you grew up. You hope that there's no one there who will recognize you, and you get off at the familiar stop— forgotten just enough to feel uncanny, as if its coincidence with your memory is a miracle, like Jesus seen in a sandwich. Your hopes are dashed the moment your foot touches the asphalt—a high female voice calls your name.

"Look at you," babbles a middle-aged woman, red coat, face painted with too much enthusiasm and not enough artifice. "You haven't changed a bit." She clearly expects you to say the same, and the lie would be easier if you could remember who she was.

"Natasha," she reminds you. "Romanova. We used to be in the same class through the sixth grade. I live one building from yours." She walks along with you, oblivious to your cringing away from her. "What are you doing here? Visiting someone?"

"Vorobyev family," you say before you can come up with a decent lie.

"Oh," she says. "I think they moved—well, the kids had all moved out."

"I heard Vasya's dead," you say.

She looks at you strangely. "Well, stop the presses."

"I just heard."

She looks at you, concerned. "What do you mean? I thought it was you who had found him."

You shake your head at her nonsense, and yet the quiet nightmare dread grabs you by the heart and squeezes harder, as you mumble excuses and break away from the talkative friend you don't remember having and you race ahead to the poplar row that seems fatter and taller and more decayed than before. The asphalted path leads between the trees to the yard surrounded by six identical brick buildings, each nine stories tall with two separate entrances. Your house is the last one on the right, and you race past your entrance. You find their apartment not by the number but by muscle memory—your legs remember how to run to the fourth floor, taking two steps at a time, how to swing abruptly left and skid to a stop in front of a brown door upholstered with quilted peeling pleather diamonds, how to press the doorbell that is lower than you expected—you can reach it without getting on your tiptoes.

It rings deep within the cavern of the apartment, and you know by the apartment's position (you've never been inside) that it has three rooms—barely enough for nine people—not counting a kitchen, and that the balcony looks out into the yard, above the puddle.

A boy with soft brown eyes opens the door, still the same, still in his coat, water dripping down his sallow face, his hair slicked into a toothed fringe over his forehead. You are mostly surprised by the differential in your heights now—something that was just beginning to manifest around the time you left home, when you were sixteen, and would rather have moved in with your first boyfriend (so much older than you) than stayed here, near those stairs that trained you in your lizard defense. Now you're towering over him with your adult, aging self, crow's feet and sagging jeans and all, and he is still twelve (thirteen?), and he looks up at you nearsightedly, his pale face looming up at you as if from under water. You accept it with the fatalism of someone who has bad dreams too often to even attempt to wake up.

"It's you," he says without much surprise. "Come on in."

You do, as you would in a dream. The apartment has suffered some damage—there are water stains on the ceiling and water seeps through the whitewash, dripping down the browned tracks over bubbling, peeling wallpaper. The windows also weep, and the hardwood floors buckle and swell, then squish underfoot like mushrooms.

The boy stands next to you by the window, looking through the water-streaked glass at the sunshine and fluffy clouds outside, at the butter-yellow poplar leaves tossed across the yard by the rising wind. "What is it that you want?"

You are well familiar with logic of dreams and fairy tales, of the importance of choosing your words wisely, of the fragility of the moment—waste your breath on a wrong question and you will never know anything. "How did you die?" you finally ask. "I cannot remember." Other questions will just have to go unanswered.

He points to the puddle outside, wordlessly, and you remember the hands pressing his face into the water, and you standing there, watching, helpless, until there are no more bubbles. Afterward, you tell the grownups that you found him like that, and you don't know who did it.

"Why didn't you tell them?"

You're an adult now, and the words come out awkwardly. "I was afraid of what they would do to me if I told. I'm sorry."

He's too much of a gentleman to rub it in your face that he had been defending you then, that he could've walked past and stayed alive.

"It wouldn't have mattered," he says instead. Dead in Chechnya. Dead in Osetia. Disappeared one night without a trace. Dead in a kayaking accident. You remember all his deaths and they crowd around the two of you, suffocating and clammy.

And then it's just you again, standing on the sidewalk outside, watching the eddies of yellow leaves spiraling around the ankles of your brown boots with worn, lopsided heels. And then it is just you, walking to the bus stop, promising to yourself to never return here, to never look back at the fourth story window and all the dead faces of the boy pressed against the weeping glass.

MOTHER URBAN'S BOOKE OF DAYES

Jay Lake

In a basement that smelled of mold and old cleansers, Danny Knifepoint Wielder prayed down the rain. The house wasn't any older than the Portland neighborhood around it. Most driveways were populated with minivans, children's bicycles, heaps of bark dust and gravel accumulated for yard projects postponed through the dark months of winter. None of Danny's neighbors knew the role he played in their lives. They would have been horrified if they had.

Not making it to church on time carried scarcely a ripple of consequence compared to what would happen if Danny didn't pray the world forward. Lawn sprinklers chittering, children screeching at their play—these were the liturgical music of his rite.

"Heed me, Sky."

Danny circled the altar in his basement.

"Hear my pleas, freely given from a free soul."

Green shag carpeting was no decent replacement for the unbending grass of the plains on which the Corn Kings had once vomited out their lives to ensure the harvest.

"I have bowed to the four winds and the eight points of the rose."

Wood grain paneling echoed memories of the sanctifying rituals that had first blessed this workroom.

"Heed me now, that your blessing may fall upon the fields

and farms." With a burst of innate honesty he added: "...and gardens and patios and window boxes of this land."

"Daniel Pierpont Wilder!" his mother yelled down the stairs. "Are you talking to a girl down there?"

"Mooooom," Danny wailed. "I'm buuuusy!"

"Well, come be busy at the table. I'm not keeping your lunch warm so you can play World of Warships."

"War*craft*, Mom," he muttered under his breath. But he put away his knife, then raced up the steps two at a time.

Behind him, on the altar, his wilting holly rustled as if a breeze tossed the crown of an ancient oak tree deep within an untouched forest. Oil smoldered and rippled within the beaten brass bowl. Rain, wherever it had gotten to, did not fall.

That night Danny climbed up the Japanese maple in the side yard and scooted onto the roof. He'd been doing that since he was a little kid. Mom said he was still a kid, and always would be, but at twenty-two Danny had long been big enough to have to mind the branches carefully. If he waited until after Mom went to her room to watch TiVoed soap operas through the bottom of a bottle of Bombay Sapphire, she didn't seem to notice. The roofing composite was gritty and oddly slick, still warm with the trapped heat of the day, and smelled faintly of tar and mold.

The gutters, as always, were a mess. Something was nesting in the chimney again. The streetlight he'd shot out with his BB gun remained dark, meaning that the rooftop stayed in much deeper shadow than otherwise.

Sister Moon rising in the east was neither new, nor old, but halfway in between. Untrustworthy, that was, Danny knew. If Sister Moon couldn't make up her mind, how was Sky to know which way to pass, let alone the world as a whole to understand how to turn? This was the most dangerous time in the circle of days.

He had his emergency kit with him. Danny spent a lot of time on his emergency kit, making and remaking lists.

Nalgene bottle of boiled tap water
The Old Farmer's Almanac
Mother Urban's Booke of Dayes
~~Silver~~ stainless steel knife
Paper clips
Sisal twine
Spare retainer
Bic lighter (currently a lime green one)
Beeswax candles (black and white)

That last was what he spent most of his allowance on. Beeswax candles, and sometimes the right herbs or incense. That and new copies of the *Almanac* every year. The *Booke of Dayes* he'd found at a church rummage sale—it was one of those big square paperback books, like his *The Complete Idiot's Guide to Magic*, with a cover that pretended to look like some old timey tome or grimoire. The entire kit fit into a Transformers knapsack so dorky looking he wasn't in any danger of losing it on the bus or having it taken from him, except maybe by some really methed-out homeless guy or something.

Danny had figured out a long time ago that he'd get further in life if he didn't spend time worrying about being embarrassed about stuff.

This night he lay back on the roof, one foot braced on the plumbing vent stack in case he fell asleep and rolled off again. The black eye he'd gotten that time had taken some real explaining.

It hadn't rained in Portland for sixty days now, which was very weird for the Pacific Northwest, and even the news was talking about the weather a lot more. Danny knew it was his fault, that he'd messed up the Divination of Irrigon specified in the *Booke of Dayes* to shelter the summer growing season from Father Sun's baleful eye. That had been back in June, and he'd gotten widdershins and deosil mixed up, then snapped the Rod of Seasons by stepping on it, which was really just a dowel from Lowe's painted with the Testor's model paints he'd found at a rummage sale.

You could never tell which compromises the gods would understand about, for the sake of a good effort, and which ones brought down their wrath. Kind of like back in school, with his counselors and his tutors, before he'd quit because it was stupid and hard and too easy all at the same time.

Anyway, he'd gone the wrong way around the altar, then broken the Rod, and the rain had dried up to where Mom's tomatoes were coming in nicely but everything else in the yard was in trouble.

Since then, Danny had been studying the almanac and the *Booke of Dayes,* trying to find a way to repair his error. He was considering the Pennyroyal Rite, but hadn't yet figured out where to find the herb. The guy at the Lowe's garden center claimed he'd never heard of it.

He'd finally realized that having offended Sky, he would have to ask Sky how best to apologize. And so the rooftop at night. Sky during the day was single-minded, the bright servant of Father Sun. Sky in darkness served as a couch for Sister Moon, but also the tiny voices of the Ten Thousand Stars sang in their sparkling choir. Sometimes a star broke loose and wrote its name across heaven in a long, swift stroke that Danny had tried again and again to master in his own shaky penmanship.

Tonight, as every night for the past week, he hoped for the stars to tell him how to make things right.

A siren wailed nearby. *Fire engine,* Danny thought, and wondered if the flames had been sanctified, or were a vengeance.

More likely someone had simply dropped a pan of bacon, but you could never tell what was of mystic import. Mother Urban was very clear on that, in her *Booke of Dayes*. Even the way the last few squares of toilet paper were stuck to the roll could tell you much about the hours to come. Or at least the state of your tummy.

He listened to the trains rumble on the Union Pacific mainline a few blocks away. Something peeped as it flew overhead in the darkness. The air smelled dry, and almost tired, with a mix of lawn and car and cooking odors. The night was peaceful. If not for the scratchiness of the roof under his back, he might have relaxed.

A star hissed across the sky, drawing its name in a pulsing white line. Danny sat up suddenly, startled and thrilled, but his foot slipped off the vent pipe, so that he slid down the roof and right over the edge, catching his right wrist painfully on the gutter before crashing into the rhododendron.

He sat up gasping in pain, left hand clutching the wound.

"That was not so well done," said a girl.

Danny's breath stopped, leaving his mouth to gape and pop. He tried to talk, but only managed to squeak out an "I—."

Then his Transformers knapsack dropped off the roof and landed on his head. The girl—for surely she was a girl—leaned over and grabbed it before Danny could sort out what had just happened.

"Nice pack," she said dryly. He was mortified. Then she opened it and began pulling his emergency kit out, piece by piece.

Miserable, Danny sat in the rhododendron where he had fallen and looked at his tormentor. She was skinny and small, maybe five feet tall. Hard to tell in the dark, but she looked Asian. Korean? Though sometimes Mexicans looked Asian to him, which Danny knew was stupid. She wore scuff-kneed jeans and a knit top with ragged sleeves.

He had no idea if she was twelve or twenty-two. Of course, Danny mostly wasn't sure about himself. He knew what his ID card said, the stupid fake driver's license they gave to people who couldn't drive so those people who were completely unde-serving of pity or scorn could get a bus pass or cash an SSI check. His ID card said *he* was twenty-two, but lots of times Danny felt twelve.

Almost never in a good way.

"This your stuff?" She turned the retainer over in her fingers as if she'd never seen one.

"Nah." Danny stared at the broken branches sticking out from under his thighs. "They belonged to some other guy I met up on the roof."

She laughed, her voice soft as Sister Moon's light. "You should tell that other guy he'd get farther with a silver athame than with a stainless steel butter knife."

"It's the edge that counts," Danny said through his pout.

The girl bent close. He could almost hear the smile in her voice, though he wouldn't meet her eye. "You'd be surprised how many people don't know that," she said, so near to him that her breath was warm on his face. "A sharpened paper clip and grass cuttings will serve for most rituals, if the will is strong enough and the need is great."

Now he looked up. She *was* smiling at him, and not in the let's-smack-the-stupid-kid-around way he'd grown used to over the years. Then she reached into her sleeve and pulled out a short, slightly curved blade that gleamed dully under the gaze of Sister Moon. "Try this one," she said, handing it to him, "and look on page 238 of the *Booke of Dayes*."

Danny stared at the knife a moment, then glanced up again. She was gone. Not mysteriously, magically vanished—he could hear the girl singing in the street as she picked up a bicycle and pedaled away with the faint clatter of chain and spokes. But still gone.

The knife, though.... Touching it, he drew blood from his fingertip. *Wow,* he thought, then raced inside to read page 238 by flashlight under the covers.

Reversal of Indifference

Betimes the Practitioner hath wrought some error of ritual, perhaps through inattention, or even a fault of the Web of the world in disturbance about zir sacred space, and so the Practitioner hath lost the full faith and credit of the kindlier spirits as well as the older, quieter Forces in the World.

Zie may in such moments of tribulation turn to the Reversal of Indifference, which shalleth remake the rent asundered in the fabric of the Practitioner's practice, and so invite the beneficent forces once more within zir circle of influence. Thus order may be restored to the business of the World, and the Practitioner rest easier in zir just reward.

Zie should gather three mice, material with which to bind their Worldly selves, and all the tools of the Third Supplicative Form before attempting the exercise in the workbook for this section.

Danny didn't have the workbook—he'd only found *Mother Urban's Booke of Dayes* by accident in the first place. He'd checked, though; the workbook wasn't available on Amazon or anywhere. So he'd done without. Most of the time he'd been able to sort out the needed ritual, trusting in his own good faith to bridge any gaps. This was not so different. He understood the Third Supplicative Form well enough. Still, he'd never noticed the Reversal of Indifference before.

It was such a big book, with so many pages.

Mice, and binding, though. There were mice in the basement, in the heater room and sometimes in the laundry closet. He went to set out peanut butter in the bottom of a tall trash bucket, built a sort of ramp up to the lip of the bucket out of a stack of dog-eared Piers Anthony novels, then considered how to bind the sacrificial animals once they were his.

The answer, as it so often seemed to be, was duct tape. Danny was excited enough to want to try the Reversal of Indifference that same night. He had his new athame, and the star had certainly sent him a detailed message in the mouth of that strange Asian girl. A practitioner could only be so lucky, and he aimed to use his luck for all it was worth.

Danny had harvested four mice within the hour, so he left one inside the trash bucket for a spare in case he made a mistake. One by one, he took the other three and wrapped them in duct tape. They were trembling, terrified little silver mummies, only their shifting black eyes and quivering noses protruding.

"Sorry, little guys," he whispered, feeling a bit sick. But magic was serious business, the lifeblood of the world, and he *had* failed to call down the rain.

No one would miss a few mice.

Then Danny made himself sicker wondering if one of the mice was a mother, and would little mouse babies starve in some nest behind the walls.

He shifted his thoughts away with the heft of the athame in his hand. The knife was tiny, but nothing felt like silver. The Third Supplicative Form—as best as Danny understood without the workbook available—was a long chant followed by the delivery of the sacrifice. Usually he sacrificed a candy bar, or maybe a dollar bill. In tonight's case, the sacrifice was obvious.

This time Danny remembered to take the battery out of the smoke alarm. Then he lit his candles, purified his hands in the bowl of Costco olive oil, and began the chant. The mice shivered on the altar, one little mummy actually managing to roll over and almost fall off onto the green shag. He nudged it back into place and tried to concentrate on magical thoughts instead of what he was about to do.

When the moment came, the mice bled more than he thought they could. One managed to bite his finger before dying. Still, he laid them in the hibachi, squirted Ronson lighter fluid on them, and flicked them with the Bic. The duct tape burned with a weird, sticky kind of smell, while the mice were like tiny roasts.

Guilt-ridden, Danny grabbed the trash bucket to go free the last mouse into the yard, but halfway up the basement stairs he had to throw up. By the time he got outside, the last mouse had drowned in the pool of vomit, floating inert with the potato chunks and parsley flecks from dinner.

He washed his mouth and hands for a long time, but still went to bed feeling grubby and ill.

Morning brought rain.

Danny lay in his little bed—he had to curl up to even lie in the blue race car, but Mom kept insisting how much he'd loved the thing when he was seven—and listened to water patter on the roof. Portland rain, like taking a shower with the tap on low. It didn't rain so much in August, but it was never this dry either.

He'd done it.

Sky had heard him, and returned blessings to the land.

Danny didn't know if it was the girl's athame, or the mice, or just more careful attention to the *Booke of Dayes*. He wanted to bounce out of bed and write Mother Urban another letter to her post office box in New Jersey, but he wanted more to run outside and play in the rain.

Then he thought some more about the mice, and looked at the red spot on his finger where one of them had bitten him, and wept a while into his pillow.

It rained for days, as if this were February and the Pacific storms were pouring over the Coastal Mountains one after another. Danny performed the Daily Observances and leafed through the *Booke of Dayes* in his quiet moments to see what else he'd missed besides the Reversal of Indifference. Mostly he let Sky take care of the land and wondered when he'd see Father Sun again.

Mom seemed distracted, too. Danny knew she loved him, but she was so busy with her work and taking care of the house, she didn't always remember to hug him like their therapist said to, or feed him like their doctor said to.

That was okay. He could hug himself when he needed, and there was always something to eat in the kitchen.

So mostly Danny mooned around the house, watched the rain fall, and wished he could take the bus to Lowe's to look for new magical herbs in the garden center. He wasn't allowed TV, and there wasn't much else to do except read Mother Urban or one of his fantasy novels.

Except as the days went by, the rain did not let up. First Mom became angry about her tomatoes. Then he saw a dead puppy bumping down the gutter out front, drowned and washing away in a Viking funeral without the burning boat. The news kept talking about the water, and how the East Side Sewer Project wasn't ready for the overflow, and whether the Willamette River would reach flood stage, and which parks had been closed because the creeks were too swollen to be safe.

Danny watched outside to see if the Asian girl came by again on her bike. He wanted to ask her what to do now, what to do next. There was no point in climbing the roof to ask Sky — the only answer he would get there was a faceful of water and Oregon's endless, featureless dirty cotton flannel rainclouds.

If anything, Sky was even less informative in such a rain than when Father Sun shouted the heat of his love for the world.

So Danny sat by the dining room window looking out on the street and leafed through *Mother Urban's Booke of Dayes* for anything he could find about rain, about water, about asking the sun to return once more.

He read all about the *Spelle for a Seizure of the Bladder*, but realized after a while that wasn't the right kind of water. *Maidens' Tears & the Love of Zir Hearte* had seemed promising, but even from the first words, Danny knew better. Still, he'd studied the lists of rose hips and the blood of doves and binding cords braided from zir hair. Closer, in a way, was the *Drain Cantrip*, though that seemed more straightforward, being a spell of baking soda and vinegar and gravity.

Danny tried to imagine how much baking soda and vinegar it would take to open up the world to swallow all this rain.

The news talked about people packing sandbags along the waterfront downtown. All the floodgates were open in the dam at Oregon City. A girl drowned in the Clackamas River at Gladstone, trying to feed bedraggled ducks. A grain barge slipped its tow and hit a pillar of the Interstate Bridge, shutting down the Washington-bound traffic for days.

All his fault. All this water.

He prayed. He stood before his altar and begged. He even tried the roof one night, but only managed to sprain his ankle slipping — again — on the way down. And he read the *Booke of Dayes*. Studying it so closely, Danny realized that Mother Urban must have been a very strange author, because often he could not find the same spell twice, yet would locate spells he'd never seen before in all his flipping through the book.

Meanwhile, his own mother complained about the weather, set buckets in the living room and bathroom under the leaks, and sent Danny to the basement or his bedroom more often than not. Something had happened to her job—too wet to work outdoors at the Parks Department—and she stopped using the TiVo, just watching TV through the filter of gin all day and all night. He wasn't sure she slept anymore.

Danny was miserable. This was all his fault. He never should have listened to the Asian girl, never should have killed those mice, not even for a ritual. If only he could bring them back to life, or set that stupid, fateful star back into the sky.

He couldn't undo what was done, but maybe he could do something else. That was when he had his big idea. It couldn't rain *everywhere*, right? If he worked the ritual again, somewhere *else*, the rain would leave Oregon behind to move on. Things would be better again, for Mom, for his neighbors, for the people fighting the flood. For everyone!

Excited but reluctant, Danny caught five more mice. He put them in a Little Oscar cooler with some newspaper, along with cheese and bread to eat, and pounded holes in the lid with a hammer and a screwdriver so they could breathe. He gathered the rest of his materials—the silver athame, duct tape, the brass bowl, the bottle of Costco olive oil, the Ronson lighter fluid—and stuffed all of it in his dorky Transformers knapsack.

All he needed was money for a bus ticket to Seattle. They wouldn't even notice the extra rain there. Mom never really slept, but she was full of gin all the time now, and spent a lot of her day breathing through her mouth and staring at nothing. Danny waited for her noises to get small and regular, then crept into her room.

"Mom," he said quietly.

She lay in her four-poster bed, the quilted coverlet spotted with gin and ketchup. Her housedress hung open, so Danny could see her boobs flopping, even the pink pointy nipples, which made him feel weird in a sick-but-warm way. Her head didn't turn at the sound of his voice.

"Momma, I'm hungry." That wasn't a lie, though mostly he'd been eating the strange old canned food at the back of the pantry for days.

She snorted, then slumped.

"Momma, I'm taking some money from your purse to go buy food." There was the lie, the one he'd get whipped for, and have to pray forgiveness at the altar later on. *Mother Urban's Booke of Dayes* was very clear on the penalties for a Practitioner's lying to the Spirit Worlde.

But without the money, he could not move the rain. Besides, surely he'd buy food on the way to Seattle. So it wasn't *really* a lie.

He reached into her purse, pushed aside the pill bottles and lipsticks and doctor's shots to find her little ladybug money purse. Too scared to count it out, Danny took the whole thing and fled without kissing his mother goodbye or tucking her boobs back in her dress or even locking the front door.

Danny's pass got him on the number 33 bus downtown. Even in the floods, Tri-Met kept running. The bus's enormous wheels seemed to be able to splash through deep puddles where cars were stuck. The rain had soaked him on the way to the bus stop, and at the bus shelter, and even now its clear fingers were clawing at the window to drag him out. Danny clutched his Little Oscar cooler and his Transformers knapsack and stared out, daring the rain to do its worst.

If he made the rain mad enough, and Sky who was both mother and father of the rain, maybe it would follow him to Seattle even without the Reversal of Indifference.

* * *

The Greyhound station downtown had a sign on the door that said "NO SERVICE TODAY DUE TO INCLEMENT WEATHER." Danny wasn't sure exactly what "inclement" meant, but he understood the sign.

He sat out front and stared at the train station down the street, crying. It was in the rain, no one would notice him in tears. The Little Oscar emitted scratching noises as the mice did whatever it was mice did in the dark. He knew he should draw out *Mother Urban's Booke of Dayes* and try to work out what to do next.

Then the girl on the bike showed up again. She came splashing through puddles with a big smile on her face, as though this flood were a sprinkler on a summer lawn. The bike skidded sideways in front of him, splashing Danny with grimy water. She leapt off like she was performing some great trick, and let her bicycle fall over into the flooded gutter.

"So how's your edge, Danny?" she asked brightly.

He couldn't remember that he'd ever told the girl his name. It wasn't like he knew hers. "Th-this is all your fault!" he blurted.

Somewhere out in the rain a ship's horn bellowed, long and slow. The bus station was near the waterfront, Danny knew.

The girl's grin expanded. "Somebody's going to hit the Broadway Bridge."

"You s-set me up."

"No, Danny." She leaned close, her hands on her knees. "I just told you how to do what you wanted. *You* set you up. A Practitioner must know zir Practice."

He was startled out of his growing pout. "You know everything about the *Booke of Dayes*, don't you? Tell me, how do I fix this?"

Another laugh. "Think," she said. "Smart kid like you doesn't have to go to Seattle to stop the rain."

"I been doing nothing *but* think for days!" The tears started up. "People been drowning, that p-puppy, Mom's got no w-work, the tomatoes are rotting...." Danny screwed his eyes shut to shut the tears off, just like Mom always made him do.

When the girl's voice spoke hot-breathed in his ear, he squeaked like a duct-taped mouse. "What's the name of the ritual, Practitioner?"

"*R-reversal of Indifference.*"

"What does that *mean?*"

He wasn't stupid! Danny concentrated, like they'd always tried to make him do in school. Reversal...reversal.... The meaning hit him suddenly. "You can turn something around from either direction," he said with a gasp.

She clapped her hands with glee. "And so...?"

"And so...." Danny let his thoughts catch up with his words. He could see this thread, like a silver trail in the sky, tying a star back into place. "And so I can make Sky stop thinking about rain on Portland, make Sky take the rain back."

"Bravo!" Her eyes sparkled with pure delight.

"Wh-what's your n-name?" he asked, completely taken in by the girl's expression.

"Geneva," she said, serious but still amused. "Geneva Fairweather."

He squatted on the bench in front the Greyhound station and opened the Little Oscar. Five sets of beady eyes looked from a reek of piss and damp animal. Danny already had his duct tape out, but when he reached for the first mouse, he remembered that it was the edge that counted. Geneva Fairweather had said you could work most rituals with a sharpened paper clip and grass cuttings.

So maybe he didn't need to kill three mice. Or even tape them into tiny mummies to bind them. His fist would hold the mouse. The athame was sharp enough to prick three drops of blood from the mouse's back. The poor animal squirmed and squealed, but it was not dead. He folded the blood into a corner of paper torn from *Mother Urban's Booke of Dayes*, and followed the ritual from there.

Within moments, the rain slackened and Father Sun peeked down for the first time in three weeks. Danny turned to Geneva. "See? I could do it!"

A distant bicycle splashed through the puddles. She was gone.

Still, it didn't matter. Danny knew he'd done something important. Real important. And Geneva Fairweather would be back, he was sure of it.

As for Danny, if he could do this, how much more could he do?

What effect would a Reversal of Indifference have on his mom?

Clutching his bus pass, Danny walked back toward the Tri-Met stop. He would study *Mother Urban's Booke of Dayes* all the way home.

On the bus, he noticed for the first time the tiny illustration of a girl on a bicycle that appeared somewhere on every page of *Booke of Dayes*. Sometimes inside another illustration, sometimes tucked within the words, sometimes on the edge.

Had she been there before?

Did it matter?

The mice rustled in his jacket pocket. A pungent odor told Danny they were already making themselves at home there. That was fine with him. Smiling, he pricked his finger with the athame, right there on the bus, and watched the blood well like a fat-bellied ruby. Once he got home, some things would begin to change.

THE MAD EYES OF THE HERON KING
Richard Dansky

There was a lake or something like one near Leonard's office, and it was to that lake that Leonard occasionally took himself after work. He did so in order to relax, to avoid thinking about work, and to generally sidestep the possibility of doing anything he might later regret.

But mostly, he did it to watch the herons.

Leonard liked watching them, finding something soothing in their manner. He admired the way they moved, standing still for untold minutes before suddenly striking, or advancing robotically back and forth on some secret avian agenda that only they would ever know.

And thus it was that when his workday was done, Leonard would come to the lake and watch the herons and do nothing else because nothing else needed doing. At least, not until the day the Heron King spoke to him.

He had been watching this most impressive specimen of avian elegance for a while, through the course of several hour-long visits, during which he would simply sit down in the mud, pull his knees up to his chin, and observe with a faint but palpable air of envious longing. Once or twice he thought he had seen this particular heron, a magnificent specimen of the great blue variety, look back at him with head cocked and beak angled and eye agleam with something that stood in for curiosity. Leonard had dismissed all such thoughts out of hand, of course. Herons, even great blues, were not curious creatures. They were placid, and they were predatory, and they soared above the still waters while giving their great calls of *gronk, gronk, gronk* that would not have sounded amiss in the epoch of the dinosaurs.

On the fourth visit of that week, however, or perhaps it was the fifth, the great blue heron abruptly changed its course when Leonard settled in, squelchily, for his customary period of observation and contemplation. Hardly had Leonard seated himself in his accustomed place in the grass, which, in truth, had become matted and pressed down under the repeated and weighty attentions of Leonard's posterior, before the heron, with great lanky strides, crossed the water to stand directly before him.

Leonard looked at the heron, a faint *frisson* of fear wafting deliciously through him. He had felt fear before, had felt it all day, as a matter of fact. That had been a small man's fear, though, the fear of humiliation and of being yelled at, the fear of losing a job he hated but needed and the fear of being trapped in it forever. This was different; tantalizingly so. Even in the most civilized of deskbound men, the most thoroughly domesticated pusher of paper and pencils and long-tailed electronic mice, there remain the atavistic remnants of the hunter his forefather once was. It was this long-buried fragment that Leonard felt now, the fear of the lone man facing a wild creature whose habits and perils were unknown.

Carefully, Leonard counseled himself in the tactics he felt most conducive to an unscathed escape. He would make no sudden moves. He would not show fear. He would not make eye contact. He would—

"Have you come," the heron said, "to pay homage, to make obeisance, to show the proper respect that is my due?" And it cocked its head to the side and stared at him through eyes that, even in the lowering twilight, he could see were golden and flecked with deepest black.

"Err," Leonard heard himself saying, and then, "Umm." He opened his mouth, closed it, and shuddered once, violently.

"Bah," said the heron, and waggled its head in disapproval. "Stupid, speechless, dumb. Unworthy of our time, and thus guilty of a crime against our person." Without warning, the slender head came down and the stiletto beak stabbed forward, and Leonard found himself thinking most sincerely that he was about to die a most ridiculous and unbelievable death. Then, at the last second, the trajectory of the lunge changed, the beak lowered, and there was a sickening crunch as the heron instead impaled a moderate-sized frog of immodest ambition that had hopped up to a position near Leonard's feet. Then, the heron lifted its head until its beak pointed directly toward the zenith, shook itself in quick fashion, and wolfed the remnants of the unfortunate amphibian down. It made a lump in the heron's neck as it slid slowly down the bird's gullet, until it disappeared from view and the predator once again lowered its gaze to meet Leonard's.

"Next time, show respect, present yourself, be not a fool," it said. Without a further word, it turned on one foot and stalked back across the submerged mudflats with imperial disdain.

Watching the retrograde advance of his erstwhile conversation partner, Leonard did not think, "I could have died." Nor did he think, "I must be dreaming," or "That's impossible," or even "It talked."

Rather, he held one thought and one thought only to his feverish mind, and held it close with a secret glee: "It talked to *me*."

For several days, Leonard did not return to the lake. Every day, he would walk out the front door of the office building where he worked, stride down the sidewalk to where his car sat in the immaculately paved lot, and then hesitate and turn and get behind the wheel. He did not walk past, did not stride further toward the pond and the marvelous creature that dwelt within it. Instead, he heaved himself into his car and drove himself home, taking care to travel by a route that would not provide temptation.

It was, he admitted to himself, an act of fear. The memory of the Heron King speaking to him was one he treasured. He turned it over in his mind at night, searching it for meaning. He found himself pondering it during the day, when the numbers that lined up in serried ranks on the spreadsheets before him should have occupied his entire attention. But mostly he found himself terrified that it had all been a hallucination, a fever dream of wonder that a return visit to the lake would strip bare. He dreaded the possibility of returning to the lake, of seeing the majestic heron and hearing it intone nothing but that familiar *gronk*. In short, he did not wish to put his memory to the test, for fear that it be found wanting, illusory, and less than true.

But the lure of the lake was strong, and the thought of another conversation with the Heron King was strong as well, and not too many nights had passed before Leonard stopped at the place where his car was parked and then, after an endless, agonizing hesitation with his foot suspended in mid-step, kept moving.

The sun had commenced scraping the tops of the trees when he reached the lakeside, and the fat red light washed low over everything. Leonard's eyes strained against the unnerving light as he strove to pick out the wading birds from the red-reflected waters in hopes of spotting the Heron King. At first he could see nothing except a blinding glare off the still surface of the lake, but then gradually, by increments, his eyes adjusted. There was one shape standing motionless amongst cattails at the water's edge. There, further on, was a slight and slender bird, picking its way through the shallows. There, in the distance was a delicate and predatory creature standing on one leg, its beak stabbing down suddenly to pierce the waters.

And there, gliding slowly across the face of the waters, blue-grey wings turned black by the sun's red light, was the Heron King.

He circled the lake once, silently. Leonard crouched down, feeling as if he ought to make some gesture of recognition that he was in the presence of royalty and yet paralyzed between a bow and a kneel and a simple stance to show respect. The bird made no sound as it flew, nor did it speak, nor did it give any sign that it recognized Leonard and acknowledged his presence. Leonard watched it fly, and his heart sank, and he imagined he could already hear the sound of the edifice of his imagination crumbling. He had imagined it after all, had dreamed or wished the conversation, and the one special thing that had happened in his life had not, in fact, happened at all.

And then the heron turned, wheeling toward him in a great silent arc. He watched in wonder as it glided toward him, its legs skimming the surface of the water before finally settling to rest a scant five feet away.

"You have returned, rethought, reconsidered," it said to him without preamble. "We would know why."

Leonard licked his lips, which were dry and chapped despite the humid summer heat. He knew that these words would be perhaps the most important ones he would utter. He knew that, despite the fact that his heart was doing leaps of joy in his hollow cave of a chest, what he said now could not be light-hearted, or flippant, or ill-considered.

He was, after all, in the presence of royalty.

"Your majesty," he began, and flicked a glance at those impassive golden eyes before continuing. They remained golden and utterly impassive, and gave no clue as to what the Heron King might be thinking. "I wished to make an apology for my previous rudeness, and to see if it might please you to converse with me further." It was a tidy speech, and one that he had spent much time writing and re-writing in various templates and formats in those too-lucid moments when he thought that his encounter had not been a dream.

"Ah," said the Heron King. "We will think on your words, ponder, consider. You will return and know our decision." Two stilt-legged steps backward he took, and then leapt into the air with an ear-splitting call of *gronk* that left little uncertainty that the interview was indeed over, at least for the nonce.

Leonard watched him go, and his fingers scraped up a little mud from the lakeside. Without taking his eyes from the retreating silhouette of the magnificent bird in flight, he rolled it into a tiny ball, and then placed it in his pocket, a tangible memento of the moment that had just passed. No more would he doubt. No more would he question. He would remember, and in due time he would return, and in the meantime a tiny ball of clay and mud would serve to sustain him.

He lifted himself to his feet, and then walked away.

"You see them, do you not?" asked the Heron King, gesturing in the direction of the other wading birds stalking the shallows of the lake. One by one his beak pointed them out, near or far or hidden by reeds and cattails, and as he identified each, he bobbed his head and quirked his neck, as if to see if Leonard were paying attention.

He had been waiting for Leonard when Leonard returned, and had wasted no time in pleasantries or preambles before speaking.

Leonard, privately, was quite thrilled, and hung on the Heron King's every word.

"I do," he said. "Are they your subjects?"

The Heron King wheeled to face him, eyes blinking twice in incredulous confusion. "Subjects? Servitors, lessers, vassals? You are more of a fool than you look."

"But...but..." Leonard scrambled back a foot or two, muddying the palms of his hands. "But if you are the Heron King, and they're herons, you're their kind, right?"

A violent shake of the head was his first response, followed by an angry, bellowed gronk.

"You are hopeless, stupid, ignorant of our ways! How dare you insult my brothers by calling them lesser?" The heron raised itself up to its full height and spread its wings, the great arc of which cast a shadow over Leonard where he sat. "How can one such as I be less than a king?"

"But if you're the king—"

"Silence! We are all the Heron King! Each of us born ineffably noble, royal, of ancient and proper lineage!"

"Oh," Leonard said. His mouth hung open. "So you're all kings?"

"King," the Heron King corrected him. "Each of us is in fact and deed and word, in right and privilege and in honor, the Heron King."

"How can that be?"

The Heron King stamped one muddy foot onto the grass. "Where I stand, I am absolute ruler, king and unquestioned. Where he stands," and its head whipped around suddenly so that its beak could point out another, particularly impressive specimen of mature heron. This one stood, one leg in the air at the edge of a clump of rushes, and even from halfway across the lake Leonard could feel the jagged weight of its stare. "Where he stands, he is king and monarch, unquestioned sovereign. At any time any of us lay absolute right and proper claim to the ground beneath us." It turned back to look at Leonard, its head canted at a forty-five degree angle. "If the particulars of that land change, it is nothing to us. Our rule remains."

Solemnly, Leonard nodded. "But what happens if two of you are together? I mean, which one is king?"

"We are all king," the Heron King said, and his voice was soft and dangerous. "And we are all jealous, as is our right, our duty, our honor, of our role as king. You would do well to remember that."

"I will," said Leonard, thinking that under no circumstances would he ever try to bring two herons together. His mind briefly put forward some awkward possibilities dealing with mating, but he quickly tamped the thoughts down to focus on the here and now.

"I speak to you because you are nothing, worthless, baseborn. You are not a king. As such, you may be in our presence without fear or worry."

And with that, the Heron King turned and walked away, pausing only to give an admonition over his bony shoulder that Leonard should return another day.

Return Leonard did, again and again. He learned much of the ways of the Heron King, who seemed almost appreciative of the opportunity to unburden himself to another thinking being. Leonard even flattered himself to think that the Heron King liked him, enjoyed his company and his presence, and thus had told him more than was strictly necessary.

And so he had learned that no creatures of the lake dared strike at the Heron King, for fear of upsetting the divine, righteous, and proper order of things. Neither snake nor turtle nor great toothy fish would tempt fate or the heavens by daring to bite at a single heron's foot placed in muddy water. Alligators might, but alligators were uncouth beasts unworthy of discussion, and besides, their foul presence did not sully this lake.

At work, some noticed that Leonard was...different. He was no longer the last one out of the office every night, for one thing. Indeed, he was rarely seen in the office after sunset, and gossip ran wild that he had at last found a lover, or a hobby, or at least a favorite restaurant with early dinner specials.

They noticed, too, that his behavior had changed. His speech, for one thing, was now more formal, and he was fond of stating things in triplicate for effect. His posture had also changed, his usual shuffle giving way to a long-legged tiptoe that could only be described as stalking down the carpeted hallways and tiled floors of his place of employment. As for his eyes, few now cared to meet them, as they seemed too bright, too fierce, and altogether too unblinking to be quite comforting. Or perhaps it was the way he held his head now, always cocked at a slight angle when he thought no one was watching.

But since they had never said anything to Leonard before, they did not say anything to him now. Besides, it was not as if he were any less efficient, or useful, or productive. He was simply odd in a different way, and to most of them, that made as much difference in their daily lives as would the vast bulk of the planet Jupiter suddenly turning purple.

Leonard, for his part, did not particularly care what they thought of him at work. Instead, he did his work and daydreamed of the evenings when the secrets of the Heron King would be imparted to him. He thought of hours spent sitting on the cool grass, and imagined what it would be like to do as the Heron King did, to stalk across muddy bottoms in bare feet and feel no fear.

Once he even slipped his shoes off at work, but only for a moment, and without anyone noticing. Then he put them back on, and carried with himself a secret smile the rest of the day.

It was not that day, nor the day after, nor even the day after that, but some time as much as two weeks later when Leonard arrived at the lake to find that the Heron King was not waiting for him. This was in and of itself unusual, in that not since their second conversation had there been a time when Leonard had not reached their appointed rendezvous second. Anxious, he walked down to the water's edge. The sun, he noticed, was lower in the sky than it had been even one week before. Summer was going, and with it the long evenings of discussion that he treasured so dearly. Soon enough it would be fall, with its leaf smoke smell and early nightfall, and the migration of the herons southward.

Soon enough, he realized, it would be over. Perhaps the Heron King would return in the spring, perhaps not, but one way or another this magical summer of clandestine wisdom and blue-feathered magic was winding down.

There were, he noticed, no herons near him. A few unfamiliar shapes in silhouette were visible in the distance, but nowhere did he see the Heron King, nor any other shape that he recognized.

The thought chilled him. The Heron King was not here. Perhaps he had forgotten. Perhaps he had grown bored with Leonard and would not be returning. Perhaps there had been—and he shuddered at the very notion—an accident of some sort, and the Heron King was wounded or struck down, assassinated by a hunter or a passing car.

It was all terribly confusing, and so he sat himself down on the lakeshore to think. The water lapped against the mixed bank of sand and grass and mud, mere inches from his loafer-encased toes. The sound was soothing, wave upon tiny wave, and it gave him an idea.

The Heron King was not here, after all. Nor were any of the other herons nearby. Surely, Leonard told himself, this was a golden opportunity, a chance to walk as the Heron King did. It was his moment, his turn to feel the muddy bottom between his toes and understand all the things he had been told.

After all, the Heron King had left him here alone.

Quickly, he shucked off his shoes. His socks he slipped out of and rolled up neatly, each tucked into one loafer for later use. His pants, slacks he'd bought some six years prior and husbanded fiercely, he rolled up to nearly his bony knees. Barefoot, shivering with excitement and the first touch of cold water against the tips of his toes, he stood on the brink transformation. One last look around for the Heron King, whose regal figure he did not see, and Leonard set one tremulous foot in the water.

It was, as he'd previously discerned, cold. The mud of the bottom gave slightly under the pressure of his weight, but maintained a spongy strength that kept him from sinking. A tickle at his ankle told of a passing brush with a small fish. He looked down, and could see the wavering outline of his pale flesh, the edges blurred by mud and silt stirred up by his footfall.

Nothing else happened.

After a minute, he put his other foot in the water.

Again, nothing happened, and that was indescribable joy. Minnows darted through the water around him. Grass waved in the slow shallow current, beckoning him to step into deeper water. A dim shape in the near distance could only be a turtle, paddling in its best ungainly fashion. And there he was, in the middle of it. Observing it, feeling it, ever so much a part of it. At last he understood what the Heron King had told him, comprehended the sheer ineffable power of it all. As if of their own accord, his feet rose and fell, and he moved away from the shoreline. Mud between his toes, water licking at the sagging cuffs of his pant legs, a trail of silt billowing behind him, Leonard laughed. Truly, he understood now. He could share in what the Heron King had told him, could give back his comprehension as a gift equal to the knowledge he had been bequeathed. At long last, he could show his respect properly, his thanks definitively, his delight emphatically. He threw up his arms, in imitation of the raised wings of the one who had led him to this place, and let out a shout of pure joy. Echoes followed it, startled frogs splashing into the water and surprised birds leaping from the trees.

And behind him, a solitary, quiet susurrus, the pressure of air against the nape of his neck, the hint of a wave washing against his muddy calves.

"Your Majesty." Leonard knew what that portended, could barely wait to greet his blue-feathered magister. Trembling with excitement—how the Heron King would be pleased to see he understood—he turned and bowed, then lifted his eyes to meet the royal gaze.

For indeed, the Heron King was staring at him, intently and unblinkingly. Those golden eyes that had seemed so strange at their first meeting were stranger still, flecked with black and hazel and slivers of bloody red. Through them the Heron King regarded Leonard, his head canted at an angle both quizzical and alarming.

"Your Majesty?" Leonard asked, or at least intended to. For no sooner had he opened his mouth to speak than the Heron King stepped forward, and drove his great stiletto of a beak into the soft hollow of Leonard's throat.

Leonard's eyes widened in shock, and in horror and pain. The hands that had so recently been upthrust in imitation of wings clutched at his punctured flesh, blood leaking through the gaps between his fingers. "I don't...understand," he started, and then collapsed to his knees. He looked up in supplication, and in return the Heron King placed one clawed foot flush against the center of his chest.

"You do understand," the Heron King said, and pushed.

"Oh," said Leonard, and went over backward so that the waters might close over him.

"Impostors, traitors, fools," the Heron King said. "We do not suffer them gladly." His royal judgment thus rendered, he turned and walked away, having spotted a fish, perhaps, or a particularly succulent amphibian in the nearby shadows.

PAINT BOX, PUZZLE BOX

D. T. Friedman

An aspect of Death came to a great Artist, the most celebrated creator of beauty that had ever illuminated the face of humanity. It found him in his studio, blending a background on an immense canvas.

"It is time," said Death, and the Artist turned to face it.

"That can't be. I ain't old yet."

"It doesn't always work that way," said Death, "especially not with artists." It looked thoughtfully over the barely-begun mural. "It is a shame, though. I would have liked to see what this was to have been."

"It was gonna be my masterpiece," said the Artist. "A whole world, full of love and hate and kindness and evil...." He looked up at Death, piercing it with eyes that could capture the vitality of existence and spread it on canvas with a paintbrush. "Give me time to finish. When my work is done, I'll go with you without so much as a grumble."

"How much time?" Death looked around the Artist's studio, at the stacks and stacks of unfinished paintings, each promising a taste of the pure delight that could be found in all his work.

"One year." The Artist clutched his brush in his fist, willing Death with all his might to give in to his proposal. "Give me one year, and I'll create the greatest masterpiece that has ever been gifted to this world."

Death stood for a few moments, contemplating the canvas as

if it could already see the wondrous creation that the Artist promised.

"I have always loved your work," it said. "One year."

The old folks had their easels set up in front of the pond that first warm day when spring started to tip into summer. Willows and flowers were already starting to bloom on the canvases, and the jars of water were muddy with the sludgy drippings of dunked brushes.

Unbidden, Carlisa's eyes jumped around, counting them. There was little Rose, and Martha, and James, and Ella, and... flutter of panic surged through her before she saw the unoccupied easel. Leo wasn't missing; he was there across the duck pond, holding his paintbrush to the sky to compare the colors. Carlisa let out a breath. Everyone had survived the winter. She ran down the hill to greet them.

She had seen them for years on her way home from school, and then work. A little cluster of geezers, chattering in their sunhats in those precious days after the chill left the air and before the sun got too hot for them. Something about them called to Carlisa, and they were often the subjects of her sketches.

Leo had noticed her one day and waved her over to chat. The friendship they struck was easy and cheerful; the whole group had murmured appreciatively over her drawings and Ella had kissed her on the cheek with her purse-string lips. The next time she visited, Leo handed her a paintbrush and a small canvas that she set on her lap like her sketchbook. She never really liked working with paint, or even really with color, but Leo's gentle suggestions brought a new life into all of her work, not just the amateurish pictures that the squiggles of her brush left behind.

"Look deep," he'd say. "You gotta paint the whole depth of the object, not just the surface." He'd show her on his own painting, a woman in the distance walking a dog that looked for all the world like it was wagging its tail.

"Don't just see the colors," he'd say. "Feel them."

"Smell the colors," teased James from the other side of him. "Taste them, eat them for breakfast and sleep with them at night!"

"Oh, you leave them alone, silly," said Martha. "Don't listen to him, dear, he's colorblind."

That got a laugh from everyone; James' paintings showed he was anything but.

Leo held a dab of green on the end of his brush, stared at it hard. Carlisa focused her attention there, too.

"Feel where that color comes from," he said, his voice low. "See it for what it really is."

Carlisa could have sworn the color changed to blend in with the grass before he smudged it onto his canvas.

"Did you see it?" he asked.

Carlisa felt her head nodding, but she couldn't take her eyes off the delicate green of the grass in his painting. It was perfect in hue and value, but felt...wrong somehow. As if the color had been tipped askew.

"Ain't this a world," Leo said.

When Death entered the Artist's studio a year later, a mural of incredible beauty and complexity awaited it. Images danced across the canvas, illustrating every imaginable aspect of human existence from birth to death and before and beyond. The composition was breathtaking; each tiny detail begged closer scrutiny even as it drew the eye to the next, and the next, and the next.

Death stood for hours, studying the Artist's creation. Eventually it realized how much time had passed and pulled itself away. There would be eternity to appreciate the masterpiece, but Death had a job to do. It called to the Artist to appear, praising his work with a choked-up voice that it barely recognized as its own.

But there was no answer to its summons; the Artist was nowhere to be found.

Death found the Artist's wife in the cramped apartment below his studio, stirring a kettle of stew over an open fire. The stones of the hearth were blackened with soot, and the room was filled with the comfortable clutter of daily life.

"Where is your husband?" Death asked. "We had an appointment, and he has disappeared."

"Don't be ridiculous," said the Artist's wife. "He's upstairs, working on his masterpiece." She ladled a spoonful of stew into a wooden bowl and dunked a chunk of bread into it. Death followed her up the rickety ladder to the studio and stood behind her as she looked around.

"He must have stepped out for a bit," she said after a moment. She held out the bowl. "Would you like some stew?"

Something about the woman's manner made Death very suspicious. He reached for the bowl, but took her hand instead. The woman shuddered, but did not flinch away.

"He did not step out for a bit," said Death, "and this ruse does not fool me. You know exactly where your husband is."

"You're mistaken," she said, and disappeared down the ladder. Death watched her go, and didn't miss the quick glance she threw at the Artist's mural.

Carlisa watched Leo carefully, studying his technique and squinting to catch a glimpse of that moment when the color would shift out of phase at the tip of his brush. Leo's paintings flowed with life and energy, at the same time organic and carefully orchestrated.

He'd direct her occasionally as she painted, sometimes fitting his leathery fingers over hers to demonstrate a brush stroke. The others gave her pointers too, and her paintings developed as her eye matured to the new medium. She often stayed long after her friends had given up for the day, lost in the strokes and the dabs of paint on her cardboard palette.

Sometimes she'd round the duck pond to stand in Leo's spot, trying for hours to see the world as he did.

Death waited for days and days, but the Artist did not return. The Artist's wife and daughter took turns offering it food and drink, and chasing away the children who occasionally climbed the ladder to gawk at it and giggle.

Death passed the time as it waited for the Artist to return by studying the mural. As the weeks turned into months, it realized that as amazing as the mural was, there was not much to separate it from the Artist's other work. This could not be the masterpiece that he had promised. Death tried to feel anger at being cheated, but all it could really feel was loss.

"You have to eat something," said the Artist's wife. "At least drink some mead."

Death declined, and caught the longing glance toward the mural that she stole as she retreated.

Death returned to studying the mural with new eyes. It was energetic and complex, as if it held a life of its own just beyond the painted surface. Death closed its eyes and reached out its hand. It was not entirely surprised when it met no resistance.

Death's first step into the mural was tentative, though as only one part of Death itself, the aspect that entered was expendable. It was not fear that checked its progress, but awe.

The mural was but a portal, a doorway into a world beyond. And in it there was love and hate and kindness and evil, everything the Artist had promised. And there was beauty and grace and ugliness and art and waste....

But no Artist.

* * *

The days kept warming, and the humidity began to get the better of Rose. She only showed up in the early mornings now, the brims of her straw hats umbrella-like and floppy.

"How do you see past that, dear?" asked Martha.

"I love it when the weather gets hot enough to bring out the big hats," said Rose. "More surface area to play with."

And her summer hats were certainly a sight to see, painted with scenes of forests and deserts, with fake flowers and ivy bunching from the crown. James lifted the front of the brim to grin into her face.

"Oh, there you are," he said. Rose rolled her eyes and dabbed a yellow splotch of acrylic across his nose. "Watch it, lady," James said and laughed with everyone else as he wiped mustard streaks onto his handkerchief.

Leo stole Rose's hat and replaced it with his own beige cap. The straw brim drooped nearly to his neck when he pulled it over his head, and the silk flowers bobbed in the breeze as he nodded to the rest of them.

"I can see just fine," he said and made a big show of walking straight into his easel. Carlisa nearly fell over laughing.

The aspect of Death split itself into many parts, and together they scoured every corner of the world the mural revealed to them. The Artist was not hiding from them there, not even by darting into the areas that Death had searched and dismissed.

Death gathered all its parts into the original aspect and sat in a sculpture garden with a glass of lemonade. The Artist was not in the world of his birth, and he had not disappeared into this new world, no matter what his wife seemed to think.

It got up to walk around, passing welded amalgamations of steel scraps, stone drums, and a long bronze log with a half-hitch knotted into the middle. The world the Artist had created even had its own artists, and their work was as creative or cheap or obscure or thought-provoking as art could be in their own world.

It paused next to a sculpture of nested boxes and leaned over to see what was inside. Through the rainwater that had collected in the bottom of the center box, Death could see a tiny bronze fish that looked like it was swimming when the water rippled.

Death stood straight, feeling as if it had been struck in the back of the head. It looked at the museum that the sculpture garden surrounded and had to restrain itself from running across the lawn.

Just as it suspected, every painting in the gallery opened onto its own world. Death split itself into an uncountable number of parts and sent them to explore the worlds that lay beyond the portals in the Artist's mural.

A stranger wearing a blue business suit approached Carlisa as she held up her brush, trying hard to make the color turn like Leo had showed her that June morning. It was now the height of summer, and the heat of the day had chased her friends back indoors for a few hours. Carlisa's paintings and charcoals had improved drastically since that first spring. A small gallery in the city had slated her for a show later that year, and she was determined to bring the same life into her work as Leo seemed to breathe into his.

"I'm looking for a friend of mine," said the stranger. "An artist like you. I haven't seen him for years, but...." His eyes flicked over to the spot across the pond where Leo always stood, communing with his paintbrush, "I heard he spends some time here in the summer."

The stranger's eyes were warm and his face was open, but something made Carlisa want to look into him the way Leo had taught her to look into the depths of her subjects. Something froze and boiled inside the man who stood before her, and she withdrew her gaze as if she had been burned.

"I'm sorry," she said. "The only other artists I've seen stay around the flower gardens at the other end of the park."

The stranger regarded her for a long moment, and his eyes found Leo's spot across the pond again.

"My mistake," he said. "I'm sorry to disturb you." He turned to leave, and then he stopped, his gaze lingering over Carlisa's painting. "It's beautiful," he said. "I haven't seen that kind of vitality in a painting since...in a long time."

As the stranger strode off to wander around Leo's spot, Carlisa couldn't help but think of the time when Leo had twitched his paintbrush toward one of the daisies on Rose's hat. The paint on the end of the brush turned as yellow as the center of the flower, and Leo had dabbed it into one of his own daisies on his canvas. The color was perfect, but felt sideways.

The stranger ambled off, leaving Carlisa to stare across the pond. She didn't tell Leo about the stranger the next morning, but she watched for him all day.

Leo went to his spot often, twitching his paintbrush at the sky. Carlisa wondered why the colors over there were so much more fascinating than the ones on their side of the pond.

It was as Death had feared: each part of itself returned with the same report. In every world they found artists, and the works of art all contained worlds of their own. And worlds within worlds within worlds, without discernable end. The Artist was still nowhere to be found.

Even though it was worried about the complexity of the maze the Artist was hiding in, Death couldn't help but smile. It riffled through its memories of the search, wave after wave of appreciation and awe washing over it as it remembered the wonders it had encountered.

More shades returned to the sculpture garden as the years

wore on. Some of the more adventurous ones reported that they nearly lost themselves as they wandered deeper into the labyrinth. But there was no news until the last straggler made its way into the garden, pale as if it had split itself but glowing with excitement.

"I have found a sign of his passage," said the part as it merged with the rest. "I have sent a shade of myself to investigate."

The blue-suited stranger appeared many times that summer, thankfully after even the mornings became too hot for her friends to tolerate.

"He's an elderly man," the stranger explained. "A great artist. Dark of face, light of hair. He often wears a beige hat, and he has this habit of holding his paintbrush up in front of his eyes. You're sure you haven't seen him?"

"Why don't you believe me?" asked Carlisa. The stranger thanked her for her time and left to round the duck pond. She stared at his retreating back and tried to see into the core of him. Suddenly something in her gaze *shifted*, and she could see only a concentration of cold silence, floating over the ground. She gasped, and her gaze shifted back. The stranger had reached the far side of the pond, headed toward Leo's spot once again.

Carlisa looked away and knelt to focus on a puffball dandelion. When she concentrated hard, she managed to shift her gaze again. The fuzz stood out in her vision, and all she could see was the life aching to burst out from the seeds at its root. It felt dizzy, unbalanced. As if in a trance, she reached out her paintbrush and dabbed the grey-white onto its end. Her gaze shifted back once more and she stared at the unsteady, ashy color at the tip of her brush for long minutes. When she managed to tear herself away from her woozy sense of triumph, the stranger had disappeared once again.

What was it about that spot? Leo spent a lot of time there,

sure, but so much that the stranger was drawn there like a dog following a scent? She left her canvas and paints where they were and rounded the pond.

There was nothing special about Leo's spot. She stood where the grass had flattened under his sandals and tried to at least tease out a difference in the colors, or in the patterns of the clouds in the sky. Nothing suggested even to her that her mentor stood there day after day, twitching his paintbrush at the trees.

Until her view shifted.

A riot of colors assaulted her eyes, in streaks and dots and swirls. They swam around her in a whirling haze, forming and reforming into strange shapes and hues she had never seen before. It was as if she had fallen into the visions of a kaleidoscope psyche, immersed in a tank full of swarming, tropical fish. Something was wrong with its alignment. She couldn't think in a straight line or hold the ground beneath her feet.

No wonder the stranger knew Leo was here. This spot was a beacon of creativity, a celebratory proclamation of the existence of her mentor. Leo couldn't have known that it would attract such a frightening visitor. Her mind reeling, she carefully reached out her brush to touch a swirl of bright yellow and eggplant. The colors came away from the chaos around her and she smeared them across the sky.

The chilling stranger would not find Leo, she promised herself. She would hide every change he made to this spot, until the stranger dismissed it as abandoned and moved on. And she would try to heal the wrongness she felt, try to correct the dizzy distortion until it felt right.

If Leo noticed, he never said anything. The stranger didn't approach her again.

The shade returned to the sculpture garden, discouraged.

"It was a dead end," it sighed. "I thought I had tracked him to a world deep within the labyrinth, and indeed it seemed as if he meant to lead me there. But the signpost where the trail led fell into age as I watched. The Artist has left it behind and moved on to hide somewhere else."

The shade merged with the rest of itself, and Death sat dejectedly on the knotted bronze log to think.

Carlisa practiced all summer whenever the heat of the sun drove Leo indoors. She learned the patterns he had created, their rhythm and flow, and did her best to blend every change he made into something that seemed like it had always been there. She straightened skewed diagonals, trued uneasy swirls. And as she learned more and more, she came to realize that this was not just an artist's creation of beauty for the sake of beauty; bits of the beacon seemed to warp parts of time and space themselves. She learned to manipulate these aspects as well, weaving them through the creation that had become as much hers as Leo's.

And then she began to set a trap.

The days became cooler as summer faded late. Carlisa's elderly friends could stay longer and longer into the day. She invited them to display some of their own work in her upcoming gallery show, and they buzzed with excitement as they touched the colors of the turning leaves to their canvases.

Leo had begun staring off into space a lot, often pausing from his painting for long minutes. The others noticed, and Carlisa heard them whispering to each other sometimes. Leo was getting older, they said. But Carlisa saw where his gaze fixed, and felt a flush of shame whenever he looked over to his spot. How could she have presumed to correct her teacher's creation? But the blue-suited stranger had not found him, and she comforted herself with that thought.

"I had a wife," Leo said once, suddenly. Everyone looked over at him; he had never spoken of any family. "A wife and children and grandchildren. Beautiful." He sighed, shook his head. "Ain't this a world, though?"

No one said anything. James clasped his shoulder before turning back to his work, but only Carlisa noticed that Leo used a clean paintbrush to dab a tear into the sky of his own painting, favoring his garden with a soaking rain. She stopped erasing the changes he made to his beacon. It was his, after all.

If the Artist had bothered to create a false trail for it to follow, Death decided, there must be more than one. A spaghetti tangle, perhaps, the better to confuse and mislead. It journeyed through worlds at random, casting around for another trail. It left a shade of itself at the portals of each world to make sure it could find its way out again. It stumbled across many similar paths, but they all led to the same center locality. The starburst trail was the only sign of the Artist's passage.

It sent a part of itself down the trail again, unwilling to believe there was nothing special about that world at the center.

"Be sure," it told itself.

An elderly man sat on a park bench in Carlisa's painting, his face mostly obscured by the fuzzy grey hair of the woman who was leaning down to kiss him. A pigeon stood next to him on the bench, leaning over to peck at the sandwich that they were both ignoring. Behind them was the rest of the park, full of life but blurred into a barely perceptible background. The original charcoal sat next to Carlisa on the grass, one of her first and favorite sketches. It seemed flat and lifeless now, compared to its canvas copy. At Leo's instruction, she sat for hours with the lovers, thinking about them as if they were real people.

"Because they are real," Leo said. "They're as real as you and me. So you gotta find out who they are and how they live, and listen to them when they tell you."

So she sat and asked them every question she could think of, shifting in and out of that strange world that offered her dabs of color if she would only reach out her brush. And suddenly, she felt them. The man was about to reach up and encircle his lover's waist with his arm, gently pulling her down into his lap so their hearts could beat against each other. The woman ached for intimacy. And Carlisa was no longer a painter but a child wiping at a steamy window, each dab of paint rubbing a clear spot in the fog until the scene behind was revealed. But the window was tipped to the wrong angle; it was so hard to balance the strokes.

The dusk was gathering purple shadows when she tore herself away. She vaguely remembered her friends' departure as the light faded, the faraway clatter of paints disappearing into baskets and easels loaded onto drag-along frames. Only one easel still stood, canted on the uneven lawn, its canvas showing a man straining for an apple he just couldn't reach. She felt his desperate hunger as the tree teased him, raising and dropping its branches in the hot breeze.

A movement caught the corner of her eye and she shifted back into the real world. The blue-suited stranger had returned and was rounding the duck pond. Leo stood in his spot, his back to them both, oblivious to the approaching danger.

"No!" Carlisa shouted. She ran along her side of the pond, knowing she would not be able to reach him in time. Leo turned at the sound of her voice, just in time to see the branches of a weeping willow wrap around the stranger and stuff him through a gash that Carlisa had cut into the fabric of their world. It would dump the stranger far away in time and space, somewhere not even Carlisa would be able to find again. Her trap had worked.

Leo gave a wordless cry and ran with a speed that belied his age to the place where the stranger had disappeared. But the rift had healed itself after swallowing its prey, and Leo's gnarled hands met only the bare branches of the willow. Leo stopped pawing through the wooden curtain and dropped his head in defeat. Carlisa thought to call to him, but she could do nothing but stand frozen and watch her friend clutch the branches in his hands.

When at length he looked over to her, his eyes were old and empty of hope. Carlisa backed away and ran, leaving her paints spread on the lawn around the kissing lovers.

The message arrived at nightfall, passed in whispers from portal to portal between the Artist's renditions of Death in each world.

"Follow the trail, but beware the girl!" "Follow the trail, but beware the girl!" "Follow the trail, but beware the girl!"

The shade that Death had sent to investigate the starburst trail never returned.

It rained almost constantly the week leading up to Carlisa's show, so she only saw her friends when they stopped by the gallery to drop off their work. Carlisa fussed with matting and framing, but as much as she occupied herself, she couldn't help but notice that Leo never stopped by. Ella brought one of his paintings when she visited and watched solemnly as Carlisa arranged it next to one of her early charcoals. Leo faced out of the monochrome sketch, holding a paintbrush aloft as if he were about to twitch a bit of color from the eyes of whoever stood before it.

"It's just a bad time for him," Ella said. "He'll be back soon, don't you worry."

But behind her comforting smile, Carlisa could see the set resignation of a woman who had watched her friends disappear over the years, one by one. Carlisa hugged her, swallowing back the lump in her throat.

"He'll be fine," she said, and tried to believe it. The stranger was gone, wasn't he? Leo was safe.

* * *

Death stood at a distance from the beacon, regarding it with curiosity and a little fear. This was where a part of itself had disappeared.

"I am," the beacon announced with its color riot. "I exist!"

To Death, it said, "I am here."

Death began to search.

Opening night at the gallery was everything a young artist could have hoped for. People actually came, lured by the promise of beauty and cheap wine in clear plastic cups. Carlisa laughed as her friends posed pseudo-nonchalantly by their charcoal portraits, waiting to be recognized so they could launch into descriptions of their own paintings, displayed alongside. She munched a handful of Triscuits. She watched visitors point at her work and lean in for a closer look. James passed by, Rose's enormous flowered hat bumping his shoulder as she held tightly to his arm.

"Success," James said with a wink, and the two of them threaded their way back into the small crowd. Carlisa smiled, but looked toward the door for what must have been the hundredth time that night. Why didn't Leo come?

And then, as surely as she had felt the lovers' longing to hold each other, she knew he was already there. Excitement thrilled through her, and she cast her gaze around the room to find him. She saw Martha, jabbering animatedly to a woman with punk-dyed blue hair, and James and Rose chatting with another couple at the refreshment table. James was flirting shamelessly with the young woman; she played along, lapping up the attention. Ella stood alone in front of Leo's painting, a hand on her cheek and smiling wistfully.

Carlisa didn't find Leo until she shifted her gaze to the color world. There he stood in the corner, watching his friends enjoy themselves as if they were young again. If he noticed Carlisa watching him, he gave no sign. After a while, he nodded in contentment and slipped out of the gallery. No one looked up as he passed.

Carlisa threaded her way to the door to chase after him, but he had disappeared into the night. She tried to pierce the darkness with her eyes, but not even her shifted vision revealed which way he had gone. She had just given up when she felt a shiver of emptiness pass behind her.

The white-suited stranger didn't look up as he walked by, intent on the quarry that had left only minutes ago. Without a backward glance, Carlisa followed him into the night.

The stranger's steps were long and quick with purpose. Carlisa nearly ran full-out to catch up with him, her cork wedges thudding at the sidewalk like a panicked heartbeat. He didn't look up until she planted herself firmly in his path.

"I know who you are," said Carlisa, surprised that her voice didn't shake when she addressed him. The stranger stopped, focused in on her with such intensity that she fought the urge to back away.

"Ah," said the stranger. "The troublesome young lady. I've heard about you. Step aside, please."

The stranger tried to walk around her, but she did not give way.

"You can't have him."

He stopped again, tilted his head.

"I must have him," he said. "The universe is out of balance, can't you feel it?" Carlisa nodded despite herself. The tilt, the uneasy wrongness of the color world. "The Artist feels it too. He has been calling to me for a long time."

"I won't let you take him," said Carlisa. "I've set more traps, all around."

"Will you walk with me, young lady? I have a long-overdue appointment, and I'd prefer not to be late."

"You won't get anywhere near him."

"That may be," the stranger allowed, and started again on his way. Carlisa tried to block his path again, but it was clear that the stranger was done playing on her terms. Eventually she fell into step beside him, her mind whirling through arguments and plans. They walked through the streets in silence.

Leo stood among the streaks and whirls of his beacon, oblivious to their approach. He twitched his paintbrush impatiently at the colors around him, and they flowed and combined and rarified at his direction. Carlisa ran over to him, leaving the stranger behind on the path, and stood between them. The stranger approached, unhurried.

"Don't worry," she told Leo. "He can't get you."

Leo's hand clasped her shoulder.

"I've painted them over," he said. "The traps were brave and clever. I don't remember teaching you how to make things like that."

Carlisa turned to stare at him, a tickle of desperation rising in her stomach.

"Why...?" she managed.

"When I reached the end of my life—a long time ago, child—I created a labyrinth where I could escape Death. I planned to disappear into it, just long enough so Death would stumble around lost, looking for me in there. Then I'd come back and spend as much time as I had left loving my family and creating a body of work that'd be worthy to be called my masterpiece."

"So what happened?"

Leo shrugged. "I got trapped. Death got pulled in, just like I planned, but I never accounted for how fast the maze would grow. Every turn I took trying to find the way back to my family, I just got myself deeper in, and the worlds just multiplied around me."

"By then," said the stranger, standing beside them, "so much time had passed that your family had passed into my realm."

Leo nodded sadly. "I left signposts as far out as I could safely travel in every direction and still find my way back here before the labyrinth multiplied. I shoulda known how fast it would grow. I shoulda known. Damn fool." Carlisa grasped his arm protectively, lest the stranger tried to take him away while she stood there.

The stranger held out his hand.

"Well?" he asked.

Leo looked to Carlisa, who held onto him as if she were drowning.

"You can let go, Carlisa."

"But...."

Leo smiled sadly, shook his head. Looking into the core of him, Carlisa suddenly saw how very, very old he was. His gnarled hands, his comfortable wrinkles, the coffee-dark softness of his skin and eyes...they all seemed tired, now that she really looked. Leo was weary, and he wanted his wanderings to end.

Carlisa swallowed hard, trying to think of something to say that would make him stay. Plea after plea swam through her mind, but she couldn't make herself speak. Leo wasn't asking her permission; he only wanted her acceptance. And he would leave without either.

Hating herself and determined not to cry, she slowly released Leo's arm. Leo kissed her forehead, then her cheek, then her hand, and then turned to join the stranger.

"Wait!" Carlisa managed before they left her. Leo turned back. "What about your masterpiece?"

"I'd already made it," Leo said. "I just didn't know it at the time."

"Can I see it?"

Leo smiled. "Yes, child. I think you can."

He motioned all around with an open hand, and Carlisa

looked with the eyes that Leo had shown her how to use. And beyond the park she saw another world, and beyond that another, and another, and another. They bloomed before her, one from the other, each filled with love and hate and kindness and evil. As she watched, they shifted from their distortion and settled back into their proper alignment. They split off and nested into each other, universes and universes full of life.

When she came back into herself, Leo and the stranger had disappeared. The tears she had been holding back were spent on her cheeks, and she clutched Leo's paintbrush in her hands. Her chest was heavy and her throat felt choked closed, as if she would never speak again. She turned away from the beacon, now a monument, and slowly left the park.

She touched Leo's paintbrush to her cheek and swept it deliberately across the sky. A warm rain fell over the city as she made her way back to the gallery.

Death and the Artist walked side by side through the park as old friends who had not seen each other for too long.

"I saw myself everywhere in your work," said Death. "I would have thought you'd avoid me as much as possible."

"You can't have beauty without balance," said the Artist. "It just don't work that way. Especially not with artists."

"These worlds that you've created," said Death. "They are all so beautiful." It picked a sprig of gladiola, held it up to the light of a streetlamp. "This in itself is a masterpiece," he said. The Artist laughed. "What?"

"This world," said the Artist, a gleam of almost paternal pride in his eyes, "it ain't even a one of mine."

"Whose is it?"

"No idea. Ain't it a world, though?"

"Sure is."

Together, they disappeared into the darkness.

A LOSS FOR WORDS

J.C. Hay

Callie's skin tingled in anticipation as she slipped one hand beneath the pillows to brush across the pen. Her fingers found the wooden body of her Montblanc where she'd left it, caressed the cool surface a moment before they closed around it. The entire time her eyes stayed focused on her newest client, who sat on the edge of the bed and searched through his hastily discarded pants.

Robert kept glancing over his shoulder at her, his face a picture of nervous innocence. Then again, she had positioned herself for best effect—a practiced ease as she lay on her side; her curly black hair spilled across the pile of pillows, her dusky Mediterranean complexion lightly shone with sweat from their exertion, all contrasted against the white sheets. Part of her wished that a mirror faced the bed, but no such luck. Still, judging by Robert's attention, she was certain that she had placed herself properly.

He looked at her again, and she could see the tremble of desire that ran the length of his spine. She smiled, pleased at the effect. Then he pulled out his wallet.

Callie sighed quietly. "No, no. What are you doing?"

"Michael told me I'd have to be ready to pay." He gaped at the billfold in his hand and let his pants drop back to the floor.

"But he didn't mention money, did he." It was a statement.

Robert shook his head. "I don't understand."

"I want you to write on me." He blinked, and she could read the confusion in his face. Callie pulled out the Montblanc and presented it to him. "With a pen. I don't want your money, Robert. Money doesn't mean anything to you. I want something that does. I want your words."

He made a sound somewhere between a cough and a chuckle. "That's it?"

"You make it sound so cheap. It isn't. After all, they're part of who you are."

He looked suitably chastened. "It just seems like a small price to pay, that's all."

Callie kicked the rest of the sheets off of her body in a billow of white cotton and lay naked before him. When she was sure his eyes were on her, she laid the pen between her breasts. "We'll see."

Robert uncapped the pen and studied the hard edge of the nib a moment before he lowered it to her wrist. Callie caught herself holding her breath in anticipation and forced herself to exhale. She knew it was hesitation and uncertainty on his part, but the tease was going to kill her.

The pen dipped to her skin twice, three times, before he drew a line. She forced herself to smile even though he pressed too hard and the tip scratched her skin to raise a spider-fine welt beneath the ink. She wondered how long it had been since he had used a fountain pen. If he had used one at all—they were passé anymore, an affectation. It took three words before his pressure evened out, and they came with the fits and starts that made Callie wonder if her sister had misjudged his talent. Then they began.

Like a rainstorm his words fell from the pen, faster until it was a torrent along her skin. He filled her arm, then carved his words across the slightly sharp curve of her collarbone. He crossed her chest, wrote concentric circles of words that chased around each breast; he surrounded her coffee-colored areola with a spider's web of letters.

His words caressed the slight round of her belly, cased and kissed each thigh, and covered her feet before he was able to let the pen rest. Callie rolled onto her stomach, presenting him with the blank page of her back, and again he was driven to fill every space. When the story had finished, the only places left unmarked by his pen were her face and the palms of her hands. Even the spaces behind her ears had not escaped his desire to cover her and divest himself of the story.

Callie rolled onto her side so she could watch him. Robert still panted and sweat plastered the dark brown curls of hair to his forehead. The pen lay discarded on the sheets, a drop of ink still hanging from the tip. He smiled at her, out of breath, and rubbed his wrist. She knew it had to hurt—most of them were out of practice at writing longhand, and Robert had written at a madman's pace once he started. They were good words, though, in spite of his speed. She could taste the power in them without having to read them individually.

Robert let his hands drop to his knees and gave her a weak smile. "Was it good for you?"

Callie pulled him down on top of her and showed her appreciation before he could open his mouth again. She made a particular point of keeping him distracted as the words slowly soaked into her skin and vanished.

He called her again the next week. Callie knew it was him from the first ring, long before she had brushed Harmonia out of the way and picked up the phone. "Hello, Robert."

"I...hi. I need to see you." He sounded off guard, and she smiled. "How did you know it was me?"

She lied with a playful smile. "Caller ID, Robert. It's not like it's some terrible mystery."

He was silent on the other end of the line as he considered that. She smiled when he gave up and rushed ahead. "Can I see you? Please?"

"Are you able to pay me?"

There was no hesitation on the other end of the line. "Of course."

"Get a room with a view of the river. That would be perfect." Harmonia leapt back onto the table and pushed herself insistently into Callie's hand. She scratched the back of the cat's skull absently, and Harmonia responded with a throaty purr. Writers and cats had so much in common—petulant, demanding, sensuous and affectionate, but only on their own terms. "I'll meet you on the Ward Street Bridge at six."

"I...okay."

She hung up the phone before he could say anything else. Always leave them wanting more, as her sister Thalia always said. And she knew he wanted. After all, that was the point. She walked into the bedroom and tried to decide what she would wear.

When she stepped onto the bridge, he was already waiting for her. She smiled as he rushed up to meet her. "My, my. Aren't we eager?" The tone in her voice was playful enough to make it feel less like mocking, but she made certain that it established who controlled their relationship, regardless of the direction of payment.

It worked. He pulled up short, a flicker of embarrassment on his face. "Would you like to go for some dinner?"

Callie nodded her approval. "Thank you but no. I'll dine later. A walk along the river would be lovely, though." She caught his glance toward the hotel that loomed over the water, knew he really wanted only to be back in the room. She had no plans to be that accommodating so early in the evening. She led the way from the bridge to the stairwell down to the water. The city planners had placed a gently curving concrete path along the edge of the river, and she wandered along it from one sodium light to the next while he followed behind.

When he didn't offer to walk beside her, she stopped and waited for him, hand extended. He hurried to catch up and clasped her hand in his. "Are you always this familiar with your...clientele?" She could hear the note of annoyance and confusion in his voice and chose to ignore it.

"I am what I am paid to be, but I like for there to be a connection. It makes things easier for me. Besides, can a girl help it if she wants a little romance in her life?"

"No, I suppose not." He chuckled and smiled. Good. She didn't want him too uncomfortable; that might block the precious flow of words. "I just thought, with all your other clients..."

She quirked an eyebrow. "One at a time, Robert. That's the way I prefer it. I like to be able to give you my full attention." She let a little hurt creep into her voice, as though his suggestion offended her, and he quickly glanced away. Her sisters might keep a cadre of courtiers around them, but she thought that sort of competition diluted rather than improved the pool. "You haven't said how your writing is going."

The distraction worked. He smiled again, and seemed to bubble with boyish eagerness. "It's so much better, thank you. The manuscript looks exceptional—I sent it off to Andrea, my agent, yesterday. I can't wait to hear her thoughts on it."

"So you think it will sell?" It was a trick question; she already knew the answer.

He hesitated a moment, and then fixed her with an earnest stare. "It's the best thing I've ever written. I couldn't have done it without you."

"Perhaps. Or perhaps it was always inside you, and I just helped you find it." She chuckled, one hand curled in front of her mouth to hide her teeth. "Besides, you paid me well."

He smiled. "I still wouldn't have found it without you. If it sells, you'll be in the acknowledgements."

"That's unnecessary, Robert. I get all the thanks I need from you already."

"I brought a quill pen," he offered suddenly. "It's in the hotel room. I—I thought it might make it more special."

She felt her cheeks blush as a little shiver of desire rippled along her spine. Damn, she thought, she hated when her lust grabbed hold of her. It clouded her judgment and made her want to mistake need for genuine emotion. Callie lifted his hand to her mouth and dragged her teeth across the base of his thumb with a mischievous grin. "Let's not keep it waiting then, shall we?"

His hand was more aggressive this time. The timidity of his first visit had been replaced by an almost desperate desire to get the words out of his head and onto her skin. He leaned over her as he worked, ink bottle tightly grasped in his non-writing hand. When he had filled her front, he didn't wait for her to offer more—instead he flipped her roughly, needing more space to empty himself. The nib in the quill was sharper than her Montblanc, and his frenzy made it catch and tear at her skin, cutting the ink into her flesh. She didn't care—found herself gasping and urged him on with soft sighs, moans, and finally, cries of ecstasy.

When he finished, he collapsed on top of her. Callie shifted until she could wrap her arms around him and quietly stroked his hair. Part of her brain still basked in the warmth of his words, a low fire that glowed with each letter that she absorbed into her flesh. She couldn't help but smile at the barely restrained force of his narrative—raw, it was true, but somehow more delicious for its earnestness. Like a home-cooked meal, there was a sense of comfort carried in the very nature of Robert's prose, and it left her feeling blissful and sated. She let her eyes drift closed.

When she opened them again, the sounds outside the hotel had changed from the commerce of the early evening to the club crowds of late night. Even the cars sounded different— boisterous music that thumped and resonated, growling engines and shattering mufflers rather than the safe, quiet murmur of commuters. She blinked twice before she remembered where she was. She sat up with the sheet clutched to her chest and pushed her hair out of her face with her free hand.

Robert sat at the small desk in the room, still naked, and typed away in the glow of a laptop monitor. She slipped out of the bed and brought the sheet with her.

Callie stepped out onto the balcony and watched the river below. The sodium lights cut cylinders out of the darkness, their edges blurry with mist coming off the water. In the streets on the other side of the river, revelers drifted from one club to the next, laughing and clinging to each other for support. Callie glanced over her shoulder at Robert.

If he had noticed she was out of the bed, he had yet to acknowledge it. A light sweat graced his hairline as his fingers attacked the keyboard. She had seen it before; so many authors tried to recapture the stories they had offered as her payment. A part of her regretted that Robert was no different from all the others. He'd get close, she knew, though he'd never recreate the story perfectly—it was hers now. As he rewrote it, he would introduce changes, things he wished he had thought of before, and other elements that would fundamentally alter the story from the one he had given her.

She stepped into the room and dropped the sheet, let the moonlight kiss her skin. He still didn't look up. "Robert, I want you to take me to a club. I want to dance."

His eyes never left the monitor. "Does it have to be now? I want to get this down before I forget it."

She took a deep breath and tried not to feel hurt that her

nudity didn't sway him. "I'd like it to be tonight, with you." She walked up behind him and brushed her breasts against his back. Her fingers trailed out along his arms. "Do you think I could convince you?"

He chuckled a bit too roughly and said, "Get some clothes on, then, and we'll go. Let me know when you're almost ready, and then I'll get dressed. I just want to get a few more lines down—it's really flowing well."

Of course it flowed well, she thought. What did he think he paid for, mere sex? That was just the means to an end, the familiarity that allowed her to inspire more easily. She gave an exaggerated sigh and walked into the bathroom. "Very well, but don't expect it to take me too long. I hate to be put off, even for someone like you." She turned the shower to just short of scalding and stepped in.

"Callie, I've got the best news! I had to tell you as soon as I heard." The excitement in Robert's voice was infectious, and she sat down on the arm of her couch to listen. As soon as she was seated, Harmonia was up in her lap, insistent. Her other cat, Discordia, dragged itself along her calf to demand equal time.

She adjusted the phone so she could clutch it with her shoulder while she lavished attention on the two cats. "Okay, I'm sitting down. Tell me."

"Andrea just called. Simon and Schuster wants a three-book deal."

She squealed. It was hard not to—he was so proud, almost out of breath with his own enthusiasm. "That's wonderful! I'm so happy for you!"

"I owe it all to you. I can't thank you enough for what you've given me."

She felt herself blush and furrowed her brow at her own foolishness. "It was there inside you all the time. You just needed some help finding it, that's all." It wasn't entirely true, but it was better to feed him a palatable lie than to tell the outright truth—that if she hadn't unlocked it, if he hadn't come to her ready to pay, it likely would have stayed locked up inside him forever. Better to let him have his moment of glory.

"I want to see you again. I need to see you."

Harmonia pressed up into her hand, and Callie smiled. "You're not sure where those other two books might come from, eh?"

She heard his embarrassed chuckle carry over the line. "Not a clue. But I've got a good idea where to find them."

"Can you put us up in the same hotel?"

"I already have reservations. A suite, so hopefully my typing won't disturb you."

"Last time, I disturbed your typing, not the other way around."

"You won't hear me complain, either. See you this evening."

Callie started to respond when she realized he'd already hung up the phone.

The tone had changed; she could feel it. Robert seemed distant, like he held something back. When his words spilled onto her skin, they were released begrudgingly, as though he refused to pay her for the inspiration. No, it was more than that. It was like he punished her for being essential. Because he couldn't do it without her.

His pen was still rough, but now it smacked of carelessness rather than passion. Callie couldn't help but feel like he paid her out of necessity, rather than any desire on his part. By the time he finished, he had to write larger and larger letters to completely fill her skin. She pulled him down to lie beside her and tangled her fingers in his hair while she absorbed his words. They sated her, no less potent than his other stories, but they lacked the wild fire that had suffused his earlier efforts.

After a too-short time, he untangled himself from her embrace and went into the other room. The blue-white light of the laptop monitor flickered on and cast strange shadows beyond the door. Callie watched them from the comfort of the bed and listened as the sound of fingers on the keyboard grew steadier. Even if his payment hadn't been perfect, she wasn't going to hold out on him. The next time would be better, she was certain.

She suddenly missed her cats. Even their insistent cuddling would be better than cooling sheets in an otherwise empty bed. Callie gave up trying to sleep and rolled out of bed, the comforter wrapped around her as a makeshift robe. Whim and mischief made her open the duffle bag he had brought, though it hadn't prepared her for what she found.

A box from the copy center on the corner held a ream of paper, as well as the empty box that his pen had come in. Below that sat his toiletries, a hairbrush, and a change of clothes. All the things she had expected. She flipped through the first few pages of paper and found his manuscript lying beneath. No doubt he needed to do a round of final revisions for the publisher. She carried the paper back to the bed and curled up. It wouldn't be as personal, but she could still enjoy his writing on its own merits.

The first few pages confused her—she thought it was a joke, so she skipped to the middle of the stack. The same characters in the same clichéd situations waited for her. She gathered up the manuscript and walked into the next room, her concern and anger outweighing the cool air.

She set the manuscript on the coffee table, then went to the bar and fixed herself a Scotch before she sat down. Robert regarded her as she folded herself onto the couch, his skin washed out by the monitor glare. His voice carried the short clipped tones of annoyance. "What's that?"

"I was about to ask you the same question."

"What do you mean?"

"Is this the novel you just sold?" She tapped the manuscript with her toe for emphasis.

"Did you take that out of my bag?"

"That's not an answer."

He scooted the chair around the end of the desk. "So what if it is?"

"Because it's crap, and you know it." Anger crept into her voice, despite her best efforts.

"That 'crap,' as you put it, got me my three-book deal."

"You used my gift to churn out the same clichéd shit that's been done a thousand times before. And better, I might add."

"Andrea says it'll be a best-seller."

"As though that helps somehow."

"If that's what the people want, who are we to give them something different?"

"Artists!" She shouted the word, her frustration filling her to the breaking point. "You have so much potential, could write something truly fantastic."

"And I could languish away in obscurity and starve, too. No thanks. I'd rather be popular and rich."

Her blood went cold. "Then you'll do it without my help."

"What do you care? You get paid either way."

She recoiled as though he had slapped her. "Is that all this is for you? A commodities exchange?"

"The question you need to be asking is, 'why did I think it was something more?' You had something I needed — inspiration. I had something you wanted. We traded. Welcome to the basics of supply and demand."

Callie dashed back into the bedroom and dressed quickly. She grabbed her shoes off the floor and hurried toward the door. When she turned to take her last look, he was already bowed over the keyboard again.

* * *

All the furniture had been moved into the hall; nothing remained on the wood floor of her living room. The only items to ruin the emptiness were a deep silver bowl, a dagger, and a multitude of candles. Callie finished lighting the last one and put it in the proper place. When she was satisfied that everything was arranged properly, she slipped out of her robe and crossed into the center of the room. Beyond the candles, Discordia and Harmonia mewed softly, but they would not break the circle.

Callie knelt down, took the bowl into her lap and finally allowed the tears and grief she had held off to wash over her. How many times now? How many had she thought loved her for her, only to discover they were using her for what she could give them? Why had she let herself believe he could be different? She pulled her hair back and leaned her face over the bowl as thick ink-rimed droplets gathered on her cheeks and splashed into the basin. Sobs rippled through her as the pain and humiliation welled up again. Damn her for being foolish, true. But damn him twice over for treating her like a resource to be used. Soon, a small layer of grey liquid had built up in the bottom of the bowl. She reached for the knife.

It had been several years since she'd had to use the blade, but on principle she kept it polished and sharp. The skin of her wrist leapt apart before it. Thick black ink welled from the wound and flowed over her fingers to fill the bowl. There was an emptiness as the words left her, but she relied on the warmth of her anger to battle away the chill.

When the ink started to slow, Callie split her other wrist. The second arm seemed to empty faster, and then it, too, slowed and stopped. She pinched the wounds closed until her skin knitted, and then picked up the bowl. When she swirled the black liquid inside, she could see individual letters that scrabbled at the polished sides of the bowl before being pulled back into the soup once again. She waited until the ebony liquid had stilled and her face reflected back up out of the bowl at her.

Her voice was quiet, but it seemed to thrum against the walls of the room, suffused with ancient energy. "Robert Angelo Vojna, you gave me these words of your own free will. I held them for you in trust, but now I accept them in the spirit they were given. Mine now, and yours no more."

She lifted the bowl to her lips and drank.

She was walking through a little locally-owned bookstore when she saw Robert's book on the shelf. The twist in her chest was sudden, unexpected, and Callie steadied herself against the end-cap as inconspicuously as possible. She chided herself for still feeling the pangs at his name—it had been too long, and that was a wound that should have scarred over by now. Her new protégé, Linda, was shaping up so nicely. He shouldn't be able to hurt her anymore.

She picked the book up with a bitter chuckle. Who was she kidding—they all hurt. A long list, which only got longer each year. They had shared a part of themselves with her, but she had given something too, and it ripped at her with phantom pain when she saw them again. She turned the cover over, found Robert's familiar eyes staring up at her out of an unfamiliar face. He appeared drawn, his eyes deep-set and haunted, his once rounded cheeks hollow and pale. She remembered seeing something in the industry rags that his next book was behind schedule. Not a surprise—it was tricky to write when you couldn't find the words. Her lips lifted in a melancholy smile as she brushed her fingers over the thick paper of the dust jacket before she put the book down and walked slowly from the store.

He found her a few weeks later.

His knock on the door caused her to jump, and Harmonia leaped off her lap in protest. She tried not to be impressed that he had actually found her, but failed. None of the others had managed it—she made an effort to keep her home hidden from her beneficiaries. It made things easier should the relationship not work out.

Her plan had been to peek at him, just see him through the spyhole and return to her cats, but when she saw what remained of him in the hall she opened the door for him.

Robert stumbled into the entry and fell to his knees, then smiled up at her. Triumph gleamed in his too-bright eyes. "Knew it." His voice was a dry rattle that made her wonder guiltily if she should offer him some water. She could see he was a wreck—he was easily fifty pounds lighter, his skin papery and thin. In contrast, his feet seemed swollen to bursting, and his shoes cut so deeply into the flesh at his ankles that she could see stains where he had bled into his socks. His hollow cheeks had been covered over by an unkempt mat of beard, and his eyes had yellowed and begun to bulge from their sockets.

She felt a moment of pain in her chest for the wreck she had made of him, and then she noticed the knife in his hand. Callie took a step back out of the entryway and positioned herself closer to the phone in case he turned violent.

Robert pressed his hand to the wall and lurched to his feet to follow after her, but didn't make any threatening gestures. Instead he made his way into her living room and collapsed again. Harmonia and Discordia, offended at the invasion of their domicile, retreated down the hall to the bedroom while Callie, curious as well as nervous, closed the apartment door and took a few steps closer.

His back arched, and dirt-caked fingernails ripped at his stained shirt until he managed to get it removed. His eyes rolled and sought her out, and she found herself pinned by his gaze. "You thought you took them, but you couldn't. I know how to get them back."

She smiled. "And this was your plan? To be such a wreck that I might be moved with pity? That won't happen. I learned my craft at Megaera's own knee—your appeal is lost on me."

He coughed, a dry, wretched sound that she realized may have been laughter instead. "Hardly. No pity from you. I can do it without you—I just need to keep my focus up. Wanted you to see I could do it without your help. That you didn't win."

He jammed the blade into his arm and began to carve. Thick blood pooled in the wake of his cuts and dripped onto her carpet. In a matter of moments he had extended the words up the length of his arm. Callie watched, torn between ripping the knife away and applauding his courage.

She took a step forward and he pointed the blade at her, his eyes afire with madness. "No! This one is mine. You had too many of my words; these are for me." He paused and gasped for breath. "I want you to see it and know you can never consume it." With that he brought the blade back to the canvas of his skin and opened more words into his flesh.

It took almost an hour for him to finish and die, and Callie watched the entire time. Eventually her legs grew tired of standing, and she moved to the sofa, still well out of his reach. She sat there long after he was done, reading the words he had carved. Her sister Mel would have been impressed at the depth of sorrow he had managed to convey so succinctly.

She read them again and debated coming up with some way to transfer them, or to at least recopy them by hand, but that would involve moving the body, and that would lead to more questions than there would be already. She'd have to move, too, not that it was much of an inconvenience. There were always other apartments.

In the end, she opted to give him his small triumph. She'd treasure the story, even if it didn't nourish her. Despite all her efforts to undo him, he had managed one last, fatal bit of brilliance.

She read the tale one final time and stood with a sigh.

Harmonia and Discordia padded to the end of the hall, and she smiled wistfully back at them. "No, I'm not going to get all maudlin again. Go on, I'm coming." She stepped around the body and walked to the bedroom. After all, she was meeting Linda tonight—she needed to look her best.

SCRAWL

Tom Piccirilli

As usual, I didn't know where I was or why I was there.

It had something to do with a couple of my ex-pat New Yorker buddies inviting me out to San Francisco around the same time a big erotica reading was happening at the Puss and Whips sex shop. I'd been dabbling with erotica tales for the past couple of years and they were starting to catch some attention.

Some of the editors who'd picked up my work were throwing something called "The Hussy Hootenanny" at the store. I still had trouble with some terminology others had embraced, probably because I still remembered when calling a woman a bitch was a bad thing that could get you iced by the sisterhood of Gloria Steinham.

My buddies dragged me around the district, hitting bars and hot spot tourist attractions. I took a trolley for the first time in my life. I enjoyed it but felt strange admitting it out loud. They showed me some of the streets where McQueen had torn it up in *Bullitt*. We looked at the bridge. It was a nice bridge. They told me it was the number one place in the world to off yourself. I didn't think it was quite that nice a bridge.

I mentioned the hootenanny and showed them the flyer. It mentioned latex, rubber, adults in diapers, Mistress Vixen, twinks, ponygirls, bears, nipple clamps, and a codicil that clothing was optional. They made some nasty jokes but didn't seem interested in attending. Like me, they had already started their shrieking slide into middle age.

My buddies had lured me across the country with promises of excitement and trolley adventure. Now it was eight p.m. and they had to go home to their wives before they got the shit beat out of them. They gave me directions and wished me well. I sensed our youth was long behind us.

The P&W sex shop was close enough for me to walk. The front window featured a big hootenanny sign and stacks of books written by the participants. Several anthologies I was featured in were on display. There were also mannequins dressed in leather regalia and bad wigs. The mannequins looked a little embarrassed. So was I.

I stepped in.

There were guys in diapers. I'd never seen guys in diapers except my great-grandfather, and he didn't carry a giant rattle and a milk bottle around. I met Mistress Vixen. She yelled at me and called me slave and told me to kneel and lick her shoes. I smiled pleasantly. It was the only comeback I had. She gave me a disgusted sneer and stormed off. The forty-year-old babies cooed and cried mama. I smiled less pleasantly at them and thought, *Jesus Christ, what the fuck am I doing here?*

One side of the store had rows of chairs set up. A topless woman with a pierced septum was reading to a packed audience. I had trouble hearing the words. She had very nice breasts with figures and symbols and Chinese characters tattooed on them. They were not conducive to my concentration on her fiction.

The reading went on for more than an hour. One of the diaper guys read some dirty haiku. Mistress Vixen and two of her buff, well-oiled slaves did a little skit. She read a poem and every time she got to the word "dick" she'd reach out and smack one of the slaves in the nuts. When she got to the word "cock" she'd smack the other one. She used the words to the point of serious repetition, I thought. My critique was not asked for. The slaves tried to look modestly unhappy.

After a pony girl clip-clopped to the podium in her hoof-boots, wagging her horsey-tail backside around, and read a piece I couldn't understand because she never took the bit out of her mouth, a speaker asked, "Is there anyone else?"

I almost raised my hand. It would've made a bad impression. Instead I lifted my chin, which wasn't all that much better. The speaker pointed to me. I introduced myself and there was a constrained round of applause. I grabbed one of the anthologies and turned to my piece.

It was a funny tale. Most erotica isn't. It was also a true story. Most erotica isn't that either. I was alone up there without benefit of a slave or milk bottle or nipple clamps or any other visual aid. I felt a little lonely.

Afterward, I sat with Evie, a small press editor who'd bought a few of my tales over the past couple of years, and an accomplished author in her own right. I'd never met her or even seen a photo of her before, and I was surprised by how attractive she was. Girl next door prettiness with a core of phosphorus, glossy black hair that fell into glistening eyes. Her stare burned intensely and started heating up my guts.

She was the original dark lady with smoky, assertive attitude and a casual smile with a lot of sweet mileage behind it. She looked at my pudgy belly and my bifocals and the disappointment and pity showed in her lovely features. I made commonplace comments. I asked common questions. I flirted with a common agenda. I was a commoner.

Still, she seemed to think me kind of cute. In that stupid, ugly fat dog sort of way.

After the hootenanny, everybody went to a bar next door.

The diaper guys put on three-piece suits and knotted their power ties. Mistress Vixen stowed her crop and wore a summer dress like my mother used to wear. It put bad images in my head and I tried not to make sour faces.

Evie and I sat together again. We shared more drinks. They say liquor brings out the real you. I was still the same. I was always the same. I was as real as anybody could ever get. I exerted a great deal of mental and physical energy trying not to be me, but I always failed.

We discussed our lives. The events of mine seemed dull, colorless, and downright dreary compared to hers, and she was just giving me the highlights. She had five book contracts waiting to be fulfilled, including a sex textbook on 1001 ways to please your lover in bed. I could think of only about thirty-seven, and that included serving hot cocoa with marshmallows.

She lived with two guys who took her in turns or sometimes together. She had to call one of them Sir. The other had jealousy issues except when they were double-teaming her. Just like her writing, she had a very visual style that plucked at my nerves. The kink in me kicked the fire in my chest up a notch. The prude in me kicked it back down. Evie asked if I wanted to go home with her.

"What about your, ah, roommates?" I asked.

She said they weren't due back for several hours and even then it wouldn't be a problem. Not for them. Not for her. I thought it would be for me. She didn't say where they were. She didn't speak their names. She seemed to be selling the jealous guy's heartache a tad short. Mine too, I thought.

I didn't want to cross swords with Sir while plying her thighs but I had nothing else to do in Frisco.

We took a cab. I saw the bridge again. I tried to send out vibes saying that maybe we should make out a little first, right there in the back of the taxi, which I thought was pretty hot anyway. She sent out vibes that said she didn't give a shit about getting any of the adorable soft stuff from me.

Her apartment was huge, or at least it felt that way. I sensed her roommates in every shadow and her many other lovers beyond them. According to her stories, essays, and the bios at the back of her books, she had participated in threesomes, lesbian affairs, S&M club centerpieces, and orgies that numbered to the mid double-digits. Strangers had flogged her in front of crowds. She'd been with mighty men carved from stone who had made her scream.

I was a tubby nerd already going grey. I'd had crow's feet around my eyes since I was sixteen. I had a head full of bad wiring. I watched too many movies. I had battled God and lost. I still had father issues. I couldn't wield a hammer properly. I drunk dialed old girlfriends. I was a vanilla fudge pudge. I suspected that I was not going to impress her with what limited lovemaking skills I'd managed to accrue. The world was turning all around me and I was stopped dead in my tracks.

I wanted wine. Wine was a romantic drink that implied *amour*. There was a wine rack on the kitchen counter. She led me past it directly to the bedroom. It was a king-sized bed, of course. There were different kinds of cuffs attached to the headboard and footboard. There were chains hanging from the ceiling. I'd written horror novels with similar scenes and things never turned out pretty for my protagonists.

She asked if I wanted her to tie me down.

"No," I told her. "I'd like to tie you down."

She couldn't wipe the expression of discouragement from her face as she got undressed. She wore no panties. She had on stockings, garters, and a bustier that framed and supported her breasts without covering them. I wanted to examine them. I wanted to kiss them. I wanted to *discuss* them. Maybe I was too goddamn dull after all.

I got the fur-lined cuffs and chained her to the bed by her wrists and her ankles. She looked bored. She wanted me to take charge. I was not a take-charge kind of guy. I wondered what a take-charge kind of guy would do in this situation. I had no clue. I opened the night stand. She had gags that looked like they'd choke a giraffe. I found the smallest one, the least invasive one, and placed it in gently her mouth and strapped it on her. She stared at me with the cool, hip, assured knowledge of fifteen thousand innovative, energetic hardcore fucks.

I walked around her apartment opening closets and drawers. She had rows of frilly garb draped on hangers. I discovered whips, riding crops, butt-plugs, anal beads, double-headed dildos, and stuff I couldn't even begin to name. A horseshoe-shaped mousetrap contraption with a remote control to it. I turned it on and the thing actually bit me. Jesus Christ.

In the corners of the room were chairs and swings you plugged in that moved in inhuman ways. The pressure was on. I was sweating like hell. I rooted around in her drawers some more and found a Lone Ranger mask and a roll of duct tape. I didn't want to think about how the duct tape might be used in the heat of passion. I also didn't want to think about the fact that I was geeky enough to sort of be turned on by seeing the Lone Ranger with tits. This night was already enough of a revelation.

I taped up the eye holes and put the mask on her. She couldn't move an inch, was blind and mute, and yet somehow in complete control of me.

On her shelves were all her novels. The titles were compact, sexy, and maybe a touch mean. *Bad Lady on Saturday. Sweet Sinner. My Virgin Wife. Something About Firemen. Learning to Lick It. Dark Bedroom Evening. Spank Me Until I Bleed.*

Precise, sensual, and cruel. It was the way I was starting to feel.

On a separate shelf, far away from the hot stuff, was my own novel *A Chorus of Mad Boys*. I drew it down. Evie had stamped her name on the first page, as if she owned me.

I was already owned by more people than I cared to count. By my exes and the ones who hadn't been around long enough to be called an ex. By my puppy loves and one-night stands. By my dreams and my regrets. By my publishers who couldn't cough up enough advance money for me to crawl over the poverty line. By the editors who smirked, by the critics who cut. By the audience that didn't love enough but always wanted more than I could give. By the past that was always hissing. By the future that forever cowered out of sight.

"Screw that."

I leaped on the bed, unlocked the cuffs, turned her over on her stomach, and re-chained her face down.

"Hi yo, motherfucking Silver!"

I brought my hand to her ass and the sound reverberated through the room. Evie didn't flinch. This was old hat. I spanked her harder. I had some muscle under the pudge. I put it into the next slap.

This is what we do, what we're supposed to do. Awaken one another, heat each other's nerves. We incite, we revolt, we annoy and endanger. We do it with words. We do it with our hands. We impress ourselves upon the world.

Evie's ass had some jiggle to it and I liked the way her flesh moved. I brushed my fingertips across her naked back and got more of a reaction that way. I am composing, I thought. I am finding the mythic essence of truth in this moment. She turned her face aside. Her forehead was furrowed. The soft stuff was the wrong way to go. I brought my hand down again and let the heat inside me travel. It didn't go far enough yet.

An urgency began to build in me as I watched her, lying there, getting bored. Thinking of her next book. Waiting for the roommates to come in and do it right. I changed hands. I spanked her, letting myself go, feeling a little more loose, beginning to enjoy the angry sound breaking the silence. I stared at her book covers. She had much better book covers than I ever got. I wanted to tear the novels into pieces, the way the novels tore me to bits.

I remembered her in the audience, unwilling to meet my common eye, her palms coming together with the barest applause. Hardly seeing me, not even listening.

I spanked her again. I was awed by how much she could take before even growing a tad pink. My hand didn't have enough meaning. I wasn't going to be able to ignite her this way.

A Chorus of Mad Boys had heft. I was a wordy son of a bitch. I grabbed the book off the shelf and ripped out the page with her name on it. She didn't own me. I didn't even own me. I slapped the book against my palm and it hurt. It had weight. History. A lot of my pain had been woven into its pages, too much of my heart.

I brought the book down against her ass. It slapped hard and with a much deeper sound than my hand could make. She didn't cry out but the furrowed brow eased. Finally, she was enjoying herself. I spanked her with the hardback again. This time she grunted lustily. A thread of sweat slid off her shoulder and trailed down her spine. I bent and licked. There was a hint of anticipation in her salt.

I flipped through the novel and read passages aloud. I was common but the words weren't. The poetry moved through me. My voice grew husky. The muscles in my back tightened.

I spanked her with the book again. Two, three, four times in a row. The flat loud noise of it snapped against the distant corners. I did it again and again, the wind from my movements causing a breeze that fluttered the curtains and started the windows rattling. I took her book *Spank Me Until I Bleed* off the shelf and compared the two. Hers was light as a dragonfly's wing; it would never make someone bleed. There was laughter in every sentence. I opened the window and tossed it into the night.

"Poetry is what stings."

Her ass was beginning to turn a gorgeous crimson. It worried and excited me. I was weak and fearful. I flipped through the book, whirling the pages.

"This is me. Everything in here is me. I'm burnishing your ass with the themes of my life."

It started to get to her. She began to fidget and moan. I spread her cheeks and she lifted herself up to meet me, expecting me to get naked and crawl on top of her now. Instead I lowered my face and blew a draft of cool air against her burning skin. It raised goosebumps. She whimpered.

I laid on the bed beside her. I rubbed her gently. The movement from rough to soft was annoying her. Good. It was time for her to give up some damn control. I needed to acquire some in this life. I kissed her buttocks and breathed against them. I scraped my beard stubble over her ass and then spanked her with my hand once more, this time lightly. And then letting go with the book, with my life.

I picked up her phone and started calling everybody I knew in Frisco. I called Joe, Ken, Mark, Phil, and gave them the address and told them to come on up. Held the phone to her mouth so she could moan into it.

"It's a party. All refreshments will be provided."

She thrashed even more. It gave me additional hope. It lit my inspiration.

"That's nothing special for you, is it, Evie? It's all so damn lightweight. It's hardly inventive."

I started making speed dial calls. I called her mother. I called her sister. I called Aunt Lorraina. I scrolled through the rest of the names.

"Who's Cissy? Who's Frankie? Who's Sage? Who's Professor

Conklin? Who's Tristan? Let's get them all over here."

I got out the phone book and found the number to a local church. I got a priest on the horn. Her ass absorbed the punishment of my imperfect sentences. Sweat pooled at the small of her back, and when she contorted it drooled down her thighs. I'd never seen that color of red before. I leaned forward and turned her face and kissed her cheek. She allowed it.

I called a twenty-four hour exterminator and told him I had cockroaches, it was an emergency, he had to come over right away. He'd need at least three men. It was going to be a big job.

Each stroke of my hand and each hammer of the book was like another thrust of love. I wasn't well-oiled, I wasn't a mighty man cut from stone, but I was loving her as well as I could.

The chains slapped the headboard.

She had menus all over the kitchen. Her tastes in all things were varied and encompassing. I called and ordered pizza delivery. Chinese food. Japanese food. Thai food. Someplace that promised the best in authentic Lumumba delicacies in the district. I'd had four years of higher education and a couple more post-grad. I had no idea where Lumumba might be.

I kneeled at the bedside.

"How do you say 'sir' in Lumumbanese?"

I swept my hand down. My palm was numb. She had to be too. I found lotion and spread it on her, working it in deep. I massaged her flesh and her flesh massaged me.

"Who do you think will get here first? The exterminator? Professor Conklin? Is he an old fart? Maybe he can use his cane on you. Maybe I can borrow it from him."

I talked my talk. I could be a whiny bastard most of the time, but when the need arose, I could croon. I could confide and disclose and divulge and spit from the soul, from my own dark heart. A chorus of mad boys resided within me. I scratched lightly down her ass and there was no trail of fingernail marks;

she was far too red for that. I struck her with the book again. I worked it between her legs. I wanted stains. She did too. The bruises rose across her flesh now, going purple. The book seemed to pick up on them.

"How many of these men are going to immediately drop their pants without a word? How many will be disgusted seeing you covered in juice, your bottom fire-engine red?"

She struggled violently. I stroked her hair. I scrawled my love. I thought, I know how to relish and adore. I can be a bad boy on a Saturday night.

"Is your Aunt Lorraina going to scream her head off? Maybe not. She probably knows what kind of writing you do. But what's it going to be like for her to walk in and see you getting it on with three guys from Bug Kill?"

I laughed bitterly and kissed her forehead. I lit a cigarette and let a stream of smoke dapple against her back. I carefully allowed the hot end of the butt to warm her skin without touching.

"Those fumigators have some funky equipment, maybe even more outrageous than some of the things you've got tucked away here."

I clapped my hand down again. I was emphasizing something but I didn't know what. My respect for her, perhaps. My fear and lust for her. This was positive. This was a format for caring and hope. I grabbed my book with both hands. Pinpoints of blood discolored the cover. Her body shook with orgasms. She snorted like a horse and I wavered, wondering if I should pull out the gag. But that would've been another show of weakness, and we were beyond that now, finally.

Evie writhed and groaned and I think she may have even wept as her body rocked. The mask was soaked with her sweat. Every so often I ran my pinkie along her inner thigh and watched her tremble. Her climax was ongoing. My words mattered.

I still wanted to talk with her. I still wanted to share a bottle of wine and discuss her manuscripts. I wanted to grouse about my editor, I wanted her to appeal to my vanity. I wanted to watch stupid sit-coms. I wanted to cuddle like a sap. I wanted to wash her wounds in cold water, and I wanted her to hold me until my fever passed. If it ever passed.

I heard footsteps coming up the stairs.

Gasping, she lifted her chin and started to struggle, but not as hard as she could've.

"Hey, maybe the Lumumba food has arrived. Maybe the guys from Bug Kill. Maybe Aunt Lorraina. We'll be right back."

The front page of my book was drenched with her, but I autographed it anyway.

A key scraped the door lock and a trim, young, handsome guy without any pudge stepped in. He had no crow's feet. He had no grey. He might be Sir or the jealous dude. His face was expressive but I couldn't fully understand the expression. It could mean anything. Or nothing. I guessed my own face looked pretty much the same way.

I handed him the book and her phone that I'd faked the calls with. We said nothing to each other. He walked past me and started for the bedroom. Whoever he was, he was going to get road rash when he finally cut her loose and she threw him against the sheets. He owed me.

I went downstairs and got a cab back to my hotel. I couldn't wait to get onto the laptop and write about my night with her. It was the best sex I'd ever had. A new novel churned onto the page, bloody and raw as a newborn, the poetry screaming.

C{HER}RY CARVINGS

before dawn breaks
Legion lingers
"for we are many"
razor in my fingers

despair overwhelming
legs shaking
destruction threatening
temperature baking

alone and afraid
anxiety and anger
so many emotions
to myself, i am a danger

painting a picture
not in a common place
not with a common brush
oh, God give me grace

—*Jennifer Baumgartner*

GOOD ENOUGH
Kelli Dunlap

Chris dragged the last body part from the garage. It dropped unceremoniously onto the worn living room carpet.

"Antisocial, my ass. I'm very social." Chris kicked the dismembered limb with hate and rage. "Outgoing, boisterous, happy-go-lucky...." The corner of a chapped lip curled toward a snarl. "I was at Rudy's last Friday, for Christ's sake. Where do they think I find the girls? Idiots."

Chris looked toward the television and recalled how the eleven o'clock news had offered more than just the discovery of the latest body and surgical alterations. According to the police chief, the FBI and their special profiling unit were involved—either invited or by force, it wasn't clarified and didn't matter—and they had presumed to understand a killer's mind, to explain it to the townsfolk. Chris had almost laughed at the standardizations based on studies from the 60s and an outdated understanding of psychology as the egotistical authority had claimed, "Most serial killers are twenty-five to thirty-five-year-old white males and tend to be heterosexual, but are often sexually dysfunctional and have low self-esteem." Instead of black humor, fury surfaced behind tired eyeballs and took over.

Already frustrated that the edges of the small flesh trophies had curled as they dried, Chris was further angered by the burns the iron left along the fingers of the inexperienced. Band-Aids, old and new, mingled with open blisters and freshly singed skin to make a mosaic of destroyed digits. The faint aroma of burning hair filled the room as the roughly cut squares were flattened in preparation for the scrapbook. Chris had planned to glue the news clipping that corresponded to each chunk of flesh into the center, using the skin as a frame—but the FBI, mayor and local police department had sidetracked those plans as they presumed to know Chris, to understand the motives. They understood nothing, and Chris had launched the iron across the room to shut them up, effectively moving focus from the flesh squares to the true trophies. The body parts that would comprise the perfect Frankenstein.

Perfect, however, became subjective when the news revealed plastic surgery as a link among the victims. Chris had unknowingly chosen those parts from each victim and they smugly thought it relevant.

"At first we believed the motive was linked to the operations or staff involved, but the procedures have all varied and been performed in as many different locations as victims, with no medical employees sharing a common thread. However, the killer is keeping the body parts involved in the surgeries."

"Shit." Chris had known the breasts taken were fake before cutting them off, and had noticed the thin scar on the back of the left leg, but had neither planned nor realized that each and every part was unnatural perfection.

"The perfectly *manmade* Frankenstein." A low growl, hissed through pursed lips, and a moment's pause were all Chris allowed before continuing as planned. Manmade or not, natural perfection or not, the point would be made. The present complete.

Chris scanned the bare walls of the apartment while absently arranging the body parts on the floor into the proper layout for reassembly. Water stains that hadn't been covered over the years, or had leaked through the vain attempts to hide rather than repair the damage, punctuated cracks in the plaster. The tear in the sofa that Chris had found on a curb and snagged for free was barely noticeable under the pile of unopened mail and haphazardly tossed clothing. A folding chair with a full ashtray on it took the place of an end table, its twin used as the table keeping the ancient television set off the floor. A plate of dried food, well past the time for insects and no longer recognizable, sat on the floor in front of the television.

The smoke from the broken television only added to the aromas in the room, the iron sticking out of the screen like a music video statement. The rabbit ears marked the age of the unit—a wad of tinfoil molded to each tip in hopes of improving the signal. Chris wouldn't miss the television. It was only turned on once a week to watch Terry's favorite show.

Chris studied the emptiness of the apartment and the iron hanging out of the front of the broken television set. It looked less like a video and more like a bum's hideout or abandoned frat house. In either instance, it did not resemble the standard idea of a rational, well-adjusted adult's home. Chris noted that while there were no reminders of the last failed relationship around the room, the apartment itself was a reminder. Chris had chosen to move out of the shared apartment when the affair went sour and had taken almost nothing along, starting fresh at garage sales, thrift shops, and late night curb shopping. Just as the itch for a stress cigarette started to creep, tingling through the empty spaces between the fingers that held the nicotine and tickling the underside of the tongue that longed to taste the burn, the newscast replayed in Chris' mind; the words of the FBI agent echoed.

"The brutality and warped romanticism of the mutilation leads us to believe the killer hasn't had a successful relationship in quite some time, if ever—or has an unnatural attachment to a female role model from his childhood and is attempting to nurture the twisted bond he felt there. An antisocial, if not dissociative, disorder is generally seen in these cases, and our killer is not someone you'll run into at a club or coffee shop, but rather at a laundromat or other such mundane location, as he will not be interested or skilled in socializing."

Ironically, Chris thought, *I actually met Terry in a coffee shop.*

Terry coming back to mind rejuvenated the anger that flowed through Chris, and she continued to spew at the now dysfunctional television set and the newscast that had been there.

"For starters, gentlemen, I am not a male." She plopped down onto the stained, torn carpet next to the harvested body parts. They had been gleaned, one at a time, from various bodies in the past few months and stored in the freezer until it was time to finish the project and put them all back together. Reaching inside the baggie she used as a sewing kit catchall, she retrieved the six-inch hide needle she'd gotten from the taxidermist and jabbed it into the threadbare carpet next to her. "Retards forget their own studies. Eight percent of serial killers are women, yet they always always *always* begin by assuming it's a twenty-five to thirty-five year old man." She withdrew the thick black thread the taxidermist had claimed would never stretch, never rot and had the strength to hold together a Cape buffalo mount.

"Not a man, not twenty-five—hell, I'm barely twenty-two— and far from antisocial. How can they be so wrong? Because I'm not the standard black widow killing off ex-boyfriends and spouses? Because I'm not using poison or some other less dirty method meant for the gentler sex, to lessen the guilt and truth of what I'm doing? Fuck that. I've never been a girl, why start now? I hope they're confused as hell when they finally figure this out. Maybe they'll learn something from it and realize their studies are pathetically outdated. Idiots."

She'd had home economics in seventh grade, but had failed the sewing course miserably, her buttonholes becoming part of the teacher's standard "how not to do it" lecture. She'd used thread, super glue, hot glue and no-sew iron-on seam holding material over the years to get by. This didn't need to be perfect, it just needed to make the point. She punched the thick needle through the chilled yet still pliable flesh of the leg and pulled the thick black thread through to the knot. Feeding the needle into the meat under the skin of the hip on the torso she'd found, she pushed it upward until it came out with a popping sound and pulled the thread tight, seeing the parts pull together with nothing more than the string to guide them, like a gory marionette show.

The breakup had been severe. The emotions had been high and the pain of words that couldn't be unheard had chewed into Chris' soul, ripped a part of her asunder and created something even she couldn't explain. The words were the worst, and they took a vibrant girl and made her into something dark. She mourned the relationship as if it had been a death. She went through shock, guilt, pain, denial and anger—and never got past the hatred that festered in her mind as Terry's words echoed whenever Chris least expected it. She couldn't take a shower or get dressed, get undressed or brush her teeth without thinking of those words.

And now the words of the newscast twisted the knife already placed in her back by Terry. Her lip twitched and one corner of her mouth rose up. "Leave it to men to get it wrong."

She pushed the needle and pulled the thread over and over until the first leg was finally attached. She tied a crude knot in the slick black thread and cut the needle free. Leaning back and slouching, she studied her work.

"It's a perfect leg. It's long and sleek, nicely tanned and looked amazing in nylons," she whispered with rage, her words almost hissing out of her in a rasp. Her mind finished the sentence her mouth had started, *before I shredded the hipbone to take the treasure for Terry.*

On to the second leg, she found herself not paying attention to the work in front of her, but stared blankly at the television.

"How could they be so wrong? I'm not trying to get away with anything, necessarily. I mean, in the end it won't matter so I haven't been overly careful. Of course, if they have my prints it won't do them any good, I've never been printed for anything so I'm not on their records, not part of their radar...." Her mind wandered as her voice drifted off. She continued to work on autopilot while her memories played with her emotions.

She and Terry had been so happy. Everything had seemed perfect. They understood each other. They meshed emotionally, mentally and physically. Their sex life was nothing short of amazing and their quiet time was filled with an unspoken tenderness she'd never known could exist.

And then Terry's job was downsized and something in Chris' lover's eyes had changed. Something in Terry's soul had cracked. And suddenly...suddenly nothing was good enough.

"It's really too bad you don't have longer legs. I think the athletic tone of your legs would look great across a few more inches...and then in heels."

Chris had laughed at the comment, believing Terry to be joking. Hoping enough time had passed since the job loss that Terry was coming back around to normal. They hadn't had sex for weeks and the idea of long legs wrapped around Terry, in nylons, seemed like just the high-passion sexual thing that would have driven them both crazy six months beforehand.

But Terry had been serious. Unfortunately, Chris didn't realize it until the next jab.

"If you grew your nails out, your fingers would appear longer, more graceful."

What? Chris thought. Her nails had been well manicured but short when they'd met and the comment—the passive-aggressive request—confused Chris. What had she done that Terry was suddenly unhappy with her?

The numb feeling that took over as the comments became more frequent and their message more evident was the only thing that protected Chris from a complete breakdown when the relationship fell apart. She was already damaged, already broken, and Terry's final words couldn't cut any deeper—Chris was already bleeding out emotionally.

"You shouldn't wear those kinds of shirts. It makes your arms look fat."

"If you did some exercises, you could tighten that little ass of yours right up."

The comments were all physical. They were all said without anger or sarcasm, but with a weird truth veiled in a thinly concealed desire or kindness.

"I love your eyes, but if you got colored contacts you could have whatever you wanted. I've always been partial to blue."

They didn't ruin the relationship, but they sure as hell weren't fixing whatever was broken. And they continued. They were added to and revisited in slightly different alternatives, they increased in frequency, and they started to wear down Chris' self-esteem and outlook.

Chris realized her hands were wet, and she glanced downward as the thick black thread pulled the second arm tight to the torso. The parts had begun to thaw while she worked; the blood and other fluids remaining in them had started leaking out. She knew the smell would come soon and hoped to be finished with the Frankenstein, with all of this, before then.

"Two perfect legs; two thin, muscular arms; long, graceful fingers; a skinny midriff with just a touch of definition; and breasts big enough to cup but firm enough to be perky long after they should be...Frankenstein is almost done. All we need are the straight blonde hair and perfect teeth and long, lean neck."

She reached for the head and had to stop herself from pushing her fingers into the once blue eyes, ruining the visage but releasing her jealousy of all of the women that were what she would never be—hating them a little even as they lay in pieces in front of her. Instead, she shoved the needle into the neck and began attaching the last piece of the puzzle.

Chris had given up on men long ago. They were brutal and cruel, selfish and hard. They'd always taken what they wanted from her and given nothing back. Matt had cleaned her bank account. Scott had cheated on her. Jim had outdone that by cheating on her with her best friend. Darrel had sold her collectibles. And Rob, he'd been the worst. He'd played the game, played Chris, and fooled her right up to the proposal—when he presented her with the engagement ring he'd purchased for an ex-girlfriend.

Sure, she knew she'd had a habit of dating quintessential stereotypes of bad boys and losers, but still, it was hard to believe they weren't all like what she'd witnessed, been subjected to, even if it was self-inflicted. Terry was supposed to have been different. Terry was supposed to be gentler, kinder. Terry was supposed to succeed where all the men had failed.

But she had failed Chris as well.

Or Chris had. Chris realized she was the common denominator in all the relationships and wondered for several days if that was where the problem lay. But Terry *had* been different. For a long time. Until she had become just like one of them. Until she had become just as bad as a man.

Well, if Terry was proof women could be just as cold and cruel as men, Chris would be proof women could be just as evil and selfish. She'd give Terry a present, the perfect woman. Chris' very own Frankenstein. And then she'd leave Terry alone forever.

She bit through the black thread with venom after tying the last knot and spat out the corpse's wetness that had soaked the thread and consequently touched her lips. She had given some thought to dressing the Frankenstein, but Terry needed to see the perfection, not just assume it was there under a dress and nylons.

Chris stood and stretched, looking down at the leaking grey body below her. The legs were longer than hers, the fingers more graceful. "I hope it'll be good enough." The breasts perfect little apples of perky silicone. "Those should be good enough." The flat tummy and straight blonde hair were starkly different from Chris', and she felt a pang of hurt jab her anger and then back away again. The black thread holding the pieces together in a haphazard way was the only unattractive thing about the body, but there was nothing Chris could do about those. They were necessary to make the perfect woman. "Good enough!"

She hoisted the body into the back seat of the car and went back into the house to clean up her mess. Chris looked at the fluids and thread scraps on the floor and shook her head. She had stopped cleaning the house weeks before. There was no point in starting now. She moved the squares of flesh to the counter and paused. She had hoped to finish that before leaving the house to deliver the body, but there just didn't seem to be time. Now that the body was done, Chris wanted to deliver it. She wanted give Terry the one thing she had wanted in the relationship: perfection.

The drive across town was a blur. Chris couldn't remember the stop signs, turns, anything. She questioned how she'd gotten to Terry's without getting into an accident. She pulled up to the curb and stared at the rental that had been hers to share for over two years. The windows were dark and the driveway empty. Terry was still at work. According to what she'd witnessed, following Terry around for the past two weeks, she'd be home in roughly half an hour, so Chris would have to move quickly to get everything ready.

Fishing in her pocket for the key she had conveniently forgotten to give back, she let herself in and propped the door open with the stool from the living room while she fetched the perfect girl from her car and brought it into the house. Chris walked through the dark house without thinking, knowing the layout like the back of her hand, and nudged open the door to the bedroom she had once shared.

She pulled the top cover back and arranged the body on what used to be her side of the bed, propped up slightly with a pillow to appear at attention rather than dead and cold. She looked at the mound of hair in Frankenstein's crotch and wondered if she'd have time to shave the pubes into a landing strip like Terry preferred. She made a mental note of the idea and went about the rest of the house, preparing.

A single rose in the thin crystal bud vase she'd purchased when they were visiting friends one summer was surrounded by lit candles on the dining room table. The remaining bouquet she'd purchased had been shredded, and the petals were now a trail that led to the bedroom and the present waiting there. Candles scattered here and there between the dining room and bedroom lit the path and completed the ambiance.

Chris pulled the envelope from her back pocket and read the note that had taken her over a month to write, one last time. In flowing red handwriting she had professed her love, apologized for her failures and imperfections, and offered up both herself and the ultimate perfection in exchange for Terry's never-ending love. She knew she wouldn't gain it. But knew Terry would never forget her, and that was almost as good.

She laid the note—open, wrinkled and barely holding off folding automatically into the position it had been for the last week—across the perfect torso. She sprayed the bed with her jasmine body spray to make the room smell of her, rather than death.

Chris turned away from her offering and walked into the adjacent bathroom. She bent over and turned on the water, adjusting it to a temperature slightly hotter than she would have liked, and added the bubble bath she knew would be sitting on the edge of the tub as if she'd never left. She and Terry may have broken up, gone their separate ways over angry words and hurtful accusations, but there were little things that Chris knew Terry still clung to, and she had seen her purchase more of Chris' bubble bath at the store last week.

She stripped down and thought again of the newscast. *The poor town is up in arms, afraid of some lunatic that is unpredictable and dangerous,* she thought. *They're looking for a man. They are wrong. So wrong. No man would do something like this for love, and that is what they truly need to fear—love. It doesn't matter if you love a girl or a boy, it only matters that you willingly give your heart and soul over to another person and then wait for them to do the inevitable— crush it.*

The tub filled; the bubbles expanded and filled the steamy air above the water. Chris scattered the last few rose petals around the floor in front of the tub and lit the two small sandalwood candles on the back of the toilet before stepping into the inviting water. She gasped at the heat of the water but forced herself to sit. She pulled her legs up to her chest for a moment and breathed in the smells of her old apartment. Her old life.

Chris could tell the bathroom had been cleaned recently by the faint scent of pine cleaner. She remembered the way they had once shared the chore of housework, laughing to the loud music and bad singing and taking a shower together to clean up when they were finished, continuing to giggle their way through soap and finally landing in a heap on their bed to explore freshly cleaned bodies until the combination of sex and housework took its toll on them and they collapsed into a well-deserved nap, wrapped in each other's arms. Chris remembered what love could be. She missed what she knew existed but was no longer hers. And she hated the universe a little for letting her know it existed just to rip it away from her.

Chris looked down and noticed the skin on her knees was red from the heat of the water and the bubbles were starting to fade. She needed the white foam to both catch the horror for others and hide it from herself, and pushed her legs back below the bubbles and let her hands float on top of the water. Closing her eyes again briefly, she thought about what she'd done, what she was doing. She wished the body parts were fresher. She wondered again if there had been a flesh-colored option for the thread. Then she picked up the razor.

"Good enough."

FIRST COMMUNIONS
Geoffrey Girard

A son réveil, minuit, la fenêtre était blanche.
Devant le sommeil bleu des rideaux illunés
La vission la prit des candeurs du dimanche;
Elle avait rêvé rouge. —Rimbaud

After, the bloodstains remained on the driveway for years. Two lopsided blotches joined in the middle that, depending on who said, looked like big butterfly wings or the head of a mouse or two mushroom clouds exploding or maybe someone's balls. They never really looked like a big misshapen heart. And as the stains grew smaller and fainter over time, you had to really imagine the mouse or balls or heart to really see them anymore. Or, even to see the stains.

They'd been darker, of course, when it first happened, on the newly soaked concrete. When you could still see the smallest drops frozen in orbit just outside the two main spheres. When everyone, *everyone*, took turns riding bikes or walking the dog past the West's house for another quick look to see where some girl had killed herself.

I have seen this driveway.

Mrs. West chased them all away sometimes, threatened to call the cops and even called some parents. There's a story she cursed at Lori Powell for being a "horrible little bitch" and had even thrown a rock at her. Maybe. Everyone later thought the story was very funny, but Lori might have made it up.

In the middle of the night, just after, Mrs. West scrubbed the driveway with a big wooden brush and dragged out the hose from her front porch. Someone saw. For all the others, like Alison, who hadn't seen, there was still a hint of water pooled along the curb the next morning and everyone knew what Mrs. West had done. Lots of kids swore the water was tinged pink. Alison thought so, too.

She is eight when the girl kills herself, and stands on the front porch in a worn flannel nightgown that goes down past her feet. Her toes curl under the cloth, tucked beneath her feet against the night's chill. Gawking down the street with her sisters toward the West house where the ambulance and police cars pulse in red and blue and gold and red. The lights stretch up into the darkness above and flush the entire block in sudden blooms of unnatural color. It looks just like the Fourth of July would if she were very far away. And, it is beautiful.

Alison often thinks of this night. This image of the little girl standing on the porch within the furthest edge of these multi-hued colors. She recognizes herself completely in the memory, and it is the only memory of herself she likes.

Neighbors edge onto their own porches and driveways, a few so bold as to go down to the West house for a closer look. Alison's brother, who'd been in high school then, joins these few and has ambled down against their mother's dissuasion for a closer look. He smiles when he gives the report.

"Some girl killed herself," he says, and their mother tsks behind them. "Right on the West's driveway," he says. "There's blood everywhere."

"Raymond Peter!"

"What? There is!"

"Who?" an older sister asks.

"I'll bet it was Sue Snyder," says another sister. "She's dated Brian all year."

"You're right! She does. I'll bet it's Sue Snyder."

This is true.

Susan Snyder. The girl who slit her wrists.

"Maybe," her brother says. "I couldn't tell. There's a body in the ambulance, though. Covered up."

"That's so gross."

Her picture will be in the paper and a full page for her in the *Thunderbird* yearbook that year. Susan Snyder. National Honor Society, French Club, stage crew for *Grease*. Susan Snyder. The name, for one neighborhood, becomes as fabled as Medusa or Cleopatra. Whispered and passed down for years whenever the bus passes the West house and everyone looks for bloodstains.

"Poor thing," their mother says. "It's just…oh, I don't know. Oh, the poor Wests." She retreats back inside.

"This is…this is so sad."

"Fucked up," her brother marvels, the ghostly lights of red and blue and red blushing behind him. "That's all this is."

"It's too weird. I'm going back to bed."

"Brian's gonna be messed up, I bet," a middle sister predicts.

This was also true. The boy went away for several years to some private school out of state. Everyone said he'd gone crazy or something. That he'd seen her do it from his window and hadn't done anything. Then, he went to a college for a little while. In all, four years passed since the night of reds and blues and reds, and he then finally returned home again.

By then, Alison loved him very much.

The young girl sat on the curb just two houses away. Watching and waiting. Studying her cell phone as if she were just another young teen lost to texting. The phone wasn't even on. It was spring, a month when the warnings of summer spread to every tree and the world smelled like dirt and worms. It was still cold.

He'd been home again for almost two months now but they'd not yet spoken. She'd even gone to his house and knocked on the door, selling her sister's candy bars for school band. She tried three times and only when she knew he was home. No one ever answered the door.

He looked different from his pictures in the yearbook. Four years. He'd grown out his sideburns and had a little soul patch. His hair was much redder than she'd imagined. His car was a midnight blue Pontiac Grand Prix GT and he'd driven right past once when she and her sisters were out front loitering in the driveway. Her parents arguing again.

"Was that...?" one sister asked.

"Yeah," said another. "I heard he quit college."

Alison tried to see in the window but he did not look their way. He kept his eyes straight ahead and turned quickly away from them and down the street. He always parked in the garage. Mostly, he just stayed home.

So, she waited. Wanting only to talk to him. To hold him.

Wanting only to let him know what she knew.

That Sue Snyder's death was a sacrifice.

There is lightning and so the pool is closed until further notice. The storm rumbles high in the dark clouds above. The pool club is already half empty while they wait it out away from the others. The summer shower trickles on the shelter's roof, where it sounds like scurrying insect legs, millions. The surrounding trees drip shadow.

One of the boys spins the cell phone again.

They sit in a semi-circle on one of the picnic tables. Her feet dangle over the edge. She and Gina and three boys.

The phone stops and Gina kisses the boy. Alison watches

with the others. The thought of playing the game is better than the game. The thought of kissing a boy is better than the kiss. The phone is spun.

A kiss. The phone is spun.

She licks her bottom lip. It's her now. She leans forward.

His tongue moves into her mouth and she closes her eyes against the intrusion. She thinks of Brian West and puts her hand behind the boy's neck. She knows her oldest sister lost her virginity in a car and that she was drunk and threw up afterward and that she cried all the next morning. She thinks of Brian West and draws the boy deeper inside. She knows her mother can't stand their father. That she is afraid to leave. Her mother hides her bottomless glass of scotch in the closet.

She thinks of Brian West and kisses someone worth dying for.

Alison draws back and opens her eyes slowly. Reaches slowly for the phone.

As it spins, the fingers of her left hand absently stroke her right wrist.

I know why she did it.

Get the fuck outta here, he says. 'Fore I call the cops.

I know why she did it.

Look, you creepy bitch—

She loved you.

You're, you're messed up, girl, he says. I swear to God...

You don't really mean that.

Why you always hanging around out here?

I don't want you to hurt anymore. I want you to understand.

You...you're full of shit, kid. You need to see someone. Just leave me alone.

She loved you. For-real love. The kind in stories.

Is that right?

Yes.

That doesn't make any fucking sense, he says.

Now you're the one who's full of shit.

Someone like Romeo or Lancelot. Tristan. Paris. Orpheus.

Rochester or Heathcliff. Jack Dawson.

Brian West. Brian...

That someone, anyone, could love someone, anyone, that much.

Please, God, please let just this one thing be possible.

She went twice to see the girl's grave. Stood over the rotting corpse and grass there. One time, flowers lay on the ground also. Old, brown and shrunken. She plucked them free from the grass. *Blessed are the pure in heart for they shall see God* the headstone reads. I have seen it also. Alison laughed when she first saw this, then cried. The next time she visited, she did just the opposite.

She is not surprised when the girl comes to see her.

At midnight in a dream. It *must* be a dream, yes?

The girl floats on a rolling black sea where all the stars sleep. The night strokes her breasts roughly. Her whole body aches for something. For him. For something inside her. She wakes in a stab of pain, sits up in her bed. Her bedroom window shimmers white, moonlit gleaming on the curtains as a vision of the girl emerges from the darkness between the window and the bed.

Susan Snyder's ghost drifts toward her. The ghost is naked, and a narrow ridge of black sutures splits her down the center like a zipper, runs from the bottom of her throat down between her breasts, over her stomach and between her legs. Her arms are outstretched as if to pull Alison close for a hug. The room smells like sweet metal; it smells like blood. One of the ghost's hands holds a dripping knife.

The stitches are pulled free and the black cord dangles beneath cuts that run from her palms to her elbows. The skin between is carved away completely so that the veins shift beneath like clumps of worms. The moonlight glistens on wet muscle and bone, and each gaping forearm looks exactly like a woman's vagina. At the bottom, thick black Xs remain at her wrists. It makes Alison think of her math class. Of the Xs and Os at the bottom of notes she's never written.

Susan Snyder's ghost stands beside her bed.

The girl dreams red. Blood spills down the dead girl's arms onto the carpet, where it slowly forms a big misshapen heart. The dripping fingers of one hand reach out to caress her.

Susan Snyder's ghost holds out its arms. Its eyes pulse in red and blue and gold and red. The knife slashes downward twice.

Slicing into Alison's arms. The skin separates. The blood flows down her fingers onto the sheets.

Alison screams when she wakes. Grabs her burning wrists.

Not a scratch to be found. She slips free from her bed.

The blood she finds—on her fingers and the sheets—is still hers.

Hot and slick. It trickles down her inner thighs.

I don't know, he says.

That's not true. Oh, I got this for you.

You shouldn't, he says.

Maybe. I found it at a used bookstore. It looked interesting.

It does, he says. Thanks.

It says he quit, um, writing by twenty-one. He wrote all of that by twenty-one.

It's.... That's astonishing.

Some famous guy called him the "baby Shakespeare."

Seriously, you shouldn't have. But thanks.

See. There's English and then the French side by side.

It's nice.

I wasn't sure…can you read the French?

Not really. I…I just know a couple phrases.

Someone taught you.

Yes.

She taught you.

Yes.

What did you learn?

Je t'aime. Je t'aime de, de tout mon coeur.

What else?

Je t'adore. Tu es mon amour.

She taught you this?

Amour de ma vie. C'est pour toi que je suis là. À toi, pour toujours.

What else?

That's all.

Je t'aime?

Yes, perfect. *Je t'aime.*

That's all.

He says, Isn't it? It is the first time she's ever seen him smile.

The camp trailer is parked in Megan's back yard and one of the boy's older brothers snuck them beer. They can't smoke inside because Megan's mother will know and get mad. Alison has had a beer and is nursing the second. Everyone's beer cans are collected in a bag at the back of the trailer in case Megan's mother comes out to check on things. Later, they will toss them out in someone else's trash can. A boy named Tommy Barnes presses his whole body between Alison's legs. Presses her back awkwardly on the cushioned bench. She can feel his hard-on against her right thigh. She thinks of blood running over her fingers. His hand moves onto her boob.

Gina and Megan are making out with the two other boys. She tries not to watch them. The trailer is dark and smells funny. The boy between her legs smells like beer and wet dirt. He tells her that she is cute, that she is pretty. He tells her that he has liked her for a while now. Megan's father was fucking someone at his office and left two years ago. Alison asks the boy if he knows any French and he pulls back, grins. *Voolayvu kochey avec mwah.* His braces are wet. There's spit caught between when he speaks. She can give her time and body and attention and promises and lies. Alison forces her hand between them and rubs him down there. If she cries, he doesn't notice.

Are you all right, he says. What happened?

Nothing.

Sure seems like—

Nothing, I said! Forget it.

OK. Sorry.

What's it like to be in love?

Alison…

Real love.

I told you, he says.

No, you didn't. You said you didn't know.

I can't. Words don't work.

It's everything, isn't it?

I don't…. Yes, everything. But there aren't really any words for, for *that*.

God. God means everything.

I guess. Yes, that's right. But God's just another big word like Everything.

But we can praise a God. Give ourselves to it. All, if we really want.

He nods.

Now you know why she did it.

Time passes before he speaks again. A minute, the night, four years.

Merci, he says.

I am too far away from this. This hot blood and hot spit. Holding phones to ears as both sleep through the night. Guns to the temple. Naming children ten years too soon. Every minute a second. Every hour a year. I am too far from first loves.

But I have seen this driveway. Where a girl killed herself because she already had everything. Because she'd run out of ways to show that, run out of things to give to that.

When every promise, every absolution, of love is truly believed.

And so I am never too far from pity. Or envy.

Or the possibility, the hope, that I may one day also know God.

He tossed pebbles until Alison stood at her window. She wore a flannel nightgown and there was some frost on the corners of her pane.

Brian West then sat on her driveway, his legs in a four, the one leg stretched out like he was sitting on a blanket. He cut his left wrist first.

He looked up at her for a while. Alison watched.

Merci.

Her driveway was already black, so she couldn't make out the slowly forming shape. His head dropped first. Then, the body slumped over to the right.

Someone called the police.

Alison watched from the window as her night again filled with beautiful colors.

THE GOD OF LAST MOMENTS

Alethea Kontis

Max received the package from his mother three weeks after her funeral. She had come to him just the night before in his dreams; he'd scolded her for her continued attempts to meddle in his life. Without a word she had lifted great wings and flown away, a perfect image of the guardian angels she'd always sworn walked beside her. Such was the way of dreams.

The package, however, was not a dream. It didn't appear harmful or potentially hazardous. It was white and padded and metered with the correct postage. There were a few stamps and stickers and scuffmarks declaring its delicate nature and boasting of a long and possibly strenuous overseas journey, but nothing that gave any hint as to the contents or the intent of the sender. In fact, there was nothing particularly strange or unique about the package at all, apart from two slightly odd things.

The first odd thing was that the package had his name clearly printed on it above his mother's address, the address where he and Rose had spent the last few days clearing out clutter and deciding what to do with the rest of their lives. A decision Max would have been happy to put off for just this side of forever.

The second odd thing was that it was from his mother. The return address had been penned in a neat and steady hand, neither of which his mother had ever possessed. But there in blue ink was her name and a residence somewhere in Våmhus, Sweden.

Max didn't know where Våmhus was, exactly. For a moment he imagined his mother sipping coffee in a little café, fishing on a fjord, or lounging in a chair on the deck of a ship, laughing over how she had fooled everyone, wondering about the donated casseroles and the turnout at her graveside. But Max had been there at the hospital, had seen her corpse in that ridiculously expensive casket. He had watched the mechanism lower it into the ground and had thrown the requisite rose in after it. Max might not have been sure about what he had eaten for breakfast, or the weather tomorrow, or the contents of this mysterious package, but he was sure that his mother was most definitely deceased.

Still in semi-shock, he heard Rose's footsteps skipping down the stairs. It was always a hop and a skip and a gallop with her, never the steady, predictable rhythm of most normal people. Everything about Rose was ever-so-slightly off beat from most normal people.

In many ways, Rose was much like that mysterious package. On the outside, she didn't appear to be anything more or less than your sweet, average, chubby, middle class girl next door with long dark hair and rosy cheeks and a smudge on her chin. She might have just been making cookies, or enjoying a good tumble, or fixing the lawn mower, or all three at once.

Also like the package, there were two slightly odd things about Rose: the first being that almost unnoticeable social syncopation. The second odd thing was the solitary butterfly clip she always wore in her hair. It was currently stuck in the side at random, slid to where the spirit moved it, and sparkling like mad despite the dust. That constant butterfly belied the presence of one foot still firmly set in a world of eternally optimistic girlhood. Rose, too, believed that angels watched over her from on high, that the universe spoke in fortune cookie riddles, and that there was always a bit of magic just around the corner. She even believed in him. Loved him. Max wasn't sure what supernatural force had prompted such unwavering, unconditional faith, but he wasn't stupid enough to turn down a pretty woman's heart, soul, and body when freely offered. There was also her obsessive love of strawberries. Okay, so maybe there were three odd things.

"Yay! I'm glad you got home before the storm. Did you pick up rags and polish? You did, you wonderful man." Rose often posed and answered such rhetorical questions. She had adopted this style of soliloquy so that the passengers on her train of thought would always know which station they were approaching, and which they had just left.

Max was not a wonderful man. But he didn't mind donning the clothes of the fairytale prince Rose decided he was, so he squeezed into those shoes every morning.

"I still feel uncomfortable opening your mail." She indicated the package as she moved to the sink to wash her hands. "Either you have a jealous girlfriend in Sweden you're not telling me about, or you're being stalked by a very sick individual. Or both." She smiled that enormous smile that had captured him all those months ago like a moth under glass, no doubt positing that the latter scenario would leave her much better stories to tell.

Rose nudged open the door of the refrigerator with one foot and pulled out a small bowl of sugared strawberries, her usual reward for a hard afternoon's work, a long-procrastinated task completed, or a particularly harrowing trip to the mailbox. Max could smell the red sweetness of her indulgence from where he stood on the other side of the table. "No, thank you," he said without looking up from the package, and then did when she cleared her throat. She was not offering her fruit; she was handing him his pocketknife.

"You always did like presents."

True; he liked presents as much as the next selfish man, but he hated surprises. A surprise implied that at a certain point in time, someone, somewhere, had knowledge of something he did not, and that feeling rankled him. A man should have control over his own life. There were traces of adhesive on the stout little blade. "You've been using my knife?"

"I needed it to open boxes. Don't worry; I'll clean and sharpen it when I'm done."

Max grunted. He sliced open the mysterious package and shook its contents out into his palm. It was small, whatever it was, and secured in enough bubble wrap to float the Titanic. Max set the blade to the translucent layers that blossomed beneath it. At the heart was a burgundy silk purse small enough to hold a large coin. But it was not a coin. Instead, the object was a coin-sized medallion, a tempered circle of glass edged and backed by what looked to be medium-quality silver hung on a length of dark twine. Etched in the silver was a crude gowned stick figure with wings, some idiot child's rendering of an angel surrounded by four dots like an unfinished square. Something Rose might have scribbled in her younger days...or yesterday; the butterfly hairpin winked at him. He turned the medallion over.

There was a lock of dull brown hair trapped in the circle of glass; suddenly Max realized that the cord from which the medallion hung was not twine but finely braided lengths of the same dun tresses. He knew that hair. It was his mother's. He was in the midst of recoiling from the grotesque ornament when the angel symbol touched his palm.

Time stopped, and Max received the real message his mother had sent him.

He felt a vibration, deep and basic as a heartbeat pulsing through him, emanating from the medallion. Some long-ago forgotten mysticism had preserved his mother's life force inside this piece of her, connecting them through their familial bond. Blackness enveloped him, warm, safe nothingness, and beyond it the faint beep of machinery. The beeping from his mother's sickbed. Max could almost taste the antiseptic in the hospital room around him. He felt knowledge, explanation, sink in through his skin.

Angels indeed. His mother hadn't just loved angels; she had been chasing them. If his dream had been any indication, she was trying to become one. Had she succeeded?

He knew the answer as soon as he asked it: no. She had stumbled upon her ability to sense this strange elemental power, but she had not known how to harness it or she would have shared that knowledge with him.

Somehow, through this amulet, she shared it with him now. In that moment, Max experienced his mother's frustration at coming so close to the secrets of the universe without ever achieving them. In that moment, Max knew he would succeed where his mother had failed. In that moment, Rose was yammering on about something. Max only stopped to notice when her curious fingers swam into his concentrated field of vision and plucked the medallion from his hand. There was a flash of brilliant white light and the warmth was instantly gone, the deep vibration silent in his bones. In his ears, Rose's voice resolved itself into words.

"Now I remember," she said. "Mourning trinkets. Hair jewelry. I read or watched something about this poor, small village in Sweden and the women who kept it thriving through their talents. On the History Channel, maybe. Queen Victoria was a big fan. Of the jewelry, not the History Channel, obviously." Her seemingly endless knowledge of trivial facts never ceased to amaze him, but now all he could focus on was that power, that precious, warm, golden power that she had taken from him. It had slipped through his fingers like the silk of the bag he had let fall unnoticed to the tabletop.

He held tightly to the memory, waiting impatiently for Rose to examine the fine detail, comment on the exquisite handiwork, and make another profound statement about Samson, lost art, and the determination of the female spirit. He was already forgetting the punch that had shocked him, the heat that had filled the core of him. When she paused to take a breath, Max snatched the necklace back. He pressed the angel to his palm, closed his eyes, and waited.

Nothing.

He might never experience that feeling again. He might have missed something in the lesson his mother had tried to teach him from beyond the grave, a lesson prematurely ended by Rose's annoying fascination with everything. Scowling, he felt Rose's comforting hand on his shoulder.

"You miss her."

A simple nod was far easier than confessing the overwhelming desire to return to darkness. In the pit of his stomach, in the back of his mind, he yearned to taste it again.

"It's beautiful. Your mother was beautiful."

Max had never thought of his mother as beautiful. Had she been? Was she now, vacu-sealed in her satin-lined coffin for a century-century's sake? Awaiting entropy or worms or whatever came first? Frozen forever in that silent grave to which she had so selfishly taken the knowledge he now craved?

He barely felt Rose's soft touch up and down his back, barely heard her words of comfort, recounted memories, the tale of the chest in the attic and how the mourning gift suddenly explained so much...

"Chest? What chest?" Max filled the question with false affection for his dearly departed mother. Rose gave a sparkling smile and a look that on any other woman would have meant mischief of a baser sort. But true to form, Rose took his hand and pulled him straight up the stairs and into the attic.

The precariously stacked piles of boxes and furniture had no rhyme or reason, unless Rose had simply moved objects around willy-nilly in her neverending quest for strange adventure. She deftly navigated through the leftovers from his mother's life to a low, cherry-stained box on the other side of the room. She knelt beside it and rubbed her excited palms up and down the thighs of her jeans. Max could almost smell the strawberry mixing with the dust there.

He shifted a Tiffany lamp and a weathered sock monkey and crouched on the balls of his feet beside her. "A what-type-of chest?"

"A hope chest," she said chipperly. "I always wanted one, but we couldn't afford it. A girl put inside her hope chest all the things she prepared for her wedding day." Rose lovingly stroked the lid, sliding her hands along the elegantly polished wood, tracing the initials engraved there.

"Your mother must have loved this box; it's the most well-maintained piece up here." Rose's eyes rose to the ceiling, reading the engraving like Braille, seeing dreams played out on the shadowed wooden beams overhead. "Can't you imagine your mother as a young woman, kneeling beside this box just like we are, embroidering cushions and handkerchiefs with wishes and hopes for her future?"

Max could imagine no such thing. But Rose did, so he nodded. "That's the story outside this chest," Rose said more seriously. "Inside, however, are different stories. After marriage, I'm not exactly sure what it was she hoped for." Rose gingerly lifted the lid.

Inside the box was a horror movie.

Angels—those same stick-symbol angels—were drawn everywhere inside the lid: large, small, scribbled in ballpoint, carved with a penknife, painted in watercolors, fingerpaints, and possibly blood. Some were surrounded by the square of four dots; some were not. Some of the dots floated aimlessly, angelless, like invisible dice.

"What *is* this?" He asked as a way to gauge whether or not Rose knew anything about the angel sigil. She certainly hadn't felt anything when she'd held the medallion; Rose never hid her feelings. There would have been a discussion, a question, a cry, a laugh, or a scream. And she would have forgotten about her bloody strawberries.

Rose's response was to shrug a little, raise her eyebrows, and blow out a breath through pursed lips.

Good. That feeling, that moment, had been his and his alone. What was it inside him that made him long for it? Had a demon slept beneath his skin, dormant and still, waiting for this key to unlock its cage? Had this unnatural ability only just now passed to him from his mother, having left her now-empty vessel? Was he the next step in evolution? Max reached out to touch one of the angels on the lid. He closed his eyes as he covered one with his palm.

He felt nothing.

"Maybe the contents will mean something to you," said Rose. "Trigger a memory or something."

Or something, thought Max. *I want the something. I need the something.*

She handed him a clear, thick plastic zipper-bag. Inside were clothes—a woman's button-down plaid print top and khakis. Both were covered in either dried blood or rust-colored paint. Max knew which.

"Theresa," he said. "These belonged to my cousin."

"Is that...?" Rose asked about the blood. Max nodded. "Oh, wow."

Impatiently, Max slid the zipper open. "Car accident. Drunk driver. She was on her way home from work." He reached inside. "She was only—"

A shockwave hit him. The room swam away in a sea of blue, faded to red; a scream sang in his blood. He inhaled, tasted Theresa's fear, her surprise, the abrupt snap of bone, the adrenaline that washed over her, the wet, warm pulse as her blood left her, left her, left her body in quiet drumbeats. Then the world turned white. The attic room returned. Rose had placed her hand on top of his. Comforting. Waiting. Expecting nothing. She would have sat there for him, just like that, forever if he'd wanted her to.

Max swallowed the remnants of his cousin's last seconds on earth like a fine wine aged in a cask of blood, glass, and tires.

He blinked. He was staring at Rose, her dark-rimmed golden brown eyes full of wonder and life. She was an empathetic soul, but she did not know what he had experienced in that moment or his overwhelming desire to feel it all again. More. She did not know; there was no way she could have known. It was his secret.

The thought pleased him.

He set the shirt aside and reached into the chest for something new. Rose folded the shirt delicately before returning it to the bag, as if she'd always been so neat and didn't live out of a constant pile of her own garments tossed over the rail at the foot of the bed.

The roof settled with a crack and wind rattled the panes of the window as he debated which object to pick up next: a hatbox; a jewelry box; various papers, letters, pictures; a dried bridal bouquet. The oncoming storm roiled inside him; the charge of it raised the hairs on his arms, but there was no spark of electricity when he touched the photograph.

What filled him was serene completeness and the deep, even breaths of a life well-lived. Eyelids heavy. Floating along the edge of the chasm of dreams in pursuit of the last dream, following it into the darkness, and knowing he was not alone. An ethereal presence comforted him. Urged him on. Then there was white again, and the sound of wings. *Wings....*

"He looks so much like you," said Rose.

Max focused on the picture pinched so tightly between his fingers that it was bent and trembling slightly. He went numb as the potent feeling seeped out of him, and he relaxed his grip.

"This was my grandfather. My mother's father. Technically, I look like *him*." And his wife had died with this picture in her hand. Granna had fallen asleep on the couch and never woken up again.

He was on the verge of an answer. Pieces of the puzzle were falling into place, but he couldn't see the big picture and it frustrated him to no end.

"I'm sure it was very special to your mother," said Rose in sweet misunderstanding. She brushed her dark hair behind an ear before lifting a bundle of bright cloth out of the chest. Max would have admired her restraint had he not been absolutely sure she'd already done so the moment she'd opened the chest.

"Gorgeous." Rose unrolled the long mesh scarf. It was mostly peach, shaded to gold and crimson along its elegant length. She closed her eyes as she caressed it. "Do you know the story behind this one?"

"No," he lied. "But you should wear it. The rest can wait until later." Smiling with her whole body, Rose deftly wound the fabric twice around her neck. "It flatters you," he said, though it would have flattered more a thinner woman with fairer coloring and a less generous bosom. He closed the lid of the chest as solemnly as the casket of a sleeping corpse. He was sated now, stronger and more powerful than ever before. If he consumed the memories trapped in the remaining items he had no idea what might happen. Would he overdose? Would it advance his evolution? It would trigger Rose's curiosity either way. "I have some research to do before bed, and you've been up here all day. You need a break. You must be hungry. I'm starving." Oh, how he was. But not for food. He wasn't sure he'd ever be that kind of hungry again.

The storm hit just after Rose went to bed. Max shut down the desktop and surfed his laptop on the kitchen table until the storm knocked out the wireless. Rose was used to his freelance schedule: long days at cafés and research into the wee hours. Terrorists in Russian schools, earthquakes in India, tsunamis in the Pacific—as long as there was tragedy in the world, Max remained gainfully employed.

Now he researched his own dilemma. All the objects in question had been present at a time of death. Save the one from his mother, but that had physically been fashioned out of a piece of herself. *That* had been needed to trigger this supernatural power. Or had it? Had this power been with him his whole life? Max tried to think back on a time when it might have manifested itself. He must have encountered such objects before.

Or had he subconsciously kept himself apart from them? He preferred new to antique. He never patronized auctions or yard sales. He abhorred gross displays of emotion and had subsequently avoided funeral parlors and nursing homes. He hadn't intended to visit his mother once she entered the hospital, but Rose thought it his duty. Unwittingly, he had gone his whole life without putting himself into the proper situations, and in doing so had completely hidden from himself what he truly was.

But what was he?

He spent hours reading page after page on death cults and cultures, natural selection and extinction, burial rites and stages of grief. There was a wealth of information on preparing for death and dealing with it, but not much about the moment itself. He found angels upon angels: harbingers of kindness, mischief, portent, guidance, justice. Spirits who gave dead men voices and led them to the underworld, gods who weighed hearts, and gods who guarded tombs. Gods who marked men for death and gods who hanged them.

Max did not see himself as an angel. Perhaps he was one of those spirits, a mythical being. A death nibbler. A soul taster. A time collector. An as-yet-unnamed god of last moments. Only he did not judge or protect those moments, he consumed them. They thanked him and gave him their power.

He remembered the scarf. It stared at him from the other end of the table, lustily sprawled across a pile of books, unopened junk mail, and copious lists of things to do that Rose made and never consulted.

The second moment Max experienced had been more vivid since he knew what he was looking for, but that first one had punched through his virgin subconscious. It followed: the more violent the death, the more powerful the object's essence.

The scarf begged him to test that theory. If he was right, that six-foot scrap of stained sunshine would be the most important piece of the puzzle yet.

It was a famous family not-so-secret: Auntie Marie had strangled the life out of her philandering husband with this very scarf. That crime of passion, that madness-soaked murder, had warranted being ostracized from her family and friends, locked away in a penitentiary for many, many years.

Max had a feeling...or rather, he didn't have the feeling just yet. But he wanted it. Oh, how he wanted it. It would be his and his alone.

Quietly, he moved to the other end of the table. He took two deep breaths, rolled his shoulders back, and cracked his neck. He planted his feet firmly on the hardwood floor, grabbed the scarf with both hands, and held on.

Sun boiled through his veins, searing him from fingertips to toes, burning away his vision of the dark house and branding it with some other place, some other time zone, some other time. It was molten joy and fear and sex and satisfaction, and he tilted his head back to gulp down the exquisite nectar. As this last moment played out on his soul, he was neither Marie nor her husband.

He was both.

The scarf: taut in his hands, tight around his neck. The blood: behind his eyes, in his ears. The bile: in his throat. Their throats. Two hearts beat in his chest: one speeding up, one slowing. Two screams: one in his mouth, one in his ears, both ringing with disbelief and betrayal, each from opposite sides of the looking glass. As one eye went dark the other turned bright. All the colors of the world merged into a pure, harsh white blaze. And then he saw her. With that one eye he saw blood-black hair and dark eyes, striking against alabaster skin and her gossamer shift and the white white white of each feather that made up her exquisite wings, and he wanted to be the ground she walked upon and the wind that caressed her and the tears that fell from her cheek and the fire that burned inside her being for all eternity and inthatperfectmomentgodhewanted—

Max awoke on the floor next to the chair, knees folded into his chest, scarf knotted between his fingers. The backs of his hands were tattooed with bloody crescents where he'd bit through the skin. He touched a trembling hand to his mouth. Blood there, too, fresh and wet and crimson. He was sweating, a cold sweat, and his mind felt...spent. Empty. Hungry. Starving again for that one answer he needed to find, the answer he now knew he was looking for.

Her.

He wanted her. She would fill him up and define him, give him life, give him purpose. She would love enough and live enough and burn so brightly that he would never be hungry again for all eternity. He was a hunter; she was his prey. He was a god. And he would have his angel.

He pulled himself to a sitting position, used the chair to help him stand. He patted his pockets on the way to the bathroom. He had everything he needed, but he should clean up first.

Ten minutes later, he put a hand on Rose's shoulder and shook her awake.

"What time is it?" Her eyelids fluttered. "Are you coming to bed?" When he said nothing, she sat up. "Max? Honey, is everything okay?"

"I need you to do something for me."

She shook off her dreams and suppressed a yawn. "Yes. Of course. Give me a second to come to." She put her hand, warm from sleep, over his. "My god, you're freezing. Really, are you okay?"

"I'm fine," he said. "I think I've just figured something out."

"Something about the hope chest?"

Interesting that it was the first thing she mentioned. The rest of the evening had not distracted her. That hopeless devotion of hers so often masked her intelligence. Thus remembered, Max would take care to tread extra lightly. "It's about Theresa," he said. "It's complicated—please don't ask me to explain. You'll think I'm an idiot. It will make more sense if I just show you."

"I love you. I would never think you're an idiot."

As it should be. Rose would never do a lot of things he did on a regular basis. "I need you to take me to the place where she had her accident. I can show you the way."

Rose leaned back, feather pillows crushing against the wrought iron headboard, and sighed. "You *really* need to get a driver's license, city boy."

"I will, soon. I promise."

She dangled her feet off the side of the bed and took a deep breath. "All right. I'm up." She looked up at him with puppy-dog eyes. "Would you make me some coffee? Pretty please with strawberries on top?"

He gave her a well-deserved kiss on the forehead and was pleased to see her answering smile. She fed off his affection; he gave it out in small doses so that she did not gorge herself.

He made her a travel mug of "coffee"—it was more cream, sugar, vanilla flavoring, and kitchen sink than actual brew—and handed it over as she settled herself in the car. There was a chill in the night air; she'd put the scarf over her light denim jacket. She hadn't brushed her hair, but that damnable butterfly clip still nestled in her tresses. Rose pushed a button to the right of the steering wheel and the convertible's roof slid back.

"What are you doing?"

"Driver's prerogative," she said defiantly. "Storm's passed. It's a beautiful night." She put the car into gear and winked at him.

He gave her directions in as few words as possible and she was tired enough to respond in kind, mechanically turning to his instructions without question. When they were surrounded by scrub woods and well away from the lights of the city, he told her to stop. She eased the car to the side of the road and turned off the engine.

"So this is it?"

Max nodded. He had spent the entire ride, one hand in his pocket anxiously fiddling with his knife, thinking about what he was going to say when the time came. Perfect words eluded him. It needed to be more than appropriate. It needed to be poignant. It needed to be memorable. It needed to be right. It needed to be true.

After a prolonged silence, Rose's hand pressed against his cheek and he turned into it. Her tired eyes seemed wiser than the world. "I love you," she said, which was better than anything he'd been able to come up with. In one fluid move he brought his arm up and sliced her throat. It was a swift, clean cut. She had sharpened the blade just that afternoon.

Rose opened and closed her mouth, unable to speak. Max tightened the scarf around her neck, absorbing the spray. Rose grabbed his forearms with both her hands and pulled at him, pushed at him, her voice a soliloquy of silent cries.

He knew what words she would have spoken. She would have wanted it this way. She would have been happy to sacrifice herself for his evolution, her final gift to him, a gift literally from and of her heart. She had been a creature of unconditional love, but something as trivial as love could never amount to his god-hood. So she would be his means to an end.

Max did not grieve for a future that would never be. Perhaps he had loved Rose, as much as he could have loved anything. He was willing to accept that every event that had led them to this place had been brought about by the hand of fate, or destiny, or one of those mystical convergences Rose believed in but he had not. Until now.

As Rose's grip weakened, he looked into her eyes and saw himself mirrored there, saw her idea of him through them as well. He was at once the God He Was and the Prince He Never Would Be. But Rose did not see herself in him, in either direction. One could not see a place one had never been.

Love and strawberries; she bled out love and strawberries. Max was overwhelmed with the taste of her. His body spasmed with joyous anticipation. Her essence seeped from her body into his eyes and ears and mouth, filling the empty parts of him with her vintage, this time aged in a cask of his own making. Through her he drank of himself; his control, his benevolence, his impor-tance. The memory held in the scarf was nothing; *this* was the most intoxicating spirit he had ever imbibed. It was the essence of a god. *This* was what he was meant for. *This* was the proper use of his power. *This* was what he had craved. He was not a spectator; he was a participant. He was the cause. He was a hunter. He was death. He was the creator and the controller. It was the first thing in his complicated life that had ever felt right.

And then he felt pain.

A fire burst in his chest, a heating blowtorch on bare skin that severed his precious link with Rose and stopped the feeding.

"*Enough.*"

A tall, thin woman with a halo of fire engine red hair around a pixie face scrutinized him with flames in her eyes. Her voice was a crackle, a spark, a roar, brooking no opposition. The red woman leaned over Rose into the car, one long-fingered hand planted flat upon his chest. She burned him with that hand, burned him through his shirt and skin, burned him clean out of his body entirely.

Max's demon spirit stepped back, hovering over the gruesome scene in the car, insubstantial, a spectator once more.

The red woman wiped his flesh off her flaming hand onto her tight golden pants with a sneer of disgust. On either side of her, three men appeared from nothing, each taller than the woman, as if that were possible. One was lean, with hair like sky, eyes like rain, and skin like beach sand. His robes floated about him in slow motion, as if the air was more viscous where he stood. The fabric phased and shifted in a rainbow kaleidoscope. The second man was dressed as a simple woodsman, thick arms crossed over his barrel chest. His skin was the dry reddish-purple of a fountain pen Max had once owned, his arms and face marbled whorls of dark knots and wood grain, yet his hair was rosy and fair. The third man: bald head, bare chest, black goatee; one golden earring short of a bottleless djinn with murder in his stormy eyes.

These were the four, then, the four dots surrounding the angels. The four elements escorting her. Which meant she would not be far behind. Max's spirit teeth gnashed and his tongue drooled. The fabric of the universe shifted.

His angel emerged from nothing and everything and shone like a star, blinding him with knowledge and illumination. She was a vision of extremes, both made of light and shadowed by its complete absence. Her wings were the down of a peaceful dove and the pinions of a raptor. Her soft brown eyes were a doe's and a wolf's. Her black hair burned with mahogany fire. He ached to have her, taste her, break her, bend her to his control, mold her to his desires, capture her and keep her and use her and sun himself in her divine candle all the way to immortality. But her guards would never let him.

He screamed his demon spirit rage to the skies, but though his teeth were sharp, his voice was impotent.

The woodsman reached down into the car with hard, heartwood arms smelling of loam and petrichor. He lifted Rose out, lifted her translucent essence right out of her blood-soaked and betrayed body. Her spirit clung to the man, face curled in his giant shoulder, arms around his neck, eyes staring fixedly ahead.

Max was glad those eyes could not see this new thing he had become. And yet—barring the considerable lack of substance—was it so very different from how he had been before? As long as there was tragedy in the world, he'd keep his belly full.

The man of many colors held his hand over Rose's hair, and the long, dark mass glowed with deep red, the same as the angel who now closed Rose's eyes for her. In turn, the other guardians each laid a hand on Rose's hair in a gesture of honor and empathy. The woodsman, whose hands were full, placed a kiss upon her brow.

As one they turned back to look at Max—not Max the cheap murderer sitting red-handed and limp in the passenger's seat, but Max the god-thing, Max the soul nibbler, Max the powerful, who by his own hand had extinguished a light that would shine no more. He stared back at the angel, searching her eyes for love. Devotion. Hatred. Fear. But she had no need of him. In her gaze was only the silent knowledge of who and what he really was. She pulled back the veil and he could no longer hide behind white lies and half truths.

He was but an imposter, a pilot fish, a beggar searching for scraps in the gutters of the road to the afterlife. He was a demon, a parasite, a poison. He had been a fool to think himself a god.

The djinn vanished and became wind. The true goddess spread her wings, and Max fell to knees he no longer possessed.

The universe shifted again, and she was gone.

The guardians were gone. Rose was gone. The angel-light was gone too, and Max was left with only the world in its plain, drab colors, a photograph flat and empty of the life her mere presence had infused.

Max hovered again above the bodies in the car. He wished he'd been able to at least hide the knife before he'd been so rudely excused from his corporeal existence. There it lay on the floor of the car for all the world to see, covered in her blood and his fingerprints, and Max helpless to move it. Whoever came upon this scene would have no doubt as to what had happened. If they only knew how these mystical events had transpired, how Rose's life had been willingly sacrificed in the culmination of knowledge gained after at least two lifetimes of research. But lo, no one would see that. They would only see the gory picture in blood-painted flesh before them, and their simple minds would jump to the simplest conclusion.

Max was rather glad he was no longer part of the idiot human race.

He turned to leave and something caught his eye: the butterfly hairpin winking wickedly at him in the dim starlight. It taunted with thoughts of fortune cookie riddles and magic and angels on high. It reminded him that there would be no more deaths by his hand. It promised him that Rose was so far away that he would never find her, even if he tried. This gift, his demon gift, would ever be his curse. He was doomed spend eternity hunting mortals on death's door and feeding off what he could steal. He would never know love. He would never be content. He would never be satisfied. He would never again taste strawberries.

Damn the butterfly. He would consume what moments he could and be powerful. He would meet his angel again.

His stomach growled.

He was hungry.

RING ROAD

Mary Robinette Kowal

Echoes and steam swirled around Nanna, merging with warm water to ease the tightness in her limbs. God, she had missed spas while she'd been away. The entire state of Wyoming had utterly failed to understand what a spa should be. In fact, the entire country might have failed in that.

Beside her, Eric groaned. "I may never move again."

"Told you." Lauger, of all the spas in Reykjavik, was her favorite and the first place she went after a trip abroad. The heat crept into her, peeling off layers of protection that she hadn't even noticed. She'd been away too long this time. Not that she'd admit it to her grandmother, who'd been outraged when she'd decided to stay at the university over the summer. And following that up by bringing an American boyfriend home had been...interesting.

Sighing, Nanna slid lower on the bench until the water lapped the underside of her chin. Carved into an amorphous oblong, the black granite bench had the lines of a sensual modern sculpture. Flecks of mica sparkled under the water like stars had been trapped in the bench. Nanna traced them, imagining they were an image from the big telescope at WIRO made manifest. A distant galaxy under her fingers.

Eric ran a hand up her leg and slid the tip of his finger into her swimsuit.

Glad there were no other guests, Nanna leaned in, almost close enough to kiss him. Teasing. "Maybe you need the glacial pool?"

"Glacial?" Eric raised his eyebrows. "That sounds double-plus ungood."

Nanna laughed and stood, the water sheeting down her body. "I promise, it is invigorating."

"Invigorating...fascinating word choice."

"Dearheart." Nanna leaned down and kissed the top of his dark hair, tasting the salt of his sweat. "Children in Iceland use the glacial pool."

He sighed with mock drama. "Vikings, all of you. There had better be perks following this."

She wrinkled her nose at him and let her accent go very thick. "What perks would you like, American boy?"

Without a beat, Eric stood and followed Nanna across the room to the pool. She let her hips sway and imagined his gaze tracking her heat like an infrared observatory.

Tucked into an alcove stood a massive oak vat shaped like a Japanese soaking tub. A bamboo tube brought in ice water to keep the pool filled to the brim.

Nanna climbed the ladder to the tiny platform on its side. The surface of the water was still and reflected her against the black depths. She stepped off the platform, plunging into the water.

The chill grabbed her so quickly it almost had no meaning. As she submerged, it seemed that nothing had ever existed except cold and dark. She could be a satellite hurtling through space. Her feet touched the rough wood bottom of the vat and Nanna surged to the surface, breaking into the world again.

Eric leaned over the edge, watching her. She snatched a kiss from him as she climbed the ladder, and his mouth was hot. "Meet me in the heated pool."

She left him to try the waters while the cold still had possession of her senses. Stepping into the hot pool, every nerve in her skin fired as the warmth claimed it. Her skin tingled, pulsing with life beyond the simple heat. Behind her, water splashed as Eric squealed at the cold.

She chuckled. The water lapped between her thighs as she slid deeper into its embrace.

One of the granite benches seemed to stir with the ripples of her passing. The dark organic shape uncurled.

Suddenly silent, the spa twisted around Nanna. A breeze carrying the scent of moss rushed out from the walls and the stone rose, its shape resolving into a man. Water cascading from his naked body, he stood, taller than her and immaculate. His dark skin held flecks of light within it, like stars that burned and spread until he was too bright to look at. *Baldur, beloved of the gods.*

Why did she recognize him? Everything—the curve of his clavicle—was more familiar to her than the shape of her own hands.

Nanna tried to look away, but her body did not respond. Her eyes watered at the gleaming beauty of him. The terror that she knew she should be feeling did not exist. In its place, longing spread from her breasts through her stomach to her groin. He stepped closer, water surging out from him and caressing her in anticipation. The silence subsumed the sound of her own heartbeat.

Lifting his hand, he traced a line from her hair down her nose, pausing for a tantalizing moment on her lips before continuing down, between her breasts. A distant part of Nanna realized that she had become naked.

His hand plunged beneath the water and found the space between her thighs. He leaned forward, putting his lips to her ear. The only sound was of his breath as he whispered, "Wife, I return." Hard as the stone from which he had formed, he thrust inside her, filling her with heat.

Heat like the pyre she had burned on.

Nanna gasped and sound returned.

A noise like the end of a scream bounced across the walls of the spa. She staggered forward, through the space where he had been. The stone bench lay beneath the surface of the water, a simple abstract sculpture once more. Her swimsuit clung to her, almost chafing. Heart racing, she spun, flinging water in her haste.

Eric stood in the water near her, like a statue. Her grandmother believed in the huddafólk, but Nanna had never given the hidden people more than a passing superstitious nod, no more binding than a black cat. They seemed easy to credit now. And that was crazy talk.

But she didn't want it to be. She did not want the rational part of her mind to drive out the memory of Baldur, her husband, who had dreamed his own death.

Who did not exist. There were streets in Reykjavik named after all the Norse gods. She had just been away from home too long.

She turned to Eric, who shuddered with his hands pressed to his mouth, his eyes closed. She stared at him, wondering how she had missed all his flaws before. His arms were a little too short for his torso. A pock marked his right cheek and an old scar split the hair of his eyebrow.

"What did...." Nanna wet her lips, afraid suddenly to hear someone say that Baldur had not come back for her. She rubbed her brow. Come back? She had hallucinated him, nothing else. Even if they existed, why would a god *come back* for her?

Eric opened his eyes and lowered his hands with deliberate care. "I'm amazed the temperature extremes don't kill people."

Nanna struggled to pull a smile out of her arsenal. "As you noted, we are Vikings, so this is nothing." The water lapped around her, teasing with its touch. She shivered and looked over her shoulder at the stone. It bore no hint of life.

"Hey." Eric pointed at the stone curled under the water. "Does that look like a horse to you?"

"No." She could not bear to be here for a moment longer without Baldur. Which was absurd, to be lusting after a waking dream. "Forgive me, if we're driving the Ring Road tomorrow, I should check our travel arrangements."

As she hurried out of the pool, she had the sensation of a hand brushing the nape of her neck. Nanna trembled and looked over her shoulder, but only Eric was there, still staring at the stone.

Early morning light cut across the road in front of Nanna, gilding it and the fields of moss-covered lava surrounding them. The hybrid car glided through the landscape with only the sound of the wheels against the pavement. In the seat beside her, Eric leaned forward. "What's in the road?"

She squinted against the sun, trying to see it better. At first she thought it was a boulder, fallen onto the road, but they were in a level area away from the mountains. Nanna slowed down, glancing at Eric, whose face was white and strained.

When she looked back at the road, the thing moved.

Nanna jammed on the brakes, images of stone rising through water in her mind. Her hands ached on the wheel.

Eric's voice trembled. "Is that a horse?"

The stone resolved into a black horse, lying on its side. Lifting its head, it stared at them from under a dense forelock and tried to rise. Only then did she see the blood streaking its flank and the twisted angle of its legs. Her gorge rose in her mouth as she understood what she was seeing.

"A car hit it." She scanned the sides of the road for the car that had hit the horse, but whoever had done it was nowhere in sight. They had gotten off lucky, if they were able to drive away. The driver must have been a foreigner, because no Icelander would leave a horse in this state. Fumbling for her cell phone, she tried to call the patrol, but had no service. Nanna got out of the car. The horse watched her the whole time, as calm and noble as if it weren't in pain. She wanted a gun with a physical ache.

"What are you doing?" Eric leaned across the seat, his face still pale.

"I can't leave it to suffer."

"Jesus," he said. "You're going to kill it?"

"No. It is already dead; I am making it swifter." She did not feel remotely as calm as her words made her sound. Her clothes felt too tight and she wanted to vomit rather than face the horse, but she couldn't leave it.

Rummaging in the trunk, she found a tire iron and a camping knife. By the time she approached the horse, Eric had gotten out of the car. She couldn't look at him, staring only at the horse that continued to regard her with unnatural calm. Coming closer, she saw that it was not pure black. A constellation of small white hairs marked its hide.

Eric followed, his hands shoved deep in his pockets. "I dreamed this. Sort of."

The small hairs on her arms lifted at his words. "When?"

"Yesterday. The spa. Except it wasn't quite this. I dreamt that I got lost as we were riding and fell." He pointed off the road. "I was lying in the moss and saw a car hit my horse. I couldn't move."

Nanna weighed the tire iron in her hand. Baldur dreamed his own death, too. Even through her glove, the metal chilled her fingers. "That's unnerving."

He nodded and shrugged. "Do you need help?"

She hesitated. He was tall and strong, but she didn't know if he had the resolve needed. If the horse would stop staring at her, she wouldn't feel as though putting it down was something *she* was expected to do. But expected by whom? It was stupid, really. She held the tire iron out. "Can you hit it, hard, between the ears?"

"I...yeah." He took the iron. "Will that kill it?"

"If we're lucky. At the least it will stun it, I hope."

The horse tried to rise, broken bone poking through the flesh of its hind leg. Nanna clamped her jaws together, breathing hard through her nose. She would not vomit. Kneeling, she held the horse's head, murmuring to it as Eric walked behind. As he raised the tire iron, she watched him in the periphery of her vision, focusing on the horse and keeping it steady. A blur of motion flashed and a dull thud resonated through her hands. The horse stiffened, eyes glazing. Nanna released its head with one hand. Before she could think about it, she lifted the knife and plunged it into the carotid artery where it pulsed beneath the black and white hair. Blood splashed, steaming, over her hand.

Time stretched, the wind pushing the scent of moss against her, seeking all the ways through her clothes to her skin. The pupil of the horse's eye flared white, pulsing with the heat of a god. Baldur's favorite horse had joined him on the pyre.

Someone whispered, "I return."

Eric stumbled back from the animal, dropping the iron with a harsh clang on the pavement. Blood coating her hands, Nanna kept her focus on the horse, speaking in Icelandic to the creature until it lowered its head, still staring at her.

Standing next to the old stone fence, Nanna examined the saddle of the stocky bay mare that old Toti had brought out to the trail for her. She tried to keep images of the black horse out of her head. This horse had the beginnings of her winter coat, which added a layer of teddy bear plush. When she moved forward to check the bridle, the mare nuzzled her, asking for treats.

"I said, no!" Eric shouted.

Nanna spun, startled by his outburst. Old Toti blinked in front of Eric, holding the reins of a black horse. Flecks of white hair marked its hide with stars. It could have been the twin of the horse on the road.

She hurried over to Eric and Old Toti. Still clutching the reins of the black horse, Toti turned to Nanna and launched into Icelandic. "What do you say about your outlander?"

"We had a fright on the road. There was a horse like this one that had been hit by a car." She swallowed at the memory. "My friend had a dream about it the day before. He is unnerved."

Tugging at his thick white beard, Old Toti grunted. "Does he have the sight?"

"I don't...." Her denial died away. Yesterday, she would have scoffed. Today? Today the horse from the road was standing in front of her. "Maybe."

He harrumphed. "Then you know what will happen if I try to get another horse."

Fairytales and ghost stories from childhood came back to mock her. Men who tried to duck premonitions always walked straight into them. But superstitions were no more binding than a black cat. Black cat, black stone, black horse. "I'll ride it, then."

Old Toti cursed and spat on the ground. He handed the reins to her as if he were handing Nanna her death. "You know that he'll be riding it before you return."

"What's going on?" Eric had clearly been trying to follow their Icelandic. The poor, sweet boy couldn't even pronounce the name of their hotel for all that he'd made a valiant effort to learn the language before following her home.

"It'll take too long for Toti to bring us another horse. His stables are out toward Hveragarde, so I'll ride the black."

Eric blushed. "You totally don't have to. It was a crazy weird overreaction on my part."

"It's nothing." She avoided looking at the horse, not wanting to see if it was watching her the way its twin on the road had. "We can switch later, if you want."

"Sure." He smiled, but the relief in his voice was hard to miss.

Breath frosting the air, Nanna held the black horse's reins lightly in her hand. The land around them sloped up to a series of wind-swept peaks. The low grasses had turned yellow with autumn and they were interspersed with brilliant red leaves, no taller than her ankles. Puffs of steam rose out of the ground on the slopes above them, signs of hot springs burbling above the surface.

She shifted uncomfortably on her saddle and plucked at her waistband, which had begun to cut into her stomach. Nanna stopped with her hand on her belly. Her stomach was hard and distended, straining the fabric of her riding pants. Even through the bulk of her coat, the bulge was noticeable. She went through what they'd eaten, trying to think of what could have made her so bloated. Nothing odd, not even the putrefied shark that her grandmother loved.

But the band of unyielding fabric hurt. She twisted in the saddle and stopped as pain shot up her side. Involuntarily, she groaned.

Eric brought his bay closer. "Are you all right?"

"I need to stop for a moment." She turned forward again, not wanting him to see how swollen she was. "Something I ate."

Pulling the black horse to a stop, Nanna swung her leg over the saddle. She staggered as she got down. Her center of balance was off. She put her hand against the black horse's side to steady herself. Her vision filled for a moment with a pattern of black and silver to match the animal's hide. Or granite under water, or ashes on a pyre.

Nanna shook herself. By the side of the trail, a boulder crouched like a troll caught above ground. She made her way to it, relieved when it blocked her from Eric's sight. She pulled her coat up, revealing the bulge of her stomach. Her pants cut so deeply into the flesh that it was hard to get her fingers under the fabric to undo the button. When she managed to release it, the zipper peeled itself open as her belly pushed it aside.

Nanna moaned at the relief from the constricting fabric. An angry red welt circled her waist. She squatted awkwardly, pants around her ankles. If she could defecate, then maybe this horrible bloating would go away. She ran her hand over the swell, flinching when she reached her navel. It was protruding the way her sister's had when she was pregnant.

"No." It was impossible. She strained, trying to expel whatever made her look so grotesque. She could not be pregnant.

But the image arose of Baldur sliding his hand down her body and the heat as he pierced her. A dream. It had to have been a dream.

Like the one that Eric had of the black horse.

Shaking, she pushed herself to her feet. Her fingers were numb as she pulled her pants up, almost falling over in her haste. She caught herself against the bolder and the rough stone scraped her knuckles.

She pulled on the waistband, trying to draw it shut, but the fabric would not close. A handspan separated the two sides. It had been painful before, but the trousers had been able to close. She could not be larger in this short space of time. A litany of "no" filled her mind like prayer. She yanked, trying to draw her belly in, but the hard dome belled out from below her breasts.

Something inside her kicked.

Nanna shrieked, clutching the spot. Nothing made sense. Her throat closed with fear, and wheezing, she pressed her hand against her chest. Her breasts tingled at the pressure. A spot of moisture seeped through her bra and shirt. A sob gagged her.

Footsteps crunched behind her. "Nanna?"

She faced away from Eric, wrapping her arms around her belly and hunching over, trying to hide it from him. He said something in English but her brain failed to make sense of it. She shook her head, trying to clear it.

The thing inside her beat against the walls of her stomach again. Nanna cried out at the sudden percussion. Eric was at her side in an instant. His face blanched, gaze fixed to her protruding stomach.

Huge and impossible, her gravid belly sat naked before his sight, pushing out between her shirt and her open trousers. Nanna moaned, rocking on her haunches.

He spoke, the tone clearly horrified, but she couldn't understand him. Nanna reached for English, but where the language had been was only the sound of breath. "I don't understand."

Eric looked up when she spoke, but his eyes were drawn down to her stomach. Again, words left his mouth without meaning.

A sobbing wail rose out of her chest. Putting a hand over her mouth, Nanna tried to hold the terror in.

Eric reached out, stopping just short of touching the monstrosity. His brow knit in concentration. "What is the news?" His Icelandic was slow and slid sideways in his mouth, but she understood him.

But how could she explain Baldur in the pool? How could she explain that a god had come back and claimed her as his bride? "Help me."

"How?"

She did not know. The sob returned, made louder when a cramp wracked her middle.

Eric cursed and put his arm around her shoulders. She let him lead her around the boulder. Leaning against him, she kept her gaze down, acutely aware that she could not see her feet. Eric stopped suddenly.

Nanna looked up. The black horse stood in the trail, watching them. The bay was gone. Her knees gave way and she dropped to the ground. Eric sank beside her, holding her as Nanna rocked. Another cramp twisted through her.

Eric ran to the horse and grabbed her pack off it. Tearing it open, he pulled out a blanket and wrapped it around her. He pressed a hand to her brow, as if she had a fever, and said something again in English. She could not understand him, but she could hear the disbelief in his voice. He pulled out his cell phone and glared at it, waving it around like a dowsing rod. Cursing, he scrambled up onto the boulder, still clearly trying to get a signal.

Another contraction bent her double and Nanna cried out at the pain. Eric jumped down, bounding over to her. He bounced on the balls of his feet, looking from her to the horse. "Can you ride?" he asked in his sideways Icelandic.

She shook her head, panting against the pain.

He ran his hand through his hair and crouched next to her. "Wait here." Eric grabbed her arms, forcing her to look at him. "Help. Bring."

"No!" She clutched his coat. "You can't. You can't leave me here. Don't go. Oh god. Please don't go. If you get on that horse, I'll never see you again."

Eric shook his head, anguish tightening his face. "Need help." He leaned forward and kissed her on the forehead. "I love you. I come back."

Before she could stop him, he stood and ran to the black horse. He stopped at its side, and even looking at his back, she could see the fear.

"No!" She reached for him, but another cramp stopped her. Her stomach rippled visibly in time with the pain.

Eric mounted the horse. Almost before he had adjusted the reins, the horse turned, heading back to where they had left the car.

Panting, she tried to get to her feet. A contraction took the strength from her legs and dropped her onto the ground. Between her thighs, a gush of wetness spread down her legs, warm as the spa. Pain split her center. Nanna screamed, clutching her stomach as it convulsed again. The pressing necessity of the moment pushed the impossible out of her mind. Rolling onto her back, she kicked her trousers off. The wind whipped around her, licking all the surfaces of her skin and lifting the damp scent of moss-covered stones.

Another contraction wracked Nanna with white-hot pain. She pushed, trying to get it out. Inside her, a light flared and backlit the skin of her stomach in a roseate bowl veined with blood. Twisting, she tried to escape as the space between her legs ripped open.

The contractions sped into a blur with no space between them to inhale or scream. The only sound in the world was Baldur's breath in her ear.

And then a child cried.

The light, almost too bright to look at, lay between her legs. It pulsed in time with her own heartbeat, beating down in intensity until the radiance faded into the body of a blood-covered infant. Even slathered in blood, he was so beautiful that her heart broke at the sight of him. Fair skin, a shock of thick white curls covering his head, and his eyes, when he looked at her, were the pale blue of a frozen river.

Her hands moved of their own accord and reached for the boy. No umbilical tied them. He lay between her legs, perfect and terrible as if he had been created there. Nanna pushed her shirt aside and laid him at her breast, gently turning the babe's head to her nipple. Her child suckled gently, one hand resting curled against his cheek.

Moss-scented wind riffled the white hair. "I have returned."

Nanna clutched her son to her breast and pushed away on the path. "No." Clinging to the babe, she got to her feet, staggering as warm moisture rushed down her legs. "He's mine."

The wind wrapped around her and whispered in her ear. "Mine."

Nanna wrapped her coat around her son and ran down the path. At the first bend, she looked over her shoulder, but Baldur was not on the trail. Shivering, she continued her limping way down the hill. At every boulder and dip in the ground, she expected him to appear, demanding the babe. Her conscious mind slid away from the truth of what had happened to her, focusing instead on the weight of the infant inside her jacket. Warm and comforting, he pressed against her bosom.

The world spun around her and Nanna stumbled, falling to her knees. She wrapped her arms around her son to protect him. Shivering and cold, she knelt for moment, trying to catch her breath. She had to protect him. Nothing in her life had ever seemed so clear.

Forcing herself to her feet, Nanna limped on. With each step she took, her burden grew heavier.

Full night had arrived before she reached their car. The Northern Lights crackled overhead in a denser display than she had ever seen. The coruscating bands of purple and green stretched in a bridge across the heavens.

There was no sign of Eric or the black horse. Nanna wavered a moment. There was no way she could have beat him down the hill. She could not leave him here and she could not wait for him. Sitting in the car at least would get her and the child out of the wind. Nanna reached into her coat pocket for the keys. Through the lining of the coat, she could feel her son. He seemed too still, but she could feel her heartbeat reflected from his body.

Nanna opened the car and dropped into the driver's seat.

Unconsciousness beckoned her to fall backward into its embrace but she did not have time for that. She had to get help. But from whom? Who would know how to deal with prophecies, gods and unnatural pregnancies?

She covered her mouth to stifle laughter, recognizing the edge of madness. Breathing slowly through her nose, she stared out the window at the Northern Lights. Something moved, black and sprinkled with stars like a piece of the sky had escaped to walk the earth.

She started the car. It was almost silent, just a faint internal hum. Keeping the lights off to avoid drawing attention to herself, Nanna eased out of the parking lot and over the shoulder onto the Ring Road. With the mountains behind her, the road led through an expanse of lava fields. Under the aurora, the misshapen lumps all seemed to be horses or men on the verge of rising. Nanna hummed under her breath to soothe herself as much as the baby.

As the road turned, she flicked on the headlights. The black horse stood in the road. She jammed on the brakes, but the sides of the road dropped without shoulders onto layers of lava. The horse slammed into the car, breaking at the knees. At the impact, Nanna flew forward, colliding with the airbag. The smell of sulphur and ozone filled the car. The baby. Glass shattered inward as the horse rolled over the car and crushed the roof. Baby. Tipping sideways, the car tumbled off the road. When it came to a stop, Nanna let go of the crumpled wheel.

The impact had driven the breath from her lungs. Blood trickled down her face. Wheezing, she pulled her jacket open to see the child and stopped with the fabric held away from her body.

Cradled against her body lay a stone.

Smooth, amorphous curves suggested the lines of an infant carved by a modern artist. She stopped breathing. A caul of blood coated the white stone.

Choking with fear, she pulled her coat off as if her baby could be tucked inside somewhere. He was not on the seat or the floor. Only the stone.

The car had come to rest at the foot of the steep slope leading to the road. Through the window, she saw only moss and stars. Nanna shoved the door of the car open, half-falling out when it gave easier than she expected. She used it to lever herself to her feet and stood, wavering, by the car.

Eric would be out there, caught in his waking dream. Baldur had managed to trade one dream of death for his freedom. And the child, the child was his escape.

The wind lifted her hair and chased tiny cold fingers over her naked legs. She rested her head against the hard metal of the window frame and stared at the ground, waiting for the landscape to stop spinning around her. Dark rivulets of fresh blood coated her thighs.

Weariness pulled at her eyelids, tugging her toward sleep. Biting the inside of her cheek until it bled, she turned back to the car. Nanna lifted the stone child to her breast. Setting her back to the road, she carried her burden into the moss, looking for Eric.

On the road, the black horse lifted its head and waited.

THE UNREMEMBERED

Chesya Burke

In the beginning, there was the Sun and Africa and there were those put here to remember and record. Oral scribes—griots—whose jobs were to act as a collective memory for an entire nation. But to forget is to cause injury to one's self and one's people. To forget is to be lost in thoughts of nothing. To forget knowledge is a sin.

The girl writhed in pain, lost to all around her. Her thoughts and actions had long been taken over by something she could not control. Her body, a lump of dead mass, her arms and legs moving to the beat of their own drum—that drum, pain. The aches took over not long before and it didn't matter any longer that she could not move, could not talk. She learned a long time ago that being lost in her own mind was simply the way things were, at least for her. Those outside noises and voices—many of them she thought she could remember if she just tried hard enough—were still simply on the periphery, speaking to a body that did not respond. One that could not respond, even if it wanted to—and it certainly did not want to.

Her name was Jeli. She knew this not because of those voices outside her head, but because of the ones inside, the ones speaking to her. She knew this because it was told to her. She was told she'd been put here to suffer—and suffer, she did.

Jeli's black body twisted and contorted in a way that would not have been possible if she'd had full control over her limbs. Her mother knew this, but all she could do was hold the girl in her arms. Nosipha, the girl's mother, said a silent prayer to whomever might be listening at the time. A sin, of course—one should pray to God and God alone—but it seemed as if the Lord himself had stopped answering her prayers a long time ago, so she supposed it would not hurt to ask all those with knowledge of her daughter's pain to aid her.

Something in her daughter's head broke and the girl stretched out, stiff as a board, and screamed with such fury the woman jumped despite herself. As she gathered her senses, she noticed what caused the girl's anguish. A thin, circular ring of blood appeared around her daughter's head, slowly tracing the girl's skull, as if a line were being drawn with an invisible razor right before Nosipha's eyes. Droplets of blood flowed freely and Jeli screamed from the pain. Nosipha cried.

The kingdom of the Snake. Black as those charred by the sun, hair of wool. His kingdom. In years to come, he would go on to unite both the upper and lower Egypt. His name was Narmer Menes. His rule marked the first of written history. But he could not dismiss the roles of his griots. Everything had its place, and so, too, the oral scribes. They must know the history and remember. Remember. It is a difficult and thankless job, but it must be done, as there are things said with the tongue that cannot be contained by writing, and there are things written that can never be spoken. So the griots held both the pen and the memory of an entire people.

Menes went on to rule for more than twenty years. He was a handsome man with thick lips and a wide, flat nose. He ruled with an iron fist but a soft heart. King Narmer was the first king to wear both the White Crown of Upper Egypt and

*Lower Egypt's Red Crown. The headdress was heavy and
shaped like a round golden bowel. The king often bore scars
from the crown.*

He is your father; remember him, girl. Remember him.

Nosipha rushed her daughter to the hospital. Doctor Davidson
arrived about a half hour after they did, because Nosipha had
learned, in the many years she'd run back and forth to the emergency room, to call him on the way. Jeli's head had not stopped
bleeding as the nurse unwrapped the makeshift bandage Nosipha had put on her daughter's head to soak up the drainage. The
older woman, whose hands shook as she worked, commented
that it looked like someone had placed an upside-down bowl
around the girl's head and then tried to rip it off, skin and all.
Doctor Davidson examined Jeli, looking over her very thoroughly as he always did. But before he had arrived, Jeli had been
examined by another doctor. The new man, Doctor Sanders, suspected Nosipha of wrongdoing. Nosipha had seen it before. Her
daughter was prone to cuts and bruises in her condition, and
over the years she'd been questioned on many occasions. The
doctor questioned Nosipha about what had happened to the
girl's head. Nosipha admitted, through tears, that she did not
know. She told the man the wounds had simply appeared. The
doctor looked at her suspiciously, and she expected at any moment for him to call the authorities. Nosipha couldn't blame him
for suspecting her of doing something to Jeli. Hell, if she didn't
know better, she probably would have suspected herself, too.

But what could she have done that would have caused this?
So she explained that to this doctor, hoping he would understand that she was innocent.

"I'm not sure what you could have done. I understand things
happen," the doctor responded. "Did you maybe wrap her head
too tightly or something?"

"Something," she mocked him, "like what?" She realized he was trying to bait her. He wanted to catch her in a lie. "Why would I wrap her head up when it wasn't even bleeding in the first place? It doesn't make any sense."

"Well, you're the one telling us what happened, and I assure you it doesn't make any sense that the wound just appeared on her all of a sudden."

Nosipha was upset at the insinuation she'd done something to her daughter, even though she understood it. She'd done nothing but take care of Jeli night and day since the girl had been born. "Listen to me. I have bathed my daughter, cleaned her, fed her—many times through a tube when her sickness got too bad—and I have changed her diaper since the day she was born. I have never done anything to hurt her, and I will never harm my child. Do you understand me?" Tears began to stream from her eyes just as Doctor Davidson walked into the room.

Davidson took the other doctor out into the hall, and the two stayed outside talking for a long time. Nosipha was beginning to get worried; she knew this might not be a good sign. If they really thought she'd harmed her daughter, they would call the police on her and Jeli would be taken away, and she could go to jail. If this happened, who would take care of Jeli? This was a nightmare. She thought back to what had happened. Yes, she was sure the girl had been lying in the bed, and as she convulsed, her body went stiff and the marks appeared. That was it. She knew it didn't make any sense and she probably wouldn't believe it if she hadn't been there herself. But it was the truth and it was all she had.

She thought back to the day the girl had been born. Nosipha was the happiest woman alive. She had wanted a baby for as long as she could remember. Nosipha hadn't been a young woman when the girl was born. The truth was, she'd been far past the recommended age to give birth at forty-two years old.

But she could not have loved the girl any more if she'd been a young woman of twenty years old, and that was what mattered.

As Jeli grew, Nosipha noticed she did not cry often. But she just assumed the girl was a good baby and she thanked God for this. Then Jeli would not crawl and the girl didn't begin spouting those cute little baby mumblings as most babies do. It was obvious by the girl's first birthday, when the other children were smothering cake all over their faces and crawling around and getting into trouble, that something was very wrong. Jeli simply sat in her mother's arms pretending she didn't even notice the other children. There was something very different about her daughter, and at that point Nosipha had to stop pretending she didn't notice it.

Nosipha's grandmother told her to talk to the girl, telling her stories to make her feel as if she was a part of this world. But this was ridiculous; she spoke to her daughter all of the time. She sang to her and tried to teach her colors and numbers, but it just hadn't worked. This, her grandmother assured her, was not the same. Jeli had to learn things that had been lost to her, the old woman assured her. In fact, it had been lost to them both, her grandmother said, since Nosipha's mother had died when she was two and she'd been raised by her father. She never even met her grandmother until she was almost twenty. Already in her declining years, Nosipha's grandmother alleged that she didn't remember what she had forgotten herself. In the end, the old woman died after Jeli was diagnosed, still forgetting what she could not remember, or at least forgetting to tell her granddaughter. Nosipha always regretted this; she always felt as if there was something she should have known, something she should, as her grandmother suggested, have taught her daughter.

After Nosipha noticed the problems with her daughter, she took the girl to the doctor. The doctor told her Jeli had a severe case of autism. He said Jeli had a "complete inability to communicate or interact with other people," and she would only get worse as the years passed.

It was true. The girl no longer even recognized Nosipha, her own mother, and she couldn't eat on her own; she had never used the toilet and she still couldn't walk or talk. Nosipha ran her fingers through her short kinky hair and sighed. Would things ever actually get better or would they just continue getting worse? And worse and worse?

Doctor Davidson walked back into the room. He looked tired and Nosipha knew if the man went through what he did with her for each of his patients, he should be ready to take a permanent nap. She knew she was.

"Everything's okay," the doctor said. "Doctor Sanders is just anxious and young. He doesn't understand this sickness."

"He thinks I did this, doesn't he? Is he calling the police?"

"No, no. He just didn't.... I cleared everything up."

Nosipha stared at the doctor for a long time. Did he think she had done it?

He seemed to read her face. "Nosipha, I know you love Jeli. I know you couldn't hurt her. I am not going to pretend I know what happened here, but I'm confident you didn't do it." The man walked quietly out of the room, not looking back.

Movement behind the drawn white curtain caught her eye as the drape swung open. A woman with heavy dark circles around her eyes stared at Nosipha. Neither of the women spoke for a moment, letting the silence envelop the room. Finally, the woman whispered, her voice soft and fearful, "I couldn't help but hear. These damn sheets don't give you any privacy."

Nosipha nodded. "I'm sorry, I didn't even notice you were here." She glanced at her daughter sleeping quietly in her sterile white sheets, her skin ashen and dark. "I was just so... preoccupied, I guess."

The woman shrugged, "I can't blame you. I certainly understand." She pulled the sheet back to reveal a small, frail little boy swallowed within the covers. "Leukemia."

"I'm sorry."

"Not your fault. Not anyone's fault, I guess. It's just how it is." The women held out her hand so suddenly Nosipha almost jumped from the motion. "I'm Julia."

"I'm Nosipha." She shook the other woman's hand. "Nice to meet you. Maybe we can keep each other company in this dreadful place, huh?"

Just then the girl began to convulse in her bed. Her body contorted again into unimaginable angles, her fingers and toes crooked and stiff. She didn't scream out, however, as her body threw itself from the bed and landed on the floor. Several nurses entered the room with the doctor, and they all helped get the girl back into bed. It wasn't an easy task; Jeli's body had become unbendable, like iron.

Girl, I am son of Sogolon and the Sun herself. I am Sunjuain. I united the twelve kingdoms of Ancient Mali by my iron sword. Those who knew me in life are all gone, as all people are subject to the laws of Heaven and Earth. And alas, kings are no different. I, however, get to take my place up in sky with those who have come before me. We all know and remember. I remember the kingdoms; the wealth I acquired. I know the children of kings who served in my court. I remember the beautiful golden beads and silken treasures of wealth that I traded for slaves and concubines. Those of us who remember do so because we must. Those who remember, remember because others have forgotten, and still others would steal our past. My dark skin. My memories. Those have been lost to history. They had been twisted to fit within an idea that does not represent what we truly were and who we have become. They…we must be remembered. You, my dear, must carry on. You must remember.

The girl awoke. As she lay in her bed, her head wrapped, blood seeping through the bandages, she screamed. Her mother thought she'd heard words within the scream. She'd said: Son of…song…something. But how could that be? Her daughter had not spoken a word in her entire twelve years of life. Nosipha didn't know if her daughter was even capable of speech after this much time. But there Jeli was, staring directly at her, her mouth forming as if she wanted to communicate with her mother for the first time ever. Nosipha desperately wished she knew what was happing to Jeli. What was happening to her daughter?

"What? What words?" The doctor stared at Nosipha as if he thought she was losing her mind. And now that she thought about it, Nosipha wasn't so sure that was not the case.

"I don't know. I just…thought maybe I heard her say something." Nosipha looked around for someone, anyone, to back her up, but Julia had gone out to get something to eat about a half hour before.

"Perhaps," Doctor Davidson placed his hands on her shoulders and squeezed, "maybe, it's simply wishful thinking on your part? Do you think this could be the case? Maybe?" He spoke to her as if she were a child.

She pulled away from him. "I know my daughter said something. I just don't…." her voice trailed off and she stared at the floor, almost ashamed to say anything further.

The doctor sighed. "What do you think she said?"

"Something like, 'Son of sonlay' or something like that. I'm not sure."

"And what does that mean?"

"I don't know."

"Well, my dear, if you don't understand them, then they're not words."

Nosipha walked back into her hospital room and slammed the door behind her. The doctor did not believe her daughter could possibly say anything. He, like everyone else, believed Jeli was just skin and bone; a lump of flesh incapable of human thought or emotion. But Nosipha knew better. She was sure she'd heard the girl. Doctor Davidson had said it might be time to consider putting Jeli in a home. He thought perhaps it was becoming too much for Nosipha to handle. He said he thought she was beginning to come apart and that he'd seen these signs many times before in parents in her situation. Nosipha simply stared at him, wondering if the doctor himself ever really saw his patients and their families at all. She thought perhaps the man only saw what he wanted to see. An autistic child who would never get better.

She turned to look at her daughter. Her child's eyes were moving rapidly under their lids, like she watched an invisible television screen within her sleep. The girl's frail body began to thrash and convulse again, and the tired woman who felt as if she'd grown older within the last two days whispered a silent prayer, Please, God, not again.

As the woman prayed, Jeli threw her legs over the rails of the bed, put there to protect the girl from herself. Then she sat up effortlessly, her back straight, erect. Julia walked over and placed her hand on Nosipha's shoulder and the two watched in amazement, not sure what to do. Jeli had never sat up by herself before. Not on purpose, not like now. The girl opened her eyes and scanned the room again, this time focusing on her mother. This was impossible; Jeli couldn't see—not that well. Since the day she was born she couldn't focus on objects close to her face, certainly not anything across the room. The girl grabbed the rails of the bed—again on purpose—and swung herself over the edge.

She landed on two very wobbly legs, her bare toes gripping the floor as they clenched tightly. Using the bedrails and pure will power, Jeli headed for her mother. Her legs were so unsteady she almost fell, but she held on tightly just before her face smashed into the floor.

Nosipha realized what was happening before the girl fell again, and she caught her daughter just as she got to the end of the bed. The mother and daughter fell into each other, Nosipha crying loudly just as the doctor and nurse ran into the room.

"She walked."

Moments before, the girl had remembered:

> *He traveled from Mali to Egypt on his bare feet. When he grew tired, he rode on the backs of his many horses. But mostly he used the horses as mules to carry his great load. He brought gifts, as no king before him had. They say many years after his journey the effects of his gifts of gold could still be felt. His face was so clear to the girl this time. She saw.... His words loud and clear in her head. She knew.... He spoke to her; he was of her...her blood, her body, her spirit. Her very essence belonged to him and his people. She belonged to his story, which she realized was her story, too. Her mother's story, her mother's mother's story. They were the unremembered. And, he warned her, she could not forget. To forget would be to kill them all. To forget would be the death of a great people.*

"Why are you crying?" Nosipha asked Julia. "Is he okay? Is he doing poorly?"

The woman shook her head; her son had not gotten worse. She looked up at Nosipha, who slowly bent to hold her hand. "I'm mad at myself. I'm jealous of you and your daughter. Jeli's getting better and Mario can't seem to keep food down. He's dying. I know it and the only thing I can think is why the hell can't it be my boy getting better. Why does my son have to die? I don't want to feel this way, but I can't help it. God, what a shitty person I must be, huh?"

Nosipha stared at the dying light piercing the window. "Jeli's not getting better; she's dying."

Father David came several days later. Nosipha felt a little ashamed to see him there. She had not been to church or paid her tithes in a long time. Hell, she couldn't even remember the last time she'd gone to church. She was surprised the priest even remembered her and her daughter. Then a thought came to her: maybe the man thought the girl was dying, so he had come to give her last rites. The thought scared Nosipha, but surprisingly, it relieved her more than she wanted to admit. Nosipha loved her daughter, but a person could only take so much. The man entered the room, looking around nervously as if he thought something waited in the shadows to grab him. The sight of Father David eased her mind a bit. She didn't pray often anymore and she wasn't even sure she believed God cared about her or Jeli anymore. Maybe if this holy man was here supporting her, though, God wouldn't ignore her. He could not abandon her now.

"How is she?" the priest asked.

"They don't know. She took a step...but they don't know." Tears welled in the woman's eyes and she wiped them away quickly.

The priest nodded.

The room fell silent and Nosipha felt as if the man wanted more. "I haven't been to church in a while, I know. But it hasn't been easy. I...I've had a lot...."

"We understand. It has to be hard taking care of a child like this by yourself. Expensive. The church sympathizes." He walked over to the girl and touched the bandages around her head. "They tell me she bled around the crown of her head? What happened?"

"I don't know. One minute she was fine, and the next she was bleeding."

"Did you see it appear?"

"Yeah, it just...happened. I didn't do anything to her."

"Have you been praying, Sister? Prayed with Jeli?"

Nosipha shrugged her shoulders, hung her head in shame. "Maybe not as much as I should. I know...I...I should have done more. Maybe...."

"Maybe, my dear, He still listens and understands your suffering and pain."

This revelation made the woman cry even more. He heard and understood her pain. Father David put his arms around her. She felt better, comforted. "What are the doctors saying, my dear?"

She wiped her face. "They don't know. They think it may be her last hurrah, or something, I don't know. They said her muscles can't just get stronger so they may actually be...fading. I think they think she's dying."

He lifted her face toward him. "And what do you think?"

"I don't know what to think."

"You want to know what I think?" She nodded; she did want to know what he thought, she desperately wanted to know. "I think God has chosen this child. And now I think the church could help her to bring a lot of people to Him."

While Father David discussed important matters with Nosipha, the nurses checked Mario, Julia's son. The boy stopped breathing and the doctors revived him after a very dramatic couple of seconds. Nosipha stood by the woman, holding her hand, trying to ease her a bit. But Nosipha knew there was no way to ease this pain. Just to think about the loss of a child was unbearable, and to actually watch one die was inconceivable. The woman held on to her as if the two had been the best of friends all their lives—they shared secrets. Luckily, the doctors revived Mario and the boy's vitals were close to normal again. Julia didn't seem to trust this, though, as she kept checking the boy to make sure he was okay. Nosipha heard the doctors tell Julia she might want to consider a Do Not Resuscitate order since it had happened several times now. Julia yelled for the men to get out, not wanting to accept it.

The priest held Nosipha's hand, assuring her everything would be all right.

In the bed beside them, Jeli slowly raised up and turned her head to face her mother and the priest. Nosipha, her back to the bed, followed the man's gaze until she saw her daughter sitting upright, staring into the distance. Jeli did not see her mother because her eyes were as black as coal, blacker than the girl's skin. They looked like tiny jewels stuck into her head. Jeli opened her mouth to speak, but nothing came out. She moved her lips as if she were holding a conversation the others were not privy to with someone. Then she let out a long, low moan. Nosipha rose to her feet, getting ready to go to her daughter, and the priest stopped her. "Just wait," the man said.

But Jeli did not wait. She threw her head back and let out the loudest scream she could muster. She had not spoken in over a decade, and her vocal cords seemed to be developing in her throat. Her cry was mangled and strange, the octaves wavering up and down like a person with laryngitis. Nosipha could not believe it; she didn't know what to do. She wanted to run out to get a doctor, but she didn't want to leave her daughter. So she stayed and watched.

The girl's black eyes seemed to look straight through everyone. She felt a strange sensation take over her body without knowing fully that this indeed was her body. She wasn't even sure what part of her feelings were directly related, or what parts she simply imagined as she had for the past twelve years. Her head whirled and spun with images she knew to be real, but that she could not distinguish from past or present. On some level she knew who she was; she had known it, she believed, all along. But now she knew other things, important things, powerful things. And, as she knew now, knowledge is power.

The knowledge she saw was telling. Images darted in and out of her head so fast she could no longer keep up with them. But she no longer tried. She let them run over her like a waterfall. This, too, had the same effect: it was calming, cooling. Now she simply accepted what she saw and knew to be truth.

Tall white men on tall white horses come to trade, they say, to learn…they create powerful Gods in their honor…pain, darkness, suffering…people being ripped from their homes, their masters….Remember…long voyages, desolate damp deathful spaces…the…church…acceptance…condoning… facilitating…. Remember…dark babies dying by their own mothers' hands to protect them from bearing the bonds of…. Remember…money… power…Remember…them…Remember us all. The slavery, my dear, was not the most difficult part; no, the hard part was the loss. The loss of everything past, present and future. To take away one's past is to deny them a future.

The girl shook her head, not sure she could take any more. It was overpowering. How could anyone carry this much on her shoulders? She'd been in the dark for so long, her mind cluttered, not remembering her name, much less where she came from or what she had been meant to do. Her great grandmother…. That's right. She remembered the old woman had spoken to her also, telling her what her mother, Nosipha, had forgotten. Her great grandmother remembered until she'd gotten too old to pass it on, and then she died. But she died before she could teach the knowledge. Jeli's mother was too old then, and by the time Jeli was born it was too late, the knowledge was lost, leaving her a shell of who she should have been.

But not anymore.

Jeli's body buckled, a spasm taking over again. Her arms flailed, throwing her body all over the bed. When she reached the edge, the girl threw herself over the side and hit the floor with a loud bang.

Julia gasped and ran over to the girl's side. Nosipha and Father David joined her, and the two women knelt down by the girl's side, checking for any sign of life. Beside Nosipha, the priest crossed himself and said a silent prayer. At that moment, Jeli's eye flew open, the whites clearly visible now.

Everyone in the room jumped, giving the girl a wide berth. Slowly, as if being pulled by a rope connected to a plank, Jeli rose to her feet in one fluid motion. The girl's eyes were clear; so was her mind. She could see and think clearly for the first time in her short life. As she stared around the room, she focused on each person, one at a time. Finally, she stepped forward on two wobbly legs. At first her mother didn't think she would make it, but with each step, the girl's legs got stronger. Her face had changed, too. She looked older, as if she'd aged with the years of wisdom of a woman many years her senior.

The girl walked toward Father David and he smiled, his arms outstretched, waiting to embrace her. The man was proud, as if he not only had witnessed this miracle; as if he owned it. Slowly, assured, Jeli walked past him, toward the child sleeping quietly in the next bed. She placed her hand on Mario. Fingers that once could not uncurl themselves to hold a fork now moved gracefully over Mario's flesh. The boy opened his eyes, smiled up at Jeli. She leaned down and whispered something to him the others could not hear. The boy's color seemed to darken a bit. His ashen brown face began clear into a deep, dark tone. Julia jumped to her feet and ran to her son.

When she was finished, Jeli turned to her mother and the other man. She looked at him, her eyes fixed. The man stared, as if he were a child waiting for recognition from a parent. "What you want from me, I cannot give. I hurt from the knowledge of the past. And since you can't use me, you will seek to discredit me. But I know the truth." The priest suddenly averted his eyes, as if lost or afraid of the girl's glare. Jeli tilted her head, faced the priest, and whispered so softly her mother was not sure she heard the girl properly. Then she said simply, "Because I remember."

The man got to his feet, straightened his suit coat, and quietly walked out of the room, knowing, if nothing else, that he would not be adding this soul to his flock.

Desperata
Or, The Desiderata of H.P. Lovecraft

N.B. This document was purchased as part of a Gentleman's estate upon his death in 1937, not "found transfixed by dagger among the moss-grown standing stones of Arkham" as has been so frequently claimed!

Run panicking amid the noisome wastes, and forget ye what peace there may be in ignorance.

Hope is not possible, all shall surrender, be they of sound mind or raving. Speak not this truth loudly nor clearly; and hide it from others, even the doomed and the innocent; they'll soon have their sorrows. Avoid gilled and reclusive persons; for they are the children of Dagon.

If you ally yourself with others, you may become victim, for always they will count you lesser than themselves. Enjoy your meaninglessness as well as you can. Beware of music ethereal, tuneless fluting; they are but portals to Azathoth's nethermost domain.

Exercise caution in your summoning affairs, for the spirit world is full of trickery. But let this not blind you to what reward there may be; many beings starve for maiden entrails, and everywhere life is full of virgins. Ward yourself. Especially do not display affection. Prefer debauchery to love, for in the face of all perfidy and disinterment, those you care about will be food for shoggoths.

Take kindly the counsel of the Necronomicon, gracefully submitting
to the things called forth. No familiar spirit will shield you when
Cthulhu wakes; there will be distress beyond your worst imagin-
ings; untold aeons he's dreamt his intrigues and ascendance.

Waste no time with ascetic discipline, be wanton and selfish. You
are a mote in the universe no more than a sneeze of the stars; you
have no right to be here. And though it may not be clear to you,
no doubt man's time on Earth is devolving as it should.

Therefore make peace with your gentle God, if you dare conceive
one. No matter your penance or last confessions, in the final ac-
counting of life, you will lose your soul.

With all its dread, hopelessness, and uneasy dreams, there is
worse yet to befall our world.

Be fearful. Strive to see it happen.

—Lon Prater

THE CHOIR

Lucien Soulban

Y ou awake?"

"Shut up. I'm dreaming I ain't here." Reggie tried to turn in his cot, but the miserable thing was too narrow to do anything but lie still in and give his back a world of grief.

"Wake up," Glen said, shaking him. "Something's wrong with Dottie."

It was pitch black and Reggie blinked to make sure his eyes were open. He might as well have kept them shut. "Who?" Reggie said.

"Dottie...Barry!" Glen said, exasperated.

"Why can't you just call the man by his real name?" Reggie groaned, pushing himself up though the cot above his kept him hunched over. His balance swayed, trying to tip him—or maybe that was just the ship. Reggie could never distinguish the two this early. No watches to mark the night. No windows to peer outside. No guards, either. It must have been early.

"Something's wrong with her," Glen insisted. "I heard a noise. I went to check on her and...she won't wake up."

"Jesus H. Patton," Reggie said, shaking his head. He tried to stare Glen in the face, to convey just how unhappy he was, but it was too dark to make the other man out, to see his black eyes or his cheeks, which he pinched hard every morning to bring out the red, or the way he fretted over his hairline that had retreated like the German infantry. What he felt was Glen's delicate fingers around his bicep, insistent. Reggie lowered himself down from the second-story cot, his toes instantly curling in his wool/cotton socks at the touch of the metal floor.

Glen must have had eyes like a cat to move around in the dark; it matched the sharp claws that accompanied his attitude. Most days, he was entertaining camp for Reggie and the other "degenerates" being shipped back to New York. This morning, he was just annoying.

Reggie relied on Glen to navigate the row of stacked cots that ran from the floor to the ceiling. To his right, men snored, the only peace known to them these days. Glen, or Glenda, or whatever the hell he called himself, stopped and jerked Reggie's arm forward and down to one of the cots near the floor. Reggie's hand met with skin.

He wasn't a doctor, but he'd handled enough dead men in foxholes to know one by touch. Just to be sure, Reggie searched up Barry's body until he found his hand. No pulse at the cold wrist, nothing but a slab of meat now. Just to be sure, Reggie went as far north as Barry's neck. His fingers came back wet and sticky.

"What the hell?" Reggie said, running his fingers together. "Is that blood?" He almost jumped when Glen touched his hand.

"I don't think it's blood," Glen whispered. "It feels like... slime."

"Y'sure he's dead?"

Reggie struggled to place the voice. Probably that kid John, the one scrubbed wholesome on a farm—blond-haired, barely nineteen and always fidgeting with his hands. If it weren't for Glen watching over the kid, Reggie figured one of the other prisoners would have sodomized him by now. John slept on the cot above Glen's, baby chick to Glen's mother hen.

"Yes, dear," Glen responded kindly. "We're sure."

Reggie couldn't see them in the dark, but he was sure Glen was holding John around the shoulders.

"One of them negroes died, that it? I was sleeping."

That voice, Reggie knew. Dwight, an ugly man who looked like he was tossed out of the womb in a bar brawl. Flattened nose and ugly scowl...if he hadn't been classified a pervert, he'd probably be in the hoosegow for slugging an officer. His brown eyes always carried a promise of violence.

"He was one of us," Reggie said. "Didn't matter his color."

"I ain't queer," Dwight rumbled. It was a dangerous thing to hear in the darkness.

"Sure you ain't," someone said; it was the other colored fellow, Reggie realized. The one with brown eyes and Cab Calloway's silk smile. Bo was him name. "Sure it was all some big mistake, saying you being a cocksucker."

"It was," Dwight said.

"Not me," Glen said. You could tell he was smiling. "They caught me *in flagrante delicto*."

"What's that?" John asked.

"They caught me with a cock in my mouth, dear."

A couple of the men laughed, but not Dwight. He grumbled and Reggie could hear him shifting in his cot, lying back down somewhere above them.

"Shouldn't we tell the guards?" another voice asked. Bill. Reggie liked Bill; he had his feet firmly screwed to the Kansas soil that was still under his fingernails; he had a way of drinking in the world with those hazel eyes of his. Reggie and Bill always exchanged glances, but neither felt right pursuing the other. Another time, another place—maybe The Astor Bar in New York—and both men would have found each other more accommodating.

"We tried," Reggie said into the darkness. "But either they ain't listening or they ain't there."

"Typical," Glen said with a *tch*.

"Anyone got a match?" Reggie asked. "I want to see Barry. Figure out what done him in."

"No," everyone answered, though Bo added, "but I'd kill for a cigarette."

At that the conversation fell silent. For all their bravado, they were frightened, and the darkness only added to the tally of their fears. In response, the ship creaked as it listed gently, the crates nearby groaning against the net.

Reggie and Glen hammered on the hatch until their fists were numb. The Liberty-class ship was a clunker, though, coughing her way through the Atlantic now that the German Wolf Packs were broken and Berlin lay smoldering; Reggie doubted anyone could hear anything past ten feet on this scrapheap.

Defeated, they retired back to their berths, some to sleep, some to whisper quietly over the lips of their cots, others to lie awake staring up at the canvas above them, mulling over their stolen futures. Each of them, enlisted or drafted but patriots the same, had earned themselves a blue ticket for being homosexual. An accusation was enough to earn them suspicion and unless their commanding officers vouched for them, they were sunk once the investigation began and the interrogators leaned on them for more names. Now the only comfort left to be found was in each other.

Reggie glanced down at Bill's cot, wishing he had the courage to slip into his bed. That wasn't his nature, though. He wasn't like Glen, or Harvey who shamelessly flirted with anything swinging like it was falling out of style.

He coasted in this daydreaming state, unable to sleep, not without knowing what had happened to Barry. Slowly, the whispers faded until only the rhythmic hum of the engines and the creaking of the wood cargo boxes settled in. Occasionally, the deep groan of the fifty-ton boom over Hold #2 filtered through all the metal.

Reggie wasn't sure how many minutes or hours passed in the oppressive darkness before a slithering noise caught his ear. It came from a new direction, away from their bunks.

The hold was small compared to the others aft of them, but it'd been cleared out for Operation: Magic Carpet, the repatriation of U.S. soldiers. Only, Hold #1 had been set aside for prisoners. Aft of where they slept was an open area where they could do calisthenics. The slithering, squirming noise was coming from there.

Nobody was supposed to be there, though, only a barrier of wood crates held in place with cargo nets and a web of thick ropes that anchored them firmly in place. The wriggling sound fell in between the creaks and groans of the cargo that was never given a moment to rest in the constant swell.

Reggie sat up in his cot, listening carefully, but he couldn't place the sound. He lowered himself, bracing against the cold deck plates, and cringed as the freezing metal bore through his socks' wool cushioning and up into the soles of his feet.

He walked slowly and crossed that threshold into the gap separating the cots from the crates. Sound changed, swallowed by the volume of darkness and open space. The squirming continued, like someone squashing wet mud between his toes, but offered no direction other than a sense that it lay ahead. Or all around. It was hard to tell. Reggie swept the air gently with his hands, though he must have been two dozen feet away from the crates.

Still, the noise came with small pauses and seeming shifts in direction. He was alone in the gulf, nothing to tether him except the cold permeating through his feet. Then he stepped in something shockingly cold, and wet, forcing him into a limp. Within a dozen steps, both socks were soaked with a sticky goo that appeared in puddles across the floor. He paused long enough to touch it, and then wipe his fingers clean of it on his pants. He advanced, the noise just within reach.

He hated bumping into things when he couldn't see, but the anticipation harrowed his nerves even worse. He latched onto the sound, the slithering. It was right behind him now. He spun around, trying to find it, but it shot past him.

Reggie turned again, trying to follow it with his ears, but the slithering was moving away and he felt lost in the void. He followed, steering by ear, and stumbled forward, trying to keep pace with the noise.

His fingers brushed against cargo netting and he almost jumped out of his own skin; after that first jolt, it was a relief to find anchor in this black gulf.

The slithering was up ahead. Reggie hesitated. It sounded like it was coming from among the crates themselves. No, he realized, from between the boxes, in all the gaps. A horrid stench followed: rotting fish.

Reggie curled his fingers around the netting, his frayed nerves unraveling with the noise. The ship swayed gently, adding to his grip, while the wet mud sounds continued. He didn't want to hear them anymore; he didn't know how to get back, either.

Fate wasn't done with Reggie yet, and another sound came from his right. It was a scuffing noise, something brushing against the ropes. Reggie froze, his breath held, his ears pricked. He felt it through the spider's web of the netting, a pull and push on the ropes anchoring him.

Someone was moving in the darkness—toward him, Reggie was certain. He clenched the ropes tighter, his stomach churning with anxious fear, his mind screaming drill sergeant expletives at him. He was a trained soldier, had seen combat against the Germans. He'd been scared before, so frightened that his heart frayed in the racing and threatened to unravel. This was different. This fear entwined itself around his spine and squeezed. It swallowed his lungs and suffocated him.

Reggie couldn't breathe. The shuffling was closer. He balled his hand into a fist, driving fingernails into his palm. His knuckles ached; his fingers went numb with tension.

"Who's there?" a voice whispered.

Reggie almost cried in relief when he heard Bill's voice.

"Jesus Christ, you scared me!" Reggie whispered.

"Reggie? Oh, brother. I scared you? You scared me!"

"What're you doing here?"

"I heard something."

"Yeah."

"I thought I was nuts. And that stench. Where's it coming from?"

"Don't know," Reggie said. "Wanna keep looking?"

"Yeah, sure," Bill replied.

The two men moved along the barrier of boxes, gripping the net when the sea suddenly nudged them hard. The ship took a stronger swell and tilted portside. Reggie grabbed the rope he was holding and gasped as it slid and seared his hand. It was loose.

Boxes shifted, crates groaned and something crashed to the deck, shattering against metal. Reggie jumped and Bill yelped in surprise and then surrendered a curse. Somewhere behind them, the others stirred awake.

"What the hell?" Dwight shouted.

"Who's there?" Glen called from the shadows.

"It's me," Reggie said. "And Bill. Glen, get your perfumed ass over here. We can't see shit."

"Hold on to your wigs," came the reply, drawing closer to them. "Ew! Why's the floor wet? Are we sinking?"

"We're not sinking," Bill yelled back, before the panic started.

A moment later, someone shuffled up next to them.

"My socks are soaked," Glen said.

"Me too. Can you see anything, Glen?" Bill asked.

"Not much," Glen replied. "A little. Ugh, what's that smell?"

"No idea," Reggie said. "We gotta figure out what fell. It came from up ahead."

The three men continued searching along the boxes with Glen keeping watch for them. Reggie felt a little better that one of them could see. At least until Glen gripped his bicep hard, startling him.

"Easy with those nails, Glenda," Bill said.

"Something scurried past my foot!"

"Rats," Reggie said.

"One of the tall crates fell," Glen whispered. "It's broken."

"The rope snapped?" Reggie asked. He felt forward, pulling at the loose strands. Glen confirmed what he felt.

"The netting's soaked."

"Like the crap on the floor?" Bill asked.

"I think so," Glen said. "But I'm not touching it."

"Nothing else?" Reggie asked.

"There's a...it's like a corridor?" he said, uncertain. "Between the boxes. What's that sound?"

"What about the corridor?" Reggie asked

"It's a gap. Like someone pushed the boxes apart."

"Doesn't sound right," Bill said, interrupting. "Those Navy boys pack these holds tight."

"What's in the crate, Glen?"

Glen was quiet a moment, the sound of shifting wood speaking for him. "Antiques?" he finally said, lower to the floor.

"Antiques?" Reggie and Bill parroted at the same time.

"Little statues. Ew...they look like squids. Um, clay pots— no—urns," he amended. "They look old. Some books with metal covers. More fish faces. My, someone loves their seafood. Wait...

what's...oh my!" Glen exclaimed.

"What?" Reggie asked.

"I think—I think it's a swastika."

"Where?" Bill said.

"On the antiques. Someone stamped swastikas on the antiques."

Reggie leaned down and felt around until his hands touched something cold and rocklike and pitted. It was wet, making his fingers suddenly greasy, and familiar. It was the same stuff on Barry. Before he could comment, however, the men in the cots screamed. This time, they didn't stop.

The three men shambled for the cots like a blind chain gang. Glen steered them, though Reggie stepped on a couple of soft things that squished underfoot. His socks were thoroughly sticky now, the wetness congealing into something else. He finally pulled them off in disgust.

The screams continued, but they were interspersed with movement, the thud of people hitting the deck, and the slithering wet noise. It sounded louder—larger—than what Reggie had heard earlier.

"What's happening?" Reggie shouted, but the yells continued. It was a choir of confusion, fear, panic and pain. The nearest voice was familiar.

"Dwight?" Glen said.

"Get back!" Dwight yelled, close enough that Reggie could have popped him on the jaw. "Who is that? What the fuck's going on?"

"You girls hold hands," Glen said, shoving someone's hand on Reggie's arm. He guessed it was Dwight when the hysterical voice said, "I can't see shit! What's going on?"

"Where are y'all!?" Bo cried from nearby. He sounded in pain.

"John!" Glen shouted.

No answer came, though some of the voices sounded further off, frightened or hurt.

"John, honey, where are you?"

"Glen?" John cried from a distant corner of the room. His voice trembled. "God, Glen. It hurts. Get them off me."

"I'm coming," Glen cried, breaking away from their grips.

Both Reggie and Bill screamed "No!" and tried to grab their friend, but he evaporated, his footfalls fading instantly in the dim.

"Glen!" Bill shouted.

"Oh God, oh Christ Almighty," Dwight whimpered. His fierce grip on Reggie's arm grew tighter. "We gotta get back up in the bunks."

"What happened?" Reggie said, grabbing Dwight's wrist. And then grabbing harder still. "Dwight!"

"Oh sweet Lord, I don't know," he said, almost breathless. "I was trying to catch some winks when the screaming started. I think it was that Jewboy."

"His name's Harvey," Reggie shouted, wishing he could see enough of the man to throw an honest punch.

"I came down and then some damn thing hit me like a ton of bricks, sent me flying. Jesus, what was it? It smelled like bad fish. Jesus."

They were quiet a moment, listening and thinking deep, troubled thoughts. The noises had died down; whoever was still out there had gone silent, not wanting to draw attention to themselves.

"Glen?" Bill whispered, but again there was no response. Neither to that nor to "John!"

"That thing? Is that what killed that blackie?" Dwight asked.

"Bo," Reggie whispered, ignoring Dwight. "You there?"

"I'm here," Bo replied in a low voice. "That thing cut me good. Goddamn, it hurts."

"Can you come to us?" Bill whispered. "Follow my voice."

"No!" Dwight cried, shattering the stillness. "Leave him out there. This thing ain't killing us. It's killing *them!*"

"Fuck you, cracker!" Bo shouted back.

"Who's it killed, huh? A nigger? A heeb? It's going after them, not us."

"What about John, huh?" Bill asked.

"He's a fucking sodomite!" Dwight said, his voice cracking.

"So are you," Reggie said.

"No I ain't!" Dwight roared, his grip tightening painfully on Reggie's arm.

Reggie, swung blindly with the other arm and connected with Dwight's face. Pain flared through his hand, the blow landing improperly. As Dwight reeled, Reggie pulled his arm free from Dwight's grip and stepped back. "We all are, Dwight. All of us on the same damn boat."

"No, please," Dwight said. Reggie could hear him spinning around, stumbling into one of cots. He could feel him sweeping his hands about blindly, trying to connect with someone. "Please don't leave me alone," he said, sobbing.

Reggie's heart ached at his voice. No matter his sins, Dwight didn't deserve this horror—stranded in the dark, alone, crippled. Reggie hated himself for his feminine compassion, but reached forward and found Dwight's arm. He wasn't expecting Dwight to pull him into a bear hug or feel his shoulder turn wet with the man's sobs.

"I'm sorry, I'm so sorry," Dwight cried. "Don't leave me alone here. Please. I'm sorry."

Reggie patted his back, feeling foolish for babying a grown man like this. Finally, he pulled Dwight away from him. "All right," Reggie said. "No more blubbering. Let's see who else we can find."

* * *

There were six of them left, nestled high in the cots and clustered together. The others—including Harvey—were dead, their bodies slashed and slathered with a slick layer of ooze. Where they died it smelled putrid, the spoiled cheese of advanced gangrene. Reggie half wondered if the bodies weren't decaying because of what covered them. Regardless, the squirming, wet mud sound was down there with the dead.

Reggie, Bill, Dwight, Bo and two others whom Reggie was ashamed to admit he didn't know huddled together on a handful of cots. Bo was swaddled in torn sheets, makeshift bandages to staunch the bleeding. Some cuts were deep, slashes across the chest and arms, but Reggie couldn't be sure by touch alone.

"Y'all think that...thing was in the crates?" Bo asked, his voice groggy with blood loss.

"Looks like," Bill whispered.

"The swastikas? You think the Krauts did this? Like a booby trap or something?" Dwight asked.

"I don't know," Reggie admitted.

"I was with the Third Infantry," one of the two men said, his voice as shy as his darting eyes, Reggie remembered. "They brought in these hurt Paratroopers, with the 83rd I think. Just come off some thing at Castle Wewelsburg. The brass pulled us back from that operation a week before."

"Shit! Himmler's castle?" Reggie asked.

"Yup," Bill said. "Only the craziest Ratzis went there. Sorry, Stuart. Keep talking."

"Well, these boys weren't right no more...up here. In the head," he said when he realized nobody could see him. "Before they arrested me for—you know—we were trying to sedate one of them. Guy went loony. Kept talking about what they saw up there. Kept talking about...." He paused.

"What? Spill it," Reggie said.

"Squid statues. As big as your house and these giant...worm

things. Two of the Airborne boys hung themselves that night."

"Jesus," Bo muttered.

"If that thing's from there, why put it with us?" Dwight said, but the suspicion had already laced his voice.

"What are we to them?" Reggie said. "When they needed bodies to throw at the Krauts, they didn't care what we did so long as we weren't caught."

"Wait. Y'all saying it's on purpose?" Bo asked.

"But we're Americans," the sixth man said. "They can't do that to us."

"I took a medal. At Salerno with the 5th," Reggie said. "Took out a machinegun nest chewing through my squad. When the MPs arrested me, they took my medal. Said cocksuckers didn't make good soldiers. Said I'd look better with earrings."

"They said if I didn't name names, they were going to lock me up forever," Stuart said.

"They told us all that," Bill said. "None of us would be here if we didn't name someone else who was queer. That's why we're going home. That's how come we know who we all are, Dwight. Or we'd still be rotting in some camp in Europe."

Everyone was quiet a moment, the weight of their actions pressing on their thoughts. For all of Glen's antics and Harvey's wandering hands, each of them shared a bond they preferred be forgotten. Each of them had betrayed someone else to escape the interrogations and threats.

"I ain't even getting a pension," Reggie finally said. "And my discharge papers have "pervert" stamped on them. Think I can go home with that? Face my family? Dishonorable discharge. Christ. I had a medal."

"So why wouldn't they stick us in here with a monster?" Bill asked, sighing. "Why not see what it can do. We're not protected by any laws. At worst, we're criminals. At best, we're mentally ill."

"Don't leave much room for the Bill of Rights, do it?" Reggie said. "Without the law to protect us, we ain't even citizens. Means they can do whatever they want to us. Because according to their say, we ain't even decent folk."

"The guards ain't coming," Dwight said.

"Only in New York, or in the morning. We're dead either way," Stuart said.

For a moment, everyone sat in silence. Their darkness was absolute, hope absent with the light that was stolen from them.

"So," Bill said. "What're we doing about this?"

"Doing?" Dwight said. "We're fucked. They left us to die."

"We do what we can," Reggie said. "We make amends with what we done and we stick together. We're family now. They ain't left us much choice."

"Even though we all blinder than Bartimaeus?" Bo asked.

"Actually," Dwight said. "I got something that could help."

Reggie was nervous; in the lowest cot, just above the floor that squirmed with sound, he held the lonely wood match by his fingertips and prayed he wasn't leaching sweat into the wood. The others had thrown shredded bed sheets and the torn pages from books into a pile on the floor after groping through the other cots. Finally, they broke three berths apart, wrapping cloth around the metal support frames to make torches.

With a silent plea, Reggie struck the match against the stubble of his cheek. The pain was brief; the match flared to life.

The effect was startling. The faces of Reggie's compatriots emerged from the shadows—haunted and frightened, familiar and alien in shared desperation. Bill was there, his hazel eyes glittering. He smiled at Reggie and brought the bouquet of paper up like a suitor. The bouquet caught fire and in being devoured, spread the light to reveal the rag pile on the floor and the bodies in a state of advanced putrefaction. Suckling at the dissolving corpses were dozens of fist-sized slugs. They squealed at the light and slithered for the shadows.

Bill shuddered in disgust while Dwight gasped out, "Oh Jesus." Reggie lowered the fast-burning bouquet and set the pile ablaze. The flames caught on the paper and along the edges of the sheets. The four torches followed, Bill passing them as Reggie brought them to a steady burn. It wouldn't last, this light. The flames devoured the paper and cloth with starved rapaciousness.

"We really doing this?" Bill asked.

"Yeah," Reggie replied, handing him the third torch.

"What if it's an accident? Just something that happened?"

"Them treating us like this was no accident. The guards beating me up was no accident. I fought and bled for this country and they took my medal. That ain't right either. So if takes burning down this ship to get noticed, well, then...."

"And if nobody knows what happened here?"

Reggie lit the fourth and final torch. "Then it'll happen somewhere else. But I'll tell you, I ain't dying quietly. I'm taking back my rights. It's all any of us can do."

Bill nodded and handed one torch to Dwight above him, the other to the sixth man in the cot over. Stuart was helping Bo, using the fleeting light to tend to his wounds. Reggie stepped down carefully, waving off the black slugs beneath the cot that squealed in their tiny voices and scattered into the deeper darkness.

The four men headed for the boxes, waving their flames near the floor to scatter the dozens—hundreds—of slugs, all squirming and screeching in terror at the approach of the flames like hundreds of needles scratching at records. The torchlight stretched up the faces of crates. They could see the shattered box, the netting torn wide, and behind it, the passage. A pile of slugs undulated at the corridor's mouth.

Only when their fire chased away the slugs did they see the body beneath. It was impossible to tell who it was, John or Glen or someone else, with the corpse dissolving to the bone and the clothes eaten away.

The smell grew more intolerable with each step. Fish and decay, the stench sharp. Scattered around the body lay the broken statues, their swastikas bold in the light.

From somewhere behind the boxes, something screeched louder than anything they'd heard so far. Their heads whipped up, catching movement in the gap between the crates, something larger than them.

A giant black slug came barreling out of the passageway, its oiled leather skin glistening. It was flat along its belly, its back covered in spurts of thorny growths, and its head was a mass of writhing tentacles. The thing rose over their heads, and then lashed forward like a snake.

It struck Dwight; the tentacles latched around his face. The creature slammed him into the ground, then pulled his dangling, screaming and spasm-torn body up into the air. The others cried in shock and prodded the thing with their torches. Reggie toppled over backward, killing a few of the monster's smaller cousins beneath him. That's when he saw the other slugs, racing toward their giant brother and slipping under him. No, Reggie suddenly realized as he jerked to his feet. They were joining the creature, becoming part of it.

Reggie helped Bill and the other man, prodding it with the torches, pushing it back. Dwight had stopped screaming and slipped out the creature's mouth after it screeched in protest. His face, muscles, and tendons were all melted into a mask of flesh, his hair left in patches.

Whatever the creature was, it didn't like fire. Reggie and the others drove it backward, into its alcove. The creature spun away, and as it did, its body disintegrated into thousands of smaller slugs.

Bill and the sixth man stood still in shock, but Reggie drove them forward with a cry of "Now!"

They pushed their dying torches against the netting, turning the web of ropes into a dozen fuses. Boxes caught fire next. The shadows staggered back, the hold revealed. Reggie spotted the crates deeper inside, the ones eaten through. Large statues of squid-faced monsters cracked open, the stone spilling out more slugs.

The screech of terror that followed almost stopped their hearts. The slugs were escaping the blaze in all directions.

"Run!" Someone screamed. It was Stuart. He was at the cots, using blankets to form a fire line between himself and the panicking slugs.

The three men backed away from the growing conflagration and headed for the hatch. Stuart stumbled with Bo as best he could and met them at the rusting aperture.

Smoke filled the room, the darkness burned away by the spreading blaze. Already the cots were catching fire. Soon, either smoke would quiet their lungs or the flames would roast them alive. The sixth man and Bo did their best to keep the slugs away, but the floor seemed alive with them.

"Second thoughts?" Bill asked, shouting over the screeching din as they pounded on the hatch.

"No," Reggie shouted back. "Either they open the hatch or we're all sunk."

"Right," Bill responded grimly.

They met each other's gaze and Reggie wished to God he had the gumption to kiss the man. Bill mustered the best smile he could in return and nodded. He understood.

"Come to your senses," Reggie muttered at the door as he coughed at the smoke. He continued pounding. As the heat grew at his back and the screeching rose to a piercing pitch, he prayed the door would open and that the hatred the men above bore against him and the others wasn't so absolute that it took the whole ship down with them.

But should he die, Reggie prayed, then at the very least let one man's bonfire becomes another man's beacon.

THE DAYS OF FLAMING MOTORCYCLES

Catherynne M. Valente

To tell you the truth, my father wasn't really that much different after he became a zombie.

My mother just wandered off. I think she always wanted to do that, anyway. Just set off walking down the road and never look back. Just like my father always wanted to stop washing his hair and hunker down in the basement and snarling at everyone he met. He chased me and hollered and hit me before. Once, when I stayed out with some boy whose name I can't even remember, he even bit me. He slapped me and for once I slapped him back, and we did this standing-wrestling thing, trying to hold each other back. Finally, in frustration, he bit me, hard, on the side of my hand. I didn't know what to do — we just stared at each other, breathing heavily, knowing something really absurd or horrible had just happened, and if we laughed it could be absurd and if we didn't we'd never get over it. I laughed. But I knew the look in his eye that meant he was coming for me, that glowering, black look, and now it's the only look he's got.

It's been a year now, and that's about all I can tell you about the apocalypse. There was no flash of gold in the sky, no chasms opened up in the earth, no pale riders with silver scythes. People just started acting the way they'd always wanted to but hadn't because they were more afraid of the police or their boss or losing out on the prime mating opportunities offered by the greater

Augusta area. Everyone stopped being afraid. Of anything. And sometimes that means eating each other.

But sometimes it doesn't. They don't always do that, you know. Sometimes they just stand there and watch you, shoulders slumped, blood dripping off their noses, their eyes all unfocused. And then they howl. But not like a wolf. Like something broken and small. Like they're sad.

Now, zombies aren't supposed to get sad. Everyone knows that. I've had a lot of time to think since working down at the Java Shack on Front Street became seriously pointless. I still go to the shop in the morning, though. If you don't have habits, you don't have anything. I turn over the sign, I boot up the register—I even made the muffins for a while, until the flour ran out. Carrot-macadamia on Mondays, mascarpone-mango on Tuesdays, blueberry with a dusting of marzipan on Wednesdays. So on. So forth. Used to be I'd have a line of senators out the door by 8:00 a.m. I brought the last of the muffins home to my dad. He turned one over and over in his bloody, swollen hands until it came apart, then he made that awful howling-crying sound and licked the crumbs off his fingers. And he starting saying my name over and over, only muddled, because his tongue had gone all puffy and purple in his mouth. Caitlin, Caitlin, Caitlin.

So now I drink the pot of coffee by myself and I write down everything I can think of in a kid's notebook with a flaming motorcycle on the cover. I have a bunch like it. I cleaned out all the stores. In a few months I'll move on to the punky princess covers, and then the Looney Tunes ones. I mark time that way. I don't even think of seasons. These are the days of Flaming Motorcycles. Those were the days of Football Ogres. So on. So forth.

They don't bother me, mostly. And okay, the pot of coffee is just hot water now. No arabica for months. But at least the power's still on. But what I was saying is that I've had a lot of time to think, about them, about me, about the virus—because of course it must have been a virus, right? Which isn't really any better than saying fairies or angels did it. Didn't monks used to argue about how many angels could fit on the head of a pin? I seem to think I remember that, in some book, somewhere. So angels are tiny, like viruses. Invisible, too, or you wouldn't have to argue about it, you'd just count the bastards up. So they said virus, I said it doesn't matter, my dad just bit his own finger off. And he howls like he's so sad he wants to die, but being sad means you have a soul and they don't; they're worse than animals. It's a kindness to put them down. That's what the manuals say. Back when there were new manuals every week. Sometimes I think the only way you can tell if something has a soul is if they can still be sad. Sometimes it's the only way I know I have one. Sometimes I don't think I do.

I'm not the last person on Earth. Not by a long way. I get radio reports on the regular news from Portland, Boston—just a month ago New York was broadcasting loud and clear, loading zombies into the same hangars they kept protesters in back in '04. They gas them and dump them at sea. Brooklyn is still a problem, but Manhattan is coming around. Channel 3 is still going strong, but it's all emergency directives. I don't watch it. I mean, how many times can you sit through *The Warning Signs* or *What We Know*? Plus, I have reason to believe they don't know shit.

I might be the last person in Augusta, though. That wouldn't be hard. Did you ever see Augusta before the angel-virus? It was a burnt-out hole. It is a burnt-out hole. Just about every year, the Kennebec floods downtown, so at any given time there's only about three businesses on the main street, and one of them will have a cheerful We'll Be Back! sign up with the clock hands broken off. There's literally nothing going on in this town. Not now, and not then. Down by the river the buildings are pockmarked and broken, the houses are boarded up, windows shattered, only one or two people wandering dazed down the streets. All gas supplied by the Dead River Company, all your dead interred at Burnt Hill Burying Ground. And that was before. Even our Wal-Mart had to close up because nobody ever shopped there.

And you know, way back in the pilgrim days, or Maine's version of them, which starts in the 1700s sometime, there was a guy named James Purington who freaked out one winter and murdered his whole family with an axe. Eight children and his wife. They hanged him and buried him at the crossroads so he wouldn't come back as a vampire. Which would seem silly, except, well, look around. The point is life in Augusta has been both shitty and deeply warped for quite some time. So we greeted this particular horrific circumstance much as Mainers have greeted economic collapse and the total disregard of the rest of the country for the better part of forever: with no surprise whatsoever. Anyway, I haven't seen anyone else on the pink and healthy side in a long time. A big group took off for Portland on foot a few months ago (the days of Kermit and Company), but I stayed behind. I have to think of my father. I know that sounds bizarre, but there's nothing like a parent who bites you to make you incapable of leaving them. Incapable of not wanting their love. I'll probably turn thirty and still be stuck here, trying to be a good daughter while his blood dries on the kitchen tiles.

Channel 3 says a zombie is a reanimated corpse with no observable sell-by date and seriously poor id-control. But I have come to realize that my situation is not like Manhattan or Boston or even Portland. See, I live with zombies. My dad isn't chained up in the basement. He lives with me like he always lived with me. My neighbors, those of them who didn't wander off, are all among the pustulous and dripping. I watched those movies before it happened and I think we all, for a little while, just reacted like the movies told us to: get a bat and start swinging. But I've never killed one, and I've never even come close to being bitten. It's not a fucking movie.

And if Channel 3 slaps their bullet points all over everywhere, I guess I should write my own *What We Know* here. Just in case anyone wonders why zombies can cry.

What Is a Zombie?
by Caitlin Zielinski
Grade…well, if the college were still going
I guess I'd be Grade 14.

A zombie is not a reanimated corpse. This was never a Night of the Living Dead scenario. The word zombie isn't even right—a zombie is something a voudoun priest makes, to obey his will. That has nothing to do with the price of coffee in Augusta. My dad didn't die. His skin ruptured and he got boils and he started snorting instead of talking and bleeding out of his eyes and lunging at Mr. Almeida next door with his fingernails out, but he didn't die. If he didn't die, he's not a corpse. QED, Channel 3.

A zombie is not a cannibal. This is kind of complicated: Channel 3 says they're not human, which is why you can't get arrested for killing one. So if they eat us, it wouldn't be cannibalism anyway, just, you know, lunch. Like if I ate a dog. Not what you expect from a nice American girl, but not cannibalism. But also, zombies don't just eat humans. If that were true, I'd have been dinner and they'd have been dead long before now, because, as I said, Augusta is pretty empty of anything resembling bright eyed and bushy tailed. They eat animals, they eat old meat in any freezer they can get open, they eat energy bars if that's what they find. Anything. Once I saw a woman—I didn't know her—on her hands and knees down by the river bank, clawing up the mud and eating it, smearing it on her bleeding breasts, staring up at the sky, her jaw wagging uselessly.

A zombie is not mindless. Channel 3 would have a fit if they heard me say that. It's dogma—zombies are slow and stupid. Well, I saw plenty of people slower and stupider than a zombie in the old days. I worked next the state capitol, after all. Sometimes I think the only difference is that they're ugly. The world was always full of drooling morons who only wanted me for my body. Anyway, some are fast and some are slow. If the girl was a jogger before, she's probably pretty spry now. If the guy never moved but to change the channel, he's not gonna catch you any time soon. And my father still knows my name. I can't be sure but I think it's only that they can't talk. Their tongues swell up and their throats expand—all of them. One of the early warning signs is slurred speech. They might be as smart as they ever were—see jogging—but they can't communicate except by screaming. I'd scream, too, if I were bleeding from my ears and my skin were melting off.

Zombies will not kill anything that moves. My dad hasn't bitten me. He could have, plenty of times. They're not harmless. I've had to get good at running and I have six locks on every door of the house. Even my bedroom, because my father can't be trusted. He hits me, still. His fist leaves a smear of blood and pus and something darker, purpler, on my face. But he doesn't bite me. At first, he barked and went for my neck at least once a day. But I'm faster. I'm always faster. He doesn't even try anymore. Sometimes he just stands in the living room, drool pooling in the side of his mouth till it falls out, and he looks at me like he remembers that strange night when he bit me before, and he's still ashamed. I laugh, and he almost smiles. He shambles back down the hall and starts peeling off the wallpaper, shoving it into his mouth in long pink strips like skin.

There's something else I know. It's hard to talk about, because I don't understand it. I don't understand it because I'm not a zombie. It's like a secret society, and I'm on the outside. I can watch what they do, but I don't know the code. I couldn't tell Channel 3 about this, even if they came to town with all their cameras and sat me in a plush chair like one of their endless Rockette-line of doctors. What makes you think they have intelligence, Miss Zielinski? And I would tell them about my father saying my name, but not about the river. No one would believe me. After all, it's never happened anywhere else. And I have an idea about that, too. Because people in Manhattan are pretty up on their zombie-killing tactics, and god help a zombie in Texas if he should ever be so unfortunate as to encounter a human. But here there's nothing left. No one to kill them. They own this town, and they're learning how to live in it, just like anyone does. Maybe Augusta always belonged to them and James Purington and the Dead River Company. All hail the oozing, pestilent kings and queens of the apocalypse.

This is what I know: one night, my father picked up our toaster and left the house. I'm not overly attached to the toaster, but he didn't often leave. I feed him good hamburger, nice and raw, and I don't knock him in his brainpan with a bat. Zombies know a good thing.

The next night he took the hallway mirror. Then the microwave, then the coffee-pot, then a sack full of pots and pans. All the zombie movies in the world do not prepare you to see your father, his hair matted with blood, his bathrobe torn and seeping, packing your cooking materiel into a flowered king-size pillowcase. And then one night he took a picture off of the bookshelf. My mother, himself, and me, smiling in one of those terrible posed portraits. I was eight or nine in the picture, wearing a green corduroy jumper and big, long brown pigtails. I was smiling so wide, and so were they. You have to, in those kinds of portraits. The photographer makes you, and if you don't, he practically starts turning cartwheels to get you to smile like an angel just appeared over his left shoulder clutching a handful of pins. My mother, her glasses way too big for her face. My father, in plaid flannel, his big hand holding me protectively.

I followed him. It wasn't difficult; his hearing went about the same time as his tongue. In a way, I guess it's a lot like getting old. Your body starts failing in all sorts of weird ways, and you can't talk right or hear well or see clearly, and you just rage at things because everything is slipping away and you're never going to get any better. If one person goes that way, it's tragic. If everyone does, it's the end of the world.

It gets really dark in Augusta, and the streetlights have all been shot out or burned out. There is no darker night than a Maine night before the first snow, all starless and cold. No friendly pools of orange chemical light to break the long, black street. Just my father, shuffling along with his portrait clutched to his suppurating chest. He turned toward downtown, crossing Front Street after looking both ways out of sheer muscle memory. I crept behind him, down past the riverside shops, past the Java Shack, down to the riverbank and the empty parking lots along the waterfront.

Hundreds of zombies gathered down there by the slowly lapping water. Maybe the whole of dead Augusta, everyone left. My father joined the crowd. I tried not to breathe; I'd never seen so many in one place. They weren't fighting or hunting, either. They moaned, a little. Most of them had brought something — more toasters, dresser drawers, light bulbs, broken kitchen chairs, coat racks, televisions, car doors. All junk, gouged out of houses, out of their old lives. They arranged it, almost lovingly, around a massive tower of garbage, teetering, swaying in the wet night wind. A light bulb fell from the top, shattering with a bright pop. They didn't notice. The tower was sloppy, but even I could see that it was meant to be a tower, more than a tower — bed-slats formed flying buttresses between the main column and a smaller one, still being built. Masses of electric devices, dead and inert, piled up between them, showing their screens and grey, lifeless displays to the water. And below the screens rested dozens of family portraits just like ours, leaning against the dark

plasma screens and speakers. A few zombies added to the pile—
and some of them lay photos down that clearly belonged to some
other family. I thought I saw Mrs. Halloway, my first grade
teacher, among them, and she treated her portrait of a Chinese
family as tenderly as a child. I don't think they knew who exactly
the pictures showed. They just understood the general sense they
conveyed, of happiness and family. My father added his picture
to the crowd and rocked back and forth, howling, crying, holding his head in his hands.

I wriggled down between a dark streetlamp and a park
bench, trying to turn invisible as quickly as possible. But they
paid no attention to me. And then the moon crowned the spikes
of junk, cresting between the two towers.

The zombies all fell to their knees, their arms outstretched to
the white, full moon, horrible black tears streaming down their
ruined faces, keening and ululating, throwing their faces down
into the river-mud, bits of them falling off in their rapture, their
eagerness to abase themselves before their cathedral. I think it
was a cathedral, when I think about it now. I think it had to be.
They sent up their awful crooning moan, and I clapped my
hands over my ears to escape it. Finally, Mrs. Halloway stood up
and turned to the rest of them. She dragged her nails across her
cheeks and shrieked wordlessly into the night. My father went to
her and I thought he was going to bite her, the way he bit me, the
way zombies bite anyone when they want to.

Instead, he kissed her.

He kissed her on the cheek, heavily, smackingly, and his face
came away with her blood on it. One by one the others kissed her
too, surrounding her with groping hands and hungry mouths,
and the moon shone down on her face, blanching her so she was
nothing but black and white, blood and skin, an old movie monster, only she wept. She wept from a place so deep I can't imagine it; she wept, and she smiled, even as they finished kissing her

and began pulling her apart, each keeping a piece of her for themselves, just a scrap of flesh, which they ate solemnly, reverently. They didn't squabble over it, her leg or her arm or her eyes, and Mrs. Halloway didn't try to fight them. She had offered herself, I think, and they took her. I know what worship looks like.

I was crying by that time. You would, too, if you saw that. I had to cry or I had to throw up, and crying was quieter. Your body can make calculations like that, if it has to. But crying isn't that quiet, really. One of them sniffed the air and turned toward me—the rest turned as one. They're a herd, if they are anything. They know much more together than they know separately. I wonder if, in a few decades, they will have figured out how to run Channel 3, and will broadcast *How to Recognize a Human in Three Easy Steps*, or *What We Know*.

They fell on me, which is pretty much how zombies do anything. They groped and pulled, but there were too many of them for any one to get a good grip, and I may not have killed one before but I wasn't opposed to the idea. I swung my fists and oh, they were so soft, like jam. I clamped my mouth shut—I knew my infection vectors as well as any kid in my generation. But they didn't bite me, and finally my father threw back his head and bellowed. I know that bellow. I've always known it, and it hasn't changed. They pulled away, panting, exhausted. That was the first time I realized how fragile they are. They're like lions. In short bursts, they'll eviscerate you and your zebra without a second thought. But they have to save up the strength for it, day in and day out. I stood there, back against the streetlamp, fingernails out, asthma kicking in because of course, it would. And my father limped over to me, dragging his broken left foot—they don't die but they don't heal. I tried to set it once and that was the closest I ever came to getting bitten before that night on the river.

He stood over me, his eyebrows crusted with old fluid, his eyes streaming tears like ink, his jaw dislocated and hanging, his cheeks puffed out with infection. He reached out and hooted gently like an ape. To anyone else it would have been just another animal noise from a rotting zombie, but I heard it as clear as anything: Caitlin, Caitlin, Caitlin. I had nowhere to go, and he reached for me, brushing my hair out of my face. With one bloody thumb he traced a circle onto my forehead, like a priest on Ash Wednesday. Caitlin, Caitlin, Caitlin.

His blood was cold.

After that, none of them ever came after me again. That's why I can have my nice little habit of opening the Java Shack and writing in my notebooks. These are the days of Punky Princesses, and I am safe. The mark on my forehead never went away. It's faint, like a birthmark, but it's there. Sometimes I meet one of them on the road, wandering dazed and unhappy in the daylight, squinting as if it doesn't understand where the light is coming from. When they see me, their eyes go dark with hunger—but then, their gaze flicks up to my forehead, and they fall down on their knees, keening and sobbing. It's not me, I know that. It's the cathedral, still growing, on the banks of the Kennebec. The mark means I'm of the faith, somehow. Saint Caitlin of the Java Shack, Patroness of the Living.

Sometimes I think about leaving. I hear Portsmouth is mostly clean. I could make that on my bicycle. Maybe I could even hotwire a car. I've seen them do it on television. The first time I stayed, I stayed for my father. But he doesn't come home much anymore. There's little enough left for him to scavenge for the church. He keeps up his kneeling and praying down there, except when the moon is dark, and then they mourn like lost children. Now, I think I stay because I want to see the finished cathedral, I want to understand what they are doing when they eat one of their own. If it's like communion, the way I understand it, or something else entirely. I want to see the world they're building out here in the abandoned capital. If maybe they're not sick, but just new, like babies, incomprehensible and violent and frustrated that nothing is as they expected it to be.

It's afternoon in the Java Shack. The sun is thin and wintry. I pour myself hot water and it occurs to me that apocalypse originally meant to uncover something. To reveal a hidden thing. I get that now. It was never about fire and lightning shearing off the palaces of the world. And if I wait, here on the black shores of the Kennebec, here in the city that has been ruined for as long as it has lived, maybe, someday soon, the face of their god will come up out of the depths, uncovered, revealed.

So on. So forth.

MIZ RUTHIE PAYS HER RESPECTS

Lucy A. Snyder

Andrew Dockholm straightened his navy blue JROTC uniform and stepped through the automatic doors leading to the Hillsonville Regional Airport's baggage claim area. He spotted a tall, silver-haired woman in an ankle-length black dress by the lone conveyor belt. She clutched a leather purse and a bouquet of yellow roses and white lilies in her left hand, and was leaning over to try to catch a small blue suitcase with her right. The woman looked just like her pictures on Facebook, except for the black dress; she was mostly dressed in flowery hippie clothes in those.

"Let me get that for you, Miz Ruthie!" Andrew shouldered his way through the sparse crowd so he could get to the light suitcase before his cousin did.

"Oh! Andrew. Hello there. I could've gotten that, but thank you." Ruthie blinked at him, looking surprised, then glanced past him, her expression darkening. "Is your mother or your father with you?"

"No ma'am. I got my regular driver's license last week, so I just came on out here in my truck after drill practice." Andrew beamed at her.

"Do your folks know you're picking me up?" She looked a bit worried, and maybe a touch suspicious.

"Not exactly, ma'am…. I got the feeling they don't cotton to you much. Don't know why 'cuz you seem like a real nice lady in your emails, and you always give me good loot in Mafia Wars, and we're family, right?"

Andrew's folks had never made the cause of their disapproval clear, although once when his pa had too much Wild Turkey and had gone on a drunken rant he'd called Miz Ruthie "That Frisco witch." His pa never had much compunction about calling women the b-word, so the witch thing had made Andrew curious, but later his pa denied having said it and went silent as a lowcountry clam about their cousin. Miz Ruthie had posted stuff supporting Obama on Facebook, but Andrew supposed he could turn the other cheek on that because women usually had stupid ideas about politics. And she'd posted stuff about doing Tarot readings, which his grandpa preached was Satanic, but Andrew had seen a Tarot deck at a gaming store once and as far as he could tell it was just paper and ink like a regular playing card deck. He didn't see what was so bad about it besides that one devil card. It wasn't like she was a Muslim or something.

"It's only right you want to pay your respects to my grandpa," Andrew continued. "The whole county came out for his funeral last weekend. It wouldn't be right to make a lady like you take a taxi or somethin'."

After all, Miz Ruthie had to be at least fifty, practically as old as his own grandma, but he knew better than to tell her that. Old ladies didn't like you pointing out that they were old. Andrew figured he wouldn't be much of a man if he didn't step up and offer to take his cousin out to the family graveyard. Besides, he liked showing off his new truck, a Dodge Ram with a hemi V8 engine. He'd worked three solid years of weekends and summers down at the sawmill to save up for it—had to get his pa to lie about his age to the owner at first—but at fourteen Andrew had been as big and strong as any sixteen-year-old. And besides, like his pa and grandpa had always said, all those labor laws were just dumb government meddling.

Ruthie still looked worried. "Well, I wouldn't want you to get in any trouble...."

"I ain't gonna get in no trouble! I stay out late all the time, and my pa don't care as long as I do my chores."

"What about your mama?"

Andrew blinked at her. "What about her? She don't wear the pants."

Despite Miz Ruthie's gentle protestations, Andrew insisted on carrying her suitcase out to his truck. He took a moment to pop the hood to show her the engine, clean and pretty as a prom queen's pussy, and tell her how fast it went up the road to Table Rock Mountain. And then they were off, speeding down the highway toward the turnoff to the old stone church where all their kin were buried, including Andrew's grandpa, the Reverend Robert M. Dockholm, who'd presided over New Bedrock Baptist Church for over thirty years.

"So are you going into Air Force ROTC in college?" Miz Ruthie asked, gesturing toward his uniform.

"No ma'am, I'm gonna be an Army Ranger. I already got it all worked out with the recruiter. I'm only in Air Force JROTC 'cuz that's all they have at my high school."

"What about college?" she asked.

"College? I already got a job, I don't need no college."

"Ah."

Andrew pulled his truck into the gravel parking lot in front of the old stone church; since it didn't have electricity or indoor plumbing, the congregation only used the 180-year-old building for weddings and funerals in good weather. The lights of the New Bedrock Baptist Church were visible on the hill beyond. The evening sky was a solid ceiling of grey clouds, and the piney air hung moist and heavy. Thunder rolled somewhere in the distance.

"Well, I'll do my best to keep this quick so you don't have to wait out here too long," Miz Ruthie said, glancing out the window at the ominous sky.

"Oh, I'm gonna go into the cemetery with you."

Miz Ruthie bit her lip. "It would probably be better if you just stayed here."

"No ma'am! It's gettin' dark out there, and what if you was to trip on a root, or twist your ankle in a gopher hole? I'd be failin' my duty if didn't escort you proper."

"Okay." She frowned; clearly she was turning something over in her mind. "But I need to pay my respects in my own way, and I want you to promise you won't interfere with me."

"Sure, I promise." He drew an X over his heart with his finger. "Soldier's honor."

"All right then." She opened her door and stepped out onto the gravel with her funeral bouquet, then gave him a sharp look. "You better remember your promise; if you don't like something, don't look."

Andrew squinted at her, wondering what she meant, and followed close behind as she made her way up the path into the graveyard. The first part of the cemetery was the oldest, some graves dating to the early 1800s. They walked among the mottled, decaying marble stones, some so worn that he could barely make out that there had ever been inscriptions on them. The ground was a patchwork of velvety dark moss, gravel-embedded soil, and short green grass.

Andrew ran his hands over the tops of the headstones as he walked, the worn stone rough and gritty. Some of these people were born before the nation had its independence. All had died before it was torn by the War Between the States. He felt a surge of pride; he and his JROTC squad had spent several weeks after school cleaning up the cemetery, clearing brush and weeds away from the old markers and headstones and crypts. His grandpa had told him they'd done a right fine job.

Old stones gave way to newer markers and crypts. The inscriptions became recognizable, and so were the family names. Hillson. Harris. Keller. Smith. Calhoun. Dockholm. Andrew watched as Miz Ruthie went to her mother's grave, pulled three lilies from the bouquet, and laid them on her headstone.

But then, instead of heading to the Reverend Dockholm's freshly-mounded grave near the edge of the trees, Miz Ruthie went to a headstone tucked back amongst the graves of townsfolk who weren't their kin, except maybe by marriage. She knelt at the forgotten grave, laid the bouquet down, and spent several minutes kneeling there with her head bowed.

Andrew tried to stand at easy attention while she paid her respects to whoever it was, but just as he was starting to feel really antsy she got up and headed toward his grandfather's resting place, her hands empty. Shouldn't she have some flowers to pay proper respects? Frowning, he followed her over to the grave.

She held up her hand. "Remember, you promised: no interfering."

She pulled a travel pack of Kleenex out of the pocket of her long black dress—

That's good, she's going to have a big ol' cry over him like my momma did, Andrew thought.

—which she shoved down the front of her dress, apparently into her cleavage. And then she unzipped the dress from neck to hem. Andrew felt his face flush crimson as she shrugged out of the dowdy old-lady garment, revealing that she was wearing a short stoplight-red cocktail dress and gartered fishnet stockings beneath. Miz Ruthie had a really nice ass, and Andrew felt his blush deepen as he realized he'd gotten a rubbery boner at the sight of her in the clingy satin. She was old enough to be his granny, for sweet Jesus' sake!

Miz Ruthie folded the black overdress and set it on a nearby headstone, then strode to the Reverend's grave and began dancing, sweeping the flowers off his headstone with her lean legs.

"Miz Ruthie, what are you doing?" Andrew was aghast.

"Paying all the respects I owe your grandfather." Her skirt rode up with each Rockette kick, and he saw a sterling silver flask strapped to the outside of her left thigh. "Remember, you promised. Crossed your heart and promised."

One she'd cleared the headstone of flowers, she stood facing the headstone with her legs on either side of the grave, did a half-squat and hiked her skirt up to her hips. She wasn't wearing any underwear. Andrew watched, horrified and hard, as she made a V with her fingers and pulled up on her pussy, and suddenly she was peeing in a strong arc right on the headstone, urine spilling down the words "In Loving Memory of the Reverend Robert M. Dockholm."

Andrew was rooted to the spot, unable to move or speak in his shock. A thousand thoughts crowded in his head, which was about 999 more than usually occupied the space. She was defiling his grandfather's grave! Vandalizing it! And she. Could. Pee. Standing. Up! Andrew had never heard of women doing such a thing. Was she one of those freaky chicks with a dick? He couldn't see anything like a penis, not even a little Cheeto-looking one like that kid in gym class had. No wonder his pa thought she was a witch!

Ruthie's pee stream faltered, stopped, and she swiveled around and did a deeper squat so that her ass was nearly touching the soil. And she began to shit, the poop coming out of her in a long, smooth coil, mounding in perfect circles like soft-serve on the grave. As she grimaced in concentration, gritting her teeth, grinding her hips in circles to squeeze out the poop *just so*, he began to suspect she'd been practicing. And also probably eating a whole lot of prunes on the plane ride from California.

Andrew's vision was starting to darken at the edges, his legs shaking beneath him, so he went with it and fell to his knees, shutting his eyes against his cousin's abominations and loudly repeating every prayer and psalm he could remember.

As he spoke, "The Lord is my strength and shield; my heart trusts in Him and I am helped," inside he was praying, *Dear God, strike this wicked witch down with your Almighty wrath, please dear God, oh please, strike her down.*

His hair rose on end, the air going electric, and a heartbeat later there was a sudden crack of lightning in the trees nearby and one of the tall pines shrieked as its trunk was sundered near the roots, and Andrew could hear it falling—

"Andrew, get out of the way!" Miz Ruthie shouted.

He opened his eyes to see the pine tree plummeting straight down toward his head, no time to stand up. He frog-hopped forward, but the tree slammed down on his right leg, pinning him to the mossy ground, the pain a bright blue spark arcing from his ankle right up into his spine.

Miz Ruthie was still in full squat, but was vigorously wiping herself clean with a handful of the Kleenex she'd stashed in her bra; she dropped the crumpled tissues neatly around her poo-swirl, completing the first-glance illusion that it was some kind of ice cream dessert. Then she stood, pulled her flask out of her thigh holster, unscrewed the cap, and poured the liquid inside over her shit sundae. Andrew smelled strong whisky. She stepped aside, pulled a packet of matches out of her bra, and lit up her pile, filling the air with the stench of burning feces.

Miz Ruthie strode over to him and squatted near his head, frowning down at him. He tried not to stare at the dark furry fringe peeking beneath the hem of her dress.

"Is your leg broken?"

"No, ma'am, I don't think so." His voice was a dry croak. He'd broken his leg when he fell off a pile of logs at the mill once, and aside from the initial pain his leg wasn't hurting nearly as badly as it had back then.

"Did you pray for God to strike me down?" Her sharp blue eyes bored down into his, daring him to tell her a lie.

He tried to shrink back into the tree's branches. "Yes, ma'am. I did. But...but you deserved it for what you done to my grandpa!"

She laughed at him. "Oh, I did, did I? Let me tell you a little something about just desserts, boy. Let me tell you a little something about that dead old bastard over there that you hold in such high regard.

"Dear ol' Uncle Bob there took over the church when I was about your age, still in high school. My best friend in the whole world was a girl named Jenny; she was the finest fiddle player in the whole state, sweet as orange blossom honey, smart. Would have made a hell of a doctor some day. One afternoon, one of her older cousins offered her a ride home from school, only he didn't take her home; he drove out to the old bridge and raped her. She was so wrecked she wouldn't even talk to me about what he'd done to her, but when she realized she was pregnant, she went to Uncle Bob for help. She thought he surely knew *everything*, and would make things right. And Uncle Bob, ever the student of Christ's wisdom and forgiveness, cussed her out for telling lies about her choir-boy cousin and accused her of being a whore. Jenny left the church in tears, went to her room and wrote me a letter, then went out to the woods behind her family's house and killed herself. Her father passed her suicide off as a hunting accident so she could be buried over there in this rusty old cemetery."

Ruthie nodded toward the headstone where she'd left her bouquet, then pointed a shaky finger at his grandfather's grave. "The Reverend Robert M. Dockholm might as well have loaded the shotgun, put it to Jenny's head and pulled the trigger. As far as I'm concerned, he murdered that girl. Bob deserved to be broken like he broke Jenny, deserved a load of buckshot right between his sanctimonious eyes, but instead he got thirty more years of respect as the pillar of the community, thirty years of ill-gotten wealth by spiritually blackmailing all the sick old folks in the county into signing their worldly possessions over to his church. Jenny's cousin at least had the decency to pick a fight in a biker bar and get his head caved in with a tire iron the year after he assaulted her, but that Bible-waving sack of shit over there got to enjoy a nice life and a nice quiet death. And so tonight he got me paying my respects the best way I know how."

Miz Ruthie stood up and put her fists on her hips, glaring down at Andrew. "There's a whole lot more you need to know about this fine little town and the people who live in it, but it's up to you whether you want to open your eyes and get a clue about the world, the *real* world, and get out of that nice warm pile of small-town bullshit you've been wallowing in. And here's clue number one: God isn't your personal hit man. I learned that a long time ago, because believe me, I prayed for Him to take out your grandfather. You pray for anyone else's death ever again, boy, you best be prepared for your own."

She inhaled like a diver preparing for a plunge. "So. You've got two choices here. Your first choice is to close your eyes and start praying again, pretending I'm not really here, and I'll call a cab to take me to the airport and call the VFD to come get this tree off you. You'll never have to hear from me again. Your second choice is you take my hand, I'll get the tree off you, and I'll get dressed and we'll go down the road to the Steak and Shake. I'll buy you a malt and tell you all about the skeletons in the family closet.

"So what's it gonna be, Andrew?"

The boy stared up at her, took his own deep breath, and held out his hand.

PARANOIA

You left the garage open when you left this morning,
the oven is still on, as well as the curling iron,
and all day no one's told you about the food stuck between your
front teeth.

Right now, your boss is reading your emails,
your children are having unprotected sex,
and that mysterious number on the phone bill?
Your spouse's lover. Who has AIDS.

Tonight, carbon monoxide will fill your home,
your taxes will be flagged for audit,
and your teenager will find inspiration in the writings of L. Ron
Hubbard.

Yes, it's true—your stories are derivative,
your poetry is doggerel,
and no one has made it past page three of your unsold novel.
(Not that it matters—all editors, agents, and publishers have con-
spired never to buy your work.)

That mole on you back? Cancer.
That cut on your finger? Gangrene.
That sore on your lip? Herpes. And it's spreading in unimagin-
able ways.

Friends say you are jealous, selfish, and a bad dresser;
Family says you are a disappointment, the black sheep, and unworthy of the will;
Co-workers report you are incompetent, lazy, and too hoggish
with the donuts at Friday breakfast,

and we all agree those jeans make your ass look huge, which is
why no one will ever truly love you.

That is blood in your stool,
a terrorist living across the street,
and a pedophile teaching your child.

Lock your doors.
Duct tape your windows.
Grow your own food.
Talk to no one.

They will get you.
It will get you.
We will get you.
You are not safe.

—*Kurt Dinan*

HUSH

Kelly Barnhill

They decide to buy a house. They can barely afford it, but he has been given a raise, and her company is expanding, and any day now her womb will bear fruit, her belly will swell, and they will, at last, be a family.

This is what they think when they arrive at the house with the realtor. Neither says it out loud. She rests her hand on her narrow middle, as though by sheer force of will she can make it bear.

The house is beautiful. A wealthy man's house. A foundation, uncracked and clean. Walls painted in rich hues of cranberry, linden and gold. The glass is original and warbles from sash to sash. All of this is barely visible from the sidewalk. What *is* visible are four large trees, one planted at each corner of the house. Their branches wrap and arch around each face as though holding it up.

"I love trees," the new wife says.

"Me too," says her husband. The leaves rub their papery skins together as the husband and wife step happily over the threshold, as though welcoming them home. The realtor scurries behind.

Inside, the husband says, "Look at the nursery, honey. Look at the library." He does not say how pale she is. He does not say that her sadness has become palpable. He smells it. He tastes it. It is slightly briny and off, like a tide pool. The first thing he does when he arrives at work is gargle the harshest mouthwash he can find. He feels that he could gargle for hours.

Inside, while standing in a square of sunlight on the bare master bedroom floor, she says, "It's perfect." The realtor and the husband both think she is referring to the house. She is not. Through the doorway, toddling down the hall, she sees a nest of pale blonde curls. She sees five downy fingers curving around the door jamb. A baby voice hums, off tempo and off key. She turns to her husband. "Love at first sight," she says and kisses him.

For the first time since he can remember, he smells lilac on her skin and tastes honey in her mouth. *At last,* he thinks. *At last,* she thinks. Within the week, their offer is accepted and they prepare for the move.

Their first morning in the new house, she stops taking her fertility pills. In truth, she does not decide to do it. She simply opens the pack as always, slurps her first sip of tea, which is always too hot and burns the roof of her mouth, and one by one, drops the pills into the drain and runs the disposal. She listens to the whir and metallic crunch, to the whoosh of water to wash it away. She does not think about why. *Why* doesn't exist today. Only the click of the switch. Only the sure hum of organized machinery accomplishing what it was designed to accomplish. It is complete and satisfying.

On top of the refrigerator, a shadow slips in and out of view. Not a shadow, really. It cannot be called a shadow, for it is made of light. And powder. And gossamer. It forms and unforms, a joy of being and unbeing. The young wife sees the light-shadow as it curves and straightens in the gap between the refrigerator and the cupboard. A long, dark gap where anything could hide. The shadow has an elbow. Then a pink foot. Then a nest of pale curls. Then a single open eye. She sips again and runs the disposal one more time, just to be sure, although what she wanted to be sure of she could not say. The being (or unbeing) in the gap begins to laugh—a bubbling, joyful laugh. A laugh that reaches into the young wife's heart, squeezes it tenderly, and with a click, whir and a metallic crunch, removes it completely.

"Oh," the young wife says, clutching at her chest. She feels nothing there, nothing beating. She does not miss it. The tree branches tap on the window, urgently, as though in a great wind, but no wind blows. She ignores them. She walks upstairs to shower and dress for work.

That day, she takes a leave of absence from her job.

"To help unpack," she says to her boss. "So we can settle in," she says to her husband.

Her husband takes her out to lunch. She wears a silk blouse, open at her throat, and a skirt that skims along her thighs. He watches as she crosses and uncrosses her legs, watches the line of muscles undulating under fine gauge wool and slippery lining. They sit outside, enjoying the sun after days and days of rain. The air, the street, and the sidewalk are all fresh and bright and clean. He is overcome by a sense of hopeful possibility. And she looks so good. He hears the swish of her nylons and the whoosh of her skirt with each crossing and uncrossing of those long legs. He remembers the wedding dress, how it frothed around her, how he tore it to shreds in their bridal suite, how they fell upon it, howling with laughter and sweaty love.

"Are you all right?" she says. She shakes her head. "What I mean to say is, is it all right?"

"Yes," he sputters. He pulls his eyes away from the curve of her hip. "Yes, of course it's all right. How long do you get?"

"Two weeks."

He raises his glass. "Two weeks, then." They clink and sip, and all the while, he imagines kneeling before her, grabbing her skirt, hooking inside, hanging on for dear life.

She does not unpack. She paints instead. She sets up eight canvases in the nursery and one stool that she moves from easel to easel. She has no idea what she is painting, and only applies a few brushstrokes of red and blue and greyish white to one canvas before moving on to the next.

The pale-headed figure crouches in the corner of the room. It has no face, save the one that flickers for an instant on its featureless oval and then disappears.

"I want it," the pale figure says.

"No, no," the young wife says absently.

"I *want* it," the figure says again, stamping what would have been its foot.

The young wife clucks her tongue. "So *greedy*. You already have one. You don't need two."

"I want the heart," the figure says, its voice sounding less and less like a toddler. "You can give it to me. It's not hard."

Suddenly, the wife realizes that the brush in her hand is not a brush at all. It's a very light, very sharp knife, with a slightly curved blade that gleams in the light. She looks at the picture forming on the canvas. It looks so very much like—

"You're right," she says, pressing the tip of the knife onto her index finger's pad until a bright spot of blood appears, like a jewel. "It would not be hard at all."

Five days later, he only wants to sleep. Every chance he gets, his body sinks into the negative space next to his wife, his eyes weight and close, and—though he does not know this part—he begins to snore, loudly, sensuously, and with gusto.

Eight times during the night he is awakened by the sound of singing. *Blacks and bays*, the voice sings. *"Dapples and greys."* He starts and sits up in bed. He looks accusingly at his wife. She is fast asleep, her jaw closed tight as always. He shrugs, assumes he must be dreaming, and goes back to sleep. Twenty minutes later, the voice comes back, *Coach and six a little horses.*

"Cut it out," he says to his wife.

"Hmmmm," she responds, kissing the air with her lips. "Maybe tomorrow, honey, okay," she murmurs without waking up.

He curves away from her, forcing his eyes to stay open. He peers through the darkness past the open door and into the hall, as if he expects something to come toddling in. *No,* he thinks, *not toddling. Why would I think toddling? Walking.* But nothing does, and soon, again, he sleeps.

Nothing comes into the room, of course, because something is already in the room. A small something that hovers over the bed, bumping every once in a while on the ceiling. A small something with pale curls and pink hands and two open eyes. It sees them. The trees tap against the window, more forcefully now. The small something bares its teeth and hisses. The hiss becomes a hum, and the hum becomes a song. *Hush.*

The young wife buys flowers—shade-loving flowers—and plants them in the boulevard and along the front walkway. The yard is more heavily shaded than before and the trees seem bigger, leafier, their branches pressed like arms around the house.

She sees her new neighbors out for their walks, or going from their cars into their houses. She waves. They do not wave back. They cross the street and turn away from her as they walk by. She makes a plan. She will bake cookies. She will make greeting baskets for each of her neighbors. She will fill them with jars of jam and olives and wildflower honey. She will decorate each one with a ribbon and a bouquet of dried flowers tied together with a bow of sweetgrass. This she decides to do as she walks up the stairs, and this she plans to do as she opens the door. But in the house, in the house is something else altogether. The light filters through the trees, giving the house a strange green glow as though it had been submerged in a quiet pond. Outside, airplanes and cars rumble and roar while birds shout from branch to branch. Inside, it is silent except for the sound of wet breathing. Silent, except for the sound of a heart, stolen, hoarded and hidden. A treasure. A pale head spins itself in and out of view. An upturned nose. Pink lips. A mouth full of teeth.

"Hello," she says to its formed, then unformed, then formed again self. Her voice is high, musical, lovely. A mother's voice. "Hello, my darling. Who loves you?"

You do, says the pale head. *You do.* It is not a toddler's voice anymore. It is sharp; it clicks; it is full of knives.

After two weeks in the house, most of their possessions remain boxed. Every day, the husband attempts to unpack one—just one—but the effort saps him entirely. His wife paints ceaselessly. She does not unpack. He supposes that some men might resent this, but he does not.

He arrives home from work, his shoulders slumping from fatigue and worry. His wife has continued to pale. She has continued to thin. He worries she might disappear altogether. He places his briefcase on the entryway chair and hangs his raincoat on the hook. His footsteps echo strangely through the main floor of the house, as though it were empty. It is not empty. They have the living room set that her sisters chipped in for and the dining room set that belonged to his grandmother. They have rugs and a piano and boxes upon boxes. Still, his footsteps echo, as if he were the only person in a large cavern. As if he were the only person alive.

He sits on the couch and feels his body sink in. He unbuckles his belt and undoes the waistband button. His wife approaches from the kitchen. Her feet are bare and pale and they do not make a sound on the gleaming wood floors. Her husband wonders briefly if she is floating, but he does not check. She hands him a glass of red wine.

"Sit down," he says. She tilts her head toward him and his heart breaks. *Oh*, he thinks, *how pale! How thin! And oh! Those dark circles under those pretty eyes!*

She shrugs. "I need to finish." And she whispers toward the stairs and disappears in the green.

When she is upstairs, the door closes with a soft click. He sips, rubs his belly impatiently. He has always been fit, but for the last two weeks, he has started to bloat. He would exercise but he is so very tired. He rests the wine glass against his teeth. She is silent. Then she is not.

Hush you bye, she sings, *don't you cry.* He slides the rim of his glass between his upper and lower incisors and bites down hard. The glass is cool and sharp in his mouth. He leaves it there for a moment, wondering at the taste of wine and quartz and blood, before spitting it all into his hand. He does not get up.

In their third week, he asks her a question.

"Can I see? Your paintings I mean."

They eat in the dining room, although boxes line the walls and hide under the table. He does not like eating in the dining room, and feels, on principle, that they are not dining room people. But there are too many boxes in the living room, and they can no longer reach the couch. Somewhere, somewhere deep, he wonders how there are this many boxes; surely they didn't start out with this many. Could it be that the moving company brought over someone else's by mistake?

She has made chicken cacciatore with buttered green beans and dark red wine. The light in the house has become greener in the last week, the trees at the four corners now so tall that they dwarf the house. Earlier that day, as he approached his front door, a leaf fell from the tree and smacked him in the face. It was a gigantic leaf, about the size of a sheet of notebook paper. He looked at it for a while. It was stiff with a warm sheen. Just looking at it made him feel warm. Having no clue at all what would make the leaves grow so big, he made a plan to mail it to his old biology professor and slipped the leaf into his briefcase. By the time he walked into the house, he had forgotten about it.

"My paintings," she says. She looks down at her plate and blushes. "No," she says. "No, I'd rather you didn't."

He shrugs. "When you're ready," he says and pushes away from the table, his belly feeling distended and uncomfortable. He kisses her on the top of her head. "I'll be upstairs unpacking." In truth, he will only unpack one box. Afterward, he will fall heavily onto the bed and snore. When he wakes, there will be three boxes where the unpacked box once stood. He will not notice.

She watches him while he sleeps. She does this every night. By now, the boxes block the stairway. For the last four mornings, he has had to climb over them like a mountaineer on his way to work. But tomorrow, they will reach the ceiling. They will block the hallway, jam the bedroom door, and probably squeeze out the windows. They know this or they do not. Either way, they do nothing to stop it.

"The heart," says the sharp, clicking voice. "I need the heart."

"No," she says, "not tonight. Look at him. Isn't he *lovely*?"

"Not lovely. Ours. I need his heart. We need it." Outside, the trees groan and rustle. The plaster next to the window begins to crack. The child hisses, throws its fleshy body to the wall. It has a face now, and heavy hands that hang down to its dimpled knees. It has a back that hunches over its growing weight and a mouth full of sharp, sharp teeth. The young wife loves the child. *Loves* it.

There is a knife on the bedside table. It is light and sharp and curved. It was not there a moment ago, but is there now. It gleams invitingly.

"Fine," she says. "But no dessert." She picks up the knife and holds it to his red and white striped pajamas. "It doesn't hurt," she says to her sleeping husband. "I promise." But the moment she presses the blade to his chest, the cold metal smokes, crackles and disappears. The child hisses and spits upon the floor. It holds its hand as if it has touched something hot. She unbuttons his pajamas and sees an oak leaf, ridiculously large, that curves around his chest.

"Get away!" the child yells at the window. "Get away!" But the window warbles, quakes and shatters. The husband's eyes snap open and he looks into his wife's open mouth. She is singing, he thinks. Or crying. But he hears nothing over the tinkling of glass, the groan of bending wood, as though something outside is squeezing the house in its tight wooden fist. Something near the window hisses and snarls, though what it is he cannot see. What he sees is this: a crush and flutter of leaf and blossom and ripening fruit; a woman in a dress that flows and roots and bears; a house made of skin and flesh and beating hearts, a family made of wood and water and song.

And he is happy.

And she is happy.

In a burst of strength and agility that shocks him, he reaches out, grabs the thing at the window by its sticky arm and pulls it into the bed, wraps it in the oversized oak leaf and hangs on tight to both woman and child as the house around them groans, cracks and leans.

The child hiccoughs and cries, and the body of his wife twines into his—a rose, a briar—a continuous loop of skin on skin on skin. He feels the weight of his soul lift and escape in a slow, soft sigh, in a jolt of the hips, in a brief stab of joy.

* * *

The next door neighbor hears the first thump. And the second. And the third. Though he does not enjoy the outdoors, the neighbor slides the patio door back and slips outside to investigate. Eight boxes tumble out of the window and onto the lawn, rolling to the sidewalk and into the street. Then nine, then ten. Broken glass laces second story window, glinting like tinsel at the edges. Eleven. Twelve.

"They haven't even goddamned unpacked yet?" the neighbor says out loud, though no one is around. "Goddamn crazies buying that goddamn house and waking the neighborhood with their goddamn squabbles." In truth, he has never heard a single cross word, though he assumes there must be. This is why newlyweds make poor neighbors. The squabbling. He calls the police to report a domestic disturbance.

By the time the police arrive, the entire neighborhood is in the street. They interview an impossibly old lady who says she came outside when she heard a large crack. She thought it was a bomb. She assumed, of course, that it was the Russians. Or that other dreadful man. What's his name? With the beard. But it wasn't. It was the trees.

The police stand in front of the house. They open their notebooks, turn blank pages, bring the caps of their pens to their mouths and bite the nibs in their teeth. They write nothing.

Jesus, what would they write?

The house is invisible. Or not invisible, just obliterated. All they can see is an enormous tree. A tree the size of a house. A tree with three chimneys peeking through the branches.

In the coming months, holes will be drilled into the wood, but the only signs of life will be aphids, lichen and loam. They will examine the expelled boxes. They will find things that they can not understand: a box of antique baby clothes, an ancient bible with every other page ripped out, the skeletal remains of a pregnant woman, and lastly, a large box containing a single human heart. It will still beat.

SANDBOYS

Richard Wright

When Terence saw them sitting just below the tide line, where wet brown sand supplanted fine, light powder, he thought them an optical illusion brought on by the elixir of tequila, tears and exhaustion. They stubbornly refused to disappear as he squinted, and he changed his mind. They weren't an illusion. They were a cruel joke played by one of the many people he had disappointed. How they knew where he was baffled him. Since selling the flat and quitting work, he had fled to this desolate, out-of-season retreat, contacting no one.

The salt-heavy wind off the water bit into his eyes as he tried to make out details of the shapes from the steps of the mobile home, but he was too far away. The outline was clear though. There were two of them; sand sculptures, each in the shape of a little boy, looking out across the North Sea. From where he stood, they looked like his son, Gabriel. Grief garroted his throat, clenching it hard, and he let gravity stumble him down the steps onto the crest of the winter dunes.

The mobile home was one of six lined along the marram grass, surrounded by a rotting picket fence that deterred vandals only in principle. Come summer, the homes would be spruced up and rented to tourists keen to brave the northeast coast of England with its wild Norwegian winds, but during the bleak months of winter they were the skeletal corpses of good times past. The owner, who lived five miles up the coast in the town of Hannah's Bell, had been shocked at Terence's interest in renting one through to March, had even attempted to talk him out of the idea, to no avail. Terence felt that he belonged there. Desolation owned him, and he would embrace it.

As he staggered down the slope of the dune, his feet slid in loose sand and he toppled, knocking the wind from his lungs as he rolled to the beach, sharp blades of grass poking him rudely. When he flopped to rest his breathing was ragged, and his sharp panting morphed to violent gagging. Turning his head to the side, he vomited hard, his stomach shoving a burning blend of bile and spirits out of his mouth and nose, bringing more tears to his eyes as his face purpled. The stench of tequila clouded around him, making the urge to vomit worse, until he was dry heaving uncontrollably.

Finally, it ended, and he flopped onto his back, gasping as his bloodshot stare took in the harsh grey sky. A seagull drifted on the wind, wings outstretched as it cast beady eyes across the sea to Europe and beyond. Raising a weak hand to wipe away the sand caking his vomit-moistened cheeks, he wondered how many times he had gazed across the roiling waters in recent weeks, a bottle in one hand, a cigarette in the other. Looking for Gabe.

Somewhere out there, on the continent, his baby boy might be looking back. Did a one-year-old know what he had lost? Not even that, not even one year old. Gabriel was only six months in this world when Nancy had called time on Terence's future, walking out and taking his son with her. It had been bad when she was in London, far to the south, and his time with his son measured only hours per month. Now she had made for the continent and taken his purpose for living with her.

Did a one-year-old baby know what a father was? Did a baby

care at all? He knew it was selfish to hope that Gabe did, to wish the knowledge of loss on an innocent whom he loved, but if he shared nothing else with his son, if the fog of grief was the only bond they had left, then surely that was better than nothing at all. New tears burned his eyes, like neat tequila on a dry throat, but he was used to them and the breathless shriveling of the chest that came with them.

Heaving himself up, he looked along the ragged, seaweed-strewn beach. The shapes were still there, and now they were unmistakable. Any thought that they might be detritus cast forth by the waves was impossible to sustain. He could make out the texture of the packed sand that gave the rough-hewn sculptures form. Each bore Gabriel's likeness like a stamp. The set of the shoulders, the sweet, curious tilt of the head—somebody had come out here in the morning, while the tide was turning and sleep still claimed him, and shaped these to cause him pain.

Who would do that to him?

Too many people, each of whom he had abandoned in a different way, until there was nobody left to betray.

Cold seeped through him, and he couldn't tell whether it was the deathly chill of a Northumbrian winter or his own leaking shame that numbed his flesh. Standing, a weary defiance against the sickness and dehydration he had inflicted on himself, he fumbled with the zipper of his jacket, finally slotting it correctly into place and drawing it to the neck. A quiet, familiar anger was building in him, prompted by his own self-disgust. Had he really fallen so far that childish taunts had this power over him?

Apparently so, when the thought of stepping closer to those two simple shapes froze his legs into numb inactivity. Terence stood there, listening to the chorus of the water, and imagined striding across the beach and destroying those sculptures, smashing them to powder with his feet, stamping them back into the beach that had birthed them.

Did he wish, in his secret heart, that Gabe had not been born, that his son could be undone, and a distraught father's desperate grief with him?

"What sort of man would wish that?" His voice was a sandpaper croak, but only the elements were there to mock it. The sea replied by crashing against the black, rocky headlands flanking the beach. The wind sighed of loss and sorrow.

Many things had snapped within Terence of late, so much so that it was becoming a daily occurrence. Each fiber of his old self that broke felt like a line mooring him to sanity, and he could not say how close he was to floating free entirely. The sandboys were the cause of a new breakage, and the fresh anger in him was hot enough to move him forward.

Head down against the icy wind, face taut and white with rage, he marched toward the sculptures, violence wrapped around his heart. In outline, the two figures were perfect representations of Gabriel as he had been six long months ago, and when Terence closed his eyes he ached with a longing so deep it almost swamped his fury. Both figures were identical, as though cast from the same mold.

Terence stepped in front of the first sandboy. In detail, the figure, sitting with hands placed calmly on its tiny knees, was less impressive than at a distance. Crude scrapes indicated the direction of Gabe's baby hair. The lips were a simple line, the eyes mere shallows thumbed into the face. The ears were poorly formed, protruding at the correct angle, but featureless. The sandboy had no fingernails, which further angered Terence. Gabriel was perfect. These half-foot mockeries were not. That wasn't *right*.

Unable to contain his hurt and rage any longer, he raised his foot to stamp the image away.

The sandboy moved, a motion so achingly slow that Terence almost didn't notice in time. Only the damp sand falling away in fractured clumps from beneath the figure's plump chin told him it was happening.

With excruciating care, the sandboy raised its head and looked at him, just as Gabe had the last time they had seen one another, in another man's apartment in London, his wife watching carefully from the kitchenette. Terence had said goodbye.

"Bye bye Gabe. Bye bye."

Gabe had stared, and then shaken his head in anxious denial. In that moment Terence's heart had broken irreparably, and his future was erased.

The angle of the sandboy's head was curious. *I know you,* that angle said. *I don't know why or how, but I know your face. I like your face. You're somebody important.*

Who are you?

Heart skipping, blinking stupidly, Terence looked at the other figure. It, too, was turning to look at him, sand pattering away to leave horrible gaps in the perfect line of its neck. It had the same knowledge burned into its posture. Familiarity. A semblance of remembrance. An understanding, deep within, that the man it stared at was significant.

Who are you?

"I don't know anymore." His breath was snatched away by the biting wind. "I don't know what I'm for, if it isn't to hold you."

Terence didn't hear his own words, though he felt them brush past his lips. The sandboys, garroted by their own painful motion, looked blindly up at him, expressionless mannequins once more.

Fear at what was happening, that he might have drunk away his own sanity, flushed Terence's curiosity away. Pumping out from his heart, it gushed into his legs, and he smashed his foot across the face and chest of the sandboy beneath him. Sand flew in dark, damp clumps, but the scream he had feared the tiny figure might give did not come, and he stamped down again, and again, and again, until he was breathless, until he had crushed the sandboy back into the beach, until all trace of his son was gone.

Again.

Resting his hands on his skinny thighs, sucking in breath that escaped in explosive clouds of vapor, Terence looked down at what he had done. Where there had been a little boy, there was now only scattered sand. Nothing to touch. Nothing to hold.

With a hoarse sob, Terence fell to his knees, moisture soaking into the filthy denim of his jeans, and clawed through the mess he had made. There were tears on his face, streaks of warmth that turned icy within seconds of exposure to the wind. Clawing desperately at the sand, he pulled it into a pile, trying to refashion what was lost, claim something back, but he lacked the skill, and the sand would not hold the shape. When he gave up, he had nothing but packed dirt beneath his fingernails and a boy-shaped hole in his heart.

Yet this time, he had a second chance. Looking up, he saw to his horror and shame that the remaining sandboy was no longer looking at him. Instead, it looked across the sea, hollow eyes seeking the horizon. Its neck was no longer ragged with lost sand. It was perfect again, as though the figure had never looked longingly back at him, recognition in the cock of its head.

"No. That wasn't me. I wouldn't hurt you. I'm not that man."

The sandboy stared away, motionless and mournful, and Terence could no longer be sure it had moved at all. Resting back on his haunches, he joined the mourning, his fingers still brushing absently through the grit-guts of the boy he had destroyed as the grey waters frothed and mocked him.

Time passed, and the tide reached its lowest ebb, turning on a schedule established long before men knew grief, and beginning the long voyage back to the figures far up the beach.

Terence watched the deep, cold waters crawl ever closer and wondered what would happen if he let them swallow him. The cold would wipe his mind, but that would only actualize what he felt within. It would be a relief to be so overpowered that thoughts could not form in his head and pain could not boil in his heart.

The sea would rob his muscles of power. Sitting limply on the beach as the minutes became hours, unable to find reason to move, this too felt like poor reason not to let the waters take him.

He would drown. This was nothing new either. If the North Sea drowned him, there would be a rapid end to suffering. Terence drowned daily in the shabby mobile home on the dune, except he never died, and woke each morning to start it all again.

The North Sea would kill him, but Gabriel was gone, so he was already dead. The North Sea offered him an absolute ending, desirable and so easy to claim. He would still be dead, but he would no longer have to live through it.

Eyes hollow, jaw slack, Terence hauled himself back to his feet. Endless grey waters waited for him. The sea was so deep and could smother so much.

Terence took a dead man's step toward it. The second step was easier, and the third happened without any thought or effort at all, much as used to happen when life was good and Terence felt free.

The sea would set him free. It would cleanse him of grief, and pain, and life.

Terence stopped in the instant between the third and fourth step. It was not his intention to pause, to give his urge for an ending a second to falter, but there was a noise. Something on the edge of hearing, or the edge of his mind. Something longing.

The weight settled back into his flesh and bones in an avalanche moment, but he knew he could start again. A fifth step would be a struggle. A sixth would be lighter. How many steps to the water? Thirty? All he had to do was ignore that subtle call-ing, keep his head down, not look back.

Terence looked back.

The sandboy had shifted, had tilted its head to follow him, causing crumbling cracks to reform along the line of movement. There was a damp clump of sand on its lap, and a hole in its throat.

When Terence looked at its face, he thought he heard words.

Don't go.

Don't leave me.

Again.

Too cruel. Terence screamed, shrill and infantile, his torso curving inward as his lungs emptied, spittle spraying over his drawn back lips. There were no words in his reply. It was an in-choate rejection of his worst fear and secret knowledge.

Gabe believed that Terence left him. Where there had once been warmth and love and strength, there was suddenly a deep emptiness that his son hadn't yet developed words to name. Was it a hollowness to match what Terence felt now, a sudden aware-ness that the world was no longer right, that parts of it that had been so fundamentally reliable were now vanished entirely?

Yes. Terence thought it might be very much like that.

Sucking in air, the nerves in his teeth stabbing cold at him, he babbled explanations. "I didn't leave! I couldn't leave! You left! You left me, Gabe!"

"Why aren't you here?"

The sandboy looked back at him, knowing only that Terence had been prepared to leave, that his pain had caused him to take meek, selfish steps away.

"I was trying to do the right thing." Pathetic, even to his own ears. Especially to his own ears. Running away was easy, every-thing else was hard.

Looking back over his shoulder at the sea, he tried to recapture the sense of comfort it had offered him, but now there was only the cold promise of loneliness, edging ever closer, wave by wave. Soon it would reach where he stood, and beyond.

Panic rinsed through him as the implications landed hard. Soon the tide would be in, and he would lose the boy.

Again.

Terence turned and was not surprised to see that it no longer gazed up at him. It looked out at the sea once more, only this time it was not with calm longing. Now Terence read fear in its posture, washing off it and polluting the air with half-formed terrors. Did it sense change approaching? Did it know it was going to be taken away from him?

Did it trust, to its very core, that he would keep it safe?

Rubbing his fingers against his stubble, Terence began to turn very slowly on the spot, a low moan escaping his lips. What could he do? The tide was coming in. He couldn't stop it. Nobody could. The North Sea was fate at its most inexorable.

Nobody could stop fate.

Terence hadn't even tried. While he would protest vociferously, his secret self knew that he had allowed Gabe to be taken from him. A hundred excuses had rolled him over. Gabe was too young to be parted from his mother. The courts would always favor her position. It was easier to be raised by a single mother than a single father.

All reasons. All excuses. In truth, Terence had not fought for his child because he had decided that he was fated to lose him.

How would he explain that to Gabe, if his son ever came to ask? What words would make it right? How could a son believe he was worth anything when his own father had refused to fight for him?

Something snapped inside him, but this time the feeling was not desolate and helpless. This time, Terence was set free.

Hands dropping away from his face, he stopped his slow,

shambolic pirouette, and faced up the beach, beyond the frightened figure with seaweed at its feet. Nothing stood between the waters and that tiny shape but Terence, and this time he was going to *try*.

Scanning the dry dunes, desperation welled up in him. How long had he whined and procrastinated as the waters turned back toward them? At this time of year the tides moved quickly. If he was lucky, he had half an hour.

"I'll be back," he muttered at the child of the beach, then set off at a weak run. This time, he meant it.

Terence made three trips, his arms full on each return leg. It took fifteen minutes of scouring the long grasses of the dunes and the small valleys between them, of combing the tide line and the detritus-filled recesses further up the beach. He would have hunted longer, but time and tide were against him. Already, in those brief minutes, the waters had covered half the distance to the sandboy, who looked achingly small and helpless against them.

When Terence returned the third time he dropped to his knees next to the boy, driftwood spilling from his arms. For long seconds he knelt there, bent over his knees, desperately heaving for breath. It had been a long time since he had worked himself so hard, and he listened to his heart hammering out its complaint, to the wheeze of his lungs ballooning and clenching to pull cold air into him. The tang froze the soft palette at the back of his mouth, but made him feel savagely alive.

With no time to fully recover, he forced himself to keep moving. Lungs still working like bellows, he crawled in front of the sandboy, Gabriel in a thousand thousand flecks of silica, and began to scoop up a crude wall of sand. Working quickly and clumsily, he packed the wall as tight as he could. How deep was the tide here? Not deep at all, for they were only a foot or so away from the tide line itself. The wall needed to be only inches high.

Too aware of time, refusing to look at the waters, pretending he couldn't hear their gentle, sinister wash ever more clearly with each passing minute, he worked the wall around the sculpture in a tight ring, and then snatched up the plastic bags he had gathered from the dunes, five dirty castaways from picnics long gone, and pushed them against the wall. By piling sand up behind them, he made the barrier a sandwich of hard packed sand with the waterproof plastic in the centre. The pebbles he had gathered went outside that, with the driftwood pinning them in place.

Terence was pushing that driftwood against the tide side of the wall, despairing at how flimsy and fragile a defense it was, when he felt ice cold water seep into his trousers. Leaping up and back as though the brine were acid, he discovered that the sea was upon them.

Too soon.

Terence looked down, found the sandboy looking up at him, and couldn't tell whether the terror in the air between them was his or the boy's. The wall looked flimsy with the sea lapping gently at the outer boundary, a pebble laid to trip fate.

The sandboy would be taken from him after all, and Terence's face creased up at the finality of the thought, but this time it did not stop him from fighting.

Terence threw himself into the shallow surf, scarcely noticing the cold sucking feeling from his legs, his nicotine-stained fingers scooping desperately at the beach in front of his tiny wall, his tiny boy. Great handfuls of sand flew over his shoulder, sodden with freezing water, but he couldn't dig fast enough. Water filled his tiny trench as it crept inward, and soon the ice-pains in his knuckles were too great to keep trying.

Terence watched as the water seeped past his defenses, ignoring stones and driftwood, finding gaps in his plastic-proofed defenses. He cried when the water began to puddle at the sandboy's toes. Climbing behind the futile wall, he sat behind the figure, folding his freezing hands gently around its shoulders as he sobbed.

Terence felt the sandboy's legs and feet become mush as he whispered to it. "I'm here," he muttered, over and again, the words lost in his choked grief, but the heart understanding the content. "I'm here. I'm here. I'm here."

Before the end, before the base of the sculpture melted away and the torso and shoulders collapsed in his arms and left nothing but sand crushed against his chest and lap, the sandboy turned its head, ever so slowly, and looked up at him. The eyes were blank, but at they same time they were Gabe's brilliant baby blues.

The boy was terrified, but knew Terence had stayed for him.

The sculpture collapsed, the waist giving way beneath Terence's hands, the chest toppling forward over the top of them, the head, still looking back, splashing into the foam.

Soon there was nothing, but Terence didn't move. Hunched over, the icy water barely reaching the top of his thighs, he sobbed savagely as the beach reclaimed what it had given him, and left him alone.

It felt as though he would never stop crying.

But eventually he did.

When he could draw a steady breath, he stood, finally aware that much of his shivering came from cold rather than grief. Exhausted, noticing with dull surprise that the light was failing and the evening was approaching, Terence limped up to the mobile home. Tonight he would sleep there. Tomorrow he would pack. There was fighting to be done, a long road to walk, and a tide to turn back.

Terence would try. If he could give Gabe nothing else, he would gift him the attempt, and perhaps one day, hold his boy again.

FOR MY NEXT TRICK I'LL
NEED A VOLUNTEER

Gary A. Braunbeck

"What is done out of love always happens
beyond good and evil." **Note #153**

—Friedrich Nietzsche, *Beyond Good and Evil*

Staring at the gun lying on his desk, his left hand holding
a pencil as he doodled on a piece of scrap paper, Detective Bill Emerson wondered if physical evil and moral
goodness were somehow intertwined, like the strands
of a double helix encoded into the DNA of the universe. Man
was supposedly created to know wrong from right, to feel outrage at everything monstrous and evil, yet he sometimes
thought—especially tonight—that the scheme of creation itself
was monstrous; the rule of life was to get your butt through the
door and take that smack from the doctor's hand and pull in
your first breath so you could then be set adrift, unprepared, unwarned, and unarmed, in a charnel-house cosmos packed from
end to end with imploding stars, lost souls, moldering synapses,
and bloodstains inside chalk outlines; and in thinking of these
things, he again wondered if God's love (or the love of Who or
Whatever was in charge of the freak show) was measurable only
through the enjoyment He-She-Them-or-It seemed to take in the
suffering of the innocent—but then he remembered Van Gogh's

Starry Night, the smell of fresh-baked bread, the photographs by Lewis Hine, anything with Buster Keaton in it, "…we are the hollow men…" and kindheartedness. Not that any of it helped much right now, but you took what you could find.

"What the hell are you doing?" came a voice from the doorway of his study. Emerson looked up to see his wife, Eunice, standing there, her face betraying concern, if not outright apprehension.

"I was contemplating today's Dow Jones' averages and how the market drop will affect the local dog grooming industry. Images of malodorous, disheveled pooches overrunning the streets of Cedar Hill now trouble me deeply." He looked down at the paper upon which he'd been idly squiggling, saw what he'd drawn, experienced a short-lived but clear-cut moment of something like alarm, and folded the paper in two before shoving it into his pocket.

Eunice shook her head as she came into the study; her face was expressionless, but her eyes were blazing. "Don't you *dare* do that to me, Bill. Don't you dare try to keep me at arm's length by resorting to your endless supply of wise-ass remarks. That may work with Ted Jackson and Grant McCullers when you guys gather around the bar to do your world-weary cronies act at the Hangman, but with me, goddamnit, *with me* you speak the truth!" She'd reached the desk by now, sitting on the edge and putting one of her hands on top of Emerson's gun. "I know I've said this before and that I promised I'd never say it again, but if you *ever* hurt yourself, if you ever leave me like that, I'll hate you for it. I say this out of love, of course, but that doesn't make it any less true." With her free hand she reached over and touched his cheek. "We could revisit the 'early retirement' question. You're only fifty-six, there's still time to cross things off that 'Maybe-Next-Year' list."

He looked at the business end of the gun sticking out from

beneath her hand. "Hon, think about what started this conversation, and then consider this: do you have any idea what the suicide rate is among retired cops, *especially* those who take an early retirement? Only slightly less than that of dentists—and *that's* not a wise-ass remark. Dentists, for some reason, have a numbingly high suicide rate. Did you catch that dark-humored pun I threw in to lighten the mood?"

"All I heard was 'suicide rate' and 'cops.'" She leaned down and kissed him. "I suppose that's what I get for not coming up with a better segue between subjects."

"Or *any* segue, for that matter. I feel obligated to point out your every flaw, no matter how inconsequential. It keeps you humble." He started to say something more, but the words died in his throat as the images from yesterday and today replayed themselves across the torn, patched, and stained movie screen of his memory. He tried again to speak, but was humiliated by the nearly-inaudible whimpering sound that took the place of any witty retort.

"Oh, *honey*," said Eunice, pulling her hand away from his gun and embracing him. "Don't start crying, it doesn't do any good, you know that."

"Someone should," he said, wiping his eyes with more force than was necessary as he gathered himself back into himself. "*Somebody* ought to cry for her. So why not me?"

"Because you're sad enough half the time as it is. You don't let on much—hell, Bill, sometimes you go out of your way to be cheerful around me—but a wife knows. I can tell." When he said nothing in return, she kissed him again, this time full on the mouth, and whispered, "Please tell me about it. I know this one's really been eating away at you. You can tell me as much or as little as you want, just...*talk* to me, okay?"

And he was going to, really, he was; he was going to tell her everything about the last two days, every sickening detail, but no sooner had he pulled in his breath than his beeper went off. *Saved by the bell*, he thought, but said nothing aloud. A joke right now would be an insult to Eunice.

"Saved by the bell," she said, smiling at him.

Emerson checked the beeper's small screen. "It's the hospital. I told them to page me when the mother regained consciousness. I, uh...I hate to do this, hon, but I—"

"—have to go, I know. I've been married to you for longer than either of us cares to admit in public, so I do have some idea how this works. I don't suppose you could just *call* the hospital, what with it being Christmas Eve and all that? No, of course not, that was a dumb question, I know, forget I asked." She stood, gesturing down at the gun. "At least tell me the safety's on."

Emerson slipped the gun into his shoulder holster. "It's *always* on, you know that. I do have some small idea how all of this works." He smiled at her, then took hold of both her hands. "Anyone ever tell you that you're pretty hot for an older broad?"

Eunice gasped. "'Older broad'? When did this suddenly become a William Powell and Myrna Loy movie? 'Older broad,' indeed."

"I'm not exactly *Thin Man* material myself, in case you hadn't noticed." He pulled her close and kissed her on the lips, a lingering, gentle kiss that he enjoyed as much now as when he'd first kissed her nearly forty years ago.

"What was *that* for?" asked Eunice, as Emerson pulled away.

"For putting up with me."

"Oh." She put a hand on his shoulder. "I'll wait up—well, I'll *try* to wait up. We can talk when you come home, okay?"

"Sure thing, hon. Look forward to it."

"Liar."

Emerson shrugged as he pulled on his jacket. "Maybe—but it sure *sounded* sincere, didn't it?" He gave her a quick peck on the cheek and walked to the door, then stopped, half-turned, and leaned his head against the doorframe. "Why is it...I mean...I was...reading this real interesting science article a few days ago and...did you know that the human brain can detect one unit of Thiol amid fifty billion units of air, and if the human ear were any more sensitive, it could hear the sound of air molecules colliding? The human eye possesses tens of millions of electrical connections that can process two million simultaneous messages, yet can still focus on the light from a single photon. The nervous system is a wonder, capable of miraculous things, yet more often than not it seems like everyone's system is geared toward destruction. *Why?* Or, hell, let's be specific, okay? Why do you suppose it is that people who *would have* make good parents, caring, attentive parents...people like us...they can't have kids, but then you get a pair like these two piles of puke and carbon who shouldn't've been put in charge of a fucking goldfish and they..." He shook his head. "Never mind. Makes no difference now. Not to the baby, anyway." He stared at his wife a moment longer and saw the alarm and confusion in her eyes.

"I'm sorry, honey. Maybe I've just got the Christmas Blues. I so wanted that *My Pretty Pony* play set." And with that, he left.

He stared through the window of the isolation unit at the baby lying in the incubator. The hands were so tiny, the body so frail and broken. He pressed his fingers against the glass. *I wish I could hold you,* he thought. *Seems to me that you didn't get held the way you should have. Seems to me you haven't had a good day on this Earth.*

He looked at the heavy casts on the baby's arms and legs, the brace around its neck, at the small cuts and blue-black bruises not covered by the casts, and then found himself staring at the tubes and bandages and connectors that had turned the little girl into a medical marionette. The machines surrounding the incubator blinked, spun, beeped, buzzed, and pumped. So much activity. It looked almost as if life were going on in there.

He was so lost in thought he'd almost forgotten about the doctor standing next to him.

"I'm sorry," said Emerson, rubbing the back of his neck. "Would you mind explaining this in a little more detail for me?"

"Not at all," replied the doctor, whose voice sounded as tired and soul-sick as Emerson himself felt. "Babies react to illness and severe physical trauma by shutting down blood flow to the lungs. The resulting acid buildup and low oxygen levels in the blood cause the vessels to spasm down. That, in turn, reduces the oxygen supply further. It's a vicious cycle—especially when coupled with the...*extent* of the physical trauma she's suffered—but it is reversible." The doctor—whose name Emerson couldn't remember—pressed the intercom button and directed one of the nurses to point to the various pieces of equipment being used. It was like watching a model on a game show point to the costly prizes.

"The process is called Extracorporeal Membrane Oxygenation," said the doctor. "It's an attempt to buy time for the baby's lungs, and in this case, also for its entire system. The idea is to temporarily reroute the flow of blood so that it bypasses the lungs and heart and gives the baby's body a chance to heal. Normally, low-oxygen blood enters the heart and is pumped to the lungs, where it receives oxygen, then returns to the heart and is pumped through the aorta to arteries feeding the body.

"The catheter in the baby's jugular goes to the right atrium of her heart. The other catheter threads to the arch of the aorta. The artery and vein have been clamped off above their catheter. Blood going into the jugular catheter is pumped to a silicone membrane that filters in oxygen. Once that happens, the blood is heated, flows back into her via the carotid catheter, goes to the aorta, then travels to body tissues." He nodded at the nurse, who turned her attention back to the baby. "Nationally, ECMO has an eighty-nine percent success rate. We've performed it on six other children at this hospital and we have never lost one. There is usually every reason to be optimistic, Detective Emerson," he said as if he actually believed it the baby had a chance.

Emerson looked at the doctor and smiled, but there was no humor in it. "I hope so. Christ, I hope so." He turned back toward the baby. After a few moments, MacIntyre—*that* was the doctor's name, MacIntyre!—put a hand on Emerson's shoulder, and then silently walked away.

Emerson tried focusing on anything besides the baby—the bright Christmas lights and other decorations that adorned every door or were splattered all over the nurses' station, the endless and a bit too-loud for him Christmas music pumping through unseen speakers, the gold tinsel taped around the window looking into the isolation unit—but his concentration was having no part of it, so he settled on the momentary distraction of trying to discern the reflection of his face in the glass. Except now there was another face behind him, its reflection sharper than his own.

"You should be home with Eunice, you know that, right?"

Emerson turned around. "And you should be at the Open Shelter, running the show. It's Christmas Eve—aren't you full to capacity?"

The Reverend shrugged. "We're at about seventy-percent capacity tonight, still plenty of room. Sam, Timmy, and Ethel are running the show just fine, and Grant sent a bunch of homemade bread and cookies, courtesy the Hangman's kitchen. Sam's running videos of the Grinch and Frosty and Rudolph for the kids. It's actually quite festive, considering the circumstances."

"You got a haircut."

The Reverend reached up to pat down a portion of his hair. "Yeah, well...a guy gets tired of having his friends tell him he looks like Rasputin."

"I always thought you had more of a Charles Manson thing

going on—sans, you know, the bat-shit craziness, cult, and bloodshed." He shook the Reverend's hand. "How did you know where to find me? No, wait, let me guess—Eunice called you, right?"

"Yes. And she called me because of, and I quote, '...a fucking goldfish,' unquote. You *never* drop the F-bomb, Bill, in all the time I've known you, I've never heard you utter that word."

"It seemed appropriate at the time."

"Have you questioned the mother yet?"

Emerson looked back into the isolation unit and balled both of his hands into fists. "She died before I got here—not that it's any great loss to the world. I doubt she had enough brain cells left to talk, anyway."

"Where did it happen?" said the Reverend.

"Three guesses."

"Ah...the Taft Hotel?"

Emerson nodded. "Best place in scenic Cedar Hill to crawl into the shadows of poverty and choke to death on your own vomit. Sorry—that was a bit melodramatic, wasn't it?"

"Vivid image, though."

Emerson felt his shoulders slump a little more. "Every god-damn time we have to answer a call there, it's something more terrible than the time before, something more...painful and de-pressing. And every time I wish that someone would just burn it to the ground. There are some places that are just so ruined and miserable they shouldn't be allowed to go on existing." And then something occurred to him and he turned to face the Reverend. "Why 'where'?"

"I'm sorry...?"

"You asked me *where* it happened. The first thing anyone else would ask is *what* happened, but not you. You ask where."

The Reverend looked at the baby again. "I have my reasons."

"Like?"

"Like I'm not sure right now I *want* to hear about what happened. I look through this window and my mind fills with a thousand sounds and images and not a damned one of them is anything I want in my head. I'm sorry if my tone's a bit snappy, but you're not the only one fighting a foul mood tonight."

Emerson nodded. "I just hope that dear Mommy and Daddy are..." He stopped himself, then almost laughed. "You know, I almost said that I hoped they were burning in hell, but suddenly that seemed too...*meek*. So, being a man of the cloth, maybe you can tell me—*is* there a worse punishment than burning in hell? Please say yes. It would give me a moment's comfort."

The Reverend stared at him for a few seconds, his eyes betraying nothing, then looked back at the baby and said, "If you want to be exact, Bill, the hell you're talking about—the fire-and-brimstone, souls-shrieking-in-agony, Satan's-pitchfork-up-your-ass-for-eternity—it doesn't exist, no more so than the entities that are called Satan and the Devil. They're all...storybook constructs. If you want to be exact, Bill, then I will tell you that Hell is actually a *part* of Heaven—specifically, it's located on the north side of the Third Heaven."

"How many Heavens are there?"

"Seven."

"You're kidding?"

"How do you think the phrase 'in Seventh Heaven' originated?"

"Huh. I...I did not know that." Emerson's gaze drifted down toward his shoes. They looked as old and worn-out as he felt.

"Okay," said the Reverend, taking hold of Emerson's arm and tugging him away from the window. "I'm taking you down to the cafeteria for something to eat."

"I'm not particularly hungry."

"How nice for you."

Emerson tried pulling away but was surprised at the strength of the Reverend's grip. "I really think I ought to stay here for a while longer."

The Reverend stopped, sighed, then whispered: "Listen to me, Bill," so softly that had anyone been standing one foot away they wouldn't have heard the words, but in Emerson's ears this whisper was a howl of fury from the depths of a place so terrible he couldn't even begin to imagine it; and then, just as quickly, he knew he didn't *want* to imagine it. Bill Emerson's heart and soul damn near froze when his friend continued speaking: "Do you actually *believe* that if you stand here you can heal her through sheer force of will? That you can, perhaps, wish so hard for a Christmas miracle that one will just stroll up and tap you on the shoulder? You're not a stupid man, Bill, so why stand here and look at her sad, ruined body and think about pain and injustice and broken-heartedness and every other goddamn thing you can pull out of that part of your memory where you store each ugly and hopeless thing you've seen? There's nothing—*look at me!*—there's nothing you can do for her. Are you so obsessed with lost causes that you want to become one yourself? I am very fond of you and Eunice and I will not allow..." He bit down on his lip, closed his eyes, and let go of Emerson's arm.

"I'm sorry," said the Reverend after several seconds had elapsed. "I don't usually get that self-righteous." He reached out and put a hand on Emerson's shoulder, giving it a gentle squeeze.

Emerson responded by reaching up and squeezing the Reverend's hand. "You're right, I'm being stupid. Is the offer for food still open?"

"You can break bread with me anytime you want. Elevator."

"Huh?"

The Reverend pointed. "The elevator doors are open. If we make our break now, it'll be a clean getaway."

They caught the elevator just as the doors began to close. The Reverend pressed the button for the lower cafeteria floor.

"You are a surprisingly strong man," said Emerson.

"I was just…angry."

"What was it you were starting to say? You said you will not allow…and then you stopped."

"I forget. Considering how mad I was, it was probably something supremely stupid."

"Not you, Reverend. I have never heard anything remotely close to stupid come out of your mouth. Except maybe when we're playing poker and you call."

"That's because you and Ted Jackson cheat."

"Bullshit. You just stink at it."

The Reverend grinned. "Look, I…I'm truly sorry about this case, Bill. I didn't act like it much up there, but I am truly, deeply sorry. Would it make you feel any better if we were to say a prayer for the little girl?"

"I haven't been real big on prayer, not really, not for a long while. And to tell you the truth, I guess there's a part of me that's a little pissed that, being who and what you are, you'll probably be saying one for the souls of her you-should-pardon-the-expression parents."

"I wouldn't be so sure about that if I were you."

The Reverend stared up at the blinking floor lights as they descended. "People talk about me, Bill, I know that, and I know that you've heard things. Would you be a good fellow and tell me what you've heard, and whether or not you believe any of it?"

Emerson hesitated for a moment, looking at the elevator doors and wishing the damn thing would stop and someone else would get on.

"Bill, please. We've needed to have this chat for a while now and I really need to know."

"I don't like repeating rumors and...speculations."

"You won't offend me. C'mon—'fess up."

Emerson cracked his knuckles and cleared his throat. "I've heard that you...that you can *do* things, that you know things and see things that other people can't. One time, at the shelter, both Sam and Ethel told me they thought you might be..."

"Might be what?"

"That you might be an angel."

The Reverend laughed and shook his head. "That's a good one. But you're not Jimmy Stewart, I'm not Henry Travers, and this sure as hell isn't *It's a Wonderful Life*." He looked at Emerson and smiled warmly. "I can assure you that I most definitely *not* an angel."

"Don't take this the wrong way, but I didn't much expect you were."

"Why would I take that the wrong way? Never mind. Over the years, you've seen more than a few...*odd* occurrences around Cedar Hill. Is it safe to say that?"

Emerson almost laughed. "Oh, Lord, yes."

"But you've never really questioned them—at least, not out loud. Why?"

Emerson shrugged. "I guess I trust my own eyes and judgment."

The Reverend nodded. "That's good. *Very* good, actually."

Emerson started to say something, then looked up at the elevator lights. "Shouldn't this thing have stopped by now?"

The Reverend smiled. "If you want to be exact, it should have stopped twenty seconds ago."

"Then...how's it still moving?" All of the floor lights were flashing in rapid, random order, and remained in a constant state of blinking chaos. Emerson was suddenly all too aware of the cramped space closing in on them.

"Are you all right?" said the Reverend.

"Am I all—*hell* no, I'm not all right! What's going on?"

"I know this may seem a bit cruel to you—Eunice has mentioned your problem with being in enclosed spaces for too long—but if you'll just finish answering my original question, I promise you the elevator will stop."

Emerson covered his face with his hands, groaned, and wiped away the patina of sweat that was forming there. "Fine. A lot of people say that you have magic powers—shit, even Ted Jackson has said to me that he thinks you might be someone or something more than human."

"Do you believe any of it?"

Emerson looked up at the chaotic lights. "I *didn't*. Under the circumstances, I guess I'm open to...possibilities."

"Trusting your own eyes and judgment?"

"Sure, let's go with that."

The Reverend, still smiling, nodded his head. "Thank you Bill. Oh, by the way—that 'magic powers' thing? Technically, it's correct, if a little over-simplified. You might want to brace yourself, we'll be stopping in a moment."

"Where are we going?"

"Another place. You'd better take my arm."

Emerson surprised himself by doing so without hesitation. The elevator came to a smooth, humming stop, the lights blinked out, and the doors quietly opened.

Emerson gripped the Reverend's arm with both hands. What lay before them was a wide, deep, gaping maw of blackness with no varying degrees, containing nothing he could distinguish as being part of the world he knew.

"Bottom floor, ladies' lingerie," said the Reverend, pulling Emerson along as he stepped out. Emerson expected them to plummet into a bottomless pit but it felt as if there were still some trace of *terra firma* beneath their feet.

The light from inside the elevator did not follow them; instead, it cowered against the back wall, shrinking into itself. Emerson hoped that the light would not go out; as long as he could look back and see the inside of the elevator, he might be able to maintain his composure.

He swallowed, looking into the eternal darkness, and said, "Where are we?"

"That's going to take a bit of explaining."

"Give it a shot."

The Reverend laughed. "You know, Bill, you're actually quite a funny person."

"I'll try my hand at stand-up comedy sometime next year. *Please* tell me where we are."

The Reverend reached over and squeezed Emerson's hand. "If you want to be exact, we are nowhere. We are in the moment after the end of the whole mess, where everything came crashing down, where it all scrambled into an instantaneous decay pattern and reduced the lot to a harmless spray of sub-particles that were scattered about only to be absorbed by whatever had existed here before the multiverse was born." He began flicking his thumb and index finger around as if getting rid of a bothersome insect. As the Reverend continued doing this, Emerson watched the spaces where the Reverend flicked his fingers. Something was…rippling.

"Matter is nothing more than energy that's been brought to a screeching halt," said the Reverend, "and the human body is only matter, and the fundamental tendency of all matter is toward total disorganization, a final state of utter randomness from which the multiverse will never recover, becoming more and more unthreaded with the passing of each moment, recklessly scattering itself, collapsing inward as it was destined to do since the violence of its birth. We have arrived at After All is Said and Done and the fat lady has sang."

"Sung," whispered Emerson. "It's '…and the fat lady has sung.'"

The Reverend shook his head. "Only you would correct someone's grammar at a moment like this. Be quiet, and think about this; right here, right now—if a concept such as 'now' is even applicable—you and I, we have nothing left to prove. No one has anything left to prove. It no longer means a damn thing that we once could write music or formulate equations to explain the universe, or cure diseases, create new languages and geometries and engines that could power crafts to explore space.

"And if you want to be exact, Bill, right now you and I don't exist, except in each other's perception." He flicked his fingers again, and this time Emerson was positive he saw the darkness ripple and momentarily turn to the blue of a cool, clean stream of water.

"Ah," said the Reverend, "we're in luck, I think." He flicked again, and the bluish ripple became slightly larger, brighter.

Emerson tried to swallow but could work up no saliva. "Why did you bring me here?"

The Reverend glowered at him. "Because everything that you've done, everything you've felt, dreamed, laughed at, cried over, raged against, none of it means anything here, and maybe it never did. And I figured, if you want to stare at something you have no power to do anything about, I might as well cut to the chase and show you where everything is heading. What do you think of it? I mean, aside from the lack of homey décor?"

Emerson was shaking and trying to hold himself together. "You wanted to convince me you've got magic powers? Consider it done. Could we please leave?"

"We could, but we can't go back the same way we got here."

That's when Emerson realized the lights from the elevator—lights that he'd been trying to keep in his peripheral vision—were gone. They were surrounded by blackness...yet he could still see the Reverend quite clearly.

Emerson felt as if his chest were going to cave in. "I'm pretty scared right now, so if you've got any more rabbits up your cleri-cal sleeve, now might be a good time."

The Reverend merely stared at him. "The baby in the isola-tion room? She's going to die. The damage her parents did to her is too extensive—after all, when you're her size and beaten by two junkies in the throes of withdrawal, it's all over now, Baby Blue. She will suffer a sudden brain hemorrhage in about three minutes and will be dead before the nurse can turn around. And it won't matter that her father died of a massive heart attack or that her mother went out after he was dead and got her hands on some really bad stuff that she shot into her arm once she got home." His voice was turning into a roar, his eyes filling with ungodly rage.

"It won't matter that the baby cried for nearly twenty-four hours straight before the beating because she was starving and her diaper was filled with piss and shit that had been there for four days and had dried and become so hardened that it pulled off a little of her skin when the ER doctors removed it, or that several people who lived on the same floor heard her and did nothing, even when her parents began shrieking and her sad, agonized screams echoed off the walls and down the hallway! *That's* the reason I didn't bother to ask you what happened—I already knew! You want to choke on something, Bill? You want to *look* for further sources of soul-sickness? Then imagine this; imagine knowing what was going to happen to that child *weeks, months* before it occurred—but you're powerless to interfere be-cause *it hasn't happened yet!* You want meaninglessness? Well, here it is, Bill, a fucking *feast* of futility, all around us! Be glutton-ous, my dear friend, because this is what it all comes down to. So take a moment's comfort in knowing that you were right—what good is hope? Love? Kindness? And let's not even get started on *prayer!*"

Bill Emerson had never been so terrified. His chest tightened, his legs shook, and his arms felt useless. He grabbed onto the collar of the Reverend's coat with as much strength as he could muster. "Why do this? Why show me this? If there's no point to anything, if there's no hope, no reason, then…why show this to me?"

The Reverend's expression was unreadable. "I'm sorry, I'm just replaying things in my head and—would you be exact and tell me precisely when and where in this conversation I said there was no point or hope?"

"W—what?"

"I never said anything like that, Bill. I only told you what matters in this place—or non-place, if you want to be exact. Think about it—how could anything mean something to a non-place? Or even an actually place? Answer: it can't, it doesn't, never did, never will."

Emerson felt his chest loosening; it was becoming easier to breathe. "So I…what exactly are you saying?"

"I told you that there was nothing that could be done to save that child because her suffering, her torture and death hadn't happened yet." He stood silently for several moments: closed his eyes, and released a long, heavy breath. "Now it has." He opened his eyes. "She's gone now, Bill. But if you're willing to do what needs to be done, we can act."

Emerson didn't answer for a moment; he felt a part of himself wither and surrender to the darkness. He should have stayed there, he should have been near at the moment of her death so that she would at least have been close to someone who would care, who would weep for her; and weep now he did. "What the hell are you talking about?" It was a struggle to get the words out. They might have been in a non-place, but grief recognized no boundaries, physical or otherwise.

The Reverend took hold of Emerson's forearms. "Look at me, my friend. You need to answer this question without any discussion, without any arguing. If it meant saving that child's life, would you be willing to do exactly what I tell you to, with no hesitation?"

"Yes."

"Even if it's something you're not sure you can live with?"

"Yes."

"You have to give me absolute trust."

"I know. I will. I do."

The Reverend nodded. "I sent you a message earlier. You wrote it down. Please reach into your left pocket and remove it."

Emerson did, unfolding it. Damn thing still made no sense to him. "You had me draw a sad-ass-looking Christmas tree?"

"First of all, it isn't a Christmas tree, it's a... well, it is a tree of sorts, but it's also for lack of a better term right now, a map. And you're holding it upside-down."

Emerson righted the page. It still made no sense to him:

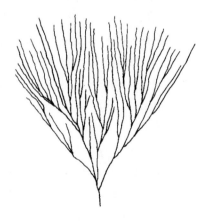

"I don't understand."

The Reverend took the page from Emerson's hand. "It's a representational diagram of theoretical collapsing probability structures that branch off one another and recombine in a simultaneous universe."

"Oh. I thought it might be something complicated."

"Very funny." The Reverend traced a path with his index finger. "Ha! I was right." He tapped the page hard. "Where you have negative space, you have negative time."

"You gonna let me in on this?"

"The multiverse sends data through our senses every second of every day and whether we are aware of it or not, our brains interpret that data, and those interpretations form the basis upon which we make choices—that's how a probability wave collapses, and that's what enables the multiverse to grow yet another branch. Just as if you were deciding whether to sit or stand, have another beer or not, choices like that. When you make a choice and collapse a wave, the action you *didn't* take goes elsewhere, to a simultaneous universe where you made the *other* choice. We don't have a lot of you-should-pardon-the-expression time for in-depth quantum physics." He turned and flicked his fingers once again, only this time when the ripple appeared, it grew taller, wider, its cold blue light beckoning.

"Right now Bill, we're just like electrons, able to travel from point to point without having to move through the space between, and that's what we're going to do. Listen: at the moment of an unchosen death, there is a very small gap between the collapsing of the probability wave and it recombining in a new branch of the multiverse."

"Okay. So what's the plan?"

The Reverend held out his arm for Emerson to take. "The plan is, we're going to fuck things up just a little bit and hope we don't cause too much trouble."

They stepped into the blue ripple as easily as they would have immersed themselves in a fountain of water…

…and emerged across the street from the Taft Hotel. It was snowing and quite cold. And it was morning.

"Bingo," said the Reverend. "Come on." He put one of his hands in the center of Emerson's back and began pushing him across the street. "Remember, Bill—no questions."

"I'll do whatever you say."

They entered through the grimy doors and began walking up the molding wooden stairs toward the third floor.

"We're still in our branch of the multiverse," said the Reverend, "but it's four days ago. Right now the baby's parents are warm and content because they've both just shot up on some really good stuff and are enjoying their powerful highs. They've got enough left for both of them to get high again when this one wears off, but after *that* one wears off..."

Emerson nodded. "I know."

They rounded the corner, hit the landing of the second floor, stepped around a puddle of something Emerson didn't want to look at too closely, and kept going. "Most of the people who are currently living here," said the Reverend, "are either out at their minimum-wage jobs or too drunk to move."

Emerson suddenly had a moment of nearly-overwhelming empathy for the people who lived here. What would it be like to be his age and living in a place like this because it was all you could afford—the best life had to offer someone in your circumstances? Working behind the counter of some greasy fast-food restaurant, or washing dishes, or being a clerk at some convenience store that had prices you couldn't afford, laboring for eight to ten hours, skipping lunch three times a week, walking home along streets that didn't have enough lights, passing among others who looked just as injured, damaged, lost, and broken to you as you probably did to them, and for all of this struggle you got to come home to...to this. Cramped, shabby rooms to contain the measly detritus you've dragged along to mark the tail-end of a shabby life. And go to sleep thinking that maybe God has decided to skip the rest of the show. Hark, the herald angels sing. Joy to the world. Early checkout available.

Emerson looked down at his shoes for a moment as if surprised they were still on his feet, or thinking maybe they were going to offer a suggestion or moral support. He snapped out of this bleak reverie when they rounded the corner and hit the landing of the third floor. He kept his gaze on the Reverend's back. You always watched your partner's back.

Two more groaning, creaking steps, and they stood in the third floor hallway. Light here came courtesy, mostly, of three bare bulbs dangling on the end of cords. Only one was working. A window half-covered in crisscrossing strips of duct tape at the far end of the hall provided the rest of the light. If you could call it that.

301. 303. 305.

"Still with me, Bill?"

"Yes."

307. It was coming up. Emerson steeled himself. Dry-swallowed.

309. He hummed a snippet of Bob Dylan's "Gates of Eden" to himself.

311. Decided that it was an oddly appropriate choice.

313. They stopped, the Reverend on one side of the door, Emerson on the other.

Instinctively, Emerson reached under his coat and un-snapped the flap of the shoulder holster.

"Hey, Bill."

Emerson nodded.

The Reverend winked. "Remember—there are no sins inside the gates of Eden." And with that, the door swung open. Neither man wasted time. They stepped into the sparsely-furnished apartment, and the door closed behind them. It was unbearably hot, the steam-heater going full-blast.

Across the wooden floor that had so many rotted boards it looked ready to cave in at any second, the baby lay on top of stained towels in a plastic laundry basket on top of a folding ta-ble. It was fussing, working its tiny hands, kicking its tiny feet, making wet, sputtering noises followed by soft cries that Emerson knew were only a warm-up.

They crossed to the table, again separating and standing on either side of the basket, looking down at the baby. Emerson felt a tight-lipped grin suddenly appear on his face and bent over to pick up the sweat-soaked baby girl. No sooner had he reached out than the Reverend's hands shot across the top of the basket and grabbed his forearms.

"Sorry, Bill—it's not quite that easy."

Emerson almost asked him why, then bit the question in half and let it drop to the floor where the two sections squirmed, stilled, and died.

Still gripping Emerson's forearms, the Reverend said: "Need to ask you something else."

"Go ahead."

"If humanity is as inherently evil as you seem to think it is, then how do you explain goodness? How do you explain kindness, love, a really infectious laugh, a haunting tune you can't get out of your mind, and the great way you feel when you smell fresh bread baking in the kitchen?"

"I can't. I don't."

"Know this: there is no such thing as a 'cosmic evil.' Evil is a human matter, fashioned by ignorance, brutality, addiction, emotional trauma—the list is endless. The cosmos doesn't feel anything, it is just a *space*, it doesn't care about either good or evil, it is simply, like Heaven itself, indifferent." He gently pushed Emerson's arms away from the laundry basket. "Any thoughts on that you'd care to share with the room?"

"We need to do whatever it is that needs doing."

"'Needs doing'? What a very John-Wayne thing for you to say. Okay, this is the part where you keep your word to me. You do remember your promise?"

"Yes."

"Good." He nodded toward the half-open bedroom door. "The two people who are lying in there completely strung-out have collapsed just about all the wave functions they're going to. The ones that are supposed to branch out later are almost completely insignificant—let me worry about those. But the...call it the 'structural integrity' of this branch, demands two deaths.

"Walk in there, pull the pillows out from under their heads. The husband first. Press the pillow to his face, jam your gun in there to muffle the shot, squeeze the trigger. Then pick up the wife's pillow and do the same to her. Then come right back here. Go. Do it now."

Emerson did precisely as he'd been told, only flinching once when the wife gave out with a soft whimper from under the pillow. Holstering his weapon, he rejoined the Reverend at the table.

The Reverend's eyes were almost moist. Almost. "I am so proud of you, my friend." He nodded down toward the baby. "Pick her up—but be careful. She just pooped."

"I can smell that."

"Wrap her in this," whispered the Reverend, handing Emerson a thick clean grey baby blanket. Emerson didn't ask where it had come from.

Once the baby was in his arms, Emerson pushed out one of his fingers to stroke her brow, but she reached up and grabbed hold of it, squeezing.

The Reverend began his flicking routine again, consulted the map, then took four steps to the left and opened the ripple. Emerson joined him, but this time it was the Reverend who took hold of his partner's sleeve.

They stepped through the ripple...

...and Emerson found himself again looking up at the blinking elevator lights. It was heading up to the lobby.

In his arms, the baby made a warm, safe sound. He could

smell her poop through the blanket. He looked over at the Reverend. "What happens now?"

"Your guess is as good as mine. Technically speaking, I'm never supposed to do what we just did. I *do* know there are going to be some consequences. I don't know what form they'll take, but they won't be immediate, not even soon. But eventually they will occur."

"What happens in the other branch? Where the wave has recombined?"

"She dies sooner. Grows up to find a cure for AIDS. We don't get there in time. Her mother comes to her senses and turns her life around. Someone sets fire to the Taft and everyone burns to death. She is placed with Childrens' Services and grows up happy and healthy in a terrific foster home. Godzilla attacks Tokyo, we finally find out who put the bomp in the bomp-dee-bomp-bomp, the Edsel is named Car of the Year, Barry Manilow never writes 'Mandy,' nobody gives a shit about who shot J.R. and *Survivor* finally gets cancelled. It's a crap-shoot with the dice loaded by Einstein."

"A simple 'I don't know' would have been sufficient."

"Says you. I rather like the sound of my voice."

"How nice for you." The two men looked at one another and burst out laughing. The baby woke up, looked up at Emerson, furrowed her brow for a moment, uncertain, and then giggled.

"What are we supposed to do with her now?"

The Reverend grinned. The elevator stopped and they moved into the lobby. Nurses laughed at their station, Christmas music was playing, the big-ass tree in the middle of the lobby was twinkling brightly; it was so warm, happy, and Norman-Rockwell-painting festive it almost made you sick.

Emerson looked at the baby. "I'm going to look up and it's going to be snowing outside, isn't it?"

"Actually, it's raining."

Emerson looked up. It was snowing.

"Yeah," said the Reverend. "I lied."

They stood to the side of the automatic doors, looking out into the night.

"Seriously," said Emerson. "What happens with her now?"

"You and Eunice always wanted a child of your own. Why not keep her? Tell everyone she was adopted."

"How the hell would I explain that to Eunice?"

"You won't have to. Say the word, and when you arrive home you'll be greeted by a wife who's been waiting impatiently for the two of you to get back because the baby missed its feeding time and needs a change of diapers."

"But...the records that would be involved with something like that!"

The Reverend looked at him and shook his head. "You and I have traveled to the end of the multiverse, experienced a state of non-existence wherein you corrected my grammar, moved from point to point without crossing the space between, technically have outrun a collapsing wave function, made it back in one piece, and, oh, what else? Oh, yeah—we saved her life. And after all of that, you're actually going to put a damper on everything by standing here on this too-perfect Christmas night—*is* a bit much, isn't it? My teeth are hurting just looking at it—anyway, you're going to stand here after all of that and bitch to me about *paperwork*? Haven't you been paying attention?"

"Yeah, yeah, yeah, you can do things, see things, know things that other people can't. I believe all of it, trust me. You have, to oversimplify it, magic powers."

"Yes, yes I do." He reached into his pocket. "And for my next trick I'll need a volunteer." He removed a thick, official-looking envelope. "How about you, sir, with the permanently perpluxed and pizzled expression? You have only to take this from my hand and—*viola!*—paperwork is no longer a worry."

Emerson said nothing. He looked at his reflection in the window. He was holding something. It moved. Giggled. Here is this minute, he thought, this breath, this second. What will you do with this minute? This minute that is passing? *You're only fifty-six*, Eunice had said, *there's still time to cross things off that 'Maybe-Next-Year' list.* But that kind of list, the kind a man like the one whose face was reflected back at him would come up with, it was for things like traveling, or taking up golf, finding hobbies, taking ballroom dancing lessons. What kind of a person in her or his right mind would even consider becoming a parent at the age of fifty-six? He continued staring at his reflection. He was still holding something. It was still moving. It was still giggling. The hands were so tiny, the body so frail. He pressed the fingers of his free hand against the glass. *What will you do with this moment, the one that is now passing?* He couldn't think of an answer; he was too busy watching as the reflection of his free hand pulled away from the glass and reached out to take something from the Reverend's hand.

AUTHOR BIOS

LINDA D. ADDISON, award-winning author of *Being Full of Light, Insubstantial* (Space & Time Books) is the first African-American to receive the HWA Bram Stoker Award. She has fiction in *Dark Matter* (Warner Aspect), *Dark Dreams* (Kensington), and *Dark Thirst* (Pocket Book). Her poetry and stories have been listed on the Honorable Mention list for the annual *Year's Best Fantasy and Horror* and *Year's Best Science-Fiction* anthologies.

JENNIFER PELLAND lives outside Boston with an Andy, three cats, and an impractical amount of books. Her short story collection, *Unwelcome Bodies*, was published by Apex in 2008 and contains her Nebula-nominated story "Captive Girl." She's also a belly dancer and occasional radio theater performer. For pictures of the aforementioned cats, plus links to her various blogs, visit www.jenniferpelland.com.

BRIAN KEENE is the author of over twenty books, including *Darkness on the Edge of Town, Urban Gothic, Castaways, Kill Whitey, Ghost Walk, Dark Hollow, Dead Sea, Ghoul* and many more. He also writes comic books such as *The Last Zombie* and *Dead of Night: Devil Slayer*. His work has been translated into German, Spanish, Polish, French and Taiwanese. Several of his novels and stories have been optioned for film, one of which, *The Ties That Bind*, premiered on DVD in 2009 as a critically-acclaimed independent short. Keene's work has been praised in such diverse places as *The New York Times*, The History Channel, The Howard Stern Show, CNN.com, *Publisher's Weekly, Fangoria Magazine*, and *Rue Morgue Magazine*. You can communicate with him online at www.briankeene.com or on Twitter at twitter.com/BrianKeene.

BIOS

WRATH JAMES WHITE is a former world class heavyweight kickboxer, a professional kickboxing and mixed martial arts trainer, distance runner, performance artist, and former street brawler, who is now known for creating some of the most disturbing works of fiction in print. Wrath's two most recent novels are *The Resurrectionist* and *Yaccub's Curse*. He is also the author of *Succulent Prey*, *The Book of a Thousand Sins*, *His Pain* and *Population Zero*. He is the co-author of *Teratologist*, co-written with the king of extreme horror, Edward Lee; *Orgy of Souls*, co-written with Maurice Broaddus; *Hero*, co-written with J.F. Gonzalez; and *Poisoning Eros*, co-written with Monica J. O'Rourke.

DOUGLAS F. WARRICK is a writer, editor, and shitty ass-wiper. His work has appeared in *Apex Digest*, *Murky Depths*, *Legends of the Mountain State*, and online at Pseudopod.org. He is the co-editor of *Up Jumped the Devil*, an anthology of short horror stories inspired by the songs of Nick Cave, due out later this year. He lives with his wife in Dayton, Ohio. Please visit him online at douglasfwarrick.com

KYLE S. JOHNSON is something of a layabout, but is mostly well-received by his friends and peers. His work has appeared in the Permuted Press anthology *The World is Dead*, and he is the co-editor of the upcoming PS Publishing anthology *Up Jumped the Devil*.

ELIYANNA KAISER is originally from Alberta, Canada but has lived in New York City for almost a decade. She spent four years as an editor for a small press magazine and currently works for the New York State Legislature and lives in Manhattan with her wife. She enjoys writing all kinds of speculative fiction, but has a special fondness for the things that go bump in broad daylight.

BIOS

RAIN GRAVES has been writing fiction and poetry professionally since 1997 and is the 2002 Bram Stoker Award recipient for her poetry in *The Gossamer Eye*, with David N. Wilson and Mark McLaughlin. Her latest book, *Barfodder: Poetry Written In Dark Bars and Questionable Cafes*, was hailed as "Bukowski meets Lovecraft" by *Publisher's Weekly* in 2009.

NICK MAMATAS is the author of two novels, *Under My Roof* and *Move Under Ground*, and of over sixty short stories, many of which were collected in *You Might Sleep....* A third novel, *Sensation*, is forthcoming in 2011. A native New Yorker, Nick now lives in the California Bay Area.

LAVIE TIDHAR is the author of linked-story collection *Hebrew-Punk* (2007), novellas *An Occupation of Angels* (2005), *Cloud Permutations* (2010), *Gorel & The Pot-Bellied God* (forthcoming), and, with Nir Yaniv, *The Tel Aviv Dossier* (2009). He's lived on three continents and one island nation and currently lives in Southeast Asia. His first novel, *The Bookman*, will be published by HarperCollins' new Angry Robot imprint in 2010.

MATT CARDIN is the author of *Dark Awakenings* and *Divinations of the Deep*, both of which explore the intersections between religion and horror. His work has appeared in *Cemetery Dance*, *Dark Arts*, *The New York Review of Science Fiction*, *Alone on the Darkside*, *The Thomas Ligotti Reader*, *Dead Reckonings*, *Icons of Horror and the Supernatural*, *The Encyclopedia of the Vampire*, and elsewhere.

EKATERINA SEDIA resides in the Pinelands of New Jersey. Her critically acclaimed novels, *The Secret History of Moscow* and *The Alchemy of Stone* were published by Prime Books. Her next novel, *The House of Discarded Dreams*, is coming out in 2010. Her short stories have sold to *Analog*, *Baen's Universe*, *Dark Wisdom* and

Clarkesworld, as well as the *Haunted Legends* and *Magic in the Mirrorstone* anthologies. Visit her at www.ekaterinasedia.com.

JAY LAKE lives in Portland, Oregon, where he works on numerous writing and editing projects. His 2010 books are *Pinion* from Tor Books, *The Baby Killers* from PS Publishing, and *The Sky That Wraps* from Subterranean Press. His short fiction appears regularly in literary and genre markets worldwide. Jay is a winner of the John W. Campbell Award for Best New Writer and a multiple nominee for the Hugo and World Fantasy awards. Jay can be reached through his website at www.jlake.com.

One of Gamasutra's Top 20 Game Writers, RICHARD DANSKY is the Manager of Design at Red Storm Entertainment and the Central Clancy Writer for Ubisoft. Formerly a designer for White Wolf Game Studios, he is also the author of the critically praised novel *Firefly Rain.* He has contributed extensively to game series including Ghost Recon, Rainbow Six, Splinter Cell, Might and Magic and Far Cry, as well as White Wolf's World of Darkness and Trinity game lines. Richard lives in North Carolina with his wife and their inevitable cats, except when he doesn't.

D. T. FRIEDMAN is a science fiction/fantasy writer and a medical student. She is a graduate of Orson Scott Card's Literary Boot Camp and a member of the Codex online writers' workshop. She lives with her Robbins Textbook of Pathology and her stethoscope. Sometimes she juggles fire.

J.C. HAY writes, knits, and sometimes writes about knitting from a secluded location in the middle of the United States. J.C.'s novella, *Hearts and Minds,* is available through Samhain Publishing, while short works can be found in Twelfth Planet's Aurealis-nominated anthology *New Ceres Nights, Crossed Genres* and *Apex*

Magazine. Part-time film snob and full-time foodie, J.C. spends too much time pushing friends into new experiences and not enough time updating the website www.jchay.com.

TOM PICCIRILLI is the author of twenty novels including *Shadow Season, The Cold Spot, The Coldest Mile,* and *A Choir of Ill Children.* He's won the International Thriller Award and four Bram Stoker Awards, as well as having been nominated for the Edgar, the World Fantasy Award, the Macavity, and Le Grand Prix de L'imagination.

JENNIFER BAUMGARTNER writes poetry in what little time she has between being a wife and mother. *Dark Faith* marks her professional debut.

KELLI DUNLAP's handwriting is atrocious. Even doctors tell her it sucks—which is why she's grateful for keyboards. And you, too, should be thankful. Not only do you get to read her sick, twisted ideas, you don't have to read it in Kelli's handwriting. Long live technology! Oh yeah, and she has a website at www.kellidunlap.com that you should stalk, a house full of kids, sometimes friends, the occasional pet that wanders through, and is lucky enough to sleep with her best friend every night, but she'll never write better than your grandma.

GEOFFREY GIRARD has appeared in such anthologies as *Writers of the Future, Gratia Placenti, Damned Nation, Harlan County Horrors,* and *Dark Futures: Tales of Dystopic SF,* and the magazines *Murky Depths, The Willows, Aoife's Kiss, Beyond Centauri,* and *Apex Digest* (which serialized his horror novella *Cain XP11* in four issues). His first book, *Tales of the Jersey Devil* (a collection of thirteen tales based on the myth), was published in 2005, with *Tales of the Atlantic Pirates* and *Tales of the Eastern Indians* following. Find more info at www.GeoffreyGirard.com.

ALETHEA KONTIS is a geek, a princess, and a fairy-godmother-in-training—not necessarily in that order. She is a big fan of life, liberty, and the pursuit of happiness, and believes that everyone has the right to be awesome. (Yes, *everyone*.) Princess Alethea recently escaped her own life of tyranny being held captive in an Ivory Tower. She now lives Somewhere Over the Rainbow, in the land of butterflies and fairies. She is still searching for the perfect magic wand, and she writes better than your grandma.

MARY ROBINETTE KOWAL is the 2008 recipient of the Campbell Award for Best New Writer. Her short fiction appears in *Strange Horizons, Cosmos* and *Asimov's*. Mary, a professional puppeteer and voice actor, lives in Portland, Oregon with her husband Rob and eight manual typewriters. Tor is publishing her debut novel, *Shades of Milk and Honey*, in 2010. She is serving her second term as Secretary of Science Fiction and Fantasy Writers of America. In addition to her writing, she also performs as a voice actor, recording fiction for authors such as Elizabeth Bear, Cory Doctorow and John Scalzi. Visit www.maryrobinettekowal.com.

With more than 40 publishing credits to her name, including the acclaimed *Chocolate Park*, CHESYA BURKE has been making her mark in the horror and fantasy worlds. Her work has appeared in such publications as *Dark Dreams I, II* and *III: Horror and Suspense by Black Writers* from Kensington Publishing, the historical, science and speculative fiction magazine, *Would That It Were*, and many more. She received the Twilight Tales Award for fiction and an honorable mention in the *Year's Best Fantasy and Horror*. Several of her articles appeared in the *African American*

National Biography published by Harvard and Oxford University Press. In early 2010 production will begin on the film *The Light of Cree*, based on her story of the same name published in *Voices From The Other Side* by Kensington Publishing.

LON PRATER is an active duty Navy officer by day and writer of odd little tales by night. His short fiction has appeared in the Stoker-winning anthology *Borderlands 5*, *Writers of the Future XXI*, and Origins Award finalist *Frontier Cthulhu*. He is an avid Texas Hold'em player, occasional stunt kite flyer, and connoisseur of theme parks and haunted hayrides. To find out more, go to www.lonprater.com.

LUCIEN SOULBAN is a novelist and script writer living in beautiful Montreal. He's written five novels including *Dragonlance: Renegade Wizards* and *Warhammer 40K: Desert Raiders*, and contributed to numerous anthologies including *Horrors Beyond 2*, *Best of All Flesh* and the HWA's horror comedy anthology, *Blood Lite*. He has also written for various video games including Rainbow Six: Vegas, Warhammer 40K: Dawn of War, Deus Ex 3, The Golden Compass, Dawn of Heroes, and Kung-Fu Panda.

Born in the Pacific Northwest in 1979, CATHERYNNE M. VALENTE is the author of a dozen works of fiction and poetry, including *Palimpsest*, the *Orphan's Tales* series, *The Labyrinth*, and crowdfunded phenomenon *The Girl Who Circumnavigated Fairyland in a Ship of Her Own Making*. She is the winner of the Tiptree Award, the Mythopoeic Award, the Rhysling Award, and the Million Writers Award. She has been nominated for the Pushcart Prize, the Spectrum Award, and was a finalist for the World Fantasy Award in 2007 and 2009.

BIOS

LUCY A. SNYDER is the author of the fantasy novel *Spellbent* and the collections *Sparks and Shadows*, *Chimeric Machines*, and *Installing Linux on a Dead Badger*. Her writing has appeared in *Strange Horizons*, *Weird Tales*, *Hellbound Hearts*, *ChiZine*, *GUD*, and *Lady Churchill's Rosebud Wristlet*. She is a graduate of the Clarion Science Fiction & Fantasy Writers' Workshop and mentors students in Seton Hill University's MFA program in Writing Popular Fiction. For more information, visit her website at www.lucysnyder.com.

KURT DINAN lives in Cincinnati with his wife and two sons. He has had stories published in *Chizine*, *Horror Library Volume III*, *Holy Horrors*, and *Darkness on the Edge: Tales Inspired by the Songs of Bruce Springsteen*. This is his first poem sale.

KELLY BARNHILL is a teacher and writer from the frozen heart of North America, where she lives with her three evil-genius children, her lovely husband and her emotionally unstable dog. Her work (fiction and nonfiction: speculative, literary and otherwise) has appeared in journals such as *Postscripts*, *Weird Tales*, *Underground Voices*, *The Rake*, and *The Sun*. She also writes novels, the first of which will be released by Little, Brown in the spring of 2011.

RICHARD WRIGHT is an author of strange dark fictions, currently living with his wife and daughter in New Delhi, India. His short stories have been widely published in the United Kingdom and USA for over a decade, most recently in magazines and anthologies including *The Anthology of Dark Wisdom*, *Withersin 3.2*, *Beneath the Surface*, *Shroud*, *Tattered Souls*, *Choices*, and the Doctor Who collection *Short Trips: Re:Collections*. His pulp novella *Hiram Grange and the Nymphs of Krakow* is available from

Shroud Publishing. If you enjoyed "Sandboys," drop by his website at www.richardwright.org and say hello.

GARY A. BRAUNBECK is the author of the acclaimed Cedar Hill cycle of novels and stories, among them *In Silent Graves*, *Coffin County*, the recent *Far Dark Fields*, and the forthcoming *A Cracked and Broken Path* from Apex later this year. His work has garnered five Bram Stoker Awards, three Shocklines "Shocker" Awards, an International Horror Guild Award, a *Dark Scribe Magazine* Black Quill Award, and a World Fantasy Award nomination. To read more about Gary and his work, please visit www.garybraunbeck.com.

ARTIST BIOS

EDITH WALTER has degrees in medieval history, art history and archaeology. She's worked for nine years as an editor before she trained to become an artist. She currently works as graphic designer on various freelance print and web projects in Paris, France.

In 1962 in the bucolic region of southern Indiana, a peculiar child was born and given the name of STEVEN GILBERTS. Being the only Indiana-bred person in a family of Wisconsin origin, this led to the unfortunate child being labeled "hoosier" by his extended family; a group collectively known as "badgers," "cheese heads," and perhaps most frightening of all, Norwegians.

EDITOR BIOS

MAURICE BROADDUS' dark fiction has been published in numerous magazines, anthologies, and web sites, most recently including *Dark Dreams II*, *Dark Dreams III*, *Apex Magazine*, *Black Static*, and *Weird Tales Magazine*. In 2008, he co-authored (with Wrath James White) the Apex Publications novella *Orgy of Souls*. His novel series, The Knights of Breton Court (Angry Robot/HarperCollins UK) debuts in 2010. Visit his site at www.MauriceBroaddus.com.

JERRY GORDON couldn't figure out a way to be an astronaut, film director, and superhero in the same lifetime, so he settled on writing about them. His fiction has been published in *Apex Magazine*, *Indie Review*, and the *Midnight Diner*. He recently completed his first novel, *Severed Dreams*, and can be found blurring genre lines at www.jerrygordon.net.

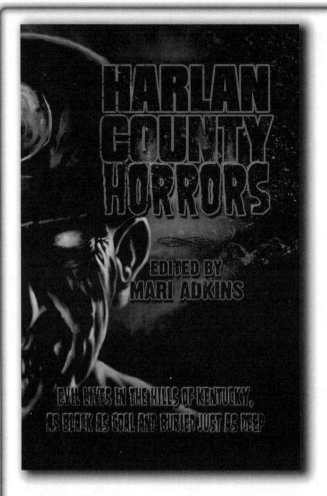

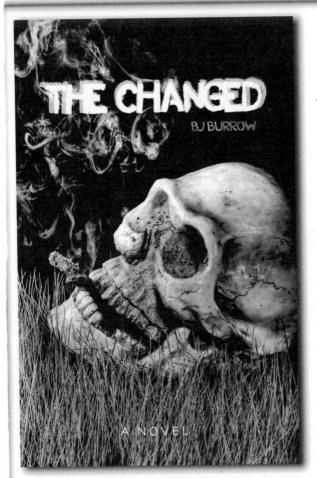

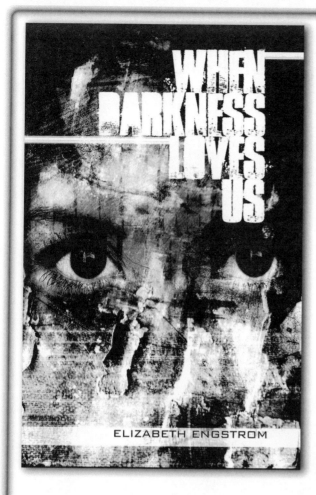